John Hallum

The Diary of an Old Lawyer

Or Scenes behind the Curtain

John Hallum

The Diary of an Old Lawyer
Or Scenes behind the Curtain

ISBN/EAN: 9783337016463

Printed in Europe, USA, Canada, Australia, Japan

Cover: Foto ©Raphael Reischuk / pixelio.de

More available books at **www.hansebooks.com**

THE

DIARY OF AN OLD LAWYER

—OR—

SCENES BEHIND THE CURTAIN.

By JOHN HALLUM,

Author of Biographical and Pictorial History of Arkansas.

NASHVILLE, TENN.:
SOUTHWESTERN PUBLISHING HOUSE.
1895.

TO THE BAR ASSOCIATION OF TENNESSEE THIS VOLUME
IS AFFECTIONATELY DEDICATED.

A native of Tennessee, the Author loves with filial devotion all that
relates to the achievement of her sons. A galaxy of noble and chivalrous
characters, laborers in every department of human greatness, fill and
crown the Pantheon builded by her sons, in every era since her "Commonwealth Builder" crossed the mountains after the revolution and
made Watauga a nucleus of men and principles, from which a great
Commonwealth has sprung, second to none in devotion to those great
fundamental principles which enfranchise, expand and ennoble man.
In this Guild of Builders, her Bench and Bar have won renown. With
her, as with every people governed by liberty and law, the Bench and
Bar have been the strongest pillars of State.

Nashville, Tenn., May 1st, 1895.

INDEX.

ANCESTRY.

WILLIAM AND HENRY HALLAM, brothers, immigrated from England under the patronage of one of the Lords Baltimore, about 1760, and settled at Hagerstown, Maryland, both being men of resolute purpose, marked individuality, and possessed of the courage of their convictions in an eminent degree.

Sturdy Englishmen from Hallamshire, where their ancestors had lived loyal to their king for many generations, they did not approve the encroachments of the crown on the rights of the colonies, nor did they join the rebellion against it, but maintained a strict neutrality, and were honored and respected for it. General Van Rensalier, of the revolutionary army, was their warm personal friend, and often visited them after Washington became President.

William Hallam was in the vicinity of Germantown when that battle was fought, was taken by scouts and carried to a British officer, who accused him of being a spy, which he vehemently denounced as false. The officer then drew his sword and slapped him in the face, and he shot the officer dead on the spot, and made his escape to South Carolina, where he became the owner of a large plantation and numerous slaves, and the ancestor of numerous descendants. His sons, William and Henry, emigrated to Tennessee in 1790, bought lands and opened farms near Carthage, in Smith county, Tennessee on the Cumberland and Caney Fork rivers. William is the grandfather of my wife, and Henry is grandfather of the Author, my wife and self being related in the fourth degree.

Hallam is the correct authography of the name; the a,

in the last syllable was substituted by the u, which is a corruption attributable to the illiteracy of early frontier conditions. Gov. Helm, of Kentucky, is a worse corruption. All their descendants were ardent supporters of General Jackson.

EARLY STRUGGLES.

Poverty is a fruitful stimulant, unknown and unfelt by the boy reared in the lap of wealth, and supplied from sources not created by himself.

Early knowledge of the practical affairs of life is generally a sealed book to him, and he knows nothing of the stern, heroic virtues which are the surest foundations on which to build robust manhood. Poverty in the lexicon of aspiring youth, is often a blessing in disguise, when wealth is an effeminate poison, a upas tree, under whose fatal shades mistaken parents raise mournful failures. The history and destiny of the world have ever been, and always will be, made and moulded by men who learn to grapple with, and master difficulties in the early formative period of life.

Wealth has made a thousand drones and fools of young men, to every one it has lifted and advanced to the nobler plains of true manhood.

The age preceding, and succeeding the revolutionary period, was eminently calculated to mould and elevate man to the higher standards. Our fathers were strangers in those pioneer times, to that sordid and corroding avarice, which drives men to crowd and elbow each other in the race for wealth, and power, and place. Their lives, habits and wants were few and simple, and the great majority were honest in all the relations of life, whether private or public; they were hospitable, noble, and generous. Their dangers were common, wants few, and they were true to themselves and fellow-men. Then that was the rule, now it is the exception in all classes. Want, during the early days of the commonwealth, was a Spartan nursery for the heroic and social virtues. Since 1861, war and avarice have driven the people mad, and drifted them hellwards from primitive moorings.

My father had nine children, of whom I was the eldest —he was poor—there were no public schools then, none in the vicinage, but the old log school house, with indifferent teachers whose methods were as primitive as the log house. Make a crop and then go to school, were alternate employments until I was fifteen years old, with no prospect disclosing a brighter horizon; a yearning for what seemed impossible of fruition, an opportunity to learn; insatiate desire, only gratified partially by reading all I could get my hands on. But fortuitous circumstances, not in the least expected, sometimes rise up in our pathway, and open desolation with a rainbow of promise and fruition.

Two of the greatest surprises of my long and eventful life were in store for me. There was a man "who went about the world doing good," who knew me, had watched over all the boys in the vicinage. Hickory Grove adorned a charming landscape near the old homestead in Sumner County, where men worshiped God in the purity of primitive simplicity, and when

"Simple faith was more than Norman blood."

Barefooted at fifteen years of age, I attended these meetings, a rustic plow boy in honest poverty and garb.

"Uncle Billy Malone" was a tower of moral strength and grandeur at these meetings. He

"Allured to brighter worlds and led the way."

At one of these meetings he announced to the people that he wanted fifteen hundred dollars subscribed to be paid in installments, for the purpose of classically educating two boys at Cumberland University for the ministry, without naming the boys. The money was raised before the meeting adjourned, and he then announced that Rorbert M. Slate and myself were the boys.

The first great embarrassment then almost over-whelmed me, and for a few moments I knew not what to say, but recovering, I told him and the people I could never be a preacher, and for that reason declined the offer; that I had something else in view for which I hoped some day to educate and prepare myself. My good mother was greatly disappointed; her anguish and sorrow greatly disturbed me, and it required much firmness to resist her appeals, but I was resolute. To have accepted the charity without living the life it imposed, would have been deception and larceny of the funds.

My resolve was to become a lawyer, but my father was so opposed to the profession, I did not disclose the fact to him. The secret was locked in my heart; I was too mod-est and bashful to disclose it to the most intimate friend, for fear of being laughed at and ridiculed beyond the endurance of a sensitive nature.

In less than two weeks another event occurred. Wirt College, then a flourishing seat of learning, was but one mile from my father's house and could be seen from the porch. Prof. W. K. Patterson was President. He came to father's with William Ralston, a local merchant, and they all retired to a shade near the orchard, and after a while called me from the plow. To my inexpressible joy, delirious ecstacy of delight, words can never paint, the kind Professor told me that he and the merchant and my father had arranged for me to matriculate at that College at the approaching session [fall of 1848].

But I knew father was not able to send me and defray the heavy expenses, and mentioned it. When this seemingly insurmountable object was mentioned, the kind Professor, with a smile as gracious as a sunbeam, said: "John, that is all arranged in this way: I will furnish you all the books you need and wait with you for your tuition and all other College expenses until after your education is com-pleted, and Mr. Ralston will furnish all the goods you need on the same terms. After you get through college, I will find you a good school to teach, and you can thus pay us, and not be dependent on anybody for your education. Your father will board you."

That was the proudest moment I ever felt. I cannot conceive that human happiness could be greater.

I had dreamed of this entry at College as a goal far beyond the reach of my poverty; the crown of an empire with all the honors man can confer on his fellow-mortal, could not have added an ioto to the transport of that delicious hour. My little cup was full and running over. I had been a spectator at College commencements, and shed tears because of the poverty which shut out those riches.

I was more sensitive than wise, and did not have ken enough to divine the ruse resorted to to make me feel that I was educating myself. Noble and generous men, they respected a foolish boy's pride, and that independence of character that can alone make a man. The idea that I was to be qualified to enter a sphere of life where I could honestly earn and pay the charges, lifted me above the clouds, and I did earn and pay every dollar, a sum little less than eight hundred dollars.

My father gave me three acres of tobacco ground the next year, and I cultivated it in tobacco, and often worked in it until the moon went down, and then when I became sleepy over my lessons, bathed my head in cold water to drive off sleep, and thus kept up with my classes and made two hundred dollars, every cent of which I gave my creditors.

The highest prize on commencement day was a medal for oratory; one hundred boys competed for it, including myself, the second session. I had not the remotest idea of winning the prize, but entered the contest for the benefit the exertion would impart, and to my surprise, the Faculty and Board awarded me the honor.

Here gratitude inspires a vivid recollection of another good man, "Uncle Jacky Wilkes," of the vicinage. I needed some money to send to Nashville for a new coat for commencement day, and after much hesitation, went to his residence to ask a loan, but my heart failed me, and I returned home without making my business known, sad and sorrowing. I wished for a less conspicuous place which my humble garb would better become. I had no security to offer, poverty and the prospects for a better day for a boy already in debt, made me tremble at the idea of asking such a favor. But after thinking over the matter, I summoned enough courage to go again to "Uncle Jacky;" and after much hesitation, asked for the loan of ten dollars; and the good old man said, "yes, John I will let you have all you want," and handed me a roll of bills and said: "You need at least fifty dollars, take all you want, I am not afraid of losing it, unless you die, and then I would only regret your death, not the money."

Good old man in Israel—his soul sped the astral depths many years ago. I paid him out of my tobacco crop, and he said, "always come to me when you want help, and you will never fail whilst 'Uncle Jacky' lives." Typical of a generation now past the Old South, all honest men and boys then had credit, and it was rare to hear of its abuse. No distrust then, no cut-throat mortgages, no stratagem and treason for spoils.

I took no vacation during terms, but worked hard on the farm every day, and thus kept up at healthy equipois that healthy inter-dependence between the mental and physical man, without which neither can attain maximum strength.

There were many wealthy young men at "Old Wirt" from Tennessee, Kentucky, Georgia, Louisiana and Mississippi, and not one of these high-born young men ever offended my pride because of my poverty.

Vattel's Law of Nations was one of the advanced studies at College, and I was eager to devour this book, but was a green Freshman, and it was at least a year before

I could reach that goal, and get into that guild of College lore. I therefore resolved to study it privately at odd times which could be spared from other studies; John Stark, an heir of great wealth for that day, gave me the book. That volume was a treasured jewel of the highest import to me, and I devoured it with ravenous hunger. My father caught me with it one day and shook his head ominously, as though the omen was a bad one from his standpoint, and I prevaricated about my intentions, by telling him that it was a school book which I would soon be required to study, and my boyish rainbow was thus disguised.

When the time arrived to take up this study, the Professor was glad that I had already accomplished that task, and after examining, passed me.

The vicissitudes of time sweep all things onward and away. Not many years ago I bent my pilgrim feet to that hallowed and sacred College ground, so full of loved and cherished memories. I went alone, and gazed in solitude, and meditated like Marius over the ruins of Carthage. There stood the ruins of ancient Wirt, like some maedevil castle mournfully attesting the perished hopes and memories of departed years. Even the spring in the Beechwood Valley, where so many boys laved their thirst 'neath the widespread foliage, had sank into the earth and gone, as if nature had shrank at the appalling dissolation.

What a panoramic crowd of blessed memories, now fringed with time's dessolation, come in solemn procession, proclaiming the mutability of all things.

I was glad to be alone, so no tempest of feeling, no storm of thought, could shake no heart and dim no eye but my own. How awfully sad it is to gaze on the ruins of time, the mausoleum of hope, the silent, yet eloquent tomb of cherished idols. How many boys came in review? Hundreds from the spirit land, but few among the living.

There was John P. Andrews, the senior of all, the Nestor of the Campus, whom all respected for his accurate learning and high moral worth, but John maintained with rigorous exactness the privileges of seniority, and an exalted dignity far beyond the comprehension of the average college boy.

In fact, it was universally conceded that John had the "make-up" of a courtier of the Chesterfield school, and that his polish, and exquisite dignity, would have imparted luster to any Court of Europe. He was the paragon, the Beau Brummel of College, without any of his infirmities. He was the ideal of integrity, but too exalted to ever enter into the sport and hilarity of the campus. John was another one to the "manor born," and yet lives to enjoy the honors of a well spent life in a fine mansion near Hartsville, on his "native heath."

He was a Captain in the service of the South in the late rebellion, and many a bloody field attests his martial bearing as a dauntless soldier.

There was Joseph Holt, born in the icy embrace of honest poverty, with a lofty ambition to scale the rugged heights of Parnassus, and he toiled "with an eye that never winked, and a wing that never tired." Never was mind better balanced. His was a lovable character, pure, and true to all the demands of life. Born in Belote's Bend, on the banks of the Cumberland, in Sumner County, a few miles from the College.

Here is another example of the good accomplished by W. K. Patterson, the President, and one of the founders of the college. Through his nobility of character and generous aid, Holt achieved a classic education, taught school, and repaid every farthing. A long roster of noble boys were thus educated by Prof. Patterson. The good, this man has achieved for society, reaches out to the bosom of the Infinite, like the child with uplifted hands, extended for the embrace of its mother.

Yet, who of all these boys who have drank so deep at

the fountain of his blessings, have stopped a moment in the onrushing ebbs and stormy currents of life, to record the untold deeds of this good Samaritan, who stopped by the wayside, picked up many a waif, lifted them to the higher planes of manhood, and gave them as blessings to the world. One such man is worth more to his fellowmen than all the Goulds since the days of Crœsus. Holt graduated several years before I matriculated, married a good and beautiful woman, Jane Davis, the sister of my mother, and died a few weeks after his marriage, in Hartsville, while principal of the Male Academy at that place. His extraordinary thirst for knowledge and severe application undermined his health, and led him to an early grave. He had been my teacher. I loved him, and was with him when he died in the house of Dr. Dyer, on the hill, my wife's father. Had he lived long, he would have become one of the most learned ornaments of the Bar, a goal to which he aspired, and was fast laying deep foundations.

There was Granville Bledsoe, another classmate, born in the neighboring county of Macon, who was as beautiful as sculptured marble, the perfection of physical symmetry and noble bearing, with an eye as quick and keen as that of an eagle, and an aptitude for learning and comprehension rarely equaled. Granville was one of the idols of the school—no lesson was too severe, no task too difficult to master. When he "unbent the bow" for recreation, for hilarity and innocent mirth, he became the center of attraction, the soul of wit; none surpassed him in the display of that rare combination of wit, mirth and dignity. He had no enemies, all loved and admired him for his noble worth.

Granville "pointed his arrows to the sun." To be a great lawyer and jurist was the goal of his ambition, and he toiled to lay deep and strong the foundations on which to build his ideal of honorable fame. On many lines he was the parallel of " Bob Duncan." He read law, was admitted to the Bar, and chose Louisville, Ky., as the field for his triumphs, and was fast climbing the ladder in a field which brought him in contact with rivals and "foemen worthy of his steel," but consumption seized and carried him to an early grave, before he had reached and achieved that splendor which was so enticing and dear to him.

Judge A. B. Williams, of Arkansas, graduated at Old "Wirt," in 1847. He was raised in Hempstead and Pike Counties, Arkansas, has served his state ably in the halls of legislation, on the Bench, and later the United States, as a member of the Utah Commission. He is an able lawyer and jurist, and a perfect cyclopedia of the events, men and history of the State; and no man could write a history of the State and times in which "Baz Williams" lives, equal to him, if he would only perform that office.

Prof. J. M. Birney, one of the "old boys" who graduated at Wirt College, in 1848, died in Prairie county, Ark., fifteen years ago. He was my client many years ago, and was a gentleman in all the relations of life.

President Patterson studied law under Judge Ridley, his father-in-law, and in 1853 settled at Jackson Port, Ark., where he became very popular and successful at the Bar, and was, in 1854, elected to the legislature. He declined a re-election, but made a successful race for the lucrative office of Prosecuting Attorney for the third Judicial Circuit, to which he was elected in 1856.

At that time his grateful pupil was in the full tide of success at the Memphis Bar, where we frequently met in that attic communion of congenial spirits, which is much easier felt than described. We called over the long roster of the College, and discussed with tenderest fidelity of purest friendship, episodes of college life, and the prospects of each who had drank at that shrine of Minerva. He possessed magnetic force of character, was a charming conversationalist, and as pure in diction as the most refined lady.

Prof. H. E. Ring, of Ohio, succeeded him at the College. He was a very strict disciplinarian, rough and brusque with his pupils, but for all that, a pure diamond of inestimable value, but the contrast between him and Prof. Patterson was too great to prevent invidious comparisons.

During these school years a mountain of debt accumulated, and I felt overwhelmed at its contemplation, although not one of my creditors had asked for pay, and I urged the President to send me to the next applicant for a teacher, and one soon came from patrons of Bar's school house, in Wilson county, Tenn., offering board and fifteen dollars per month for a trial of three months, with the promise of a six months school and eighty pupils, if the community was satisfied with the trial teacher. I accepted the proposition, and went to work determined to command approval, and on the first of October the pay roll of my roster of girls, boys, young ladies, and young men, in this school of co-education commenced with eighty pupils. There were no free schools in the State at that time. It was what we now call a "pay school" in distinction from free schools. At the end of the session I paid every dollar of my debts, and had $2.50 left, to which my mother added her mite of $2.50. The mountain of debt, now paid off, had greatly distressed me, though no creditor had ever presented his bill, and I felt a horror of going in debt.

I had a change of clothing, a small trunk, and some school books, and five dollars; and although I could have borrowed any reasonable amount for a poor boy, I preferred getting to Memphis on the five dollars, if I could. Before starting I gave my life secret to my mother, and exacted a promise to keep it from all the world, until I could redeem it on my next return to the old homestead, however long that might be. I told her my intention was to return to her with authority to practice law in the Courts of my country, and that I did not want my father to know it, because he would oppose it, and a knowledge of the fact would distress him: that I did not want the outside world to know it, because the prospects for success was so remote, the attempt would excite derision. She kept that secret as sacred as a shrine, until the world knew it, two years later, from other sources.

It was ten miles to Gallatin, my trunk was light, and I carried it on horseback, a younger brother riding behind me. I would have walked from there to Nashville, but was compelled to take the stage because of the trunk. That reduced my funds to $3.50, and a night's lodging took another dollar.

The steamer Iroquois, a Nashville and New Orleans packet, was anchored at the landing, and was advertised to leave that evening. Cabin fare to Memphis was ten dollars, and deck passage four dollars. Here was a dilemma. I sought the kind-hearted Captain, showed him my election as teacher, and some books with my name written in them, to identify me and remove any suspicion of my being an imposter, and asked him if he would take two dollars and credit me for the remainder until I could teach school and pay him; and told him that only left me fifty cents to subsist on, until the boat reached Memphis, and he kindly assented. I bought some cheese, crackers, and a piece of dried beef with the fifty cents, and carried my trunk on my shoulder to the boat, and put it in a convenient place under the boilers. It was a cold March, and I slept under the boilers to keep warm.

The steamer was heavily laden with tobacco, pig iron, and cotton—the cotton extended up to the cabin guards. The boat stopped at every landing, and made very slow progress, and was four days reaching the Ohio river, and my provisions gave out. I had a fine pocket knife, and traded it to a "roustabout" for crackers.

At the confluence of the Ohio and Mississippi rivers the sun was warm and bright, and I crawled out on top of the cotton bales to enjoy it. I knew deck passengers were prohibited the freedom of the cabin, and did not go in. I sat on the cotton in front of the boat, and I suppose looked in a serious mood, I certainly felt so. A dozen or more well-dressed passengers eyed me rather closely, and to escape their supposed criticism I started below. They hailed me to come to them. I reminded them that the regulations did not permit me to come either in or on the upper cabin, because I had not paid for, and was not entitled to such privileges. "Yes," said the leader, in a kind, gentle voice, "we have come to the conclusion that you are a Southern college boy, and by some misfortune—we do not care to know—have lost your funds; here is fifty dollars, take it and come into the cabin, you are evidently a gentleman."

I admitted the latter conclusion, but told him briefly the facts, thanked him courteously for the kindness which prompted the offer of assistance, but resolutely declined it, and told them the Captain of the boat knew my condition, and had generously extended all the aid I asked.

All then crowded around me and strongly urged me to accept their hospitality and generosity, and it was with embarrassment, and difficulty I made my escape to the lower deck.

A few minutes after all these gentlemen came down, bringing the Captain with them, who kindly took me by the arm and said: "I am commander of this boat, and have authority to put down any insubordination on board; come with me, young man, without rebellion or resistance." I was thus kindly forced to accept a stateroom the remainder of the journey, and a seat by the Captain at the table. I was never treated more courteously in my life.

Fortunately the steamer landed at Memphis after dark, and thus saved me the humiliation of being seen much in the role of butler carrying my trunk.

I went to a boarding house, at the southwest corner of Main and Washington streets, on the opposite corner of which I had an office some years afterwards, and was in the full tide of success.

The Academy to which I had been elected as Principal at a salary of one hundred and fifty dollars per month, was twenty miles from the city, near Morning Sun. I had an uncle, Ferdinand Thomas, husband of my Aunt Betsy, my father's sister, who lived in the vicinage, and was in fine circumstances; the stage fare to that point was two dollars, of which I was conspicuously minus.

Here was another difficulty, the wind was to be raised before I could proceed any further, and I knew of but one man in the city on whom I could call for assistance; J. Rich Ray, who knew my parents, and was born in Cairo, where they were married, in 1832, and where I was born. He was a very prosperous merchant at that time, but I was two days in finding him, and began to feel hungry. When I approached and made known my condition, he pulled out a large roll of bills, but I took but three dollars. He remonstrated, and insisted that I should accept not less than one hundred dollars, but I declined, and said three dollars is much easier to pay than a much larger sum, I can get along on that very well. But, to my horror, the landlord charged me for meals I did not eat, and more than the sum I had borrowed. The stage coach was at the door, and my little trunk had already been strapped on behind. When the coachman found I was "strapped" he took my trunk off. Then the landlord took compassion, and loaned me two dollars to pay the fare. Before daylight I was at my destination, nearly famished, but did not make that fact known.

But a still greater difficulty awaited me, the keenest disappointment, challenging my pride and manhood. The Trustees, who had elected me at a salary of $150 per month, were composed of a Board of five gentlemen, and my election had been unanimous. But after I had, under so many difficulties, got there, William Walsh, one of the Trustees, reconsidered the matter and withdrew his support, without stating his reason or objections, but I knew the source of his wounds full well.

He had had a personal difficulty with my father, who was a very resolute and firm man, and revenge was to be taken out of the son, to soothe enmity which his manhood denied at the hands of my father. Thomas B. Crenshaw, a wealthy planter, and a gentleman of the "Old South," who dispensed his hospitality with the courteous bearing of a prince, together with the other Trustees, vehemently insisted that four to one was majority enough, and that I ought to disregard "Bill Walsh's" desires. But I resolutely declined to take charge of the school, on the ground that no consideration on earth could induce me, to seemingly become under obligations to an enemy of my father, whose good name and honor I loved and cherished above all the possessions of earth. In such a juncture, to even hesitate would have been to dishonor my father and degrade myself.

My four supporters were more chagrined than I was, but on reflection they approved my course, and to-day (now they are all long since dead), it is one of the dearest memories of my life, to know they were my warm friends and unswerving supporters when I came to the Bar and ever afterward.

Ferdinand P. Thomas was my uncle, and he never had a dollar or credit that I could not bank on.

Thomas B. Crenshaw, as the years rolled on, bringing the losses and misfortunes of war, came to me when I had it in my power to be of great assistance to him, and it was the greatest consolation to render it without reward.

J. Rich Ray, who loaned me the money when penniless and hungry, lost nearly all in the vortex of war, and just after its close, came to me with almost a worthless claim for $4,000, and offered me one-half of any part of it that might be collected. I offered to lend him any reasonable sum he wanted, and reminded him of his kindness to me, but he declined it. I made no reply to his offer of so large a fee. It so happened that I was the only man possessed of information and power to collect it, and in time succeeded, sent my office boy for him, handed him every dollar, and said nothing about a fee.

He divided the pile and handed me half. I threw it back in his lap, and told him I lamented his misfortune, but was glad of the opportunity to serve him—that my recollections of him and his noble generosity to me, when I was in distress, made me a better man.

Whilst teaching school I employed every leisure hour in reading law—night, morning, noon, and Saturdays. I bought several reams of paper, and made rude and copious notes of all I read. When I became drowsy or sleepy at night, I bathed in cold water and aroused myself up —five hours was my allotted time for sleep—and it was enough.

Whilst teaching my last school, a series of conflicts began, which have followed me at intervals through life, always unsought and wholly unexpected.

I had been raised by the gentlest of devout mothers, and in refined society, free from broils and fights and bullies, and looked on the world as a gentle carpet, spanned by a rainbow, where denials and honest toil are rewarded without unpleasant strife. But I was now entering on man's estate and a new life, in a country where frontier conditions had not passed away, where the ruder phases of life had to be met and confronted.

All people had been kind and considerate with me, and I thought this smooth sailing would last forever, without storms to ruffle the placid waters of life.

I had never indulged the slightest inclination to invade the rights of others, nor had I ever given occasion or foundation to encourage or provoke such feelings towards myself.

One William Rogers sent his daughter, Mary, to my school. She was near sixteen years of age, and thought herself about grown, and too large to submit to mild school discipline. She was insubordinate, and her example was exerting a bad influence. I remonstrated with her in vain. She was too large to subject to ordinary punishment, and my gentle reproof inspired laughter and derision until patience ceased to be a virtue. As a last resort I wrote the kindest of notes to her father, and informed him of my inability to govern Mary, and advised him to keep her at home. To my amazement, and terror of the school, within thirty minutes Rogers took a seat in ten paces from the school door, with a double-barrel shotgun in his lap, to await the dismissal of the school, and settle with me. This looked critical, and necessitated my being placed on a war footing as soon as possible. There was a fine double-barrelled gun at the place where I boarded, and within a walk of ten minutes of the schoolhouse, and I sent one of the students for this in haste, and he made a quick trip. When Rogers saw him approaching with the gun, he divined the import, and left with a double-quick step, and with much better judgment than he came. This was as gratifying to me as it was ludicrous, serio-comic, and all laughed at his sudden exchange of gun for legs. He was a giant in physical proportions, an overseer of negroes by occupation, and naturally overbearing from his calling. I thought this ludicrous episode an end of the matter. The next day, being Saturday, I went with one of my school boys on a fishing expedition, through a lane, where this overseer was watching negroes at work.

The gentleman with whom I boarded begged me not to go, and said Rogers would kill me if I passed along the public road where he was. I replied that my engagement to go that way was made before the trouble arose, and that I never had, and never intended, to break an engagement, to keep out of the way of a blustering bully, or any type of man, and declined to put a pistol in my pocket, saying that it ill became a teacher, and was cowardly in any man, except on urgent necessity.

But the gentleman, W. H. Sneed, followed me quite a

a

distance, and vehemently insisted that I was in great danger, and finally I consented to put the pistol in my pocket, but felt humiliated by the act. Sure enough, Rogers sat on his horse awaiting my approach with the school boy, and angling rods, and as I was passing his horse he cursed me, lit off on the opposite side, and rushed at me with uplifted Bowieknife. But I had cocked my pistol, and as he approached, rammed it in his mouth, cutting his upper lip severely, and breaking two teeth out.

He was paralyzed with fear, dropped the knife out of his powerless hand, and ran in the yard of a neighbor, Monroe Coleman, and asked for a gun. Coleman berated him for his cowardice, and ordered him out of his yard. I thought the matter surely ended there, and went on about my fishing, with the little school boy. But some three hours after, the constable of the township came to the creek, with a posse and warrant, charging me with assault with intent to kill. By this time excitement was running high, and every man in the community was my friend, and many went with me to Raleigh, the county seat, to see me through. I employed George Bayne to defend, and demanded a trial, which lasted late in the night. Rogers employed Jesse L. Harris to prosecute. The lawyers came to blows, and Harris drew his pistol on Bayne, who was unarmed, but put up his pistol when he looked down the mouth of mine.

The Court discharged me. My friends were armed, and if Harris had fired, an awful tragedy would have been enacted in that Court room.

In the meantime I had denounced Rogers as a base coward, and said I could run him in Wolf river with a goose quill. He heard the denunciation, and did not resent it, and I regarded the matter as ended, but he owed me, would not pay, and I brought suit to recover the debt. Many predicted serious consequences on the day of trial, but I did not, and went to the trial, at Raleigh, unarmed. The Court room was full of spectators, who expected trouble, but I had no apprehension whatever because of his previous cowardice of pronounced type.

My friends came to me and asked if I was armed, and told me that Rogers was going to shoot me as soon as the Court adjourned, and James M. Coleman, my brother-in-law, put a derringer pistol in my pocket, and told me to look out. The Court gave judgment in my favor, and as soon as I stepped out of the room, Rogers followed and fired at me before I could get my pistol out, but missed me, and wheeled to run into a saloon. As he entered the door I ran up on him, and fired as he closed the door, but the ball only cut through his clothing. He was the worst alarmed man I ever saw; ran through the saloon into a ten-pin alley, burst through the end of it into a garden, knocked off the palings and ran around to where his horse was tied. While he was engaged in this chivalric performance, I was loading an old muzzle-loading shotgun, handed me by Mrs. Bolt, the wife of a minister of the Gospel; she handed me powder, ball and caps. By the time my gun was loaded, Quince Cannon, the constable, had arrested Rogers; the fight was on now to the finish, and I intended to end it then and there, and drew down on him, but he made breastworks of the constable, and shouted murder as loud as a calliope, to the infinite disgust and derision of the crowd.

I threw away my gun, and walked off, and and let him go home.

Paradoxical as it may seem, to me, Rogers was an evangelist, preaching in the wilderness, teaching that there was either some fighting, or a great deal of unpleasant running to be done, and that one horn or the other of the unpleasant dilemma had often to be quickly taken and promptly met, from which there was not likely to be any honorable avenue of escape under the social conditions then prevailing.

It was a revelation, teaching that cravens and cowards

are generally the men who insult gentlemen, and the first to run from the danger they provoke, and that a truly courageous man will never intentionally give offense in the absence of well considered and honest conviction that it is merited.

It was "a condition that confronted" me, growing, to a great extent, out of the peculiar structure of Southern society, at that time and place, since much modified by patent causes, which I will not here discuss. At that time gentlemen were often compelled to conform to the established order of things by defending their integrity, or submitting to humiliations intolerable to a proud spirit. The *Code Duello* was recognized as part of the *lex non scripta* of gentlemen.

I was then preparing to enter on a profession, which, above all others, demands the exposition and probing of fraud and crime, an office, an offense, never forgiven when robust Saxon is indulged in exposing it. I realized that a negative, passive character, who wires and worms and edges his way through life, without contact with its rough and rude phases, is incapable of coping with the great emergencies of life, in society as then organized and dominant.

Here was "a condition confronting me," at the threshold of a profession which was the idol of my boyhood dreams, the inspiration to arduous toil. To follow it up with that sense of self-respect, which had been imparted by education and association, would certainly change that line and mould of character, which the simplicity of boyhood, without any knowledge of the practical affairs and stern relations of life, had marked out. What was I to do, now the rainbow had faded in the dawn of a new existence, a new life; meet or shrink from its demands?

Not one moment of hesitation, with that consoling philosophy of Socrates, "do the best you can and let consequences take care of themselves." I "plunged into the Rubicon," realizing and knowing full well, that the first

chapter in my life was forever closed, and that its beautiful rainbows were a thing of the past. And I realized
that there are two characters equally detestable—the
bully and the coward—from both of which the true gentleman instinctively shrinks. The true analysis is each
of these characters resolve themselves into one, and
I realized that the occasion would be rare, when two gentlemen come into irreconcilable conflict, and that such
radical difficulties could only occur where both were honest and sincere in maintaining their self-respect; also that
acute sensitive natures, of all others, ought to be cautious
in fixing standards and making demands—that to steer
between " Charybdis and Cylla " would often be difficult,
requiring the finest discrimination to be decided and acted
upon instantly, and herein lies the chief difficulty with
all men, when compelled to act in emergencies, generals
in the field, as well as men engaged in the private affairs
of life. During the crysalis and formative period of most
lives, it is easy to commit, and hard to avoid errors, and
every life is moulded to a greater or less extent by the
circumstances, influences, and condition of society which
surrounds it.

Society is a revolutionary, vacillating pendulum, which
oscillates in sentiment, and the periods marking these revolutions are measured by short decades and cycles. What
is popular to-day in science, literature, art, philosophy, nay
religion, and Government, may be the reverse to-morrow.
The man of great popularity to-day in politics, Government, literature, or religion, may be dashed to pieces as
an idol to-morrow, and become a living " back number."
This is the rule, rather than the exception. Look down
the ages, scrutinize the records of time and facts in confirmation of this. These infirmities influence the great
majority of men to desert deliberately formed convictions,
" that thrift may follow fawning," politicians to become
knaves and sycophants, " bending the pregnant hinges of
the knee " to popular ebbs, tides, and currents.

What is a young noviate starting out in life to do, but fix his own standards on the best and highest foundations his judgment and surroundings permit, and work with the courage of his convictions to attain the summit, regardless of the whims and caprice of that sometimes worst of all tyrants, public opinion.

The highest functions of capable men are to lead and mould public sentiment, to scorn the "political tramp," that parasite on the body politic who, knowingly, encourages a false sentiment to promote self interests. Such are the prevailing conditions now in the organized elements of power, represented by an aggregation of vast capital in the hands of a few, from which the liberties of the people are in greater danger than from all other sources. The Government of the Roman people existed for centuries before it finally developed into a tithe of the corruption we now find in the administration of public affairs, apparently without the power to prevent it.

ADMITTED TO THE BAR.

In May, 1854, I was admitted to the Bar by Judges John C. Humphreys and William R. Harris, at Raleigh, and immediately opened an office in that now ancient town. I had then been married six months, to Virginia W. Sneed, the daughter of a prosperous planter living in the vicinage. The first office I performed as an attorney was to write a bill of sale, conveying twelve likely negro men of the value of $18,000, on the day I was admitted to the Bar, from my brother-in-law, Captain Angus Greenlaw, to his wife, Elenora. The Captain had just lost the Mary Agnes, a fine, new, palatial steamer, of the value of $80,000, running in the cotton trade between Memphis and New Orleans, and shortly before that had lost another steamer on Red river, without insurance in either loss. Ten weeks before my admission, he instructed me to draw a conveyance of these negroes to his wife, to the exclusion of the husband's marital rights, as he desired to protect her in the money she had invested in those negroes and boats. Court was in session, and my office was full of friends when the Captain called for the instrument, and in the confusion I drew the bill of sale without excluding the marital rights of the husband. This oversight in drafting my first instrument the day my license was signed, caused me infinite trouble, three years afterwards, when the negroes were attached, in New Orleans for the debts of the husband, before Judge King, of the Fourth District Court. Local attorneys were employed, who informed me that the rights of the wife depended altogether on the construction to be given the instrument, under the laws of Tennessee, where the conveyance was made. As I was unavoidably a witness in the case, I declined the relation of attorney.

A commission issued to take my deposition, with more than two hundred interrogatories attached to the cross-examination, which for a while perplexed me very much, and imposed much labor. A thorough investigation of the origin and introduction of slavery into the United States, the colony of North Carolina, thence into Tennessee, which once formed an integral part of North Carolina, and the laws governing the sale and transmission of title to slaves in North Carolina and Tennessee, were extensively investigated. It required much investigation to answer these questions intelligently and correctly, and I devoted two months to it. Had the interrogatories been properly framed, ten or twenty at most could have been made to cover the whole ground. After all, the statutes of three years' limitation gave the slaves to the wife, and saved the negroes.

After writing out this voluminous deposition, I submitted it to Judge Archibald Wright, a very eminent lawyer, and took his deposition, which corroborated and confirmed my statements.

When the deposition was read, to my infinite joy, Judge King gave judgment for the wife. The case was so plain that it was not argued by either side. From that, to this day, I have never drawn an instrument that did not effect the objects designed, save one assignment in bankruptcy, hereafter explained.

On the fourth of July, 1854, an immense barbecue was given at Raleigh, and I was the orator of the occasion; near the close of my address, and almost under the rostrum, John Branch plunged a carving knife into a negro man, who had wiped a greasy knife on his coat, and I was engaged to defend him at the following September term of the Court. Clients poured in on me from the day I opened an office, not because of my ability by any means, at that time, but a large number of them had known my father, who lived there in my early boyhood; he was a man of much reading, engaging conversational powers, and had many friends, many of whom had grown to be wealthy. Then I had an uncle living in the county. Ferdinand Thomas, who married Betsie, my father's sister; he was an influential man, and one of the best friends I ever had. His purse and name were always at my command.

These fortuitous circumstances gave me a large practice, and I realized four thousand dollars cash the first year of my practice.

> " Kind hearts are more than Coronets
> And simple faith than Norman blood."

But it is a great mistake in a young man to desire a large patronage at the beginning. A very few, well studied and argued cases at the beginning, is far more conducive to a solid and lasting fame. Lord Eldon achieved national fame in the argument of one case, Arkroyd against Smithson. Many of the ablest men at the Bar in both hemispheres served long probations. This large practice caused me to labor at the start almost beyond the powers of mental and physical endurance, and prevented that concentration of time and thought on a few well considered cases.

At the September term, 1854, in the defense of Branch on indictment for assault with intent to kill a slave, I made my maiden speech. This case I had mastered thoroughly. I announced this proposition: that less provocation from a slave to a white man, than from one white man to another, justifies violence.

This was in the language of the South Carolina cases. The Court denied, and argued the point with me, before I produced the authorities in answer to a statement that no such authority could be found. This was what I expected, a triumph over the Court and the Judge's admission that he was wrong. This was the pivotal point in the case, and, after a lengthy argument to the jury, a verdict of acquittal was rendered.

The Appeal contained a flattering account of my defense and address to the jury, and I sent a copy of the paper to my father, and he said to my mother: "I have never heard of that Hallum before, do you know who he is?" "Don't you know your own son; have you forgotten John?" And he replied with his favorite exclamation of surprise: "Goodly God! I was afraid that boy was going to read law. I caught him with a law book when he was at College, but the rascal made me believe he had to study that book at school; I was afraid some bad end would come to him when I saw him with that book, and sure enough it has; but it did not happen whilst he was under me. A poor father can't tell what his children will bring him to."

Then he asked my mother: "Minerva, did you know that boy was studying law?" "Yes, sir," she said. "Then why did you not tell me?" "For the best of all reasons; he confided his secret to me under promise that I would keep it, because he did not want to give you any pain, and he had obstacles enough to overcome without your opposition. I encouraged him all I could, and I have no fears that he will dishonor his parentage."

For an allwise purpose, the Creator has made the

mother the guardian angel of her children, and her heart goes out to them through storm and sunshine; she never deserts them; no matter how great the calamity which overtakes them, whether they adorn a throne or swing from a gallows, they are still her children, and nothing can destroy her love.

The little bird that sings on a limb, and flits through the air, an emblem of innocence and purity, will strike at hawk or eagle when it swoops down on her young. Little mother fish will strike at a snake when it invades the spawning nest.

In due time, my father condoned the offense, and gave me his pardon, when he learned that there is nothing in the character of the true lawyer to mar the fame or cloud the loftiest aspirations of man. Every relation of life, every calling of men, may be abused, are abused, but because some are derelict, it is the crystalization of cruelty to charge odium on all.

I have ever labored to keep my feelings green and fresh towards my fellow-man, and do not want to survive the hour when I must suspicion all.

Immediately after the trial of Branch, Wm. Yarbrough retained me in many cases on the criminal docket against him.

He was large in physical proportions; had been an overseer of slaves, which occupation of itself brutalizes the nobler elements of manhood. He had been engaged in many fights and broils, and was considered a desperate and dangerous man, and the people were afraid of him. Many submitted to his tyranical and overbearing invasion of their rights, at the expense of their manhood. He had run a long career, and had an established character as a bully, and thought that every man must quietly submit to his insults.

It was notorious that he always carried a pair of pistols and a bowie knife, and a large roll of money on his person. After trying many of his cases, and being his attorney for more than one year, I presented my account for the small balance of ten dollars, during the session of the Circuit Court at Raleigh, in 1856.

At the time he was sitting in the grand jury room, all the sixteen jurors being present, but not in session. Judge Humphreys was holding his Court in the room above. To my surprise, he assumed a contemptuous scowl, and asked me if I wanted to know his opinion of me, to which I replied that I wanted the ten dollars he owed me, but if he was anxious to express an opinion, he was at liberty to do so; and he said, "I think you are a d—d rascal." To which I replied: "You have deliberately and wantonly insulted me. I will immediately go across the street and get Jim Coleman's pistols and return, and if you do not apologize one of us must die."

I secured the arms from James M. Coleman, who was my brother-in-law, and while I was gone for the pistols, Yarbrough moved from the jury room, and took a position at the entrance to the open hallway leading through the basement story of the Court house, and stood up against the wall, facing me as I hastily approached him. By this time the large crowd of men was intensely excited, but all moved off a short distance out of range of pistols.

I walked up to him and demanded an instant retraction and apology, and he said, "I am not armed;" and I said, "You are lying, you cowardly cur; but here are two pistols, take your choice. I did not load them." And handed him both weapons to choose from.

He refused to take either, but retracted and apologized, and paid my bill, and his knees smote each other like Belshazzar's. Another Rogers, another bully, another lesson. All bullies are arrant cowards, and one don't exist, never did exist, who will fight on equal terms at short range. His cowardice, when the mask was torn off, was a revelation to the community, as well as myself, and the insight it gave me into character, has been of infinite service and has served me many times.

Yarbrough, after that, demeaned himself well, but sold out in the fall and moved to Crowley's Ridge, in St. Francis county. Ark., where he now lives, with grown sons and grandchildren around him.

Here was an ordeal forced on me, without the slightest provocation. Nothing could be more foreign to my education, associations, and desire.

Will any gentleman—Christian, Heathen, or Pagan—tell me how I could have avoided that collision, or rather prospective clash, in a better and more satisfactory way?

Some would advise, resort to the law, a suit for slander for instance, and, if I was afraid of a thrashing, a peace warrant—heroic remedies, infinitely worse than the disease and far more disgraceful." Peace warrants and slander suits are sometimes appropriate, but these remedies did not apply to this sort of case. If General Jackson had relied on such remedies, his name would have been a buzzard's roost.

If a man's honor is not worth defending, his life is not worth living.

I know many ministers of the gospel in the West who would face the cannon's roar, and rattle of musketry, rather than "swear out a peace warrant," and they are good and true men.

"NO ROSTER KEPT OF THE MEMPHIS BAR,"

Writes the accomplished Miss Maud R. Layton, to whom I am indebted for assistance in getting up this Roster. I have added one hundred and fifty names from memory alone, and am conscious that many have been forgotten. I have indicated the nativity as far as my memory serves me.

The capital letter, S., indicates born in the South, and the capital letter, N., born in the North.

When I glance down this column a thousand memories elbow their way for recognition. Memories long in abeyance come to the surface, like the faint outlines of a cloud on the distant horizon, until they assume vivid outline and form.

ROSTER OF THE MEMPHIS BAR FROM 1835 TO 1870.

Avery, W. T., 1846, S.
Ayres, T. S., 1846, S.
Ayres, John, 1857, S.
Anderson, James A., 1857, Tenn.
Anderson, B. P., 1867.

Anderson, Van A. W., 1865, Miss.
Adams, John T., 1859.
Adams, Gen. Chas. W., 1865, Mass.
Adams, W. S. J.

Bailey, Judge Sylvester, 1835, S.
Barry, Judge Valentine, 1838, Ireland.
Brown, Judge W. T., 1840, Tenn.
Blythe, Wm. A., 1845, Tenn.
Bankhead, Smith P., 1849.
Barry, Henry, 1848, S.
Beecher, Ed. A., 1854, N. Y.
Brown, B. C., 1855, Md.
Baine, Geo. W., 1853, Tenn.
Brett, James, 1857, S. C.
Brooks, John Mc., 1857, Tenn.

Barnes, D. B., 1857, S.
Beard, Judge W. D., 1857, Tenn.
Belcher, E. L., 1860, N.
Bland, Peter, 1865, Mo.
Bullock, John, 1865, N. Y.
Brown, T. W., 1865, S.
Black, J. S., 1865, S.
Brizzalara, James, 1869, Italy.
Bigelow, 1865, Mass.
Bigelow, 1865, Mass.
Burglehaus, R. J. 1869, Germany.
Buttinghause, F. W., 1857, Germ'y.

Coe, Levin H., 1840, S.

Cummings, 1859, Miss.

2

Curran, David M., 1847, Ky.

Coleman, Walter, 1847, Tenn.

Caruthers, Judge John P., 1848, Tenn.

Carmack, John M., 1849, Tenn.

Carr, Wm., 1852, Tenn.

Carr, Lewis, 1856, N. C.

Collins, Richard, 1853, Miss.

Crockett, Robt. II., 1853, Tenn.

Carpenter, L., Ky.

Carpenter, 1858, Ky. } Brothers.
Carpenter, 1858, Ky.

Clements, Hon. Jere, 1858, Ala.

Craft, Henry, 1856, Miss.

Carrol, W. II., 1867.

Cooper, Henry, 1858, Tenn.

Crockett, Robert II., 1853, Tenn.

Carter, 1859, Tenn.

Conde, II. Clay, 1865, N. Y.

Combs, M., Jr., 1865, N.

Craig, W. M., 1867, N.

Castles, I. C., 1868.

Chambers, T. P., 1865, Miss.

Chalmers, Gen. Jas. R., 1865, Miss

Cameron, Chas., 1865, N.

Cherry, John II., 1865, N.

Cook, G. W. T., 1865, N.

Choate, C. A., 1865, N.

Collins, Charles, 1869, Tenn.

Dunlap, Judge W. C., 1835, S.

Douglass, Judge Addison II., 1840, S.

Daniel, Lu. W., 1840, S.

Davidson, 1850, S.

Delafield, 1845, N. Y.

Dickey, Cyrus E., 1858, Ill.

Dashiel, Geo. T., 1858, Tenn.

Duncan, Robt. A. F., 1855, Tenn.

Duff, W. L., 1857, S. C.

Dixon, L. V., 1865, Miss.

Dixon, Judge George, 1847, Ky.

DuVal, W. J., 1867, Tenn.

Dix, II. F., 1866, N.

Dyke, Van W. L., 1866.

DuBois, Dudley M., 1854, Tenn.

Dunlap, W. A., 1866, Tenn.

Eldridge, T. S., 1848, Tenn.

Estes, Judge B. M., 1854, Tenn.

Edrington, T. B., 1868, Ark.

Ethridge, Hon. Emerson, 1868, Tenn.

Ellett, Judge Henry T., 1866, Miss.

Farrington, John C., 1848, S.

Foote, Judge Green P., 1848, S.

Frazer, Selem B., 1848, S.

Frazer, C. W., 1857, S.

Frayser, R. Dudley, 1857, S.

Fowlkes, W. C., 1868, Va.

Finnie, John G., 1857, N. Y.

Farrelley, John Pat., 1854, Ark.

Finlay, Luke W., 1858, Miss.

Flournoy, 1858, Va.

Flippin, W. S., 1850, Tenn

Flippin, Judge John R., 1856, Tenn.

Flippin, Judge Thos. R., 1856, Tenn.

Foote, Gov. Henry S., 1856, Va.

Foote, 1858.

Felton, 1850, Va.

Fentris, F., 1866, Tenn.

Goodall, Gen. John D., 1848, Tenn.

Gregory, J. M., 1857, S.

Gammon, Sam, 1857, Mo.

Gilliam, George, 1857, S.

Greer, Hugh, 1857, Miss.

Gause, Hon. Lucien C., 1859, Tenn.

Glisson, W. B., 1865, S.

Griffin, Gerald L., 1868, Ind.

Green, John, 1868, Tenn.

Gantt, George, 1865, Tenn

Galloway, Judge J. S., 1866, Tenn

Geomano, S. P., 1869.

Gallagher, James, 1866, Ireland

Glisson, Rufus, 1865, S.

Hurlburt, Henry, 1845, S.

Herron, John, 1845, S.

Haynes, Hon. Lanon C., 1866, Tenn.

Hawkins, Gov. Alvin, 1866, Tenn.

Harris, Judge Wm. R., 1847, Tenn.
Harris, Gov. Isham G., 1847, Tenn.
Haskell, Wm. T. 1846, Tenn.
Harris, Jesse L., 1853, Tenn.
Harris, Howell E., 1853, Tenn.
Hallum, John, 1854, Tenn.
Hamilton, Capt., 1858, Tenn.
Harlow, John P., 1858, Canada.
Heath, Judge R. R., 1858, N. C.
Hammond, Judge E. S., 1858, Tenn.
Haynes, A. B., 1858, Tenn.
Humes, W. Y. C., 1858, Tenn.
Hunter, Judge Wm., 1863, N.
Hatch, 1865, Mo.
Haynes, Robert, 1866, Tenn.

Hart, Henry N., 1866, Mo.
Hart, Newton, 1866, Mo.
Horrigan, L. B., 1866, N.
Hill, M. P., 1866.
Hutchinson, Robert, 1866, N.
Heiskell, Gen. J. B., 1866, Tenn.
Heiskell, Judge C. W., 1866, Tenn.
Halsey, Irvin, 1866, N.
Hudson, H. E., 1866, N.
Heathman, J. M., 1866.
Hermans, 1868.
Henry, D. L., 1866.
Hanson, George, 1866.
Hanes, Milton A., 1857, S.

Jarnagin, Hon. Spencer, 1846, Tenn.
Jones, 1849, S.
Jarnagin, Milton P., 1866, Tenn.

Jackson, Judge Howell E., 1854, Tenn.

King, Judge Ephraim H., 1842, S.
Kortrecht, Charles, 1846, N.
Kerr, John S., 1858, Tenn.

Kellar, Col. A. J., 1856, Ohio.
Kelley, John F., 1868, D. C.
Kitridge, A. S., 1866.

Leath, Jas. T., 1843.
Looney, James, 1845, Tenn.
Looney, Robert F., 1845, Tenn
Leatherman, D. M., 1847, S.
Lamb, James, 1847, Tenn.
Lindsey, 1848, S.
Lanier, John C., 1848, S.
Lyles, Col. O. P., 1850, S.
Lee, James, Jr., 1851, Tenn.
Logwood, Gen. T. H., 1856, Tenn.

Luster, John B. 1858, Tenn.
Loague, Hon. John, 1860, Ireland.
Lewis, Judge Barber, 1863, N.
Lewis, 1866.
Lehman, L., 1866.
Lehman, Eugene.
Lee, Pollock B., 1858, Va.
Lee, H. S., 1866, Va.
Lowe, Thomas, 1857.

McKiernan, Judge B. F., 1846.
Massey, B. A., 1848.
McKissick, L. D., 1851, S.
Morgan, Judge R. J., 1859, Ga.
Morgan, E. De F., 1859, Pa.
Micou, T. B., 1859, S.
McMea, Hon. Duncan K., N. C.
Moore, James, 1858, Tenn.
Messick, Wm., 1857, Tenn.
Martin, Hugh B., 1857, S.
McConnico, L. D., 1859.
Mulligan, Gen. Thos. C., 1866, Ky.
Metcalf, C. W., 1866.

McDowell, Judge E. C., 1866.
Matthews, 1866.
Marye, L. S., 1866, S.
Morgan, W. H., 1867.
Martin, A. J., 1866.
Miller, U. W., 1867, S.
Minnis, T. S., 1867, S.
McFarland, L. B., 1868, S.
McSpadden, Jasper, 1859.
Megenden, Ben. D., 1868.
Moyes, 1859, La.
McDavit, J. C., 1858, Tenn.
Mallory, T. S., 1868, Tenn.

Miller, R. B., 1866, Ohio.
McHenry, P., 1866.
Myers, D. E., 1866.

Mulvihill. Pat, 1866, Ireland.
Malone, James H., Ala.

Noe, Judge John A., 1857, Ala.
Neal, John T., 1857, Tenn.

Nabors, Ben., 1857, Miss.

Orne, W. T., 1857.

Onley, John A., 1858, Tenn.

Pope, Leroy, 1845, Ga.
Preston, 1845, Ky.
Perin, E. O., 1845, N. Y.
Poston, W. K. 1847, S.
Pettit, Judge J. W. A., 1850, Ga.
Paine, R. G., 1857, Tenn.
Peyton, James T., 1858, Tenn.
Parham, Richard, 1858. Tenn.
Putnam, 1857, Mass.
Porter George D., 1858, Tenn.
Pickett, Ed. Burke, 1858. Tenn.
Pickett, Ed., Jr., 1858, Tenn.

Pike, Gen. Albert, 1865, Mass.
Pierce, Judge James O., 1865, N.
Pike, Ham, 1865, Ark.
Poston, D. H., 1868, Tenn.
Perkins, M. L., 1868, Tenn.
Peebles, J. C., 1858.
Purviance, J. W., 1868.
Pillow, Gen. Gideon A., 1866, Tenn.
Patterson, Hon. Josiah, 1868, Ala.
Phelan, Hon. James, 1866. Miss.
Phelan, Hon. Geo. R., 1866. Miss.

Richards, L. R., 1840.
Ray, Hon. J. E. R., 1847, Tenn.
Ralston, John, 1856, Tenn.
Rives, L. O., 1857, Tenn.
Rogers, Henry A., 1857, Tenn.
Rose, John, 1858, Tenn.
Rowell, C. H., 1858, Ala.

Rainey, W. G., 1859, S.
Randolph, W. M., 1866, Ark.
Robertson, J. R., 1855, Tenn.
Raney, T. A., 1866.
Reeves, Willis G., 1856, Tenn.
Rogers, W. F., 1866, Ky.
Richards, Channing, 1865.

Searcy, John Bennett, 1840.
Smith, Thomas G., 1843, N.
Stanton, Frederick P., 1843, Ky.
Searcy, George D., 1843.
Smith, Gen. Preston, 1847, S.
Sneed, Judge John L. T., 1847, S.
Sale, Gen. John F., 1847, Ky.
Small, Henry D., 1848, Tenn.
Swaine, Judge John T., 1847, Ohio.
Stewart, M. D. L., 1854, S.
Stovall, W. H., 1854, S.
Scales, Joseph W., 1854, S.
Stockton, 1856, Tenn.
Scott, W. L., 1857, Tenn.
Scruggs, Judge Phineas T., 1858, Miss.
Sullivan, T. L., 1858.
Seay, Chas., 1857, Tenn. } Bros.
Seay, W. A., 1857, Tenn. }
Scott, Chancellor Edward, 1857.

Sykes, Joseph, 1866, Tenn.
Stephens, W. H., 1866, Tenn.
Stephens, Charles M., 1868, Tenn.
Stephens, A. M., 1868, Tenn.
Sharp, 1863, Mo.
Smith John M., 1867.
Smith, Judge Wm. M., 1866, Tenn.
Sale, H. T., 1868, Ky.
Swingley, A. L., 1866.
Smith, Thomas R., 1865.
Smith, Canning, 1866.
Stahl, Geo. E., 1866, N.
Stockton, F. D., 1866, Tenn.
Somerville, J. A., 1866, Tenn.
Sneed, W. M., 1866, S.
Swan, Wm. G., 1856, Tenn.
Sanford, Val., 1866, Tenn.
Sanford, R. A., 1866, Tenn.
Serbrough, Thos. G., 1867.

Tuley, Thomas J., 1835, Va.
Topp, Robertson, 1840.
Turnage, R. K., 1847.
Temple, J. E., 1847.
Trezevant, John Timothy, 1847, Tenn.
Thompson, Wm. G., 1849, Tenn.
Thompson, Philip, 1856, Tenn.
Taylor John A., 1854, Miss.

Unthank, J. H., 1852, Ga.

Vollentine, Hiram, 1850, Tenn.
Vance, Calvin F., 1853, Miss.

Williams, Henry B. S., 1840, Tenn.
Wickersham, James, 1840, Ind.
Wheatley, Seth, 1845, S.
Williams, Kit, 1848, Tenn.
Wright, Judge Archibald, 1850, Tenn.
Wright, Gen. Marcus J., 1852, Tenn.
Walker, J. Knox, 1849, Tenn.
White, Moses, 1853, Tenn.
Waddell, B. B., 1854, Tenn.
Welch, M. D., 1855.
Watson, Sydney Y., 1856, S.
Woodward, J. B., 1866, N.
Williams, C. H., 1855, S.
Yerger, E. M., Tenn., 1847. } Bros.
Yerger, Orvill, Tenn., 1850. }

Thornton, Col., 1852, Va.
Thomas, Asa, 1857, Pa.
Trousdale, Chas., 1858, Tenn.
Turley, Thos. B., 1866, Tenn.
Thurmond, T. B. M., 1865, Mo.
Thurmond, 1865, Mo.
Thompson, Judge Seymour D., 1865, Ohio.
Townshend, Hosea, 1866, N.

Vaughn, Gen., 1867, Tenn.
Venable, Judge S., 1857, Tenn.

Wilson, W. P., 1855, Tenn.
Waddell, V. B., 1860, Tenn.
Winchester, Hon. Geo. W., 1866, Tenn.
Wynne, Val. W., 1868, Tenn.
Washington, Geo., 1868, Ky.
Wright, Gen. Luke E., 1869, Tenn.
Wood, 1866, Tenn., } Father & son.
Wood, 1866, Tenn., }
Warriner, H. C., 1866, Mo.
Walker, Judge S. P., 1867, Tenn.
Westcott, J. W., 1866, N.
Webber, W. W., 1867.
Wallace, Gen., 1867.

> " 'Tis weary watching, wave by wave,
>   And yet the tide heaves onward.
> We climb, like corals, grave by grave,
>   Yet beat a pathway sunward.
> We're beaten back in many a fray,
>   Yet ever strength we borrow,
> And where our vanguard camps to-day
>   Our rear shall rest to-morrow."
>   —GERALD MASSEY

RECOLLECTIONS OF MEMPHIS.

I WAS born in the month of January, 1833, at Cairo, on the Cumberland river above Nashville, Tenn., where my parents, Bluford and Minerva Hallum, and maternal grandparents, John Davis and Sarah his wife, with their eleven children lived. My father was born in 1806, in Smith county, Tenn., where he grew to manhood, when frontier conditions still obtained. He was one of the best gunsmiths and marksmen in the world. I have often seen him shoot matches for a thousand dollar stake, and he won four fifths of all he shot. One hundred yards "off-hand" was his favorite distance. It required steady nerves, and his were as near iron as human organism permits, in every emergency of life. He passionately loved beautiful streams, wild forests, and majestic mountain scenery. The Cumberland mountains were a "joy forever" to him, and he was one of the most industrious readers I ever saw in every field of literature and science. His mother, Jennie Hallum, was born in the territory of Alabama, on the Tombigbee river, and was a woman of extraordinary energy and will power. My grandfather, Hal Hallum, had the will power, without the energy, and sometimes "rode a high horse." All of my other grandparents were born in North Carolina. Grandfather Hallum came in his youth to the Cumberland Valley in that living stream which poured its flood across the Alleghanies after the Revolution, and was an humble factor in the guild of "Commonwealth Builders," under John Sevier and William Blount, when the inspiration of liberty and law radiated the frontier from Watauga. In the summer of 1837 my father and grandfather, Henry Hallum, built a floating house on the Cumberland river, which some would call a flatboat, but it was divided into six comfortable rooms, with all the conveniences and comforts of a dwelling. In this they embarked late in the fall with their families, in all consisting of eleven persons, my father, mother, and three children, of whom I am the eldest, my father's apprentice, Robert Brown, Grandfather and Grandmother Hallum, and Aunts Patsey, Minerva and Luamma. Father and grandfather were of the best river craftsmen, having often descended to New Orleans with keel boats loaded with produce, which was exchanged for merchandise, and the reloaded keel boats were cordelled up the river to Nashville and upper Cumberland ports. Six months was the usual time occupied in the up river trip.

The embarkation was impressive, many gatherings and dinings with kindred and friends preceded it, and finally a dining on board the craft. My maternal grandfather, John Davis, and grandmother, Sarah Davis, with many kindred and citizens, stood on the banks of the Cumberland and bade the voyagers farewell; many tears attested hallowed associations, and my mother was inconsolable—she said it was the last time she would behold her mother on earth—and the prediction was true.

As the craft floated around the island below the town the last handkerchief waved in pathetic farewell. I felt as though my heart would burst in sympathy with my weeping mother, and my sympathetic father could not restrain his emotions. I paid little attention to the others. My mother was a devoted Christian, of orthodox Methodist faith; one of her favorite hymns was that good old devotional song that yet stirs a thousand memories in my soul—"I would not live alway."

After the shades of night gathered over that frail craft, the social circle was formed around the family altar as it floated down that loved stream, and my mother and aunts sang that hymn and others that yet ring in my ear and heart like the voice of angels.

The frail craft swept by Nashville one October evening, with the onward flood, and the first sight of the city left a photograph yet vivid in outline. At night they generally tied up the boat, and after passing out the Cumberland often stopped several days at a time; wild game was found in great abundance, bear, deer, turkey, squirrels, ducks and wild geese, and our table was bountifully supplied with meats, vegetables, and delicacies. I remember one time seeing a large deer with antlers peering high above the water, swimming the Mississippi river just below the boat—father and grandfather entered the skiff, chased and caught it.

A few steamboats were then navigating the river and were always a source of alarm to my boyish heart, when they came near the craft, as they often did, seemingly in a spirit of mischief, our boat would rock and ride the waves, and dip and plunge as though it would go to the bottom every moment.

After a voyage of six weeks our craft was moored in Wolfe river, near Memphis, where we remained three months prospecting for a location in the new country. Father located on the Memphis and Summerville road, twenty miles from Memphis, where he remained until 1840, after which he removed to what was then known as the Mississippi Hills, eighteen miles north of Memphis, where he improved a farm, leaving it in 1844 to return to Sumner county, Tennessee, at the urgent request of my mother. Grandfather moved to Mississippi, and located on the Yocnapatawka, where Aunts Patsy, Luamma and Minerva were married respectively to James Davis, Wm. Morrison, and James Owens, planters.

My grandparents died there in 1846 and 1848. Memphis was then a very small village on the bluff—the exchange of produce and merchandise was almost exclusively confined to trading boats anchored at the wharf. The city was laid off in 1826 by General Jackson, General Winchester of Craigfont, Judge John Overton, and John C. McLemore, who were proprietors of the " John Rice Grant" of 5,000 acres granted by the State of North Carolina in 1786, and by him coveyed to the grantees above named, who also owned the adjoining grant of 5,000 acres, on which Jackson Mound and Fort Pickering stands. Gen. Jackson was the moving spirit in this land enterprise and location of the town. He always had an eye to business. At that time he owned a large trading post or mercantile establishment in Mississippi, on the Yazoo river. Randolph, sixty miles above, was then thought to be the successful rival of Memphis for commercial honors, and but for the sagacity and enterprise of Gen. Jackson and co-owners of the third Chickasaw Bluffs would to-day have been the great commercial mart between St. Louis and New Orleans.

In 1838 a large number of Indians were removed from Mississippi, Alabama, and Georgia to the Indian Territory, and were camped for fifty miles at intervals out along the Memphis and Sommerville road and Memphis and Hernando road, and on the Pigeon Roost road. They were the first Indians I ever saw. My father, in prospecting for a location, carried me with him for company— in fact I was more of a companion than a child to him. My Grandmother Hallum, nee Jennie Gillespie, was born on the Tombigbee river in Alabama, and when three years old was captured with others by the Indians and held in captivity for many months before the whites surprised and routed the Indians and rescued her. She had an inveterate dislike to the Indians, from whom I really imbibed her feelings, and yet appreciate that memorable saying of the celebrated Kit Carson: "I never knew but one good Indian, and he was dead."

I have since seen many thousands of various tribes ex-

tending from California to the Mississippi river, and am
not yet much improved in this opinion.   The Indian has
an inborn hatred for the white man, whom he regards as
a usurper and robber—restraint and fear are the only
agencies which quiet the torch, tomahawk, and scalping
knife.   Let moralists in their easy chairs write and de-
claim until Gabriel blows his trumpet, but the fact remains.   One rifle is worth a ton of Bibles in the march of
civilization and empire, and has been the only evangelizer
as yet.

In March, 1838, the steamer Fulton was lying at the
wharf at Memphis to transport these savages to the
Indian Territory; after receiving her cargo of human
freight she steamed up the river a mile, cracked on a
good head of steam, turned and came with flying colors
at the masthead, and when opposite the wharf every Indian leaped into the stream and swam ashore.   I was
looking on, with my hand in my father's, the chiefs with
clubs in hand made the blood fly from the recalcitrants
and forced them to re-embark on the steamer.

Forty-eight years after this incident a very tall old
Creek Indian came to my office and employed me to defend him against an indictment for larceny in the Federal
Court at Fort Smith.   He was a minister of the gospel,
well educated, and spoke English perfectly, his name
was Chickatubby.   I mentioned the incident above related, he laughed heartily and told me he was one of the
number that swam ashore.   He was acquitted of the
charge of larceny.

At that time and up to the advent of plank roads in
1852 the dirt roads leading to Memphis were almost im-
passable in the winter season, cotton for a hundred miles
in the interior was hauled principally by ox teams to
Memphis.   I have seen trains of these teams several
miles in length, with wagons stalled and broken down at
every mile of the road, and often oxen either dead or worn

out and abandoned on the roadside. Plank roads were, afterwards in 1850, extended out to the county line, with toll-gates every five miles, but they did not last long and were ultimately abandoned. I filed a quo warranto in 1857, and had the charter of the Memphis and Sommerville Plank Road Co. declared forfeited for noncompliance with the charter. This had to be done before a ferry over Wolf river at Raleigh could be established, and hands appointed to work the road.

In 1840 Memphis began to grow rapidly and to assume metropolitan airs, and the old commercial and common law court, a chancery court and a criminal court were established at Memphis in the decade between 1840 and 1850, with many changes and modifications since to meet the growing demands of the city.

The Appeal, a democratic paper, and the Eagle and Enquirer, a whig paper, were both published in Memphis, and were the first newspapers I remember to have seen.

I learned the alphabet, and in fact learned to read quite well from the old Appeal, sitting on my anxious and patient father's lap, to whose memory I can never estimate the standard of obligation.

In 1839 I went to my first school, when but six years old, and was regarded as a prodigy because I could read with great facility, all the New York series of readers, and spell every word in Webster's spelling book. Jarrett Edwards, one of the world's best men, was my teacher, and when I was admitted to the Bar was still my very kind and affectionate friend, a word of encouragement from him was worth a coronet to me. The first political speech I ever heard was delivered at Green Bottom by Frederick P. Stanton, afterward a member of Congress from the Memphis district, and Governor of the Territory of Kansas under Buchanan's administration. The next political speeches I heard were delivered in "the

Mississippi Hills," by Tom Avery "the dray driver," who, I think, succeeded Stanton in Congress, and Thos. Turley, the able lawyer, father of Thos. B. Many of the men in Shelby county whom I knew in early boyhood grew to be wealthy, and with rare exceptions were my strong friends, when I returned to them in 1852, after an absence of eight years.

It has been my fortune in life to have strong friends and aggressive enemies, aggressive because my profession made it an imperative duty to unearth and expose fraud. A negative, passive character is not adapted to cope with the emergencies which often arise in the discharge of professional duty, particularly as society was then organized, every gentleman was expected to resent any imputation of his courage or integrity, and the man who disregarded these primal laws became at once a back number. When the glove and gage of battle was thrown in his face, there were but two ways to meet it, bravely like a man, or coweringly like a cur.

Every age and people admires one, despises the other. Ornithologists and the sailors of the sea tell us of the brave little petrel that plumes its wing and rides the storm when larger birds hie away to the windward islands. We were still near frontier conditions. Perhaps the chivalry of those days can be better illustrated and understood by stating an incident or two in the life of one of the ablest lawyers of Mississippi, the Hon. Reuben Davis, cousin to President Davis. In 1842 Judge Howry was holding court at Athens, Mississippi, and during the argument of a question of law arising in the progress of a trial the Judge, without justifiable cause or provocation, fined Davis fifty dollars. He was amazed and thunderstruck, and in a blaze of indignation drew his knife and threw the point in the table—it quivered and vibrated ominously—his object was to force the Judge to order him to jail to complete his arbitrary action, but the foresight of Judge Gholson, in moving an adjournment, prevented a death scene in court. (Recollections of Mississippi and Mississippians, by Reuben Davis, 144.)

In 1844 Judge Gholson of the Federal Court of Mississippi, adopted the arbitrary rule of not permitting lawyers to argue their cases in his court. Davis had an important case pending in that court, and rose to argue it, and was ordered to take his seat, which he declined to do, upon the ground that he was only demanding a right in the most respectful terms. The Court again ordered him to take his seat, and stated that if obedience was not yielded he would send him to jail. Davis said: "You have the arbitrary power to make that order, but execute it if you dare."

The Bar stood up and crowded around Davis, and the Court receded. An attempt to execute such an order would have resulted in instant bloodshed. He proceeded with the argument.

With all this, I never knew a more chivalrous and courageous gentleman in my life than Reuben Davis, none more cautious of invading the God-given prerogative of his fellow men, and none quicker to repel their invasion. His daughter Bessie lives here in the city where I live, came here a stranger several years ago (1890) to take charge as principal in a Conservatory of Music, for which she was splendidly equipped. He left her in my charge, and the last time I ever met him he grasped my hand, spoke of his great affection for his daughter, and with tears streaming down his cheeks bade me farewell. Within a year from that time he passed away at his home in Aberdeen, Mississippi. He presented me the book, of which he is the author; it is a work of much interest and I prize it as I do the poems of Gen. Albert Pike.

LOVE OF NATIVE LAND.

LOVE of native land is a primal law with all races of men. The Laplander, with his dogs and deer and vast solitudes of snow and ice, thinks his home the chosen spot of earth; the Bedouin in the desert loves his native waste of sand and cloud; the Esquimaux, in his snow hut, surrounded with eternal fields of snow and glacier, feels the inspiring touch of love for the everlasting solitude of his arctic surroundings no less than he who comes into life surrounded by a wilderness of tropical splendor. The Irish pilgrim loves his Erin. The Swede his native Alps. So I love every hill, valley, stream and purling rivulet that adorns and abides my "native heath," where the mind first unfolded its petals and flowers and drank the glories of nature and life on a vivid landscape painted in fresh and fadeless colors that knows no guile. And I love all the good people that swarm in the front and background of that hallowed landscape who comforted and made glad my boyish heart, and planted so many flowers in its virgin soil, when hope and aspiration, stimulated by a father's counsel and a mother's prayers, reached forth and looked upward with tenderest yearnings, like the tendrils of the ivy, for support while it climbed higher.

There was Col. Alfred Wynne a mile down the pike, wealthy in this world's goods, but with a far greater wealth of head and heart, the son-in-law of Gen. James Winchester, with broad acres of field, and pastures filled with lowing herds and fine horses, he so much loved, stretching away to the old baronial Cragfont, that towered like a medieval castle on the Rhine or Mose, overlooking Bledsoe's creek, that famous stream that came pouring its crystal waters from the spurs of the Cumberland mountains. A house full of noble boys and girls, the richest heritage of the State, a fine library of choice literature and science, and the best periodicals of the day. My father's friend in all the term implies in those good old days when head and heart were the standards of manhood. The postoffice was a few rods away from that old hospitable mansion, the old stage coach came and went, the driver sounded his bugle a mile away coming and going, its shrill and tuneful notes echoed through valley and glen. I, my father's barefooted postboy, with a heart as lithe and light as the bird that sang in the foliage.

A thousand times the "Colonel," as we called him, filled my arms with books and papers "for Bluford," my father and his boy, and made me feel as comfortable and happy as his own dear girls and boys. What a charm he threw around and over the social circle. Integrity was the standard by which he measured men. He came often to my father's—father as often went to him, they were great talkers, both of Jackson's faith in politics—they had a rule to divide time in social converse. Social caste, that corroding curse which measures men by dollars and cents and teaches a shoddy and effeminate offspring that God exalted them above all who have less of spoil and plunder, never tainted their hearts. His sons, Bolivar and Val. W., became lawyers—the latter is on the Roster.

Two brothers, the "Gillespies," my father's relatives, lived near by in the valley of Greenfield, at the foot of the Cumberland spurs, near Hopewell church, with two fine, handsome sons, Graham and Marion, my boon companions.

I loved to steal away at the end of the week from the husbandry of the fields and go to them. Forty and five years have come and gone since then, but Miss Belle, the daughter of Marion, often picks up a racy pen and writes

me a bonnie letter. On the way hither I often stopped
at Jerry Belotes' to see Miss Betty, the happy and beautiful blonde, who acknowledged that she liked me, but
there was an ocean before me with stormy breakers to be
crossed, with a poor bark, too frail to risk the fortunes of
such a girl in such a craft.

In the vicinage lived "Uncle Jacky Wilkes," deeply
imbued with that practical religion that lifts and makes
man great in the light of apostolic creeds. When the
professors gave me first place on Commencement day,
he volunteered to loan me all the money the occasion required. May the sod rest lightly on his grave, and God
bless all his descendants. There was "Uncle" Billy
Malone, who "went about the world doing good?" One
of his sons became prominent in the legal guild, and Bettie, the bright flaxen-haired little girl, my classmate when
we were children, married Mr. Wray, a prominent lawyer in the Lone Star State, and Mildred, that princess of
beauties, my boyish love, "who weighed the world as a
feather" against her girlish troth. At that lordly mansion hospitality was only limited by the horizon.

On the adjoining farm lived Jonathan Wiseman, a Baptist minister, who practiced the religion he taught.

> "Tried each art, reproved each dull delay,
> Allured to brighter worlds and led the way."

Over the hill from the old homestead, beyond that
stately grove of poplar forest with its burthen of fra-
grance in the spring, lived "Uncle Johnny Shaver," the
prototype of all that is true and good in man.

To the northwest of the old home, across that sylvan
scene of woodland forest, lived Gen. William Hall, who
spent a long life doing as he wished to be done by. He
came in the early days with ax and rifle and cleared the
wilderness of Indians, and could "shoulder his crutch
and show how fields were won."

Bushrod Thompson, whose kind and amiable nature

was only exceeded by the best of wives, with a house full
of boys and girls. Ike, George, Willis, Davis, Emily and
Martha, all schoolmates in the pioneer log house, near
the rocky spring and Hawthorne grove. Martha would
risk her life for a practical joke. All the boys wore the
gray, and George and Davis fell in Shiloh's battle.

"Uncle Davy Chenault," on Greenfield's fat lands,
with a fine farm for each of his many children, the best
of farmers, the kindest of neighbors, would send his carriage for "John" to come and dine with him. His sons
"wore the gray," and after Appomattox came to me.
What a delight it was to serve them, and when I once
more met "Uncle Davy" he gave me his blessing. Addison Jones lived half way between the old homestead
and the college—his banquet hall was always open to
the college boys—and lad and lassie were lavishly entertained by his hospitable wife and beautiful sisters.

"Uncle Billy Reed" came over the Cumberland mountains when the virgin forest was full of buffalo and Indians, and helped build blockhouses and forts to protect
the early settlers from Indian depredations. The Misses
Neely, two brunette queens of beauty, his granddaugh-
ters, gave many entertainments to the college boys.
"Uncle Jimmy Harrison," with his boys Nat and Tobe
and Tup, lived on the hill to the west. He preferred
Clay to Jackson, and about that he and father never
could agree. They called each other "Jim" and "Bluford," and walked over Stoner's Hill, that looked down
on the valley over the old homestead, and walked and
talked over the battleground where this Indian fell, and
that one died, and where the rescued women and children
sat and prayed when the rifle was cracking and pealing
through the forest, and where old Tom, the slave, performed prodigies of valor in hand-to-hand contests with
the Indian. He, too, was fighting to rescue his son.
Within the radius of a few miles lived many families,

3

early settlers in Sumner county—the Mentlows, Harlans,
Morgans, Winchesters, Jamisons, Crenshaws, Lauder-
dales, Seays, Winstons, Wrights, Hibbets, Pattersons,
Bushes, Bates, Heads, Tyrees, Youries, Turners, Ma-
lones. All the elder members, and ninety per cent of
their children are dead, the ceaseless waves have "swept
them onward." All of these people were as kind as kindred to me, and but one lived in the circle whose name is
not in this little Roster, was ever unkind to me. I went
to his house, was his guest, solicited his patronage to a
school I was competent to teach, and he rudely drove a
thorn where a rose might have been planted. "I will
rub my head against the college wall and qualify myself
for something great." At that time it was the rudest
blast that had ever shocked my sensitive nature. Years
rolled away and the Civil War piled him up in the debris
where opportune aid would have saved him. When on
one of my annual visits to the old homestead, where many
friends of my boyhood congregated on these attic occasions to thrice welcome me, he came and solicited aid,
which I could have easily then extended, just as he could
have done when I wanted and needed his patronage to a
little school.

It was not a Christian spirit in me to remind him of
the bread which he could have cast upon the waters, but
I did it, and told him I was not a Christian in that spirit
which returned good for evil.

Read the Saviour's parable of the sower. I cannot embrace that injunction which commands us when one cheek
is slapped to turn the other. The theory of religion is
much easier acquired than the practice of precepts; the
mote is easier discerned than the beam.

Many a note came from, and went to, Hawthorne Hill,
where the Misses Turner entertained youth and beauty
in sight of the old homestead. The body grows old, the
limbs weak, but the mind, the memory, ever drinks at
the fount of youth.

THE CODE DUELLO.

HE Code was part of the *lex non scripta* of gentlemen when I came to the Bar, and with no class or profession was it of more primal force than with lawyers, the army not excepted. It was a condition confronting society and had its advocates and opponents. Those who provoked, yet denied its obligation, were regarded as pseudo moralists and their sincerity and courage were alike doubted. S. S. Prentiss, from Maine, General Albert Pike, from Massachusetts, General Jackson, Robert Crittenden, the Conways, from Tennessee, the Rectors from Virginia, with their numerous descendants of public prominence in the West, Governor Henry S. Foote, a native of Virginia, Henry Clay, John Randolph, Thomas H. Benton, Charles Lucas, Governor B. Gratz Brown, Governor Reynolds, Davidson, Lindsey, Nolan, Pope, Graves, Cilley, Henry G. Smith, afterwards Judge of the Supreme Court of Tennessee, John Taylor, of Memphis, General Preston Smith, of Memphis, to which might be added a long roster of prominent and noted men, recognized and fought under the rules and requirements of the Code, and all, with two exceptions, were members of the Bar. It was of primal obligation with a class of chivalrous men, who adorned the highest class of society. Humanitarians and theologians and professed Christians, who are more conversant with theory than practice, may preach and teach until Gabriel sounds his trumpet, that when one cheek is slapped we must turn the other in meekness, and yet there always has been and always will be a chivalrous class of men who will fight upon terms of equality in defense of their reputations and honor. Nations equally as advanced in civilization as our own, the highest classes of

France, Germany, Spain, Italy, Russia, recognize and
enforce the rules of the Code regardless of all penal laws
that can be spread on the statute books, and public sentiment in all these countries frowns on the enforcement of
penalties against duelling. So far as these penal laws
are concerned they belong to that class of dead letter law
which lie buried under the frowns of public opinion, and
justly so. When gentlemen go to the field they are on terms
of absolute equality, and nothing can be devised by man
fairer and more equitable. Nerve and will forces may be
unequal but nothing else. No street broils endanger the
lives of innocent people; when gentlemen are governed by
the high punctilious laws of the Code encounters are not
near so frequent. The percentage of death by conflicts
vastly decreases, the bully and braggart and spaniel are
never found on the field where terms of equality prevail.
These were the considerations addressing themselves to
every young man entering the profession, he could choose
for himself, and had it to do. As for myself I recognized
the obligations of the Code, always believed in it, and always will. And with all the changes the supposed advance in civilization has made, I would, if my life were to
be acted over again, act on the same conviction, with the
same conditions confronting me. Rainbows are nice
things to talk about, but they fade from the college boy's
lexicon when he enters the field of practical life in a law
office where his chief occupation is to checkmate and expose fraud. Every man's life is to a greater or less extent moulded by conditions which confront him in action.
During the formative period of character it is difficult to
avoid, easy to commit error, and every man must fix his
own standard in the best foundations his own judgment
admits. His highest function is to first mould his own
guides on a correct basis, then to lead and mould public
opinion without being led by it, because it is sometimes
the worst of all tyrants.

HOISTED ON MY OWN PETARD.

I WELL remember the first shot of sarcasm and biting irony thrust at me like a javelin sent home by Ithureal. Mr. McGilbra Rogers, a well-to-do planter living near Collierville, had subscribed ten dollars to build a Baptist church. When it was finished he made some objection to the cornice, refused to pay his subscription, and the church brought suit to recover. It came on appeal from the Justice to the Circuit Court at Raleigh, and the congregation retained me. Many witnesses were in attendance, and the cost amounted to ten times the amount involved. I made a five minutes' talk in a conversational tone, and told the jury that it had become a notorious fact that Mr. Rogers, although possessed of ample means, was piteously afflicted with a disposition to dispute all claims against him, however just and honest, so much so that all demands against him were finally collected by an officer of the law, and that it ill became juries to encourage such petty litigation, and then took my seat. The jury decided against him, and I thought no more about it. Coming up the steps leading up to the court room after dinner, I met him, and he stopped me, with an angry scowl on his face, set off with an angular hawk-bill nose, which gave him a formidable appearance, and I expected some trouble. He said with a sarcastic grin, "You say no little suits ought ever to be brought to this court. If there were no little suits, how in the h—l would you ever get anything to do?" I ought to have laughed and enjoyed it, as I do now, the insult was more in the manner than the words. I caught his Roman nose and pulled it until the blood spurted all over my shirt bosom. He did not resent it, but stepped back and gave me an example of Christian forbearance that cut deep and made me feel penitent in a moment. "Why, John, I was only joking." I expressed much sorrow at not having interpreted him correctly. I was retained by him in all of his litigation from that day until his death.

A KISS TENDERED IN OPEN COURT.

IT is said the law is a dry subject. I deny the allegation, and cite the following precedent:

There was a beautiful young widow, living in Shelby county, on whom the law cast the administration of her husband's estate. I was retained and she attended court and made oath that she would lawfully administer the estate and account for all the assets. In those days deponents were required to place their hands on the Holy Bible and kiss the book when an oath was administered. Most all ladies are embarrassed when they first attend court. She stood up by the clerk's desk when the oath was administered; the clerk told her to kiss the book; she seemed dazed and amazed and stood motionless. The invitation was repeated the third time, when with trepidation she turned and said, "If I have to kiss anybody I will kiss Mr. Hallum."

AN UNEXPECTED STRANGER IN MY OFFICE.

IN 1855 a gentleman of tall, commanding and majestic mien, called at my office quite early in the day, of whom I had heard and read much but had never met him. With a princely salutation which of itself told that he was no ordinary man, he said: "Mr. Hallum, I presume?" His personnel was such that I could not possibly mistake the man, and I said, "Yes, General, I will salute you by that title though I know not which of your many great titles you prefer, but to a young man whose kindred have followed a hero to victory and empire there is no greater title than General. San Jacinto was to you what Waterloo was to Wellington. Thrice a member of Congress, Governor of two States, President of a Republic, and Senator in Congress are illustrious titles, but that of hero of San Jacinto in its vast results is greater than all. If I am not mistaken I have the honor of General Houston's presence." That little speech touched a tender spot in his heart. That curious compound of dress imparted an individuality as striking as that of his life, which had been one of frailty and greatness. Holding me by both hands he asked, "Whose son are you? William's, Robert's, Andrew's or Henry Hallum's?" I said, "The grandson of Henry, and the son of Bluford. You will perhaps better remember my Uncle Henry Hallum, and Cousin Rance Hallum, who footed it from Tennessee to share with you the dangers and glories of San Jacinto. My Uncle Henry's body rests in an unknown grave in Texas, and though no marble shaft marks the spot, we know it is consecrated ground to a soldier's rest. You see, General, my family have a pride in your name, and interest in your fame, and inheritance in

(31)

your renown.   Remote and humble it is true, but none
the less cherished by them."   A tear came to the eye of
that unique character which towers in the solitude of its
own originality.   I was but twenty-two years of age ; he
put his hand on my head and gave me his blessing.   He
was to speak that night in Odd Fellows Hall.   His
brother's widow, with whom I was well acquainted, then
lived in a fine mansion at the northwest corner of Madison
and Third streets.   His business was to have a land title
investigated for her, and he charged me with the commission.   I wanted to call in the local gentry and introduce
them, but he was in no humor for that and declined.
When I finished the work in hand, he asked my fee, and
when told that I made no charge, he said, "No, sir, you
are just commencing in life and can't afford that," and
laid a ten dollar gold piece on my desk.   I rode with him
from Raleigh to Memphis and drank deep at the fount of
his animated and magnetic inspiration.   He would have
me sit on the platform from which he spoke, and although
an older and abler man had been selected to introduce him
to the audience, he requested that honor should be conferred on me, and I introduced him to that vast auditory.
His speech was one of the most impressive and impassioned pieces of oratory and eloquence I ever heard.   He
said: "I have won an empire, and like a dutiful son, laid
it in the lap of my mother, and I have won a name that
will survive long after my traducers are forgotten."   He
spoke two hours, and held a levee after the speech was
over.   Then taking me by the arm he insisted that I
should go with him to his sister-in-law's and stay all
night with him, which I did.

JUDGE JOHN C. HUMPHREYS.

THE Eleventh Judicial Circuit of Tennessee was at that time, 1854, composed of the counties of Shelby, Fayette, Hardeman, and Tipton. John C. Humphreys, of Fayette county, was Judge. He was first elected under the old system by the Legislature, and after *vox populi, vox Dei* supplanted that method, was elected by the people. He was a pure man, an able, upright Judge; in person tall, and of delicate mould, with a tendency to consumption, which ultimately carried him off. Usually he was very sedate, and dignified, and inclined to be austere, not fraternizing much with the Bar, but I have occasionally seen him carried off his feet in a paroxysm of mirth at some outburst of wit or repartee. He viewed it as a great and unpardonable infringement on his judicial dignity to ask him a question, even at chambers, on an application for an injunction.

If an injunction was applied for during a session of his court, the attorney could hand him the bill and say what it was for but not one word more touching that case, unless he was on the bench in open court. He threatened to send me to jail once because I asked him what conclusion he had come to on my application for an injunction, after he had had it for several days. "When court opens I will tell you all about it, sir, but ought to send you to jail for thirty days for asking me that question when off the bench, and I only excuse you because you are a mere boy, and evidently quite a fool." I was greatly shocked, and my first impulse was to knock him down and learn him some extra judicial ethics, but before I could catch my breath or speak he said, "Come on into court and I will tell you my conclusion." The application was for an injunction restraining the sheriff from selling quite a variety of personal property, including cows, bulls, sheep, rams, and a stud horse. He granted the injunction as to every thing except the stud horse, the reason for the exception I did not then perceive, nor have I ever discovered it since. After writing his fiat and handing it to the clerk, he raised up and said: "Brother Hallum, have you not yet learned that the law does not permit injunctions against stud horses?" I said: "No, sir, I have not so discovered, although your Honor so holds. You must excuse me for not believing your ruling to be good law, but if you will further excuse me—now you are on the bench —I will say that I have discovered you are very partial to stud horses, and draw invidious distinction between that noble sire and bulls, and rams, animals equally under the protection of the law." "Sir," he said, "are you determined on a jail sentence for contempt?"

"No, your Honor, I think perhaps as much of studs as you do, but cannot throw around them the same protection you do, but let us get to something more pleasant. I hold in my hand, Judge, one of the finest witticisms I ever read, and am sure it will relieve me from servitude in jail and restore you to your normal good humor," and proceeded to read what always amuses me. It was a letter from a raw son of Erin to his brother in Ireland, and ran thus:

"Dear Pat—Potatoes in this country are two bits a bushel, and whisky the same, and one man is as good as another, and sometimes a damn sight better."

This restored the *statu quo* and he roared, and said, "I see the application, I guess I'll not send you to jail this time."

Judge Humphreys was universally beloved by the Bar, these little sallies of occasional temper were over in a moment, and always ended in closer relations. He was eminently an upright man, and I have often thought the ablest *nisi prius* Judge I ever appeared before. I have argued a thousand cases before him, and I revere his memory.

A CANDIDATE FOR OFFICE.

IN 1856 "some of my friends" had no trouble whatever in persuading me to "run for the office of Attorney General for the 11th Judicial Circuit." As the English say, I "stood for the office," and was left standing.

Thos. R. Smith, of Bolivar, and Wm. Hardin, of the same place, in the upper end of the District, were my competitors.

Being the only candidate from the lower end of the District, and from much the larger voting county, it was erroneously thought that I had the enemy corralled, at least by far the best chance.

But I was no politician and never have been; the backset I then received in that direction dwarfed my future growth in that line, and deprived the country of much valuable public service. I had not then learned the potential value of the biblical admonition, that "the race is not always to the swift nor the battle to the strong," but at the end it was fully impressed. I innocently bluffed up against the "Snollygoster in politics."

My defeat was compassed by one of the most unscrupulous politicians Tennessee ever knew. "Old Phil Glenn," of Sommerville, had a lot of circulars issued and distributed at the polls all over the Circuit on the day of election, in which it was stated that I had withdrawn from the race. The only railroad then in the Circuit ran from Memphis to Moscow, thence to Sommerville. The great mass of votes were deposited in rural districts, not reached by telegraph, and there was no chance to discover and expose the fraud. It was a success, and Mr. Hardin was chosen. He was an elegant gentleman, but Smith was the best lawyer of the three.

"Old Phil" carried a bay window in front that weighed something under a ton, and was always ready to do the questionable work for the Democratic party.

He was elected to the legislature once, and made the canvass on foot, and would arrive at the hustings about the time his opponents were closing their addresses to the horny-handed sons of toil. He reminded them of his poverty and of the great disadvantages he labored under in trying to keep up with his aristocratic opponents, who rolled around in carriages and luxury, while he toiled and sweated on foot over dusty roads trying to keep up with them.

Phil "got there."

Once during the canvass of Gov. Harris and Netherland for Governor, Phil advised the former to "Fling dirt at him, Governor, and fling it lively." Old "Snollygoster" again.

I bear no malice to the memory of "Old Phil." We have had many a hearty laugh. After all, I regard his circular as a "blessing in disguise." Peace to his ashes—may the daisies bloom and the sod rest lightly on his grave.

L, simply "Lu," was the brotherly greeting of all his friends, and they were numerous enough to embrace everybody he knew. A Chesterfield under all conditions, a royal bird of tropical plumage, in the social realm. He owned a farm "down in the Point," near Raleigh, and spent most of his time there. He was of the generation which was retiring to give place to the one in which I made advent. In physique he was small, with one short leg that found difficulty in keeping up with the robust limb. He had a joyful smile that took in the earth, was the soul of honor, scrupulously courteous, rigidly polite, with a shrill metallic voice. He was deeply learned in ancient lore. Coke upon Lyttleton, Selden, Fearne on Contingent Remainders, and the Pandects of Justinian, were his favorite authors and studies. Modern authors, if they happened to differ from these ancient headlights, were considered untrustworthy innovators. His repository of legal learning came from these Silurean bed-rocks. He had two distinct identities, one for his coterie of friends, the other for the courts. He was cast in a severe antique mould and believed in the mace and black gown for judges, and everything else that was stiff and unbending in court. He was stiff and methodical in arranging his geological specimens of law. He never indulged in rhetoric, never shot an arrow at the sun, or sat on a rainbow in court; but these qualities he had in tropical luxuriance for the social circle. When he calmly rose to address the court, supporting his short, restless leg on a cane, he looked as cold as an arctic glacier and as stiff as a monumental shaft; then the lawyers would whisper while he was clearing up his throat,

"Listen, now we will learn more of my Lord Coke and wherein he differs from Lyttleton, and catch flashes from the Pandects of Justinian, and if anything more modern gets in his way it or him will catch hell." When court was over Lu. would gather up his friends and "unbend the bow," sample the vintages from the Rhine to the Moselle and eulogize all the classics in literature. He was one of the rarest and best of the F. F. V.'s that ever came West to grow up with the country. None knew him but to love him. He did not want office. He was comfortable and self-reliant, and died in the last years of the fifties.

TRIAL OF CADY AND STANTON FOR PASSING COUNTERFEIT MONEY.

1855.

IN December, 1855, I was employed to defend two men—Cady and Stanton, strangers, who on that day drove out from Memphis to Raleigh, and passed a ten dollar bill to James M. Coleman, a merchant. They drove off on the road leading south from Raleigh to the Macon road. Very soon after they left, Coleman discovered that the bill was a genuine one dollar bill raised to a ten dollar bill, and sent an officer in hot haste after them. They were caught and brought back.

None of the "queer" was found on them, but a suspicious circumstance was developed. They had driven a few yards from the road, lighted a match and burned something, what was not known. They claimed to have lighted a cigar at the spot, and that the match, without design, thrown into the dry leaves, caused the fire, but they had no cigar when arrested a few furlongs farther on, and why did they turn out of the road to light a cigar?

They had no money to pay me, but Stanton had a valuable farm near Pomeroy, Ohio, and wealthy connexions. He so represented to me, and the facts as to that afterwards proved to be true. They gave me their joint note for two thousand dollars to defend them, and mortgage on the Ohio farm to secure it.

Stanton was about twenty-five years old, and of but ordinary ability. Cady was thirty-two, and one of the shrewdest men I ever saw.

It was evident if guilty, that Cady was the leader.

As most criminals, where the probative facts charged are not clear, they solemnly protested their innocence in consultation with me, but I felt perplexed and doubtful as to their innocence, none as to my ability to successfully defend them.

The Committal trial came on next day, and they were held to answer at the January term and committed to jail. They told, when questioned, where they boarded in Memphis, at Mr. Smoot's, a painter by trade. Before being carried back to jail I found that a search warrant had been quietly issued by the Justice and that Quince Cannon, the Constable, and Jesse L. Harris, the attorney employed to prosecute, had started in a buggy to Memphis with the search warrant to discover evidences of their guilt, if it existed.

I told Cady of this and that he must truthfully answer in a moment, and give me an order for their baggage if it contained any inculpating evidence. He turned pale as death, and trembled as a reed in the wind, and said $300,-000 was in their baggage. I had the fastest trotter in town, and could overtake and pass the officer and attorney although they had a mile the start and were urging their horse.

While the order for the baggage was being written, my horse was being hitched up. I gave him the whip and at the five-mile post passed them. Safe, then I knew, no telegraph or telephone to checkmate. I obtained two

large valises, paid their board bill, and took things easy,
very complacently, and I confess, with a degree of satisfaction at having headed off my elder rival, a rivalry not
justified when viewed from that high standpoint of the
profession which, without envy, welcomes a young man
to the guild.

I never for one moment in my life envied any man because of patronage and success, and do not know the un-
happy sensations of an envious nature, but have had it to
contend with all along the line for forty-one years, not much
before, but much since, the war. I carried the valises to
my residence, then with my father-in-law, near the site
of the National Cemetery, since established. After all
had retired but the old man, whom I had taken into my
confidence, I opened these valises, and after counting until we were tired, but without finishing, we were satisfied that there was at least three hundred thousand dollars in counterfeit bills, many sheets of which had not
been cut and signed.

These bills were consigned to the fire, and it took quite
a while to burn them.

We retired late, feeling that the destruction was complete, but next morning George, the negro foreman on the
plantation—black as the ace of spades—came running in
with a cotton basket full of these new, crisp bills, with
his white eyes rolling heavenward in an attitude of adora-
tion and wonder which would have furnished the brush of
a Raphael or an Angelo with a fine subject. He was
followed by all the negroes on the plantation, who thought
freedom at hand and the days of labor ended. Charles,
my hostler, patted his thighs and hands alternately, while
others danced on the lawn an "old Virginia breakdown."
Others sang plantation melodies.

While I was amused I felt somewhat alarmed for the
safety of my clients. Such a miracle in the eyes of the
slaves was a difficult matter to explain and suppress,

and my youthful anxiety to defeat an older fox might,
after all, overleap and defeat itself.   I told the negroes
that it was the work of the devil, and burnt it up before
their eyes, and had the field gleaned for the remainder,
which might have escaped their attention, and they found
a lot more.   While counsel could not be put on the stand,
nor negroes testify against the whites at that time, all
others could have been forced to testify, had the secret
got abroad; but it did not, and the men were acquitted,
the inculpatory circumstances in proof not being sufficient to warrant or sustain conviction.

This clientage presented questions of morals, ethics,
and law, requiring profound consideration, in the solution
of which moralists and jurists arrive at opposite conclusions.

A condition confronted me, in determining for myself.
I had to steer through the waters of the mad, seething
straits—Charybdas on the right, Scilla on the left.   If
I looked to the standard of moralists alone I found many
converging, many diverging lines, and but few parallels
to purely legal standards applied to the administration of
criminal codes.   That standard would not fit all, while it
did many cases.

My oath of office fixed, ethics and loyalty enjoined
the strictest fidelity to clients, and the law imposes it.
Their secrets were confided to me alone ; the depravity in
which they were so deeply involved was imparted to me
after the relation of client and attorney had been fixed by
contract, by law, imposing rigid fidelity to the exclusion
of debatable questions.   The constitutions and laws of
all the States and our federative system guarantee a fair
trial, and hermetically seal the lips of counsel from exposure of facts coming to him in that relation.   But view
these oft-arising questions as we may, we tread on delicate ground; debate with ourselves on lines as delicate as
those of the rainbow, we cannot fix the junction where

3

one color separates from another to form a luminous background of distinction.

Had I determined these fine, delicate questions against them at the supreme moment, requiring instant and decisive action, they would have been ruined by an error of judgment in the man in whom they had trusted all. I acted right from every legal standpoint.

The question would have been very difficult, and would have admitted the widest scope of option, had I known all the facts before employment.

A REMARKABLE SCENE IN COURT—THE TABLES TURNED.

AT the January term, 1857, of the Circuit Court at Raleigh, Mr. Hardin, of Bolivar, the Attorney General, was absent, and at his request I was sworn in as Attorney General pro tem.

One Mr. Burke was tried on an indictment charging an assault with deadly weapon with intent to kill. He was a gentleman of high standing in the community, and in the Masonic order, but impulsive and quick to resent an injury. He was forty years of age, and the step-son of an old gentleman seventy-five years old, who was in his dotage, but possessed of a very ungovernable temper. His name, if my memory is not at fault, was Bryant; however, that is not important.

These impulsive gentlemen were sitting on opposite sides of a small table for the purpose of adjusting mutual accounts, some of which the old man disputed, and gave Burke the lie, and on the impulse of the moment Burke jumped up, and shot the old man with a small brass-barrel pistol in the breast; the ball knocked him down but did not penetrate the cavity or produce a dangerous wound.

Although it was a clear violation of the law, it was not attended with other presumptive malice, and was not one of those crimes for which jurors of the South would readily impose a degrading sentence by sending the defendant to the penitentiary, and I did not expect a conviction.

Burke was defended by Selem B. Frazer, one of the best and most successful jury lawyers. He was a consummate master of irony and ridicule, and when he had the closing argument in a case admitting any play or scope for this talent, was almost invincible. He was popular with everybody, knew the religion and politics and peculiar traits of character of every man offered as juror or witness. He never tried to argue a controverted question involving knowledge of law.

The evidence in the case was concluded a moment before the court adjourned for dinner. Selem and myself occupied adjoining rooms at the hotel, with plank partition between them which did not obstruct sound sufficiently to prevent ordinary conversation from being plainly heard. I preceded him to the hotel, and was sitting in my room examining a law book when he, together with Mr. Garrett, entered his room in high glee. I did not stuff wool or cotton in my ears. I had no interest in their conversation, but could not well avoid hearing it. To my utter amazement and horror at the idea of deliberately packing a jury, for any purpose whatever, Selem said: "Garrett, we have played that hand finely, Hallum has yet to learn how to select a jury. In fact I may say he is as innocent as a virgin, and as green as a goose, and has no capital but main strength and awkwardness. Selecting a jury was the easiest and simplest job I ever had in that line, we have a high Mason on trial, and twelve Masons in the box." They took a drink, and pledged a "bumper," and laughed immoderately at my virgin simplicity.

It was the unembarrassed criticism of a fool that took the starch out of me. I could scarcely restrain myself, but did, and "nursed my wrath to keep it warm."

I thought of Goldsmith's retort in the ballroom, "the fool who came to scoff, remained to pray," and resolved to paralyze the whole outfit, regardless of consequences, let them be what they might. A Comanche Indian on the warpath for scalps, I wanted fifteen in my belt—Garrett, who aided in packing the jury, Selem, Burke, and the twelve jurors.

When court opened I told the scene in extenso. Garrett was a hog, if a mulatto wench as mistress could impress that seal on a man's character; that fact was open and notorious, a degrading parasite, whose touch was contamination—a pretty man to be engaged in packing a jury of peers.

I told the jury that their selection, under the circumstances, carried with it the implied conviction that they were rotten, and ready to pollute the administration of justice—that I had fifteen men instead of one on trial, that their verdict would necessarily confirm or repudiate the slander. Selem and Garrett were paralyzed, the jury was amazed, confounded, overwhelmed, red hot with indignation. The truth is they were all good men, good citizens, and had been outraged. Snow was on the ground. Burke was the most pitiful object I ever saw, great drops of sweat rolled in profusion from his face.

There was no denial of the facts stated by me. The jury did not retire from the box to consider their verdict of guilty.

This was not a fair and impartial trial. Burke was simply crucified, with his counsel on the right, and Garrett on the left. The jury was forced to consider their own honor and nothing else.

Next morning, of my own motion, I asked the court to set aside the verdict, and give him a fair trial. Judge

Humphreys commended me, and granted the motion, and at the next term of court Burke went free.

In this connection I must say of Frazer, that he stood high, and was always regarded as an honorable man, and was never before or after that caught in such a bad box.

Garrett was the real criminal in the transaction, and Frazer did not have the moral courage to repel and kick him out of the court room.

THE MISER.

ALL misers are curious compounds of frailty; they embrace strange hallucinations in their desire for accumulation, and sometimes embark the savings of a lifetime in a single venture, the ultimate results of which they are wholly incompetent to judge. They are generally self-conceited, stubborn, and hard to convince of the folly on which they have made up their mind to enter. James H. Markham was an example of this class. Born in Sumner county, Tenn., he moved to the "Point," six miles from Memphis, before my birth. He was uneducated, could neither read nor write his name. By severe economy, unremitting energy and industry, he accumulated a little fortune for that day, of $30,000 in money, stock and farm. During the cropping season he would walk to Memphis with baskets of eggs, butter, and vegetables and fruits. Distrustful of banks, he kept his accumulations at home. In his advanced age he married a young woman, who bore him children. He knew my parents before my birth, and as soon as I opened a law office I became his legal adviser, until he thought he was wiser, and a better judge of human nature and its frailties than I. One day he came with Mr. Moore, a merchant of Memphis, to my office at Raleigh, and asked me to draft a copartnership agreement between them in the mercantile business, by which Markham was to put in ten thousand dollars cash, and the old man had his old socks and greasy bags of money with him to pay over as soon as the contract was executed. I had studied physiognomy and phrenology, and I saw, as plain as Belshazzar did, the handwriting on the wall, that caused his knees to "smite each other," that Moore "would not do." He was then a stranger to me, and at that time had a business established in Memphis.

I took "Uncle Jimmy" out and urged him to abandon the idea at once, for reasons above stated, and told him that he was utterly incompetent to cope with such disadvantages as those under which he labored ; that not only the cash he put in would be absorbed, but his whole fortune would be endangered. He was offended, said he knew what he was doing, and that all he wanted me to do was to draw up the papers. I then declined to do it, and told him that I would not be the passive instrument by which his family would be reduced to poverty. He then went to another lawyer and had it drawn up, and handed over his hard earnings.

In less than fifteen months his $10,000 was "gone where the woodbine twineth," and the firm was in debt $20,000. This broke the old man's heart, and he died under it: the lawyer who drew the instrument administered on his estate, sold his slaves and filed a bill to sell the realty. The war closed the courts and for years suspended this proceeding, but when the courts were opened the land was sold, leaving much of the debt still unpaid.

In another instance death was caused by the financial shock of a man the opposite in character in every respect to Markham.

ELIJAH BROOKS,

Of the old ante-bellum firm of Brooks & Suggs, contractors and builders, came to me to wind up the business of the firm. Suggs died during the civil war, and it devolved on Brooks as surviving partner to attend to the settlement of the business interests of the firm. He was one of the best of citizens, full of hope and energy, but exceedingly careless in his business.

The assets of the firm consisted in one mortgage on real estate for $10,000, and some improved and unimproved real estate far out on Beal street in Memphis, from the whole of which he thought I ought to realize fifteen to eighteen thousand dollars. The debts of the firm he guessed did not amount to more than half the value of the assets, but no books had ever been kept by these men. On the strength of this statement, and at his urgent request, I was fool enough to advance him $5,000 as a loan. I immediately proceeded to foreclose the mortgage, on which I realized in due time the full amount of $10,000. The other real estate I subdivided, and by judicious management realized on it $28,000 more, making the total of cash assets $38,000. In the meantime while the necessary legal steps to reduce the assets to cash were in progress I advertised for all debts against the firm to be filed with me, and was greatly astonished to find that the debts were largely in excess of the assets. Brooks lived near White's Station. I wrote, asking him to come in and assist me in classifying and arranging the claims. Then I said, "Mr. Brooks, you are a bankrupt beyond all question unless your private means are sufficient to pay the large number of claims that have been brought in, besides this you have involved me in a loss of the $5,000 I loaned to you, because the partnership debts have priority over individual debts." He turned as pale as death, was sick in less than three minutes; the immediate pathological effect severely disturbed the bowels. He went home to bed, and to death in a few days. He was an honest man, no man ever doubted that, but careless, with no books to show credits and debits; the war period having intervened he had forgotten the debts until his mind was refreshed. Of all the wonderful creations in the universe, all of which proclaim the infinite wisdom of God, none to me are so wonderful as the subtle mechanism of the human mind. That awe-inspiring work of infinite subtility which has so many secret springs which move and act their part at the most delicate touch. A harp, the brain with its little box of springs and strings on which the soul of man plays its part; the tabernacle in which it dwells but a day, then across the river through astral depths in upward and onward progression, through eternal realms of light, with new and greater and greater beauties forever unfolding. We are but a chrysalis here. When we crawl out of the ground in the spring time, like the worm, we are transformed into a higher and nobler state of being. We see the dormant chrysalis, we witness the transformation of that chrysalis into the ugly worm, and then into the beautiful creature of wings. God's ocular demonstration of changes, and each one a higher progression. Can man, the noblest of created things, reason from cause to effect in the light of God's revelation, either assume that he passes to nonentity or to retrograde standards?

A DEVOTED WIFE.

IN September, 1855, I was employed to defend a man by the name of Adams, indicted on a charge of larceny, all of the criminative facts being admitted. He was connected with some of the best families of the county, and I sent for several of his kinsmen, but they felt so chagrined and humiliated they would have nothing to do with him. On investigation I found that insanity ought to be and could be successfully set up, and sent for these relations again, and found they were possessed of knowledge that would establish that much abused defense in later days. I had them subpoenaed, but they were so morbidly sensitive they refused to attend, and I had an attachment issued. The insanity was intermittent; at times he would secrete himself for weeks in the forest, and make his bed of leaves, raked up by fallen logs; when greatly hungered he would go to the farm houses and ask for food. This narrowed the inquiry as to whether the alleged crime was committed during a lucid interval, on which point the proof was not satisfactory. The Attorney General made a strong appeal for conviction. I did not reply to his argument, and only spoke about three minutes, criticising the remote civilization to which he appealed. Not guilty was the verdict.

Adams lived in Weakley county, Tenn., and was married to a beautiful little woman, whose devotion was simple and pathetic. Like the widow who threw her mite into the treasury, she exhausted all the resources of her humble home to raise fifty dollars, and then walked a hundred miles, weary and worn, stopping at the wayside farm houses for hospitality. Late one cheerless, rainy night, this little woman, weary and forlorn, knocked at

A DEVOTED WIFE.

IN September, 1855, I was employed to defend a man by the name of Adams, indicted on a charge of larceny, all of the criminative facts being admitted. He was connected with some of the best families of the county, and I sent for several of his kinsmen, but they felt so chagrined and humiliated they would have nothing to do with him. On investigation I found that insanity ought to be and could be successfully set up, and sent for these relations again, and found they were possessed of knowledge that would establish that much abused defense in later days. I had them subpœnaed, but they were so morbidly sensitive they refused to attend, and I had an attachment issued. The insanity was intermittent; at times he would secrete himself for weeks in the forest, and make his bed of leaves, raked up by fallen logs; when greatly hungered he would go to the farm houses and ask for food. This narrowed the inquiry as to whether the alleged crime was committed during a lucid interval, on which point the proof was not satisfactory. The Attorney General made a strong appeal for conviction. I did not reply to his argument, and only spoke about three minutes, criticising the remote civilization to which he appealed. Not guilty was the verdict.

Adams lived in Weakley county, Tenn., and was married to a beautiful little woman, whose devotion was simple and pathetic. Like the widow who threw her mite into the treasury, she exhausted all the resources of her humble home to raise fifty dollars, and then walked a hundred miles, weary and worn, stopping at the wayside farm houses for hospitality. Late one cheerless, rainy night, this little woman, weary and forlorn, knocked at my residence, opposite the jail where her husband was confined. She told me her story with a sweet and simple pathos that brought tears to my wife, then untied a worn rag and said, "Mr. Hallum, here is fifty dollars for you, it is not enough, but it is all I could raise. I tried my best to get more but failed." My heart came into my throat, and in a voice scarcely audible, I said, "No, my God, my little woman, you can't pay me anything, neither you nor your husband owe me. I make no charge, the kind providence of God would desert me were I to use the opportunities he has given me to earn your money under such circumstances, but I will serve you with as much zeal as I would a queen." She looked astonished, and said: "Papa told me to tell you that he is a poor man, with a large family to support, and that we all did the best we could to get some money up for you."

My wife directed the preparation of a warm and generous meal, late as it was. While eating she asked me when she could see her husband, and I said "As soon as you finish your meal," and she said, "I am done." John Branch was then jailer; he threw open the doors as soon as he could dress and gave them a well furnished room.

he told with the effective zest of President Lincoln, and Ben's graphic, laconic description of the puffing engine amused him very greatly, and he said, "After all. Hallum, that description is hard to beat." He was quite corpulent, large, portly, with a massive and well-shaped head, one leg was a little shorter than the other, and he walked with a strong hickory cane, in a rambling gait from side to side as he advanced, necessitated by the defect in the short limb. He lived in a day when the political atmosphere was not surcharged with dishonest scheming as it is now in too many places. Dishonesty then in politics was an unknown factor in elections. "The snollygoster in politics" was then an unknown quantity, but he has a roost at every cross roads now.

JUDGE ADDISON H. DOUGLASS.

THE first time I distinctly remember this walking library of good humor and exhaustless reservoir of anecdote and hilarity, he was Mayor of the city, on tap, and "felt his oats."

The Memphis and Charleston railroad had just been finished, connecting Charleston with Memphis by rail. A tierce of water dipped out of the Atlantic pond had been hauled to Memphis and carried down to the margin of the mighty river; a huge squirt-gun, with silver nozzle was attached to a hand fire engine, with one end of the hose in the Atlantic water and the silver nozzle pointing to the Mississippi.

The ceremony to be performed was denominated "the Marriage of the Atlantic Ocean to the Mississippi River," and Addison, dressed in regimentals of startling flash and fit, cockade, hat and plume, was the biggest city dad, and the ceremony devolved on him, *ex officio*. Twenty-five thousand people witnessed the magnificent banns. The oc-

casion furnished the inspiration. When the hour arrived all
heads were uncovered. A choir sang "Yankee Doodle,"
Addison, naturally tall, mounted the still taller Atlantic
tierce, handed his cockade hat to the chairman of the judiciary committee, his gloves to the chief of the fire de-
department, and his cane to the chief of police. He then
took the eagle bird in hand, smoothed her tail down until
he got her confidence, and then proceeded to pluck every
feather before he turned her loose. The choir then
touched off "Hail Columbia," while Addison directed
the nozzle where to spill. The vast auditory was wild
with enthusiasm, the nozzle holder turned pale with patriotic upheaval of heart, and bowed with quivering lips
of pride. He could have been elected President had he
offered—thousands pronounced it the happiest marriage
they had ever seen, and that the bride and groom, although "which from tother" was not announced, and
gender made no difference, would obey and love and
cherish each other without a ripple of discord: *Vox
populi, vox Dei.*

Addison, do you yet remember the little dude with hair
parted in the middle, and reed with a gold head? You
crucified him on the pavement, near the Irving block,
twenty-five years ago. That dude is my client.

Fun aside, Douglass was one of the best and most
jovial men I ever knew; he could make a mourner laugh
at a funeral, and the world is far happier and better for
such men. I wish we had thousands, and many such in
every community. He was a fine speaker, an orator
without effort.

Not long ago my heart was deeply touched and made
very, very sad. I met Addison in Memphis, and rushed
up to him with hands extended, forgetting that I had
turned old and gray, and was no longer the joyful youth
I once was I exclaimed, "Don't you know me, Addison?" He drew back and said, "Where did I ever see
you? Was it in Louisville, or Nashville, or Washington?"

And before I could answer two ladies called him, and I was left standing alone as they drove off in a carriage. I did not say "It's John, simply John." A tear stole in my eye. Could I help it? I would not have restrained it if I could. There is a divinity sometimes in a tear— we are all better for them. Angels sometimes come in a tear, they clear up the heart, and soothe the soul, and are gathered in God's garner. Reader, whether strong man or gentle woman, if you have never shed tears you have never been near your God. It was neither the Addison nor the John of old in external appearances, but I am sure we yet have the same joyous hearts. Since writing this Judge Douglass has crossed over the river. Farewell, dear Brother, yours was a gentle, happy life here on earth, its bliss is now fadeless.

EDWIN M. YERGER.

EDWIN M. YERGER, one of seven brothers, all eminent lawyers, born in Lebanon, Tenn., of humble parentage, located in Memphis about 1840. He was in the zenith of professional splendor when I first met him in 1853, and he made in September of that year the first great legal argument I ever heard.

It was the contested will case of Crenshaw *vs.* Crenshaw (rather it should be so styled), but technically denominated an issue of *devasavit vel non*, barbarous butchery of idiom, coming down from the days antedating My Lords Coke and Lyttleton.

Yerger spoke seven hours; he had a marvelous command of language, a fine voice well modulated, was martial in appearance, Ciceronian in delivery, and as majestic as the flood of a mighty river. His legal attainments were vast, his accomplishments great, his capacity for social enjoyment almost unlimited. If he had any professional weakness it lay in his aversion to work on the dry details of preparation; he always cast this labor on associate counsel if possible. I have known him to go into the trial of many important Chancery cases without ever having previously read a paper in the case. He would listen attentively to the reading, and then make a luminous argument, manifesting as much familiarity with details as if he had made the most thorough preparation. He had a marvelous memory and relied, I have thought, too much on his genius.

I was associated with him in many cases. When a young man I often required my clients in important cases to let me choose associate counsel, and in this way became quite a tributary to "Ed. Yerger" (as we called him) and Judge Brown.

In after years Yerger often reciprocated the favor, not so much because of my legal ability, for I do not think he would have regarded Kent, Story, Marshall or Reverdy Johnson as necessary in any case he was assigned to argue, but the often arduous labor of preparation, and the necessity to give bonds for foreign clients, as well as a spirit of gratitude and generosity, brought him to me. He was equally great in every department of the law, chivalrous and devoid of fear. I remember we were associated in 1859 in a case involving a plantation and negroes in Arkansas. Madison Jones *vs.* Bedford Forrest, since the celebrated rebel general. Jones was one of those quiet, passive, negative men, who instinctively shrink from personal collision. Yerger, Jones, and myself, were in Yerger's office in consultation; we had taken some move which checkmated Gen. Forrest, alarmed and greatly angered him. While we were in consultation Gen. Forrest came in unexpectedly, and, without taking a seat, commenced abusing Jones violently. Yerger rose from his chair, his eyes flashing fire, and in the most imperious tones said to Forrest: "Jones is in my office and under my protection, if you utter another word of abuse I will cut your throat."

Gen. Forrest was well known to be a man of unquestioned courage of the highest order, but he realized he was in the wrong, and left the office without saying another word. Gen. Forrest, after the close of the civil war, was indicted for treason in the Federal Court, and Yerger and myself were his counsel, and I drove down to Joiner's farm on the Hernando road, by appointment, to bring the General in, and give bond. The cause never came to trial.

Yerger and John P. Caruthers, before the elevation of the latter as Judge of the Common Law Court of Memphis, were partners. Judge Caruthers was a little stiff before the harness got well set, and Yerger did not think he extended to him that consideration on all occasions the subject demanded, and chafed over it until explosion came, sudden, terrific, startling.

Yerger rose during the morning hour and proceeded to argue a motion for a new trial with great earnestness. The Judge picked up a newspaper and held it up before his face hiding that of the speaker. The lawyers began to laugh, but the advocate continued, unnoticed by the court; finally the latter revolved on his chair, and stopped with his back to the speaker, still intent reading the paper. At this Yerger took his seat, the lawyers still laughing. After a few minutes the Judge turned on the chair, and asked Yerger if he was through, to which he replied, "No, but I don't intend to speak to your d —d back while you are absorbed reading advertisements." A fine of five hundred dollars was imposed, but was afterwards remitted.

When Fort Sumter was fired on, a party of congenial spirits were together at the "Alcove" discussing the situation, and I asked Yerger if he intended going to the front, and he replied, " What, join the army ? No, unless I go in a coach and four, or to Montgomery to assume the office of Attorney General for the Confederate States, any other position would be beneath my dignity." It was said that he was vain—true, but it was clothed in radiant, ornate and the most charming language. All men of eminence are *vain*, it is the driving wheel which propels the most delicate machinery of the human brain, that most wonderful of all the creations of God. It is the electric motor, the God-given incentive which moves, directs, and drives the higher aspirations of man. Withdraw its inspiration and you reduce man to the level of the ox. Clay and Benton are eminent examples of its extraordinary development.

When I hear the superficial and hypercritical inveighing against vanity as a deformity of character, I am reminded of the seagull skimming over the mighty waters of the ocean, without seeing or knowing anything that lies hidden in its depths, yet the bird's plumage is beautiful and well adapted to the purposes for which it is created. If I had a child without the noble impulses of well-founded vanity, I would regard it as a deformity.

Yerger's income was large, like that of all good lawyers in those days, but he knew no more than a child of the value of money, and spent it as rapidly as he made it. He was a Whig, and I think in 1854 was nominated for Congress and made the race against Frederick P. Stanton, an eminent lawyer and Democratic politician of that day, and was defeated only by one vote.

4

HON. JOHN LOAGUE, MEMPHIS.

SINCE England's oppression of Ireland, centuries ago, her sons have been pilgrims to every shrine of freedom where its altars have been set up; they have crossed every sea, braved every danger, and have fought in every great battle for freedom during the last four hundred years with chivalrous courage surpassed by none of the children of men. Every town and cotter's home, where her sons dwell, have drank the farewell tears of her people, and they have contributed their mite to aid her immigrant sons on their pilgrimage, and no country of Saxon and Norman blood has been so much enriched as our own by Celtic absorptions. They have always fought for the land of their adoption with chivalric devotion, and no Irishman has ever deserted his flag or disgraced the Shamrock.

John Loague was born in Londonderry in 1829. He received a liberal education, and in his twentieth year came to the United States, and settled in Memphis in 1860, since which time he has been continuously in honorable office for a period of near thirty-five years.

Memphis has never had his equal in political sagacity—a natural politician, with inborn intuition to judge of ebbs and tides and currents of public sentiment—with the ability to subordinate and utilize it. A local Talleyrand, a political magician, who controlled men and votes for a great period almost at will, all of which is attested by his many offices. To say nothing of his novitiate in the political arena, he was four years in the school board, three years tax collector of privileges, member of the constitutional convention of Tennessee in 1865, when and where his every vote was to enfranchise the people—here he rose above the clamor and mad frenzy of revolution and opposed Brownlowism and fanatic ostracism.

He was surveyor of the port of Memphis, under President Johnson, four years clerk of the county court, when that was the most lucrative office in the State, was mayor of the city of Memphis, a member of the Legislature of Tennessee, cashier of a bank, public administrator of Shelby county. His success is without a parallel in the history of Memphis. A warm and true friend, he never deserted one in the hour of need, and is now actively engaged in pursuing his profession, being a member of the Memphis Bar.

HON. JOE. B. HEISKELL.

HE is a native of East Tennessee, ex-Attorney General and Reporter, and deserves special mention, not only as a very able lawyer in his day, but as one of the best of citizens and men. His record as a lawyer is amply preserved in the records of our jurisprudence, and of that it would be superfluous to further speak.

Our offices were for years in the same building, and we saw and knew much of each other. Generals Pike and Adams were in the same building, also that of General Chalmers, who was with the author. Four Generals and one layman. What elysian moments of recreation we had. Heiskell was a great lover of pungent, dry wit. It was worth ten dollars to get off something that would make "Joe" laugh, and the coterie never failed. If Pike and Adams failed to shake him up, Chalmers would catch him, and sometimes we all bagged the game.

He was profoundly logical and analytical, and when greatly pressed became profoundly technical; this was

his last resort, the redoubt, where McGregor determined
to die.   He has retired from the Bar to enjoy the golden
fruits of a ripe age and well spent life.

'Tis a pity that threescore and ten is the allotted span
of man.   Joe Heiskell belongs to that class of men who
enrich and ennoble the heritage of the State.

WALTER COLEMAN.

WALTER COLEMAN was in the meridian of
splendid manhood and achievement when I was
teaching school and reading law; full six feet
high, a perfect model of physical perfection.   A
native of Middle Tennessee, he came to Memphis, I think,
as early as 1848.   Scrupulously neat in dress, his carriage was proud as that of an emperor.   He was a profound lawyer, his eyrie was in the crags around the summit.

The greatest intellectual conflict I ever enjoyed in my
youthful manhood, was in listening to the battle of the
giants, when he and Ed. Yerger were opposing counsel
at Raleigh, in 1853, in the contested will case of Crenshaw vs. Crenshaw.

They were as perfectly matched as any men I ever
heard.   They had met and broken lances on many a field
before, and each knew that he had no resources that could
lay dormant in that mighty conflict.   They were each
masters of that rarest of all gifts, a combination of powerful logic, ornate language, and perfect modulation and
intonation of voice.   I adjourned my school for a week to
hear them, from the beginning to the finish of the trial.

A day was allotted each to speak, and each occupied
seven hours.

Coleman was an indolent man, and did not desire that
large volume of business Yerger had, but he was always

thoroughly prepared when he tried a case. He was rather reserved in his habits, and did not mingle and fraternize much with his brothers at the Bar.

WILLIAM T. HASKELL.

HASKELL was in the zenith of a splendid fame in 1854. As an orator, Tennessee never produced his superior; he ranked with the greatest in the galaxy of renowned speakers. But was an erratic, meteoric genius, indolent and careless of his talents and fame. An old line Whig in politics, no man ever hurled more brilliant phillipics at the Democratic party. He smote it, hip and thigh, and gave it a brilliant funeral. I heard him in the presidential campaign of 1852; he was with our army in Mexico, with Gen. Franklin Pierce, then candidate for the presidency. It was said a part of our army had to retreat from a charge of the enemy at Cerro Gordo, both Haskell and Pierce being in the retreat, and it was charged that Haskell lost his hat and that Pierce did not. In reply to this Haskell admitted that he lost his, but said, "you could not have pulled Pierce's off with a pair of pincers: I was by his side in the run, and, although time was a little pressing, I observed that."

I heard him at Sommerville, in 1853, at the celebration of the completion of the Moscow and Sommerville branch railroad.

Twenty-five thousand people were present. In one of the finest flights of oratory of which man is capable, he took up a glass, held and shook its crystal waters in the sun and told of the revolution steam applied to mechanics had produced in the world—a splendid theme in the hands of a wonderful genius, whose soul was as light and radiant with inspiration as a cloud on fire in the heavens. A giant, a Colossus stirring and playing with the passions of men. His voice was perfect, his gesticulation natural and admirable, his person tall, and of commanding mein, his eyes radiant with stirring emotions of the soul, when speaking. After all, what is man? God alone can answer. He died in an asylum.

WILLIAM THOMPSON.

WILLIAM THOMPSON was an old and feeble man when I first knew him, in 1854, he came from Middle Tennessee, had been the law-partner of the Hon. John Bell, and was heroically struggling to keep his place at the head of the column. It is very hard for some old men to realize that it is foreordained in primal law that they must give way. He was a courtly, dignified, charming old man.

In 1859 I was a candidate before thirty-five justices of the County Court for the then lucrative office of notary public, against Hume F. Hill, who had made a fortune out of the office, which was then worth ten thousand per year, there being but one such officer in the county, who had the business of the banks in Memphis, and quite a volume of marine business. On the first and fourth of the month, the days on which the largest volume of notes, bills of exchange and drafts went to protest, I have often protested as many as four hundred, these fees ranging from two to five dollars each, and marine protests from ten to fifty dollars.

Hill became alarmed before the election and gave Mr. Thompson $250 to disparage my pretensions and elevate himself on my ruin. I was not aware of the programme until the moment when the justices announced that they would now "go into the election."

Mr. Thompson then arose to address the Court, and "give it to be informed" that the business was of a weighty nature, requiring profound consideration for the public good, with uplifted, half palsied, arm, weak but silvery voice, he entertained the thirty-two justices on the Bench for half an hour.

The old Roman, the Nestor of the bar, placed much stress and emphasis on the charge that Mr. Hallum had on a few unfortunate occasions looked too deep in the wine bowl, and said a man through whose official hands hundreds of thousands of dollars must pass, ought not to aspire to such responsible positions.

At the conclusion of his classic phillipic, I merely said to the court that my beloved and honored friend would make the same speech for me to-morrow for a quart of champagne and a fifty-dollar note, and took my seat.

The ballot was then taken and twenty-nine of the thirty-two votes were cast for me, and while the ballot was being counted two more justices took their seats and asked that their ballots be counted for me. The office was for four years. I gave bond and immediately entered into office.

Bro. Thompson, in his brighter and better days, would not have made the speech he did before that court; but there was some foundation for what he said about the wine, a thimble full would soon master my tongue, and a decayed apple would make me drunk, a glass of lemonade dashed with port wine would soon put me to bed, but I was in no sense of the term an intemperate drinker, and very seldom took a drink of wine.

I have often said that I could make more reputation for drinking on a quart of wine than most men could on a barrel of whisky. For many years I have not touched a drop —have been president of the State Temperance organization four terms, and have materially aided in the accomplishment of a vast and beneficent work in Arkansas on that line, and that work is the pride of my life.

I may be indulged in saying this, lest some friend or descendant of mine should draw erroneous conclusions as to my habits and life.

There was then a much larger volume of water transportation than since the advent of railroads, a large capital was invested in marine carriage, and marine protests were much more frequent than now, and the fees ranged from ten dollars to fifty. This business was the introduction to quite a volume of marine conveyancing and other business, all of which did not materially interfere with my law practice, as I transacted the major part of my notarial business through efficient clerks.

RECOLLECTIONS OF RETURN J. MEIGS AND JOHN MARSHALL.

THESE great lawyers were in the meridian of a splendid fame when I came to the Bar, and I looked on them as idols of the profession. But in personal appearance it is difficult to conceive of a greater contrast in men. Meigs was tall and slender, and scrupulously neat in his dress. Marshall was very corpulent and utterly regardless of dress. In the summer he wore a three-dollar suit of checked cotton goods, and brogan shoes suited him as well as the finest congress gaiter. I have seen him in this dress arguing cases before the Supreme Court, where he handled every question he touched like Jove playing with his thunderbolts. He had a massive head, flowing locks, and flashing eye that compassed the intellectual horizon, a master, Meigs his equal. To be in the shadow of these men, enjoy their courteous consideration and instruction, was very gratifying to a young man. I met them together in Mr. Meigs's office in 1856. I met Meigs often, Marshall less frequent. The war came on and I lost sight of Meigs until March 1869. He was then Clerk and Recorder of the District of Columbia, and still maintained that methodical precision which distinguished him at the Bar. I was married in Washington on the 6th of March, 1869, and was not thinking of Meigs when I entered the clerk's office for license. When the document was made out the deputy stepped into an adjoining room for the signature of the clerk, and in a moment the great lawyer came hurriedly and greeted me with the greatest cordiality. He insisted on the marriage taking place at his residence, but I was compelled to regretfully decline, because arrangements were already consummated at the residence of another friend. That was the last time I ever met the truly great and grand old man.

SETH WHEATLY.

SETH WHEATLY was one of the earliest members of the Memphis Bar, and I suppose that Bob Looney and myself are the only living members of the guild who recollect him. Perhaps Governor Harris recollects him. Seth was a very prominent man during the early days of Memphis—was possessed of high legal attainment, and financial ability, but quit the Bar in the meridian of life, embarked in banking and other financial enterprises which he found more remunerative than law. He finally established himself on a fine cotton plantation some twelve miles south of Memphis.

In those days it was the ambition of many able lawyers to become wealthy planters, especially those possessed of financial ability, and many quit their alma mater for the mistaken Utopian idea of reaching a higher sphere in social life and position. Seth had a commanding physique, and was very tall, full of life and energy, and relished wit and humor. What a treasure he could have left us had he recorded a history of those early days and men of Memphis. I knew him well, before I became the "kid of the guild."

SPENCER JARNIGAN.

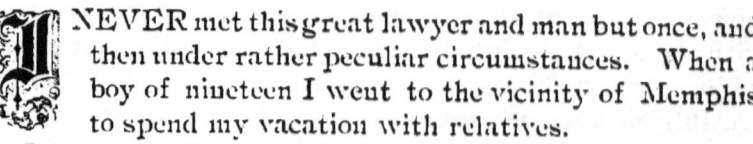 NEVER met this great lawyer and man but once, and then under rather peculiar circumstances. When a boy of nineteen I went to the vicinity of Memphis to spend my vacation with relatives.

I was standing on the corner of Main and Madison streets talking to Seth Wheatly, who for the first time I had met. Wheatly was in one of his fine conversational humors, and took more interest in me than men generally do in boys, and I was as much flattered as pleased. He took me for a Yankee at first, and put the direct question to me. Jocularly I demanded an apology, and he laughed heartily. I had just finished a severe reading of Comb's Phrenology, and was then as I have always been an admirer of fine heads.

While engaged in this conversation, a man with one of the finest heads I ever saw nodded to Wheatly and passed on. I gave expression to my admiration and inquired who he was, and Wheatly called Jarnigan back and introduced him. I knew him as a politician, and of his fame as a great lawyer, and gazed on that splendid head, where God had placed his seal of nobility, with far greater admiration than I could have possibly looked on the wearer of a crown. His history is part of the heritage of the State. Not long after I sorrowfully read of his death.

W. A. BLYTHE.

 A. BLYTHE was from Wilson county, Tenn., and at one time was associated with Ed. Yerger, but retired from the Bar as early as 1852, and occupied his time with his private affairs.

He built a three-story house at the corner of Second and North Court streets which brought him a handsome revenue. I never will forget an incident which happened on the stairway to this building in 1860. L. Q. C. Lamar, of Mississippi, afterward representative and Senator in Congress, member of Cleveland's Cabinet and Associate Justice of the Supreme Court of the United States, was visiting the city, and lodged with a friend in Blythe's building. Quite a number of lawyers, including myself, hired a band of musicians and serenaded Lamar. He came half way down the flight of stairs, in his night dress, and delivered a short speech of touching pathos and beauty. It would be difficult for the most facile pen to paint the mental abandon of that delirious hour. I have heard him address the Senate, and have seen him in the black gown on the Supreme Bench, but never could drive back the vivid scene I witnessed on the stairway.

ROBERT H. CROCKETT.

ROBERT H. CROCKETT, grandson of the celebrated Davy, and son of John W. Crockett, who succeeded his father in Congress, was born in Paris, Tenn. His maternal grandfather, John A. Hamilton, was one of the first Circuit Judges in West Tennessee. He was educated at the Military Institute in Kentucky.

Overflowing with life, redundant with superabundant vitality, he ran away and joined the Ocean Marine, shipped before the mast for a year. Not yet satisfied with romance and adventure, he joined the Fillibuster expedition of Lopez for the conquest of Cuba, but was not long on the island before reaching the conclusion that the United States might possibly contain him, if he could get back.

In 1851 Bob became a student of law in the office of Harris & Ray, in Memphis, and was enrolled there in 1853, where I first knew him, and since that time the warmest friendship has mutually existed. For a time he was associated with Smith P. Bankhead, as associate editor of the old Eagle and Enquirer, a staunch Whig paper.

He honors his noble pedigree, inherits the wit and humor of his celebrated grandfather, is a wit, humorist, lawyer, sage, philosopher, and one of the most attractive lecturers and speakers. He was a gallant Confederate soldier, where he proved and showed the spirit of the Alamo on many fields—was Colonel of the Eighteenth Arkansas regiment at the close of the war. A man of great popularity and magnetism, a warm and devoted friend, true to all the relations of life and manhood:

We met in the roseate days of youth and drank from the fount of its "bright lexicon" as Bob and John. He frequently writes me charming letters. Everybody in Arkansas loves "Bob Crockett."

JOHN TIMOTHY TREZEVANT.

TREZEVANT was one of the "Old Guard," but had retired in the interests of railroads in the early fifties. He was possessed of much oratorical and persuasive power, and enjoyed breaking a lance on the hustings as much as any man I ever knew, and I knew him long and intimately. He canvassed the South extensively in the interests of railroad enterprises.

A gentleman in all the walks of life and a very charming entertainer in the social circle. Noble type of a past generation. In 1887 I was driving through that rich belt of alluvial farms known as the "Richwoods," in Lonoke county, Arkansas. When opposite a residence on one of those plantations I heard an anxious voice hailing, "John, stop and come in." I was not a little surprised. On the porch stood a fine old gentleman, with hair as white as snow, and a negro boy came running to take charge of my animal and vehicle.

As soon as I vacated the carriage the old gentleman, who had hailed me so familiarly wheeled and entered the house, instead of coming out to meet me—rather strange, I thought, still not recognizing the man, but the servant told me it was Col. Trezevant.

We have an unlimited supply of military titles in the South, and none below the grade of Captain; and as to privates, they were all killed off in the civil war.

We had not met for more than twenty years. When I stepped up on the porch he met me with both hands extended—heartily grasped, and the two old white-headed

Johns, one still of slender mould, the other with fine bay-window addition to his physical residence, shook and re-shook hands and clasped arms, and dropped a tear of joy sacred to the memory of brighter days. Cicero has so beautifully and charmingly described the wealth of old age—Yes, it has its pleasures as well as its thorns, and its golden fringes on sunset clouds when the sun kisses the day farewell.   After being seated in a room piled up with a profusion of papers, periodicals, and books which defied order and arrangement, I said, "John, why did you not run out to the gate and meet me?"   "Why, I thought of that bottle of Burgundy, and ran to my trunk to unlock it and get it, and call the servant—the key was missing, and I was delayed.   I wanted it ready for you as soon as you entered, this chilly morning.   I have been saving it for you.   I knew you frequently passed, and told the negroes to keep a lookout for you."   "Well, John, I will accept that explanation, it is abundantly satisfactory."   He was looking after the interest of his charming daughter who owned the plantation, and for two or three months was living there, the life of a hermit absorbed in literature. A thousand things, episodes and incidents of early life, were renewed and reviewed by those garrulous old broth-ers, both voluble of speech, with tongues impatient to work off the wares and cares, the loves and joys of hearts still young.   I took out my watch, and John fearing I was about to leave, anxiously asked if it was true, but I relieved him and threw him into a roaring peal of laugh-ter, when I said, "fair play, John, you must divide time." Attic hour, a "pearl of purest ray serene," a beautiful islet in the river of life.   How ambition in a thou-sand multiform shapes misleads us—causes us to overlook the fact that life is not made up of great things; but we strain heart and eye and soul looking far beyond for the dim outlines of mountain ranges that lie hid in the mists of doubt and uncertainty.

If we would only stop and look down at our feet and

all around us everywhere, what an eden of flowers we could pick up and out of the common-place affairs of this little, feverish, short life. These are the places where God has poured in exhaustless profusion of wealth, the glories we overlook and trample under our feet.

Ambition for crowns and coronets and wealth, station and power are fruitful nurseries of human misery. I had it in my power to render John some little business service, and he became the guest of my Arkansas cottage. Peace to his memory, God bless the urn that holds his ashes, and long may our beloved country be fruitful of such men.

THE ROMANCE OF A WILL.

IN December, 1859, I was summoned to the dying bedside of Miss B., to write her will, and was ushered into a small box-house with only one room; all the surroundings presented the appearance of abject poverty. There, on a mattress of straw, lay Miss B., in the last stages of pneumonia, without having a physician called. Why? "They charge too much." The ruling passion of avarice, strong in death.

What could be found in such a hovel of wretchedness and death to be solemnly disposed of by last will and testament? She motioned me to draw near, her voice scarcely audible. Three ladies, all young, and three children were in the house—relations. She commanded all to retire, and then whispered in my ear her dying testament, which I wrote on a greasy pine table. She disposed of more than $20,000 worth of real estate and securities. After I read it over to her, slowly and carefully, she said it was correct. Then she said, "Take it to your office and lock it up." After the witness to the will retired, she said, "Now look out carefully and see that no eye beholds what I am going to do—hang the towel over that keyhole—be careful." I did as directed. "Now," she said, "I have one dying request to make, and you must grant it. Promise it on your honor before I make it." I promised—was nervous to get away— she proceeded: "There is a dark closet in my family. That little niece, to whom I bequeath two thirds of my fortune, is the illegitimate child of my sister, who died when the child was born, in a land far away from here. My sister was a pure and beautiful woman, but. alas, the old story, 'loved not wisely, but too well.' In an hour of transport she permitted the solemnization of the banns before man pronounced the benediction, and the father, not her, that was faithless. To you I have un-bosomed a secret which has gnawed at my heart ten long years. Now I am in the embrace of death, it may be. I don't know, the child's interest, after I am gone, will be served by making you the depository. Take it, keep it, guard it, as I have, but never divulge it, unless neces-sary to the child's protection. I am glad, so glad, that God is calling me home. Now one thing more: I want to pay you before you leave the room—reach around under the head of my bed and you will find ten pounds of spoons and plate, of silver, and six gold teaspoons, take them as yours, but never let mortal know from whence they came." "But," said I, "I cannot consent to that, it would haunt me all my life." "But did you not give your promise to a dying woman a few moments ago, will you break it and destroy my faith in my dying moments?"

Here was one of the most painful dilemmas a promise had ever given me. I did not, would not, add one pang to the dying woman's heart. I resolved at once to take them, and as soon as I got out, to call those women who stood waiting in the yard shivering, and make them my confidants, and take one of them with me to the bank, and let her see the plate and spoons labelled and deposited in the vaults as the property of the child, to be delivered to its guardian after the death of the testatrix, which I did deposit in the vaults of the Franklin Insurance Co., a banking institution at the corner of Jefferson and Front streets, owned by S. D. McClure, a former pupil of mine, and where I did business myself. When the testatrix died I gave the plate and spoons to an uncle of the child, who was appointed guardian.

I remember writing another will, connected with many phases and complications in life, all of which I have never been able to unravel, the understanding of which needs a little prefatory explanation. Smith P. Bankhead and myself were then spare made men. One day by accident we met in Turnage's clothing store, and we bought a fine suit of clothing, of exactly the same pattern, and hats of the same make. This coincidence by itself was nothing; we were the best of friends, our acquaintance dating back before my admission to the Bar, when he was on the editorial staff of the Eagle and Enquirer.

At that time, the winter of 1866-7, if my memory serves me correctly, Dr. Jones, the father of the Hon. Met L. Jones, now of Pine Bluff, Ark., was my family physician, and had an office in the Bank's building, on the same floor where my suite of offices were located.

One day soon after the purchase of the clothing, above stated, Dr. Jones came into my office and told me he had a dying patient, a married lady living out on Adams street, who wanted her will prepared as soon as it could possibly be done, and asked me to get into his buggy and go out with him, stating that his patient was in the last stages of pneumonia. I had never heard of the parties before, they had not been in Memphis long—had recently come from a large city in the North. When introduced, the patient asked the attendants and physician to retire to another room.

The mansion had every appearance of luxury and wealth. I drew my chair to the bedside (she spoke faintly and with difficulty), and began by saying, "I am

5

conscious of approaching death, and am at last compelled by the novelty and romance of my past life to give up my secrets to a trusted lawyer, an ordeal, the inevitable. I am but thirty-one years of age. I have a classical education, have always had all that wealth could command. When but eighteen years old I became infatuated with a young man living in Illinois, my native State, and through his treachery became the mother of a daughter without the sanction of marriage. That daughter is now twelve years of age—young, pure, beautiful. She was born in Montreal, Canada, and my acquaintances have never suspected that I am a mother. I own $35,000 worth of property in my own right. Either my child must lose this or my secret must become known after my death. My husband knows all about my property, but nothing of my child. I would rather that property was sunk in the ocean or consumed by fire than to pass into his hands. He is a gambler, and loves nothing but the vices that habit engenders; he has neglected, abused, tortured me, is insanely jealous."

A flushed tint came into her cheeks, and her voice increased in volume from excitement as she advanced in her story. Dr. Jones became impatient and left before I had committed a note to paper. It was late in the evening, the gas was lighted. Although no physician, I did not believe she was going to die then. I wrote the will that night, and next day at 10 A. M. rode out with the physician, read the will to her, and had it executed in due form, Dr. Jones and myself attesting the execution. She recovered and sent for me again to write a codicil to the will. I found her a polished and charming conversationalist, but made my stay as short as possible. A few days after this visit she drove to my office, and asked a private interview, after handing me my fee. She told me that for months detectives had been shadowing her, and that her husband knew of my visits without knowing the object, and had sworn to kill me on sight; that he was furiously jealous, insanely enraged, and altogether desperate." His gambling house was on Jefferson street. I did not know him, had never seen him, but sent a reliable man to see, not to speak to him, to be able to point him out to me. He did so; he knew me by sight. That evening we met at 9 P. M., at the corner of Main and Adams streets. He attempted to draw his pistol, but I was too quick, and made him drop his arms.

I then forced him to my office and explained the innocence of my visits on the three occasions I had gone with his family physician to his residence. He pretended to be satisfied; I returned his arms and he left the office, and I supposed the matter was at an end. I often worked until late hours in my office. A few nights after that Smith P. Bankhead was assassinated, brained, under my office at the corner of Washington and Main, and I have always thought that the assassin's blow was intended for me, and that our perfect similarity of dress led the assassin to mistake him for me. Bankhead had no enemies, he was deservedly popular. I had no proof, other than the threads above indicated. The motive and the brutal, depraved nature existed in the mind and character of this man, and, without being able to prove it, I will always believe him responsible for the assassination of Bankhead.

BOLTON, DICKENS & CO., AND THE INSTITUTION OF SLAVERY.

THE institution of slavery gave rise to a large volume of litigation in the South, chiefly for breach of warranty on bills of sale as to soundness of the slave.

These bills of sale were of very simple form: "Received of John Smith one thousand dollars for Ben, a negro man aged thirty years, whom I warrant to be sound, and a slave for life. William Johnson, Memphis, Tenn., Oct. 20, 1857."

Isaac L., Wade H., and Jefferson L. Bolton and Thomas Dickens, under the firm name of Bolton, Dickens & Co., were the most extensive negro traders in the world. They had negro marts in Memphis, New Orleans, Vicksburg, Mobile, Lexington, Richmond, Charleston, and other places, Memphis being the place where they had their chief office. General Bedford Forrest was at one time connected with the firm, and his iron nerve saved the life of Isaac L. Bolton under extraordinary circumstances.

A gentleman by the name of McMillan (if my memory is not at fault), living in Kentucky, sold to Isaac L. Bolton the unexpired term of a free negro apprentice, and Bolton brought the negro to Memphis and sold him as a slave for life.

The negro, through Frazer & Jones, brought suit, and recovered his liberty. The act of Bolton in selling a freedman into slavery was a felony. By some means Bolton induced McMillan to come to Memphis, as the latter thought on a friendly mission, but really, as it was charged, to ensnare and murder him. At all events, as soon as McMillan stepped into Bolton's office, in the negro mart, he was shot down in cold blood by Bolton.

Bolton was imprisoned, and denied bail, because "the proof was evident and the presumption great," in the language of the constitution. This was, I think, in September, 1855. Excitement and indignation against Bolton was at fever heat, and a mob of several hundred broke the jail and carried him to the ropewalk, in the old navy yard, to hang him.

General Forrest threw himself headlong in the breach, mounted a box, with pistol drawn, after the rope was around Bolton's neck, and told the mob that the man or men who dared to pull on the rope and take Bolton's life, must and should die with him on the spot. This brought the mob to immediately recognize its own danger, and their intended victim was not further molested.

The iron nerve and will of this one man, so greatly distinguished afterwards in the civil war, saved the life of Bolton.

Eminent counsel were retained by both the prosecution and the defense, including Yerger, Gov. Foote, Stanton of Kentucky, Frazer, Phil Glenn, and others, and the venue was changed to Tipton county, and the jury, it was said, was bought and packed for acquittal—at all events he was acquitted. The jurymen were indicted, charged with receiving bribes, and it was often said that not one of them died a natural death.

Wade H. Bolton, after the close of the war, told me that the defense cost three hundred thousand dollars. The money expended in this defense became a Pandora's box. Isaac L. Bolton contended that the money expended in his defense was for the benefit of the firm of Bolton, Dickens & Co., and should be charged to it. Thomas Dickens contended that it was expended for the personal benefit of Isaac L., and should be charged to his individual account. This contention caused a feud, which ultimately involved the lives of thirteen men. This was the bitterest and most vindictive feud known in the annals of Memphis.

I was not engaged in the civil suits growing out of these complications, had never been retained by any member of the old firm, but had prosecuted successfully a civil suit against the firm, for the heirs of Jefferson Bolton, who died in 1852, leaving two minor children whose interest in the firm I recovered for them at the end of another and earlier bitter feud.

John Bolton, a distant connexion of the Boltons, connected with the firm of Bolton, Dickens & Co., married one of the daughters of Jefferson Bolton, and proceeded against the firm for his wife's and her sisters' interest in the firm.

During the progress of this suit we met at Cuba to take depositions for the plaintiffs in the fall of 1857 Wade H. Bolton, with a party of ten men, all heavily armed with double-barrel shotguns, and John Bolton, with an equal number of armed men, took their seats in the room where I was taking depositions, and proving beyond doubt the plaintiff's cause. Blood was in the air. It was in the village of Cuba, in the northern part of Shelby county. I was in my shirt sleeves, standing up at a desk, when the principals, Wade H., and John Bolton, cocked and raised their guns to fire. They were near enough together for me to seize the muzzle of their guns, one in each hand, to prevent their firing. Disinterested men came to my assistance, and we prevented the little office from being converted into a slaughterhouse.

Al Sigler, the brother-in-law of John Bolton, sided with Wade. This angered John beyond all control, and when Sigler stepped out, John followed him, and he fled down the street and took refuge in a storehouse.

John broke into the house, and after unmercifully chastising Sigler, threw him out of the window. Wade and his party followed to rescue Sigler, but John's party stood them off with their guns—kept them at bay—and not a gun was fired, but Sigler went home a wiser and a sadder man, and much in need of "repairs."

The next day Isaac L. Bolton challenged John Bolton to fight a duel. The challenge was promptly accepted, and double-barrel shotguns the weapons named, twenty-five yards as the distance, and Hernando county, Miss., as the place.

The cartel was arranged in all details, guns costing $150 each were bought, and the parties, with seconds and surgeons, were ready to start for the place of conflict. An hour before the time to depart, the mutual friends of the parties came to me and proposed a conference, with a view of preventing the conflict if possible.

To give time for this, a postponement of twenty-four hours was agreed upon.

The principals were men of families, and it was our imperative duty to prevent this collision, if possible, without compromising either. Finally I proposed the following terms, which were agreed upon by all, and accepted by the seconds, namely, Isaac L. Bolton to withdraw the challenge, neither to demand or make apology.

The war intervened, and the courts were closed, during which time a lull in the feud ensued.

THE VENDETTA.

BOLTON, DICKENS & CO. FEUD, MURDER, AND TRIAL.

NOW to return to the tragedies after the war. Some party or parties went at night and tried to assassinate Thomas Dickens, at his farm, several miles north of Memphis. He and his cook, Nancy, a mulatto woman, were sitting by the fire when a volley was fired through the window. Nancy fell dead. Dickens was slightly wounded in the arm. E. C. Patterson, who had married a daughter of Isaac Bolton, and Wade H. Bolton were charged with the crime. Patterson was a brother of Thos. Patterson, ex-member of Congress from Colorado.

Bolton and Patterson, expecting arrest, fled to the woods of Tipton county, and sent Frank Cash to retain me as their counsel. This was quite a surprise to me because I had never been engaged as counsel on that end of the line, but was then free from engagements against their interests, civil or criminal. I refused to go to the woods to see them, because I regarded it as unprofessional, but advised them to come in at once and give themselves up, as their flight before arrest was the worst possible move they could have made. It lent vehement coloring to the grave suspicion flight had thrown around them. The retainer was left open, subject to arrangement between Bolton and myself. In a few days he came to my office looking much downcast and troubled. He commenced the interview by saying, "Hallum, you are satisfied, I know, it is not out of any personal regard for you that I seek your aid and counsel, you have always been against my interests; but you have just cleared Ed. Bartlett under extraordinary circumstances, in the face of threats from your warm friends to desert you if you conducted his defense; and if we can agree, I am sure you will make equal exertion for me. What are your terms?"

I told him five thousand dollars for myself, with the privilege of choosing my associate counsel, on such terms as we could agree on. He said, "Why do you want associate counsel? I thought you would be enough." "Because you need associate counsel, the more so because the Republican party have control of the Judiciary, and all the machinery of government, and it stands you in hand to have one of the ablest lawyers on that side. You were a slave trader and large slaveholder, and neither of us are favorites at court. You and I are Southern Democrats." Then said he, "May I ask who you prefer as associate counsel?" "Yes, I want Gen. Wallace." "What will he expect?" "I can't tell you until I see him." "Then see him as soon as you can."

I sent for Gen. Wallace, and he demanded two thousand five hundred. Patterson was brought in. His defense was included in these fees—Bolton paying them.

We were twenty-seven days trying a writ of Habeas Corpus for bail, which was granted, and as long in trying the case. Verdict "Not guilty" in each. They were jointly indicted but severed in the trial. During the trial, my office in the Vincent block, at the northeast corner of Second and Court streets, was broken open and set on fire. Dr. Mitchell happened to be passing, and extinguished the fire, one desk and papers being ruined. The public connected the coincidences together and thought the Dickens party responsible, but I did not share in the conviction, then nor now, but charged another party with having taken advantage of this trial to fire my office to cast off suspicion. The charge was made and delivered in writing, a copy of which I have kept to this day, and no action was ever taken to refute the charge. Fifteen years afterwards, after the guilty party was dead, I learned who it was, and relate it in another place in this volume.

Wade H. Bolton had a very strong presentiment that he would be assassinated. When he left his farm in the Big Creek settlement, he never told anyone when or where he was going, not even his wife. He always went armed.

I tried often to disabuse his mind, but the conviction settled, and I found it impossible to remove it. His will had been made, but I did not draft it. He told me who his executor was, and I told him that in the choice of his executor he had made the greatest mistake of his life, but he did not think so. The end proved my prediction correct. He bequeathed five thousand dollars to the widow of Stonewall Jackson, but I am informed she never received it, because of the executor's default.

One day in July he came into my office just as I was ready to leave it on my summer vacation; my baggage had been sent to the depot. He said, "Hallum, you will be gone a month or more ; I shall never see you again." He looked very sad, still I did not embrace the idea under which he labored. He left the office and proceeded west through the center of Court Square to Main street, and just after he passed through the gate opening on Main street, old man Thos. Dickens approached him and fired, an ounce ball striking the right shoulder and shattering the collar bone. I was just entering the omnibus to leave when the pistol fired. I went to Bolton immediately, had him conveyed to the residence of Frank Cash, on East Court street, and sent for two of the best surgeons in the city, Drs. Rogers and Rice. They examined the wound and cut the ball out. It had lodged near the skin and backbone. Bolton then declared that the shot would be fatal, but the surgeons did not think so, nor did I.

Dickens was arrested and bailed out. On the fourteenth day after this shot was fired, I was in the St. Nicholas

Hotel, in New York, and in the telegraphic column read the announcement of Bolton's death.

I immediately telegraphed to have a post-mortem examination held to determine the cause of death, because it was all important to the prosecution of Dickens.

The same surgeons made the post-mortem examination. Bolton had had pneumonia many years before, and his lungs were completely hepatized; that is, small air cells were filled with a white, floury substance. This left debatable ground as to whether he died from the gunshot wound or other latent causes. The surgeons presented a bill for five thousand dollars for the post-mortem examination. The executor, E. M. Apperson, postponed consideration of this bill until I returned, which was about the first of September. I thought the bill exhorbitant and advised the executor not to pay it. The surgeons would not give an opinion as to what caused death, until their bill was settled. This devolved much labor on me. It became necessary to thoroughly acquaint myself with the nature of gunshot wounds, and to do this I must have the aid of the best medical science. I applied to Dr. Frank A. Ramsey, who occupied a very high position in the profession, having been a professor in a medical college when quite young, and medical director in the Southern army of Virginia.

I told him I wanted an elaborate thesis based on the facts developed in the post-mortem, and all the best medical books in support of the thesis.

He charged two hundred and fifty dollars for this, and I gave him a draft on the executor, which was paid. After this my labor was easy, except to grasp and retain the grossly outlandish medical technicalities which appeared to me about as intelligible as the Egyptian worship of storks and onions. But I "waded through" the tome of gunshot science. When Dickens' trial came on, and after the jury had been selected, I took the surgeons to an anteroom, told them kindly that I had undergone great labor to qualify myself to crossexamine them with some degree of intelligence, that I was thoroughly satisfied that Bolton died from the effects of the shot and not from any supervening cause. I then read them the thesis, told them I had all the books to support it. Dr. Rogers said, "Who wrote that thesis?" I said, "Never mind, it is luminous and speaks for itself." He burst out laughing and said, "You can't fool me, I see Dr. Frank Ramsey's hand in that. Bolton died from the gunshot."

I told them kindly, for they were personal friends of mine, and men of the highest standing in the profession and society, that I did not wish to be unnecessarily forced into a collision of criticism, which would be unavoidable from my standpoint, if they gave it as their opinion that death was caused by any other cause than the gunshot, and as high toned gentlemen they appreciated my motives.

Two remarkable occurrences attended this long and tedious trial.

John F. Sale was associated with me in this trial. We were perfectly satisfied that a jury was being packed for acquittal, and that Dr. Sam Dickens, son of the defendant, had bought up the Deputy Sheriff, who summoned the talesmen, but to prove it was quite another matter. Where so much publicity is given to the facts by the press, the enlightened community who read, form opinions as to the guilt or innocence of the accused, and thus become disqualified jurors. This is always as the jury packer desires. He can go through a city, large or small, and select his scoundrels, place them, and have the sheriff or deputy, who summons them, pick them up as easy as a chicken picks up grains of corn.

Sale and I had almost exhausted our ingenuity in examining these men on their *voir dire*, without making a lodgement in the camp of the enemy. Nine jurors had been forced on us. When the tenth was examined as to his qualifications, I thought I saw some chance. I knew

his excitable, volatile nature, his occupation, and the class
he associated with. He was a Scotchman, and kept a
saloon in Scotland, one of the suburbs of the city, near
the old Winchester cemetery.

I commenced by asking at what hour Dr. Dickens was
in his saloon, then the names of the parties at the card
table in the anteroom, and said to him, "I know all about
this, and you had better tell us the truth and save yourself some trouble." He was surprised, and thought I
really knew all about it, when I was only thrusting a
probe in the dark.

He said Dr. Dickens was there the evening previous, had
a conversation about his father's case, then threw down a
ten dollar bill for a cigar and would not take any change,
and said, "If you are summoned on the jury I hope you
will help the old man out." This was a confession lurid
with guilt, and the Court, of its own motion, emptied the
panel, discharged the nine jurors already selected, cancelled the commission of the deputy who summoned them,
sent him to jail for thirty days, and ordered one hundred
talesmen summoned, and the selection of the jury proceeded.

George Gantt was leading counsel for the defendant, but had no hand in packing the jury. He would
have scorned such an office. He was as indignant as we
were, and forcibly so expressed himself. He always
fought with a keen polished blade.

When the argument commenced the large court room
was densely packed with eager listeners, a large number
of ladies being present. It was the custom of those days.
The elevating and refining influence of cultured ladies always lends a charm, an inspiration to these forensic contests. The argument continued through four days. Col.
Gantt closed the argument for the defense. He is always
eloquent, but on this occasion was grandly, majestically eloquent. And no one in that vast auditory of wit,
wealth, talent and beauty felt the sublime inspiration

more than he did.   He moved along in cadence of rhythm
and beauty, like the muse of the Grecian Isles sweeping
the harp of immortal song, until he fainted under the
glory of his own inspiration and fell to the floor.   I rushed
to him and threw a pitcher of water in his face, which re-
vived him.   He lifted and carried that audience with the
power and splendor of his polished genius to the height
of intellectual rapture.   None but a genius could have enthralled that audience with the magic of his own splendor.
Twice I have seen him faint under parallel circumstances.

Sargent S. Prentiss in a great speech in Nashville, in
the presidential campaign of 1844, fainted from the same
cause, when Gov. James C. Jones, lifted by the most exalted enthusiasm, dropped to his knees, raised Prentiss'
head and exclaimed, "Die, Prentiss, die, it is the best opportunity you will ever have."

Gen. Sale made one of his characteristic and powerful
arguments, many passages of which equaled the great
masters.   Notwithstanding our success in emptying one
panel of jurors, he firmly believed Dickens had succeeded
in organizing the jury in his interest, and plainly indicated his belief in his argument, in one of the finest phillipics I ever heard.   The appalling scenes in Dante's Inferno
are not more harrowing than his description of the crime
against society involved in the pollution of the Temple of
Justice.   The divinity of God in man, flash of the immortal soul.   I closed the argument for the prosecution, and
the scene closed with a verdict of not guilty.

The Southern people, whose hearts and natures are as
warm and genial as the sunbeams that dance in the foliage
around their homes, have always loved and admired intellectual conflicts, true eloquence, chivalric manhood, refined and noble womanhood, and these traits will continue
to distinguish them as long as the sun exerts climatic influence over physical and mental organism.

A STARVING LAWYER DYING OF PRIDE.

OW infinite the springs of human action. What delicate touches may shut off the machinery or set it in motion and change, destroy, or create character; a word, an act, a sentiment sometimes becomes immortal. One turn of that little kaleidoscope called life will move a thousand prisms and change ten thousand combinations of light and shade that none but the great Infinite can fathom and view as an harmonious whole. Hence springs the fiat to little, finite man, "Judge not." What strange compounds of frailty and greatness God has created.

That splendid genius of the British Isles, Burke, never uttered a profounder aphorism than when he said, "He who too severely criticizes the frailties of his fellow man, blasphemes his God." How frail we are, the greatest cannot win emancipation, there is no divorce from it. Frailty came with man into the world as a primal law. There are comparative degrees, that's all. The thunders that rolled around Sinai did not drive it from Canaan. The banners and lofty standards of the Savior of mankind were not spotless. The gentle Nazarene, conceived of the Holy Spirit and born of woman, disclaimed perfection because of his humanity. The sun has its spots. We turn now from the scenes in the Dickens' trial and look from my office across the street in that building with its Doric columns, it commemorates a revolution in the short and infinitely little life of myself, and holds in its urn memories as sacred as a pilgrim's shrine, of not the slightest moment to any mortal but the one little soul whose memories cluster there. The old house is gone, replaced, but it gave shelter to a penniless, hungry boy-wanderer, when he first entered the gates of a busy world—a life he knew not of.

"Hope which springs eternal in the human breast," and toil was his only capital. Kindness was there shown me, "Bread cast upon the waters."

In that Doric temple many lawyers labor and toil, some for fame, some for bread, some are hungry. One of learning and genius, and talent exalted, of splendid pedigree, has no patronage, no following. No one of the mighty throng sweeping past and over him in the river of life drops a morsel. A chivalrous Southron with nothing but the memory of an ancestral inheritance, which was swallowed in the relentless ravages of war. Pride, head, heart and genius were his all. But what are all these? Fleshless skeletons without patronage. With patronage an eyrie in the cliffs around Alpine summits. That man's name is on the Roster of the Memphis Bar, but the daisies that guard my remains may tell it. This tongue will never lisp it because of his noble pride. I would not disturb his grave. Ah! Tennyson, God and truth were in your soul and heart and on your pen when you wrote:

> "Kind hearts are more than coronets,
> And simple faith than Norman blood."

One day a noble brother of the guild, who now rests in voiceless Elmwood, came in to confer with me on some business matter. This ended, he said, "Do you know the condition —— is in, his absolute destitution and his pride, which invites death rather than appeal for help?" "Yes," said I. "I have been trying to help him in disguise, and made one miserable failure under circumstances that gave me much pain. I went to him and offered to lend him $250, and said to him he could hand it back whenever it suited his convenience, but his face flushed and he turned his head away, to hide from me the pain it gave him. He had been denied board longer, because he could not pay, and was sleeping on his office table without any pillow—using his books for that—and without covering, and was shabbily dressed. I then practiced a pious fraud on him, had some friends to go to his office and employed him to write fictitious deeds, for each of which he received ten dollars, and I had him employed in other services, and in that way made him free from want; but in a few months he suddenly disappeared, and I never knew where he went.   Thus we drop out and join the roll of the forgotten.

A thousand pearls lie hidden in the depths of the ocean to every one the storm throws to the surface.   Without opportune conditions Cæsar and Bonapart could never have worn the Imperial purple, William could not have fought and won the battle of Boyne, Cromwell could not have become Lord Protector, nor could our own great Washington have become the child of fame and one of the idols of mankind.   Some lawyers seem to "lift the latch and force the way," but fortuitous conditions must exist even with men of exceptional ability.

JOHN C. FARRINGTON.

JOHN was once the law partner of Edwin M. Yerger, and was a man of great ability.   I never knew his superior as a close logical, compact reasoner, when he would study his case and prepare it well; but, like Walter Coleman, he was inclined to be indolent, and would not often make these great exertions.

Judge Wm. T. Brown, and Ed. Yerger, came to me in the court room, at Raleigh, in 1859, when I was in the act of leaving for Memphis, and urged me to stay and hear Farrington that day, and assured me that I would be amply repaid.   The case to be tried grew out of the institution of slavery and the laws making common carriers responsible for the value of runaway slaves escaping from their masters through their agency.

A valuable man slave had boarded a steamboat at Paducah, Ky., and escaped from his master, and was never recovered.

Brown and Yerger and Farrington were retained by the master of the slave, and brought suit for damages against the owners of the boat to recover the value of the slave, the *ad damnum* being $1,500. Those who know the great ability of both Brown and Yerger will readily infer that of Farrington when informed that these great lawyers willingly retired from the argument of that case feeling that John Farrington's argument needed no supplement by either of them. The proofs were conflicting, and the plaintiff's case depended on the weight of circumstantial evidence. Farrington handled it with the touch of a master, link by link, and thread by thread; he unfolded the evidence like the orb of day breaking through the fleecy clouds. For condensation of luminous logic, it equaled the oration of Demosthenese for the crown. He crushed every remnant of hope for the defense, and destroyed it "like a cataract of fire." Selim B. Frazer, that "great jury lawyer," the master of ridicule, irony, burlesque, sarcasm, and comedy, represented the defense, but in this case he was overmatched, overwhelmed, and drowned in the waters of the majestic Niagara:

Verdict for the plaintiff $1,500.

For the last fifty years I have embraced every opportunity to hear great men, but have never, never heard Farrington's effort in this case surpassed by any man. If that argument had been preserved it would have taken its place in the classics of legal literature.

John belonged to the highest order of Nature's noblemen. He was quiet, inobtrusive, modest, temperate, and never seemed to realize the massive structure of his intellectual powers, the wealth God had showered on him. He has gone, left us, crossed the Stygian ferry, died of softening of the brain. Those were halcyon days, when my brothers of the noble guild could sit in the shadows of so many truly great lawyers, drink in so much that was great, good, and noble; a lawyer, with such surroundings, could almost become great by absorption.

When I go to Memphis now I find so many vacant places I feel solemn and sad, like a returning pilgrim "treading some banquet hall deserted."

Unless by chance I meet some of the "old boys" who go down in the urn of the golden past, I never hear the names of Farrington, Coleman, Payne, Brown, Yerger, Frazer, Caruthers, and many others, even mentioned. How quickly the wave of oblivion sweeps over us when we drop out of the moving column, FORGOTTEN, the only memorial, the waters of lethe bear us on the hidden wave. Sometimes I think the brotherhood too careless about these things, and wish they would take time from this overworked, onrushing, utilitarian age, and plant a flower here and there to inform the living where the ashes of their departed brothers repose.

ABE HERRON.

ABE HERRON quit the profession early in the fray. He was the representative of a class in those days, sprung from a parentage of ample means, he studied law as a polish rather than as a profession and science; he had talent, ability, without severe application. Inheriting a plantation and negroes, when thirty years old, he closed his law office, retired to his plantation, and never strengthened or rounded off the apex of that ambitious manhood which spares no toil, however severe, to win laurels on the higher fields of human action.

To withdraw the stimulus of poverty from such men, is to inflict lasting injury. To teach that wealth is the crowning end of human life, is as poisonous to expansion and greatness as corrosive sublimate is to human life.

When the fortunes of such men are swept away they become the most helpless of all classes. Energy, stimulus, application, vim, the very cream of true existence, sapped, undermined, dwarfed, dried in the bud, leaves the tree without fruit.

The relentless vicissitudes of war brought all this home to Abe when it was too late to retrieve. I remember a contest he had in 1864 with his former slaves about the ownership of fifty bales of cotton. The commanding general, to satisfy himself as to the merits of the controversy, disguised himself and listened to the evidence without any attache of the Bureau knowing he was present. I was present at the trial, representing the slaves who had produced the cotton, and knew the general was there in disguise—went with him to court. The evidence was overwhelmingly in favor of the slaves, and they got the cotton. An appeal to Washington was taken, and the judgment of the Bureau was affirmed.

JOHN PAT FARRELLY.

JOHN PAT FARRELLY was one of those men of quaint humor, and luxurious ease hard to describe. His father, Terrence Farrelly, was born in county Cavin, Ireland, immigrated to America, and settled at the Arkansas Post in 1818, where he married an American lady of English descent, the mother of John Pat, who thus became a cross between Celt and Saxon. His father was prominent in the early days of Arkansas, a lawyer, and member of the Territorial legislature four terms. A warm friend and great admirer of Gen. Pike. The General was married at his baronial mansion. A large cotton planter during the best days of the republic. John Pat was educated at the best institutions of the land, and supplied with an abundance of cash without knowing its value—a great and injurious mistake made by too many of our Southern planters.

John Pat was tall, with high forehead, large eyes, and a mouth that rivalled that of Henry Clay's, large enough to drink in any subject however abstruce. He loved to flip a fob chain, and equally well to take a julep, and entertain his friends wherever he overtook them, but was not an excessive drinker ; he loved an Irish bull and served his friends, but cared nothing for law briefs as long as Dad's cotton fields held out. The result is easily anticipated. There was no stimulant to "point an arrow at the sun." No necessity to fill the poor man's quiver with arrows worthy to battle with giants. No self-reliance, that Phœnix which so often rises from the ashes and soars above the Alps, while well-fed eaglets perish in their nest. His life "paints a moral and adorns a tale."

His father landed on the quay without an education and without a dollar, poor and penniless in a land of strangers. He rose by degrees and hard toil, to help at the foundation of a State, and wished to full high advance his son far above the meridian to which he had climbed, but he mistook the stimulants to soul and brain necessary to support such a flight.

John Pat, the *protege* of the Walkers, was elected to the legislature one term, and gradually faded away from the world without leaving any footprints. He was my personal friend, but would attract no attention here but for the moral taught by his life.

ROBERTSON TOPP.

TOPP was one of the first lawyers to open a law office in Memphis. He was a member of the legislature during my boyhood, and was a man of fine attainments and much force of character, but had retired from the Bar prior to my advent in 1854 to look after the interests of a large fortune for that day. He built and owned the Gayoso Hotel, which was the equal of any hostelry in the South. The acme of his ambition was the United States Senate, and he was often discussed in connection with that office but never became a formidable candidate. He was an exception to the general trend of able lawyers, a good financier. Of all the able lawyers who have graced the Memphis Bar but few have been able financiers. Topp and James Wickersham were able in that line, and William M. Randolph, since their time, has also proved himself an able financier, and James Lee, Jr., is a conspicuous success as a financier.

James Looney and T. S. Ayers made fortunes as commercial lawyers simply from the accumulation of their fees and not by speculation and financiering. Charles Kortrecht had the ability to manage large affairs, but confined himself to his law practice. Sydney Y. Watson gave evidence of much ability as a financier, but had no chance to develop before the commencement of the civil war. W. A. Blythe added his accumulations as a lawyer to an inheritance, invested in a fine building and retired from the practice. J. Knox Walker and Judge E. W. M. King were conspicuous failures as the managers of banks. There is a broadgauge liberality, the natural result of the study of law as a science, which is inimical to the close calculating banker.

L. O. RIVES.

I WAS running the gauntlet the week the episode with Sale occurred. These troubles often pop up at the most inopportune and unexpected moments. L. O. Rives was born and raised in Fayette county, Tenn., educated at the Cumberland University, and graduated in both the literary and law departments of the institution; was of small stature and morbidly sensitive. I had been his best friend on many occasions, had kept him out of a duel with McRae, for the most cruel and unjustifiable personal attack on the latter in the argument of a case in court. I had kept him out of a duel with Wiiliam J. Duval, after the challenge had been passed and accepted, on terms highly honorable to them both, and after they had made their wills, the cause being personalities indulged by both in the argument of a case. We were trying a case in the old Library Building, and I had made many well-founded objections to questions propounded by Rives to a witness, and the court sustained me in every instance, but Rives would repeat the question after it had been ruled incompetent. Finally, in the most pleasant and jocular way, I said, "I will have to ask the court to fine you for contempt if you repeat those questions again," and the Judge said he would impose a fine if he continued to trifle with him. Rives turned pale but soon recovered and went on pleasantly enough with the case, and I thought no more about it. When I descended the stairway to the pavement he was standing there with his hand in his hip pocket on his popgun. He demanded an explanation as to why I wanted the court to fine him. I could have wiped the pavement with him before he could get his pistol out, but the de-

mand under the circumstances was so ludicrous I burst
out in a hearty laugh, and said: "Rives, I would rather
run twenty miles than shoot you, and fifty miles than be
shot by you. Can't you look around and find some other
subject for the undertaker. Name your price, and if it
don't involve my life or some great bodily harm, I'll try
to accommodate myself to the terms." This flashed the
ludicrous so vividly to his mind that he burst out laughing
and paid for the cigars, and we were in a few minutes
the best of friends, the *statu quo* was restored. "How
often a kind word turneth away wrath," and it is the imperative duty of every gentleman to resort to such methods as long as honorable avenues are left open. And
when honorable escape is closed, to go in with all the
force necessary to complete vindication, be the consequences what they may. Let consequences take care of
themselves when such issues are presented. That is the
basis upon which the *code duello* is founded, and it stands
on elevated grounds.

Rives was a true friend, and never let any one harshly
criticise a friend in the absence of the latter. He once
had a fight on my account under such circumstances long
after I had left Memphis. He finally abandoned his profession and removed to his farm near Mason's depot,
where he led the life of a morose recluse, ending it in
suicide.

JOHN F. SALE.

JOHN F. SALE—this compound of frailty and greatness stands out in solitude against a background that reflects no other character, with an individuality wholly his own, a personality incapable of imitation, a rough unpolished diamond, possessed of a diversity and divinity of genius that at times soared to the loftiest heights. Those who knew him will recognize the absolute verity of this statement, those who did not know him in life will never know him, because his character defies either tongue or pen.

John came from the "dark and bloody ground," away back in the early forties, and soon took a commanding position at the able Bar of Memphis as a criminal lawyer, and maintained it as long as he lived. He had no taste for civil law, and never made but one grave and serious attempt at display of ability in that line, and for that he and I were fined $500 by Judge Reeves, but that in its order.

John was long Attorney General, a lucrative office, for which he was eminently fitted, and he finally lost it by a very forcible and impolitic speech. During the days of the Know-Nothing party, which he espoused with much zeal, he made a speech on the bluff at Memphis, not far from where the present postoffice stands—to the people, one half of whom were foreign born. In this speech he said "the Government of the United States ought to erect a gallows at every seaport on her coast as high as that on which Haman was hung, and hang every immigrant on it as soon as he set foot on our soil." This was political suicide, and when he offered for re-election he was defeated by Thomas B. Eldridge. Burch's alliteration of the three R's was nothing to compare to this speech, but financially it did him no harm. He went into an immense criminal practice as soon as he retired from office. John and his successor failed to agree as to the division of fees on indictments found while he was in office, and it was not long before he and Eldridge had a rough and tumble fight in open court. Eldridge was about to get the best of it when the lawyers separated them. John picked up his broad felt hat, jumped on a table, waved the hat over his head, and addressed the court thus: "If your Honor please, I will give one thousand dollars to any man who will show me a man I can whip. I have had a thousand fights and never whipped a man yet."

He was not methodical in argument, but never left one stone unturned or a point uncovered. At times he indulged in terrific denunciations as awful as "a cataract of fire."

Good intentions were sometimes interposed as palliation for crime. He always dashed at such defenses like a bull at a red flag. "Hell is paved with good intentions," he would say. "This paragon, who is unable to distinguish larceny from a Sunday school; this apostle of lying, who don't know the devil from a saint."

He was a fine judge of human nature, could follow the intricate avenues of cause and effect with consummate ability in unravelling and connecting acts and motives leading to crime. With all this he had many kind and amiable traits of character. He enjoyed a joke with as much relish as any man I ever saw, and could perpetrate them at the most unexpected junctures.

Once he was trying a case at the office of Justice Mallory, over the bank at the corner of Madison and Main, with "Jimmy Gallagher" opposing counsel. The law and the evidence were with "Jimmy," who read from Greenleaf on Evidence. John realized that his case was hopeless, unless he could sidetrack the justice. Turning to the preface where Mr. Greenleaf apologises to the pro-

fession for the imperfections in the book, he read it
slowly and deliberately, with emphasis on the imperfections and the humiliating apology of the honest author,
and told the justice that if he permitted such impositions
he ought to have his commission taken away. This
aroused the indignation of the court against "Jimmy"
to exasperating heat, and he said: "Mr. Gallagher, if
you ever bring that book in this court again I will fine
you to the extent of the law. You can have judgment,
Mr. Sale."

I went to John's office one day and found him in the adjoining room in his long white gown, propped up in bed
reading the Testament. "What are you doing, John?"
"I am taking notes and reading a brief of my case in the
Appellate Court. I find that I have been guilty of too
much oscillation and vibration between transgression and
repentance, with a great preponderance of transgression.
That is the difficult and pivotal point in my case. I guess
I had better retain St. Paul, as he appears to be the only
lawyer admitted to that court—all the others were dis-
barred at the beginning." I said, "Can't you ring in
some good intentions, John?" "No, all I ever said about
good intentions is in the record, and I fear St. Paul after
that affair at Damascus became too conscientious to give
a zealous defense, and I fear equally the first period of his
life, he looked so complacently on the stoning of Stephen."
"Chickens come home to roost, John, is a Persian adage.
Do you remember the fate of Haman when Mordecai exposed and turned the tide against the Know-Nothing?"
"You are too personal," he said, then kicked off the cov-
ering, bounded out of bed, and laughed, opened a box of
fragrant Havanas, and held the decanter to the sun.
"What theologians you and I would have made if we had
not wasted our time on the puny affairs of this world,
but then it is an awful dry and fiery subject."

He was careless in meeting pecuniary obligations. One
day he met and stopped me on the street and said, "Have

you time to listen to a short and earnest prayer for relief?" I knew pretty well what was coming, but said
"proceed." He threw his head back with uplifted hands
and said: "O Lord, thou knowest my distress and the
ready means of relief. I pray thee to move the spirit
of my brother and open his pockets of compassion to
the small extent of $250, a matter of no moment to
him, but of momentous interest to me, at this the most
critical of all junctures in my misspent life. I pledge my
vow to Gabriel and hosts of heaven to make it a specialty
ever before my mind to refund this loan if made now." I
stopped him short, and said: "John, you blasphemous
rascal, come along to my office and get the check, but I
know that will be the last of it." His eyes flashed lumi-
nously and he said, "What power there is in prayer, my
dear brother. I'll make an exception in your case, I feel
humiliated at your doubt." I gave him the check, and it
was a year before he ever alluded to it, in this *a la* Sale
manner. One day he called me across the street and gave
me a very long and large cigar, which he said cost fifty
cents, and said, "light it. I want to see the smoke as it
curls and floats upward. Do you know why I rushed
into this wild extravagance?" I replied, "No, why?"
He said, "Because your bump of credulity is so large.
It was enormous that morning you loaned me that $250."

He was a privileged character, and could do things with
the utmost impunity that other men dare not do.

Prince, his son, after returning from college, corrected
his father's broad English pronunciation of Don Quixote,
the inimitable Spanish satirist.

"What," said the father, rising up from the diningroom table with majestic indignation, "I'll Don Ke-ho-te
you, you trifling Sancho Panza of an ass, if I ever hear
you butcher that respectable name again."

I obtained judgment in the circuit court for a client and
gave the execution to "Bill" Moncrief, a deputy sheriff,
for collection. "Bill" collected the money, but instead

of paying it over to me, went around and bought up debts against the judgment creditor, and offered me these claims in payment, some of which were disputed. Of course I could not submit to such illegitimate methods. Moncrief consulted John, came back to my office and said he was well advised and knew whereof he spoke, and to crack my whip. · I said, "Very well, it will cost you heavily, because the statute gives a penalty of twenty per cent and a summary motion against the sheriff and sureties for such delinquencies. I read the statute to him and told him I did not want the penalty; that John Sale was a very able criminal lawyer, but I did not think him well qualified to advise in civil matters. They were both warm personal friends of mine, and I did not want either of them to get into trouble, but sent Bill to bring John to my office that I might show him the statutes and six decisions of the Supreme Court construing the statutes.

John got his Irish up to a high key and refused to come, but sent Bill back to tell me he would bet $250 that I did not know what I was talking about, and that when I brought the threatened motion he would defend it and go into the "fool-killing" business. This did not anger me in the least but I laughed heartily, and had the motion served immediately. The remedy was very simple and speedy. In a few days the motion came on to be heard at the morning hour. Court was then held in the old Library building on Third street adjoining the old Memphis theater. A murder case in which I was employed for the defense was to be taken up immediately after the morning hour, and the court room was densely packed. Many were strangers to me—not knowing that John was a privileged character—and could say almost anything to his intimate friends without giving offense. I did not care what he said within the circle of these intimate friends, but would not submit to the same privilege being taken in the presence of a hundred strangers, who would carry away with them a contempt for any

man who would submit without resentment, not knowing
John's peculiar ways and privileges within a limited circle of friends.

I did not know that any fun was up until I entered the
Court with my office boy. I then saw John in consultation with six members of the Bar, some of whom were
laughing. Immediately I knew what was up. These civil
lawyers only wanted to see some fun, and had been stuf-
fing John with fallacious and wholly untenable arguments
to be vehemently hurled at me in what he called the argument of the motion. I immediately sent my office boy
for six volumes of Tennessee Reports, containing decisions construing the statute, leaving John not a scintilla on
which to base an argument. I was then in for the fun
myself, and never felt more serene in my life, and less in
expectation of anything serious. I fully comprehended
that the *coterie* of six able lawyers whom John had consulted had excited and urged him on as a practical joke,
and nothing more. He had never read the decisions, and
to get the opening and conclusion had filed a demurrer to
the motion by the advice of mutual friends.

He rose with more animation than usual to argue the
demurrer. When he had clearly announced his first proposition I handed him a decision diametrically opposed to
it; he read it and was somewhat taken off. Then he proceeded to the second proposition, and I handed him another
decision settling the law to the reverse of what he stated,
and he read that with increasing embarrassment, left the
point and proceeded to announce a third proposition. I
handed him a third decision directly against him, and he
read it with some hesitation and difficulty.

By this time forty lawyers were laughing at John's embarrassment and he felt it keenly, but announced his fourth
proposition, and I handed him another decision in the
teeth of it, and asked him to be courteous enough to read
that. All this time I was in the best of humor and as
happy as a girl at a May-day party, and enjoyed the joke.

But John's cup was brimful, and he threw down the book without reading it, turning to the Court he said:

"If your honor please, I am convinced that Mr. Hallum's client is a d—n rascal, and his attorney no better." There was a large heavy oak table between us, and an iron column supporting the roof on Sale's side of the table. Instantly I said "John Sale you are uttering a willful and deliberate d—n lie, and you know it." He threw the Code at me, which glanced the side of my head without hurting me in the slightest, and then he picked up a glass and hurled it at me, but it struck the iron column and shattered in a thousand pieces. The room was so densely packed with men, I saw that I could not get at him except by jumping upon or over the table which separated us.

In an instant I was on the table and seized him by his long flowing hair, jerked his head many times with great force against the iron column, injuring him severely; when pulled away the hair of his head came with me. John was cut to the skull in many places and I was as bloody as a butchered beef from his wounds.

The skin was not broken on my person. John was taken to Dr. Arthur K. Taylor's office for repairs. I went to the jury room and sent my office boy for another suit of clothes. Col. Andrew J. Keller came to me and said, "You ought not to notice John Sale." I said, "You jokists ought not to have set him on me if you did not want him hurt. I know you only intended a practical joke at Sale's expense, but you knew that either of us would fight the devil, when mad, and give him the first shot. I forgive you the joke, but don't want any more strictures or comments, or advice that would lead me to play the role of spaniel." And Col. Keller said, "Yes, boys, it is now but too evident we carried this thing too far without intending such results." I regretted it because Sale was badly hurt. The Court fined us $500 each for the contempt involved in fighting in its presence.

Dr. Taylor shaved and plastered John's head. He then

went to John Creighton, an Irish justice of the peace, and borrowed his Derringer pistols, came and took his stand at the foot of the stairs leading down from the Court room, intending to shoot me when I came down. I did not know this until informed by Col. Keller, Joe. Scales and other attorneys who were now on the alert to prevent another collision. They insisted that I should go down another stairway and thus flank John. I told them that if the prince of hades and all his imps were there in waiting, that I would go down as I came up. But said, "Boys, I am not armed; I am cool and deliberate, and know John Sale better, perhaps, than any of you, and don't intend to hurt him any more. All of you pass down and across the street, and stand there until I come down; then I will speak to John and settle the matter quicker than anybody else can. We are both quick and impulsive and have been made the innocent victims of a practical joke by mutual friends." They believed me and filed down and out to the opposite pavement—about forty in all.

I walked down and stepped in about two feet in front of John—his hands were in his pockets, and I saw the protrusion of his pants made by the pistols. John was ready for anything. I said, "John Sale, you have John Creighton's pistols in your hands. Now I want to make two bets with you before this thing proceeds any further: first, I will bet you one thousand dollars that you don't know which end of the pistols to hold when you shoot; second, I will bet you another thousand dollars that you had rather take a drink than to shoot me?" "By G—d, let's go get it;" and you never heard such a yell in all your life from the boys across the street. Champagne corks flew, and I paid $55 for the drinks. All this occurred within the space of three hours.

Half of the next day was consumed by the gentlemen who got us into it, in persuading the Court to remit the fines.

The speeches were indeed humorous at our expense and

we had to submit, like penitents at a baptizing. Judge Reeves was on the bench. At the end of the speeches John and I stood up and solemnly assured the Court, that in all we had done no contempt was meant, and the fines were remitted.

John and I were always before and always after warm friends. It was not in the nature of either of us to harbor malice or be at enmity, when no premeditated or willful injury had been perpetrated. He was fined in the Criminal Court once, and not long after was elected Special Judge to try a case in which the Judge was disqualified. Immediately after taking his seat, he turned to the clerk and said, "Mr. Clerk, a fine was entered not long ago against one John F. Sale, enter an order remitting that fine."

He was garroted once on Front street. Next day he told his friends that the thief was evidently a stranger in the city, because no one who knew him ever supposed that he had enough money to justify choking him for it. I have heard him make many strong and powerful arguments. He cared nothing for money, except to serve immediate and pressing wants.

APPOINTMENT OF JUDGE CATRON TO THE SUPREME BENCH OF THE UNITED STATES.

I AM indebted to the late Hon. John F. Darby, of St. Louis, for the following interesting episode: He was in Washington at the time Judge Catron was appointed to the Supreme Bench. I have no doubt of its authenticity, and think it worthy of preservation, as I have never seen it in print. Judge Catron took the world easy, and never elbowed or pushed himself for promotion. But his wife in this was his opposite, was all energy and full of ambition for the husband she idolized, and she generally had her way. Both were warm personal friends of General Jackson, then President of the United States. The Judge was then on the Supreme Bench of Tennessee, and lived, I think, at Tullahoma, but that matters not. In those days waterways and dirt roads afforded the only means of travel, and mail facilities were retarded by these slow standards. One night after the Judge had retired, his wife picked up a newspaper and read the announcement of a vacancy on the Supreme Bench of the United States. In less than ten minutes she had the cook and hostler in her room, gave orders for an early breakfast, and for the carriage and horses to be ready at sunrise next morning. She then arranged the wardrobes for herself and the Judge, and retired without communicating her plans to him. Next morning she aroused him at a much earlier hour than usual, and with some difficulty got him to the dining room. Quoth the submissive Judge, "Good wife, what does this mean, I will be drowsy all day, you have broken in on the sweetest hour of sleep?" To which she replied, "Never mind,

Judge, you say I do all things for the best, we will discuss details after the hurry is over. Hurry up, we must be off." "Be off?" he said, "that cannot be. I have some law papers to read and write up to-day, and you must excuse me." "No, my dear Judge, the business is urgent, and requires you, too, and that settles it for the present."

From the dining room his wife led him to the carriage. After they had advanced as far as the Kentucky line, she handed him the paper containing the announcement of the vacancy on the Supreme Bench, and told him that they were on their way to Washington, and her purpose was to put him on the Supreme Bench of the United States; that she knew Gen. Jackson would appoint him if the vacancy was not filled before she could see him. Quoth the Judge again: "Wife, this is the veriest nonsense of your life, I would not humiliate myself by asking for the place for the city of Washington, and we had better turn around and go back home." The wife got just a little bit "up on her ear" at this, and said, "You don't have to ask for it. I am not taking you to Washington for that purpose. My husband is as well qualified for that place as any man in America, and if he does not get it, I will know why. You are in my hands, Judge, your honor is mine. I will take care of it. Make yourself comfortable," and the Judge, as usual, subsided. She obtained several relays of horses, they drove across the Potomac into Washington, and the carriage stood in front of the White House at sunrise. She jumped out like a girl and left the Judge sitting in the carriage, but was refused admission by the usher at that early hour. Indignantly she brushed him aside and demanded to be conducted to Gen. Jackson's presence. The General was an early riser, and was sitting at his table with his gown and slippers on, and long stem cob pipe in his mouth. When Mrs. Catron was ushered in by the frightened usher the General was as glad as surprised to see her, and before she took

her seat she asked if the vacancy on the Supreme Bench
had been filled, and when answered in the negative said,
" I ask the appointment for Judge Catron." And the old
hero said, " By the Eternal, he shall have it," and before
the sun set he was appointed and confirmed.

A REMARKABLE PROFESSIONAL VISIT.

IN 1859 a remarkable young lady came to my office
with several letters of introduction from unquestioned sources, indicating wealth and high social
standing. Her personnel was distinguished, manners polished, dress of the costliest fabrics worn with
diamonds of great value. Her command of language
almost unrivalled, a very charming woman, apparently
about twenty-five years of age.

The letters of introduction simply indicated her desire
to consult me professionally without stating the nature of
the service required.

"Have you the time, coupled with the necessary privacy, to listen to a long, pathetic story which has sorrowed my heart for years—one that has never been voiced
or found expression to a living soul on earth, not even to
my husband, who is the best and kindest of men, possessed
of an ardent and devoted desire to make life a paradise to
me? He is possessed of high social standing, much culture, great wealth, unquestioned morals, and is perfectly
devoted to me—yet there is an aching void—a wilderness
of unrest in my life, which I have tried in vain to repress
without finding it possible. That he cannot supply.

We have spent five years in foreign travel, visited all
the courts of Europe, the Holy Land, Asia, the isles of
the sea. We have climbed the Apennines, scaled the
Alps, wintered in Venice and Rome, sailed the classic seas
of Greece, where the mightiest deeds of men on land and

sea, in arms and the civic forum, where poets, philosophers, heroes and sages enacted and achieved the highest
success of man in a pagan age. All that wealth and
culture can enjoy and appreciate are mine. I crave no
more in that direction; my heart is surfeited, and yet unrest is consuming my life."

The preface of a lady's story is generally much longer
than the story itself, and is often concealed to the last.

"Have you any children, may I ask?" But she had
not arrived at that door of the closet, and did not answer,
but blushed and kept right along at railroad speed for
half an hour, then for a few minutes became quiet and
sedate, evidently embarrassed.

Then she said, "Perhaps I had better longer defer the
object of this visit and patiently await further unfolding of the divine will, it is too distressing, too embarrassing, yet the heart, mind, soul, must have somewhere to
go for consolation and advice; my heart is breaking to
accomplish the divine purpose of woman's creation. Do
you understand me? Don't you anticipate me? I believe
you do, from the inquiry. I have not answered, because
of those modest elements of woman's nature which con-
stitute her highest value." Pardon me, madam, I think
I fully anticipate you, and am solicitous to relieve you of
any further embarrassment. You are childless, and your
husband is impotent. "That is it." And she burst into
a flood of tears and covered her face.

After recovery, she said, "I came to you for legal,
moral, any advice which you think calculated to relieve
my soul from this burden."

"The legal aspect, Madam, is of very easy and ready
solution. The law, if appealed to, will dissolve the marriage. Further than to tell you that I cannot go. It would
be empiricism to attempt it. It is beyond the reach of man
to indicate to you in what that step would result, in its
relation to your future happiness. Man cannot draw back
the curtain which opens to view the purposes of the Cre-

ator, nor can he tell what discord such a disturbance and strain on your heartstrings would produce. You must be the exclusive judge of that."

She lived in a distant State, and I never heard of her again, except through a polite note in which she enclosed a bank check on New York, of which nothing was said at the interview.

CHASE AND CAPTURE OF A STOLEN STEAM-BOAT.

1861.

FOR some years prior to 1861 I was attorney for the Ætna Insurance Co., of Hartford, which did a large business of marine insurance on the Mississippi river, and during that period sustained many losses and had many controversies growing out of it. To facilitate consultation with me, Mr. Stanard, the local agent having this business in charge, moved his suit of offices to a suit of rooms adjoining mine. A few weeks before Fort Sumter was fired on, a steamboat and cargo insured in the Ætna, coming down White river on her return voyage to the port of Memphis, was alleged to be in a sinking condition, necessitating the throwing overboard of six hundred bales of cotton, which was afterwards picked up by the boat's crew. Captain Robinson, of the steamer, made a claim for salvage, which the Insurance Company vehemently disputed on well-sustained ground.

There was very strong proofs to sustain the charge that Captain Robinson, the owner of the steamer, had fraudulently thrown the cotton overboard, for the purpose of claiming salvage. There was but little doubt of this. As soon as the boat entered port I libelled her in Admiralty, as indemnity to the Insurance Company. Moses Wilson was the United States Marshal in charge of the steamer, which was run up into Wolf river, tied up and put in the hands of an engineer by the name of Mc-Nutt.   The insurance Company was owned in the north. Captain Robinson, wholly unscrupulous, was very demonstrative in his denunciation against the north, and tried to inflame the swelling war cry against the libellant. McNutt came to me and said he feared an attempt would be made to rescue the boat by force.   I directed him to take out the cylinder heads and bring them to my office, which he did, and I thought this precaution all that was necessary.

In a few days Fort Sumter was fired on, the war feeling rose to fever-heat, and was never higher during the war.   Robinson took advantage of this excitement, went with a crew to the steamer, seized McNutt, put new cylinder heads in the boilers, raised steam, and started down the Mississippi.   McNutt came to my residence about ten o'clock at night, bleeding from the maltreatment he had received, and informed me of the mob and rescue of the steamer.   I lost no time in communicating with Marshal Wilson, a resolute fearless man.   In three hours we had a crew of ten armed men, chartered a fleet running tug-boat, and started down the river in pursuit of the stolen steamer, the Marshal and myself making twelve armed men on board the little flying craft. The engineer cracked on every pound of steam the quivering little boat would bear, and she plowed the waters like a little monster, making twenty miles an hour down stream.

At six o'clock we discovered smoke from the chimney stacks rounding an island below us.   The engineer in charge gave the order to "fire up."   We soon passed close under the steamer.   The astonished Robinson standing on hurricane deck, readily comprehended the emergency that confronted him, when he saw the armed boat pass so swiftly by, and then round to, facing up stream. He hurried to the lower deck and mustered ten armed men to resist the capture.   But when the resolute Wilson bore up within twenty yards with his armed deputies, all of whom had been sworn in, and ordered Robinson to surrender on peril of being fired on instantly if he refused, the river pirates grounded arms and surrendered, and we put McNutt in charge of the engines and made the pilot round to, and take the steamer back to Memphis. Robinson's idea was that when he passed below the Tennessee Line, he would be beyond the jurisdiction and out of reach, but Wilson, in emergencies like that, did not await the slow process of courts. He was a native of Sumner county, Tenn., and knew my parents when they were young. He could be implicitly relied on in any emergency that challenged either the physical or moral courage of man.

But the courts were now closed during the long night of war, and Wilson discharged the prisoners because we could not get process to hold them, nor appropriations to feed them, but the steamer was again tied up in Wolf river, to be again stolen by Capt. Robinson. Stanard, the local agent of the insurance company, was a Union man, and saw no further encouragement to recapture the boat. He went north as soon as he could ship the books, papers, and effects of the office, and I never heard of him any more. McNutt remained too long. He was an honest, faithful northern man. I took care of him, secreted him some days in my residence, and one dark foggy night we crossed Wolf river in a skiff, having previously sent my horse and buggy across the river. I took him to the head of Island No. 40, chartered a skiff and boarded the first upriver steamer, put him on board, and bade him a hearty farewell, not knowing whether the vicissitudes of war would permit us ever to meet again. How many lost sight in the storm of relentless passion it engendered, of the nobler phases of humanity and the demands of friendship and brotherly sentiment. War is a whirlwind, tearing its way of devastation through the heart of man.

McNutt returned to Memphis as an engineer in the ironclad fleet, and as soon as the naval battle was over and his war vessel came to anchor, he came into the city and hunted me up, and manifested much gratitude and the sincerest friendship, which was in all things reciprocated. He manifested much anxiety to serve me, frequently came to dine with me, sometimes bringing an officer of the fleet with him. What a fratricidal war that was !

> " I saw two brothers to-day, cripples,
> And one of them said he fought for the Blue,
> The other, he fought for the Gray.
> Now he of the Blue had lost a leg,
> The other had but one arm.
> The leg was lost in the Wilderness fight,
> And the arm on Malvern Hill."

How infinite the impulses, countless the passions, numberless the strings, which play on the soul of man! And make—what? Character, destiny, and finally hide him out of sight.

CHALLENGE TO THE FIELD.

JUDGE HENRY G. SMITH AS PRINCIPAL AND SECOND— HARLOW CHALLENGES THORNTON.

JUDGE SMITH was an appointee to the Supreme Bench under the Brownlow administration when the wealth and dignity, bone and sinew, of the State were ostracised and disfranchised, and in no sense did he or could he under such circumstances represent the people as a jurist chosen by them. He came from the north, I think New England, at an early day prior to 1840, and located at Somerville, but when Memphis began to put on metropolitan pretensions he came to her. He was an able civil and commercial lawyer, and a laborious worker.

In the pronunciation of many words he retained the broad New England accent, and never emancipated him-

self from those pilgrim provincialisms, those illegitimate
invasions of the "King's English," which grate so
harshly on the Southern ear where treason against the
mother tongue is not tolerated, and never embraced by the
better classes.

His ability as a lawyer was admired, and he had a
large clientage, but he had no very warm friends and no
very strong enemies. Outside of his legal worth and attainments he had but little knowlege, was an unsophisti-
cated novice in the practical demands and affairs of life,
though he essayed sometimes much in that direction and
made some very signal failures.

He thought he had the refinement of the *code duello*
when in fact he knew no more about it than a pig does of
the intricacies of theology.

Late in life he fell in love with the accomplished widow
of a deceased judge and met a rival in an old bachelor
and sent him a challenge to the field, without first addressing a polite note stating the supposed offense, and
asking, in the literature of Chesterfield, whether true or
false, and if true then the challenge.

The challenged party was surprised, and replied to the
pre-emptory mandate to fight, that as he had not committed the alleged breach of gentility, he felt under no
compulsory obligation to set himself up as a target to
be shot at.

Smith said to one of his friends, "Here is a lame place
in the code, I suppose I will have to accept that explanation, but I believe he lies."

I saw him on the field of honor in March 1859, as the
friend of the challenged party, when, through blunder-
ing ignorance, audacity of presumption, and rigid code
of ethics, which there obtains, he forfeited his own
life, had the rules been enforced against him. He
advised an acceptance of the challenge when convinced
that a retraction and apology was due the challenging party, and led his principal to the field to "run

a bluff." Unsuccessful in that he advised an apology. So extraordinary were the facts I will give them, and state only such facts as come under my direct observation, for I was there and an eye-witness to all I state.

John P. Harlow, the challenging party, a Canadian by birth, an American by adoption, came to Memphis—he was a sprightly and knightly young man. I gave him the use and freedom of my office, and for his benefit let him appear in some of my cases. In one of these cases, Col. Thornton, of Virginia, but then a citizen of Memphis, was opposing council, and some rather tart criticisms passed between him and myself, but nothing beyond what often occurs in the heat of debate. We were then and always had been friends, and left the court room so feeling toward each other: at least I never knew of any other feeling, and certainly indulged none other myself.

Harlow also appeared in the case, and I thought was eminently conservative.

That evening Dr. Thorton, the Colonel's son, then quite a young and chivalrous man, asked me to deliver Harlow an offensive message in retaliation for what he understood Harlow had said offensive to his father in the argument of the case. Harlow had not said it, but all possibility of adjustment by explanation was cut off as long as the offensive language of Dr. Thornton stood unrecalled. Harlow asked for a disavowal or apology, which was denied, and a challenge was immediately sent, and accepted. The terms of the cartel were arranged in detail Saturday evening, and the duel was to be fought on the following Monday morning at sunrise, in Hopefield, opposite Memphis, with duelling pistols, at ten paces, which is thirty feet.

Judge Smith was young Thornton's second. The pistols were the celebrated pair belonging to General Preston Smith, who afterwards fell in the battle of Chickamauga gallantly leading his men.

The seconds measured off the ground, and tossed for

choice of positions, and the right to give the word or call the signals to fire, and Harlow's second won both. The pistols were then loaded, and the principals placed in position, and the arms handed them.

After both responded in the affirmative to the words, "Are you ready?" they were to fire between the words one, two, three, and not after.

The calling second stepped off a few paces and asked, "Are you ready?" and both principals responded, "Yes." "One, two," and at this juncture Smith hallooed "Stop." The principals lowered their arms. This was wholly unwarranted, unprecedented at that stage in a duel, but Harlow's second attributed the interruption to Smith's ignorance, and for that reason tolerated without endorsing it. Smith called a conference with the other second, to whom he vulgarly proposed that it be announced that the duel was off, without explanation or apology. Harlow's second indignantly spit on the proposal and proceeded at once to call the fight, and Smith rushed to his principal and advised an apology, which ended the farce, and surprised the spectators. Gen. Preston Smith, the owner of the pistols, rushed up to Dr. Thornton, took the pistol from his hand, and fired it over Smith's head, and said in language more forcible than elegant, that he never expected to see his pistols disgraced on the field. Judge Smith submitted to this without one word of response or protest.

Dr. Thornton was a chivalrous young man, in the hands of his much older second, and was in no sense responsible for his conduct.

As Harlow was not guilty of the supposed offense, the withdrawal of the language offensive to him ought to have followed his polite note, and would if Smith had been a man worthy of such trust.

Again, I repeat that every word here written is from my own personal knowledge and presence. The news in some way had leaked out that the duel was to be fought,

and the bluff on the Memphis side was lined with people,
anxiously looking across the river, many with glasses in
hand.

After being both principal and second he was appointed
Judge of the Supreme Court, and took the oath of office
prescribed by the laws of Tennessee, affirming that he
had never in any way participated in a duel or borne a
challenge.

EARLY EXPERIENCES AND EPISODES IN ARKANSAS.

IN 1861 I received $200,000 in notes, bills of exchange,
and protested drafts from the Gayoso Savings Institution, for collection, against Humphrey & Griffin, large levee contractors, who had largely
invested in Arkansas wild lands at the flood time of speculation, when they, and hundreds of other speculators,
looked upon these lands like " Mulberry Sellers " did on
his eyewater.

In March of that year, in behalf of the bank, I went to
Arkansas to look after these lands to secure the large
debt, or as much of it as possible. I landed at St.
Charles, on White river, and rode fifteen miles to DeWitt,
the new county seat of Arkansas county. The brick
courthouse was just finished; there was no fence around
it. The hotel was a pine log house just west of the
square, presided over by an estimable lady who fed bountifully and royally, juicy venison, prairie chicken, squirrels,
wild turkey, and everything from the larder in proportion. At that table I was introduced to two young lawyers—brilliant, buoyant, bright—C. C. Godden, from
Alabama, and —— Poindexter, of the noted Tennessee
family of that name. I never met more courteous gentlemen. I was quite young, but their senior by several

years. We sat out the night until the cock crew for day, talking over our professional experiences even at that early day. Poindexter had just passed through a memorable scene which was then "the talk of the town," and he "the lion of the day." I have it from his own lips:

"I was engaged to prosecute some noted desperadoes before I knew their characters, and had been paid a good retainer. I summoned many witnesses and made thorough preparation, which caused some uneasiness in the clan, and they threatened me with vengeance if I proceeded. I was informed that previous to that time they had successfully intimidated other lawyers. To quit and return the retainer, or advance was the question, and I advanced. Retreat was out of the question. I had no reputation, but had one to make in this new community where I am a stranger. I whipped them with a scorpion's lash, and when I had finished the first trial and was leaving the courthouse for dinner they blockaded my way. I picked up a piece of timber and advanced on the bullies, and said: 'I will wear this timber into frazzles on the first scoundrel who makes a move.' This astonished and dazed them, and they opened out and let me pass without saying one word. Just as I got to the corner where the saloon stands, the leader called to me thus: 'Hello, Poindexter, I'll be d—d if you ain't a man after my own heart, a gamecock; stop and let's take a drink.' All came up to the bar and drank to my health, and that ended it."

Charley Godden said: "Now, Hallum, it is your time to speak in this experience meeting; give us some Arkansas experience."

Here a box of Havanas were handed around.

"Well, boys, it is sometimes as disagreeable as the sequel is amusing to relate how Arkansians pluck pin feathers from city gents and college fledgelings when they assume an air of importance and superiority. I have some personal experience in that direction which is fresh, at least it has never been put upon the news market by me, although it transpired one year ago. The youthful idea that it might be construed in 'derogation of the common law' caused me to 'hold it up for further consideration,' as I did not wish to do or say anything rash about Arkansas and the primitive customs of her people. In fact, having been 'proved and fully initiated in the first degree,' I was not anxious for the second, and hope to escape the third altogether.

"One of my first wife's distant relatives in the collateral line lived in Tipton county, Tenn., and paid us a visit at a time when I happened to have $1,500—just the amount he happened to need *only for a few days*. My wife was anxious to make a good impression on this distant relative whom we thus met for the first time. He, a Mr. Tisdale, was good looking, well dressed, saintly in demeanor, and could excel a Methodist bishop in the invocation of blessings at the table. Nothing wrong about that man. I was also anxious to oblige and make a good impression on my wife's distant relative, if it did take my pile to clinch the impression—nothing small about me, then, when circumstances did not compel it—so I readily invested fifteen hundred in this distant relative, who knew more about the 'enchantment distance lends to the view' than I did. Impressions never grew more luxurious in a virgin soil than mine did, and I did not neglect this splendid opportunity to invest. There was no blemish in his external appearance on which a doubt could be raised, or suspicion sprouted, and I turned the cash loose, *only for a few days*. I did not even require a note or memorandum of the transaction, but our distant relative thought it best, as he might 'drop off,' which he did unexpectedly. He gave me a note, due one day after date, for $1,500, crisp and green. To conceal any anxiety which might possibly arise, he told me that he had a large lot of cotton stored with D. H. Townsend, a commission merchant on Front Row, as the street was known in those days, that he wished to hold it for a few days for a better price. This was perfectly satisfactory, and I presumed one of those beneficent presumptions of the common law, that he was O. K. In fact, I inferred from his deferential bearing that he might be offended if I were to ask why he did not get the advance from his merchant who held the collateral.

"A month rolled around before I ventured to ask my wife where that distant relative of hers lived and his post-office address. 'Tipton county,' she thought, but did not know his address. It was said he lived in that county. When I went to Memphis on other business, I casually dropped in at Mr. Townsend's and asked him how much cotton he had on hand for Mr. Tisdale, of Tipton county. 'Oh!' he said, 'did he do you up, too? He exchanged what was once supposed to be good character for all the cash it would command and jumped the country.' I had already dropped the 'distant relative' handle.

"Two years rolled away before I located him in the backwoods of Crittenden county, on the banks of the classic Tyronge. I sent the claim to that prince of good fellows, Perry Lyle. He brought suit, and in due course of time notified me that my distant relative had paid every dollar, and to come over and get it. I wrote him our courts were running, that I would be over next Sabbath. I went up on the 'Mark R. Cheek' to Mound City and borrowed a spirited saddle horse to ride four miles up the banks of Marion lake to the county seat. I took a mint julep on the steamer with some friends—perhaps two, I did not count—and felt as happy as a lord, rich as a king, and eloquent of speech, and wanted some suitable occasion to work it off to advantage.

"After proceeding up the lake in solitude and pent-up silence for about a mile, I saw a crowd of young and old men with angling rods desecrating the Lord's day. Here was my opportunity. I felt like an inspired evangelist, and stopped in the road just as one of them was landing a fine bass.

" 'Gentlemen,' said I, "in the name of the Father and the Son I command you to remember the Sabbath day and keep it holy! Is it possible that you don't know that Gen. Jackson is dead, and that Christ was crucified? I think so.' At this they laid their poles down and came up and formed a circle around my horse. I took this as an indication of the marvelous effect my superb opening in the wilderness was producing, and rose to a higher key with all the authority of John the Baptist, without the locust and wild honey. But I had reached the climax of absurdity, and was on the verge of taking the plunge from the sublime to the ridiculous, when one seized me by the left foot, another the bridle rein, and one said: 'You d—n city gent, we will teach you what it means to molest gentlemen in this way.'

" This caused the scales to fall gently from my eyes. My right foot was free with a large spur, which I proceeded to drive deeply in the horse's flesh. The poor, tortured animal jumped twenty feet and knocked one of the gentry like a pair of winding blades. I put my thumb to my nose and tauntingly worked my fingers at them, laughed, and rode on, a wiser man if nothing more. When I arrived at Col. Liles' house I found him alone with a gallon of strained honey and a ten-gallon keg of peach brandy. After 'sampling,' he counted out $1,770, which my distant relative in the collateral line had kindly left with him.

" 'Perry,' as we called him then, detained me long, and it was growing late when I left on the return trip, having completely forgotten the incidents of the morning. This crowd of Sabbath breakers 'had it in for me,' and lay in wait with malice aforethought, and took me unawares— in other words, captured me. While two held fast each foot, a third led the horse to a large log, where I was required to dismount. I had no pistol, and am glad that I

8

did not; but if I had been armed that would have been a tragic spot.

"An elder man stood off a space with a green hickory stick seven feet long. Realizing that something had to be done instantly, I said: 'Gentlemen, I have somewhat to say to you. 'Arkansas, whatever else may be said of her people, has the reputation abroad of having fair women and brave men. In my opinion, you are a disgrace and a slander on that reputation—ten men have conspired to mob and whip one. Now I have two propositions to make you, and you may take your choice: First, I will fight all of you, one at a time, with three minutes to rest between fights. With these conditions, and a fair fight, I can whip this cowardly crowd. The second proposition is one that will suit all of us better: Here is $10, take it, send to Marion, get a demijohn of fine brandy. and let's take a drink and call it square. But the gentleman with a bruised face said: 'No, we will not accept either proposition.' All this time he of the hickory stick had not spoken; but now he said: 'Stranger, you have made a fair proposition; hand over that $10 and lend us your horse to send after the brandy; if any one objects, I will peel this stick over his head.'

It is needless to say the $10 was forthcoming, and we parted under the moon the best of friends. Tom Cloah was he of the stick. He was born on the Cumberland river, in the same town where my parents were married, and was at the wedding. but we had never met. Tom was a fine man to act as umpire and arbitrator, and was never in favor of pushing matters to extremes against a man who showed any disposition to do right.

Charley Godden said, "My story is one of extreme humiliation, and I must beg you not to construe it in the light of irony and sarcasm. I, too, have taken the first Arkansas degree.

Not long since, one of my best friends kindly invited me to act as best man at his approaching nuptials with one of the most charming daughters of the land, the banns were to be celebrated in the palatial residence of her parents, who lived at Arkansas Post, on Arkansas river. I taxed my treasury in the purchase of an appropriate suit, and when the time approached left for the Post, stopping on the way to spend the night at the mansion of a very pious planter. Next morning the usual custom of prayer and toddy before the morning meal was observed. The old gentleman filled a large silver bowl with the richest nectar, and as a matter of course handed it to me first. I thought the allowance was unusually liberal but drank it all.

To my horror I soon discovered that the allowance was intended for all the family, and that the custom was to hand the goblet around, as the sacramental glass is at church—all take a sip. My mortification was enhanced by the presence of the beautiful daughters.

The wedding took place that evening. I hastened on to the Post, arrived weary and quite fatigued—the inner man craved just a little bracing—and I yielded to what was regarded as a necessity.

When the nuptials were being celebrated I was in my shirt sleeves, rolled up to the elbow, bareheaded, walking up and down the streets challenging the world for a fight and offering a reward for the accommodation.

Is the plan of salvation broad enough to throw its mantle over me? Arkansas passed the ordinance of secession that day.

Halcyon days, attic nights, effervescence of youth, communion of genial souls, that finally settle into sedate manhood.

Poindexter plunged into the vortex of war, and was lost in its slaughter. Years afterward Charley Godden professed religion, and never afterward entered the court room to argue a case—entered the Methodist ministry—has lived a pure, devotional life, stands high in all the relations of life, and is universally loved, and is yet engaged in the highest calling of life.

After arranging my business at DeWitt, I had to go to Brownsville, then the county seat of the adjoining county of Prairie, sixty miles distant, nine tenths of the way leading through Grand Prairie—that immense carpet of grass and flowers—denuded of forest except here and there a clump of trees rose up like islands in the sea.

The habitations of man were sparce and far apart. Vast flocks of prairie chickens and numerous herds of wild deer sported over that beautiful lawn, nature's enchanting landscape. The scenery was novel and new to me. Some ideas of the difficulty encountered in travel in the interior of Arkansas in those days may be gathered when I tell the reader that there were but few public conveyances of the primitive stagecoach even, and none on the route I had to travel between these points.

The best conveyance I could get was a long, lean, far-reaching, and fast traveling horse, with uncovered saddle-tree, rope bridle, and rope stirrup supports. I gave a twenty-dollar gold piece for this horse and a guide. The guide was a long, gawky, wiry, flaxen-haired boy, of fifteen summers, a product "to the manor born." His instructions were to reach Brownsville that night and DeWitt the next, all bills to be paid by me.

At sun up I was in the improvised saddle, the guide on the bareback of his charger, with well-filled basket of food on his arm. I did not salute Poindexter and Godden when I "lit out"—they were in bed at that early hour—but I left with the good landlady the kindest salutation and my blessings for them.

I was not accustomed to horseback exercise, and by noon was jaded. At that hour we halted at one of those beautiful isles in the sea of verdure and ate venison steak, eggs, etc., and gave the horses a browse on the grass. Thirty miles were behind us, thirty in advance. We mounted and resumed that far-reaching trot, trot, trot, jolt, jolt, jolt, my physical powers growing less and less, and revolting more and more.

When the shades of night overtook us we reached a dense primitive forest, some miles from Brownsville. Finally the town loomed up in sight, to my intense joy, but I had to be lifted off of the horse; my muscles seemed and felt as rigid as marble.

I retired to my room at once, called a servant, had him rub me down with hot water, mustard, and liniment.

My repast was served in my room, some friends came up to laugh and condole—mostly laugh. Miserable as I was they forced roars and peals of laughter. A good joke and laugh has always been half of my life.

I did not rise from bed the next day, but my room was full of those jolly friends. I was the best subject they had had for many a day, and they utilized the occasion.

R. S. Gantt, a lawyer of local celebrity (cousin of George, whom I propose to notice in another place), and a brilliant young lawyer, whose Christian name I have now forgotten in the flight of years—Douglass, who was editing the local paper in connection with the practice of law, E. M. Williams, a brilliant young lawyer, was also of the local Bar—brother to that great and good lawyer Col. Sam. W. Williams, of the Little Rock Bar— of whom I propose an episode before winding up these "Recollections."

I also met Judge B. W. Totten, brother of A. O. W. Totten of the Supreme Court of Tennessee, a wealthy planter. These kind and noble gentlemen made me exquisitely comfortable. My father's brother, George Hallum, and his cousin, Charles Hallum, planters, lived in the vicinage (two better men never lived), Ellis E. Dismukes, long sheriff and collector of the county, the husband of my cousin, Jane, daughter of George Hallum, lived in the vicinage.

Ellis Dismukes was a local celebrity of that day, kind, jovial, and full of life ; he would ride ten miles any day to get a good joke on a friend. He never tired of telling one on me, one that I never to this day have discovered the point. He was with me in Memphis on one occasion when I called on business to see a lady, whom I had never met, and I introduced myself as "Mr. Hallum." This was to him a custom not tolerated in Arkansas, and he embraced this occasion to repeat it as evidence of my audacious simplicity.

Judge Totten said: "Turn him over to me, Hallum, and I will revenge you." In those days supplies had to be transported to interior points from river landings. Said Judge Totten: "Ellis is a powerful man, as you see. He has not got sense enough to know when a small man is fighting him. There is Peter Cook, another giant living down on the bayou. He was jealous of Ellis' prowess in an Arkansas knockdown and drag out, and one day told Ellis to square himself for a fight. Ellis accepted the challenge and knocked him down as fast as he could pick himself up. When the last fall came, Cook lay there without attempting to rise. At this juncture one of Cook's friends, a man under the medium size, ran up and commenced thumping Ellis with his fist. Ellis stood still until the fellow struck him eight or ten blows, without moving, striking, or saying a word. Finally he asked the little fellow what he was doing, and he said: "D—n you, don't you see I am fighting you?" It was so supremely farcical Ellis burst out laughing, and told him when he got tired to go and sit down like a little man.

"Ellis was a poor judge of oxen in his younger days," continued the Judge. "Before he picked up enough to buy a plantation and negroes, he freighted supplies from White river across the prairie to the merchants and planters with a four-yoke ox team. His camp bedding was made of bear skins, an animal then very plentiful in this new country.

"On one occasion, when crossing the wide, soft prairie, his team tired, and no amount of lashing could move them.

Ellis slipped out a large bear skin at the rear of the wagon, unobserved by the oxen, and retired some distance in the tall grass, and wrapped himself up in it in imitation of the animal as much as possible, then got down on his knees and hands and crawled to the oxen. When the team discovered him they raised their heads, curled their tails, bellowed, and 'lit out.' Ellis ran after them for five miles, hallooing, 'Whoa, Buck! Whoa, Berry! Whoa, Darby!' but they kept on until ten miles distant they reached the timber, overturned the wagon, broke loose from it, and went home.''

After attending to the business in hand, I registered at the stage office for Madison, on the St. Francis river, the terminus of the Memphis and Little Rock railroad then.

The stage from Little Rock arrived at dark with but two passengers, Edwin M. Yerger and James Wickersham, who had been to the Supreme Court to argue some cases. I was much surprised and delighted with this company—with Yerger, especially. He was one of the wittiest and most jovial of men; but Wickersham was very dry, prosaic, except on rare occasions. This was one of those happy occasions—an oasis in the general desert of his life.

The night was dark as Erebus, and the roads were heavy and muddy. The old stagecoaches of those days weighed a ton. We arrived at the foot of Crawley's ridge two hours before day, and were politely asked by the driver to get out and walk to the top of the ridge. The road was what was then known as "corduroy road;" small trees laid at right angles across the road to prevent vehicles from sinking. I discovered what I took to be a smooth side path and made a spring to get on it, but to my consternation and horror landed in a ditch of muddy water up to my chin. I suffered much with cold before arriving at Madison four hours later. There I purchased a new suit of clothes.

CAPTURE OF A RUNAWAY, AND RECOVERY OF MY MONEY.

A few months after my return to Memphis I was again called to Arkansas on private business under extraordinary circumstances, which must be explained to understand the powerful motives which influenced my conduct.

When quite a schoolboy I had a classmate, named Robert Ware, who was raised on a farm in the neighborhood of Cuba, Shelby county, Tenn. He was of respectable lineage, and I thought him sound, head and heart. In the course of my early years at the Bar I became the owner of the Alexander farm, near Cuba, paid to me in discharge of a fee of $2,000, a low estimate of its real value.

Ware wanted this farm, and offered me $1,500 cash, and urged our early acquaintance as an inducement to accept this low valuation. I was in the full tide of success, and cared at best too little for money, and made the deduction, feeling at the time that it was on insufficient grounds.

A few evenings after he came to my office, and said: "Have that deed ready by 2 o'clock to-morrow. I have brought cotton enough to the city to pay you." I executed the deed and had it ready. He called about half past two, and said, "Let me look at the deed." I handed it to him, he read it over, and said, "I will step around to the bank and get the money." He put the deed in his pocket and stepped out. A circumstance I thought nothing of because his integrity was above reproach. He did not return that evening, nor send any message, and I thought some unforeseen circumstance had detained him.

Next day he did not return, and I had still no suspicion

of fraud. In about ten days I found that he had sold the farm for $2,000 cash, and had left the country, with his family, and had gone—no one could tell where. This sort of conduct is one of those injuries, willful, deliberate, for which there is no excuse in law or morals, and I never condoned it. My indignation was great, and I vowed that if ever I found out where he was I would follow him if necessary to the ends of the earth. He had shamefully abused my confidence, had robbed me, and had fled, without one palliating circumstance. He had a competence, and owed no one but me. An indictment and requisition I never thought of. I was a law to myself. I took such men by the collar, and forced restitution. It was not the loss of the money I cared for so much, but the breach of trust—the robbery made me "nurse my wrath to keep it warm." He was gone three years before I located him, and then by one of those fortuitous circumstances which sometimes rise up in our pathway. Joe Payne, an old client of mine, went to those fine "buckshot lands," in Jefferson county, Arkansas, about fifteen miles below Pine Bluff, and bought a farm. He knew Ware, and of the circumstances above explained.

When he returned he came into my office laughing, and said, "John, I have found your man Ware. He is overseeing for the Hon. R. W. Johnson, in Jefferson county, and is living on the lower farm. Be cautious, for Bob is a dangerous man." I said somebody will find out "who struck Billy Patterson." I will tame the dangerous colt, and make him as gentle as Mary's little lamb, if I ever get my hands on him.

"When are you going after him," asked Payne. The thought struck me that I had better throw Payne off the track, as he was then a neighbor to Ware, and might put him on his guard and give him a chance to avoid me when I did go over. I gave him an evasive answer, and left the impression on his mind that it might be months. There was a tri-weekly line of steamers then plying between

Memphis and Little Rock. Payne left on the steamer leaving next evening, and I followed on the next steamer, landing at Pine Bluff at daylight. I went to the law office of Grace & Bayne, and told them that I wanted the best team in the city, and an honest, courageous driver, a white man. Bayne went to the livery stable and procured a spanking team and driver, but I did not size him up as a man possessed of staying qualities when danger was in the air, and told Bayne so, but he said his reputation in the town was the best for honesty and courage. "All right," said I, " he may have it tested before noon," and off we started for the plantation. It was a beautiful May day. I gave my solitary companion all the particulars, and he pledged loyalty to me in case of danger. At noon we pulled up in front of Ware's residence, and, without hailing, I went in alone. I knew he was in—a negro had told us so.

He was sitting at the table eating dinner. I told him to finish it, that I intended to put handcuffs on him, and take him to Memphis. He sprang for his pistol, which lay on the cupboard, where he had laid it while eating dinner, but with the spring of a tiger I seized him with the left hand, bowie-knife in the right, and ordered him to drop it. He obeyed.

He wore a new brown linen coat. I twisted the tail in my left hand, holding all the time the knife in my right. Three or four negro men were standing in the hall way, and he ordered them to seize me, and threatened to kill them if they refused, and yelled lustily for help. I touched him quite gently with the point of the knife, and admonished him to be quiet, and told the negroes he was a thief, and I would kill the first one that moved. All obeyed me.

The alarm scared my driver, and he whipped up the horses and ran off three hundred yards, then stopped and looked back over the carriage, but obeyed my summons and came back.

Ware took the front seat by the driver, and I sat behind with a firm grasp on his coat, and directed the driver to proceed to Pine Bluff. Ware then said: "If you will drive down to Joe. Payne's, I will get the money and pay you for the land. I know I treated you badly, and abused your confidence shamefully. If you will give me a chance I will get every dollar, interest and all, and pay you before to-morrow morning. My credit is good. I feared Joe. Payne would tell you where I was. I knew he was going to Memphis to consult you, and I started at once to go and see him and request him not to tell you; but that would have involved an unpleasant explanation, and I abandoned the idea and took the chances, and have always been armed. If you had not come in on me as you did you would have never taken me alive. I had just sat down to dinner and laid my pistol on the sideboard."

A kind word always disarms me, and I said: "All right, Bob, restitution is all I want, and that I am going to have." At this he brightened up as though a great load was being lifted from his conscience. His wife stood at the gate crying, and that sight came near unnerving and causing me to abandon one of the most determined resolutions of my life; but when I told her husband that I would not press him beyond restitution, she raised her white apron, wiped her eyes, and recovered partially from her grief. Up to this moment she had been ignorant of the fraud practiced on me. Bob said: "John, that was the first and only bad break I ever made in my life, and it shall be the last."

Payne lived five or six miles distant, and the road led through woods and timber deadening with which the driver and myself were unacquainted. Three miles had been traveled, when the road grew very dim and we were entangled in one of those almost impenetrable forest deadenings, grown with undergrowth and chapparal.

This led to the conviction in my mind that Ware was endeavoring to throw me off my guard and make his es-

cape. If my firm grasp had once been released he would
have sprung from the carriage and in a moment been hid
in the jungle. This second attempt at treachery and deception angered me and redoubled my resolution to stay
with Bob, and I pricked him gently with the knife and
told him to find Payne's residence; that if he made a
break I would run the knife through him, and he gave up
all further idea of escape, but claimed that he honestly
got lost.

After retracing our steps to the plain road, we had no
further difficulty in finding Payne's residence. Payne
was a client of mine, had inherited quite a fortune from
his father, and had moved over on one of those fine cotton
plantations in Jefferson county—those "buckshot lands,"
so famous for fertility. The owner was noted for that
open hospitality so characteristic of the old Southern
planter and gentleman.

The residence was fronted by one of those beautiful
woodlawns and landscapes which lent a charm to every
surrounding. The gate opening into this beautiful rural
prospect was about a furlong from the residence, a large,
two-story building, built not so much for external show
as comfort and elegance.

Payne, Ware, and myself had known each other from
early boyhood, and had been warm friends, and nothing
had ever occurred to mar that friendship except as between Ware and myself, growing out of the treachery related. When the carriage stopped in front of the gate,
we looked up the avenue and saw Payne sitting on the
veranda with his wife, looking toward us. Ware's heart
failed him, and he begged piteously to be released and
permitted to walk or drive up to the residence "like a
gentleman," and I felt sure that he would attempt an escape, and knew that my driver was not to be relied on in
such an emergency, and I neither wanted nor intended to
do personal violence further than necessary to accomplish
his safety and my security, and I declined the request.

When we got to the second, or inner, gate we vacated the carriage. Payne meeting us, expressing astonishment, not at my conduct but at Ware's submission, and said: "Bob, you might have expected this as soon as John found you." Ware asked: "How much money have you, Joe? I want about $1,800 to pay John for the land he deeded to me—the Alexander place."

Payne said: "I have only ten or twelve hundred in the house; you can have that, Bob." Here I told Payne again all the circumstances connected with this debt. He went into the house, got the money, and handed it to Ware, took his note for it, and Ware handed the money over to me. It amounted to $1,100, most of it in gold coin.

Bob then said: "I know where I can get the remainder of the money. I can get it from the overseer on the upper Johnson farm. It is on your way to Pine Bluff, will you please drive up there?" "Certainly," I said. The farm was ten miles distant; the sun had set, but the moon was shining out brilliantly, and the road was level and dry. We resumed our former position and drove off; but it was two hours in the night when we arrived at the upper farm, and the overseer had retired. Bob again begged to be released, but that was silly to think about; his brother overseer was his right-hand bower, and he could easily have escaped or brought on a tragedy to supplement the serio-comic act then warily played to the finish. Bob then begged that no disclosure be made, and I acceded to that.

The overseer was called and asked to bring his cash to the carriage, which he did. Bob introduced him to me as his old schoolmate from Memphis on an important matter of business, and said he wanted the money to pay me a debt he owed me. "Get out and come in," he said, "you shall have all that I have if you want it."

He came out to the carriage with gold and bills, and counted out all he had, but that left a deficit of $150, for which I took Bob's due bill and then released him, drove to Pine Bluff, boarded the same steamer I came on, and returned to Memphis. Bob offered to include my expenses in the note, but I declined that. I had no lawful claim on him for one cent more than the consideration for the farm and six per cent interest.

A lawsuit would have been fruitless—that he cared nothing for. He had taken the law in his own hands in the first place, had abused and violated confidence and trust—in realty, stolen $1,500. His crime exceeded that of the robber who prowls by night, in moral turpitude.

In recovering my dues I did not pay the slightest attention to the law either, but did not go beyond assault and battery, and what the law denominated false imprisonment. I took the only remedy which would afford practical, substantial relief, restitution for the equivalent of larceny of my property, with whatever consequences and penalties the law might attach.

Did the end justify the means? is the question. Many will condemn, as many will approve. Desperate men, as well as desperate diseases, sometimes require heroic remedies. As a simple question of law, I did wrong; as a question of equity, I did right; as a question of morals, the ground is debatable. I have submitted the question to theologians as one of morals, and they are divided. In any event, I did not throw away $1,778—abandon it to a robber who was "lawproof"—on a question of morals.

Many a trim bark that floats like a swan on the smooth waters of an unruffled lake, goes down in the tempestuous billows of a stormy ocean. I related this unpleasant episode in my life to Col. W. P. Grace, of Pine Bluff, that long and cherished friend whose life has been full of noble deeds and eminent usefulness to his fellow men, an eminent lawyer, who lifted himself from a brickyard in Kentucky to a high and noble position in the profession, of whom it may be truly said, "He went about the world doing good;" and his conclusions were just as I have stated mine. But he illustrated with much force and power what he meant by the great inconveniences and frequent injustice growing out of strict adherence to the letter of the law. He said:

"I knew Gen. Yell, of Pine Bluff, intimately in all the walks and relations of life, and have always admired his iron will, his heroic courage; he was a patriot, a soldier, and one of the greatest jury lawyers I ever knew. I heard him once in the defense of an innocent man charged with murder. He firmly believed that the jury had been organized to convict regardless of proof or the innocence of the victim.

"Gen. Yell did not poise himself like a maiden before a mirror, but told the jury that they were organized to convict. Then rising to the loftiest flight of impassioned oratory, like an eagle with defiant wing cleaving the clouds, he said: 'If you prostitute the judgment seat, the highest office among men, to that basest of all actions, I say to you in this presence and in that of the God who made us all, you must, you will, you shall die in atonement for your own sin, whether I survive or perish. Look to your own cowardice for safety. You shall not survive such a crime!' The verdict was, 'Not guilty.' The negative, passive lawyer incapable of coping with such emergencies, would have stopped at the frontier of propriety, and would have shrunk from throwing himself in the breach, and let his client hang by rope of etiquette."

Although foreign to the restricted scope of this volume, I cannot forbear mention of the tremendous will-power of Gen. Yell, as it comes too well authenticated to be questioned. He had grown wealthy before the cival war. When Arkansas passed the ordinance of secession he was one of the first to raise a brigade of troops for the service of the Confederate States; and he advanced many thousands of dollars to pay and equip troops. He was guardian of some minors with more than an abundance of means to discharge that and all other obligations, but the close

of the war found him, as almost every other Southern
man, in debt, their slaves freed, and their hitherto valuable and large-landed interests of no marketable value.

The courts when opened were administered principally
by northern "carpet-baggers," whose contracted stock in
trade was red-hot politics and animosity to Southern gentlemen.   Gen. Yell was sued on his bond as guardian, and
a large judgment obtained against him.   With the merchantable remnants of his fortune he paid $20,000, leaving
a large unpaid balance, which he could and would have
easily and readily paid if his lands could have been sold
for fifteen per cent of their value.   All he wanted was a
reasonable time to convert these landed assets into money.
But the Republican lawyers who had the matter in hand
would not listen to any terms proposed, nor grant any extension of time.   "Your money or the jail," were their
terms.   This distressed Gen. Yell more than all the noble battles he fought during his five years' campaign;
and no braver soldier ever wore a plume or led men to battle.   An Order of Court was obtained to pay the money
into Court or go to jail for contempt of Court.   I get this
direct from Col. W. P. Grace, in whose integrity and
veracity I place implicit confidence.   He lived in the same
town, and was intimate with Gen. Yell for many years.

To relieve Gen. Yell from this distress, Col. Grace
went to him and told him that himself and others had
agreed to raise the money for him.

"No," said Gen. Yell, "I will not imperil the fortunes
of my friends any more.   I will leave an estate which will
discharge every dollar of this debt and leave a surplus.
I have lived without dishonoring my name.   I have survived my usefulness—having lived like a *man*—I intend to
die like one.   Come to my house to-morrow morning, Porter, between the hours of nine and ten, and I will show
you how a man can die."

Porter, as the intimate friends of Col. Grace call him.
tried to dissuade the General, but to no purpose.   At the

appointed time he went sorrowfully to his residence and found the General in bed in apparently perfect health. After conversing a few minutes about his business and telling the Colonel how he would like to be buried, he turned over and said: "Now, Porter, look and see how a man can die." And in a few minutes was a corpse— Thus hounded to death by men who were not worthy to "loose the latch of his shoes." A Roman among men, an exemplar in virtue, a Colossus in the legal forum, a chivalrous knight in the field, a hero who knew how to live, a martyr who knew how to die.

He was a nephew of Gov. Archibald Yell, who fell at Buena Vista, and who was sent from Fayetteville, Tenn., in 1828, as Territorial Judge of Arkansas, whose biography I have written and published in another volume. Gen. Yell, I am informed, came from the same town in Tennessee. Another noble contribution from that grand old State to her sister commonwealth.

E. O. PERRIN.

O. PERRIN, I presume, has been long forgotten. He was quick, vivacious, witty, and attentive. He came in the "forties" from Brooklyn, N. Y., and was prominent at the Bar. He returned to New York after spending some years in Memphis, where he became owner of a considerable amount of real estate in connection with Wickersham, some of which I afterwards owned. Perrin became Clerk of the Court of Appeals in New York, a lucrative position, the salary being ten thousand dollars per annum.

JUDGE JOHN L. T. SNEED.

JUDGE SNEED'S life spans a great part of the Judicial history of Tennessee. He yet survives, full of years, and full of honors. He was in the noontide of success at the Bar when I came on the stage, and was then one of the most courtly and magnetic gentlemen I ever met. He was a captain in the Mexican war, brigadier general in the Confederate army, and Justice of the Supreme Court of Tennessee sixteen years, and yet he looks as young as George Gantt, or Bob Looney, as vigorous as a lad of only forty summers, both in body and mind. Youthful patriarchs in Israel, this trio, they have almost compassed the century without loosing any of the elixir of youth. Frauds, these men, a burlesque on the efforts of time to work ravages. See to it, Methuselah, that these men don't succeed to your laurels. "Bob Looney" aspires to be the Cassius of the Triumvirate. Beautiful character. Exemplary life. What a world we would have if all could be Sneeds! On the woolsack now, as vigorous as Lord Eldon in his palmy days. No man ever held the keys to a court of conscience with better grace or greater dignity.

JUDGE WILLIAM R. HARRIS.

JUDGE HARRIS, a brother of Senator Isham G. Harris, was Judge of the Common Law and Chancery Court in 1854, but was soon after that elected to a seat on the Supreme Bench.

He was a gentleman of charming, magnetic manners, a fine lawyer, and universally esteemed. He lost his life when in the meridian of his fame and usefulness by one of the greatest disasters that ever occurred on the Mississippi river, on the up trip from New Orleans on the palatial steamer Pennsylvania, which blew up in 1858, and a thousand lives were lost, Judge Harris being one.

WILLIAM M. RANDOLPH.

RANDOLPH is a native of Clark county, Arkansas. He was Confederate States District Attorney for Arkansas, came to Memphis in 1863. His energy and commanding talents soon brought him a large following. Unlike most able lawyers Randolph has determined not to "die poor." He possesses fine executive ability, and has accumulated a fortune. Like Jim Lee, he has an eye to corner lots and fine buildings, and deserves his well-earned distinction and success.

R. A. F. DUNCAN.

BOB DUNCAN, a native of Sumner county, Tenn., was a classmate of mine at College. He was possessed of extraordinary ability, and nobility of character, and was gifted with a command of language rarely equaled.

He read law with A. O. P. Nicholson, and located at Memphis in 1856, and at once commanded a large following. But "death loves a shining mark." He died in 1859 of consumption.

GEN. JOHN D. GOODALL.

GEN. JOHN D. GOODALL, whose title was de-
rived from the civic office of Attorney General
for the Eleventh Circuit as early as 1848, was
born near Hartsville, Tenn., and came to Memphis some fiteen years in advance of me, but located in
Summerville and divided his time between that town and
Memphis. John was a man of pleasing address and magnetic character, and succeeded from the start. He had
been six years in the Attorney General's office when I first
met him at Raleigh while I was teaching school. He was
anxious for me to enter his office as a student, and generously volunteered to lend me all the financial assistance
I needed, but I was anxious to "lift the latch and force
the way" without being the *protege* of any man, and declined, but appreciated his kindness none the less. Poor
John, he finally became insane, and died in an asylum.

JUDGE B. F. McKIERNAN.

JUDGE McKIERNAN presided over the Criminal
Court of Memphis when I was admitted to the Bar
in 1854 and for many years after. He was a confirmed old bachelor, tall, spare made, high forehead, and devilish, restless eyes. His hair was long, and
hesitated between the blonde and red types, and it was
difficult to tell which type prevailed, but both were represented. I knew him well. We had adjoining offices
several years. He was possessed of average ability and
stern integrity, but was morbidly sensitive and was always guarding his toes against being stepped on.

He was as restless as a fiery stud when a motion for a new trial was argued, based on the assumption that he had misled the jury through ignorance of the law, a very common performance with a great number of judges. The ermine is luminous with such precedents. Judge McKiernan believed in his infallible luminosity, and was easily chagrined when that idea was softly impeached. George Bayne once argued a motion for a new trial before him based on the assumption that the Judge had no proper conception of the law and had greatly injured his client by charging "such stuff to the jury." This put the Judge on his mettle. It was more than he well could stand, but he wanted to conceal his irritation. "Stop right there, Mr. Bayne, this court sees very plainly what you are driving at. You are trying to get it in a fret, but you can't do. it. Take your seat, Mr. Bayne, this court don't intend to listen to any more 'such stuff' as that."

He lived a quiet, secluded life, and never became "one of the boys," never "unbent the bow." He disappeared when the revolution was put in motion, and Memphis never knew him any more.

JUDGE WILLIAM T. BROWN.

FROM the beginning, I made no department of law a specialty, but gave Law, Equity and Criminal practice equal attention. The practice of following certain branches has grown up since that day. Many of the ablest lawyers of the local Bar of that day were equally great in all departments. There was Judge William T. Brown, who was a Colossus in every department of the law, enthusiastic, at times vehement, always methodical, persuasive profoundly logical. I have heard him make a thousand arguments and every one was methodical. Of all men I ever heard, none surpassed him in profound, electrifying enthusiasm; he had a rich, melodious voice with perfect modulation and intonation. He had a peculiarity of bending his body over the table in front of him when in the zenith of his argument. When hard pressed he became very nervous and could rarely sit still.

I remember a celebrated instance which occurred in the Supreme Court at Jackson, Tennessee, shortly after I was admitted to the guild. Judge Washington, of Nashville, and Judge Brown were opposing counsel in a case of much magnitude. These antagonists were equally matched, but Judge Washington was old and quite feeble. Sometimes he would ask the Court's permission to sit down and rest, and much of his able argument was delivered while sitting. He was replying to Judge Brown. One passage I can never forget: "My Brother Brown has manifested all the nodosity of the oak, without any of its strength, and has undergone all the contortions of the fabled Sibyl, without uttering any of her oracles."

At such amusing thrusts Judge Brown manifested agonies of pain, writhed, and turned in his seat, but nothing ever provoked him to transcend the limits of legitimate discussion. He was born in Middle Tennessee and came to Memphis about 1840, when the city first began to aspire to metropolitan honors. He always commanded an immense practice, but like the great majority of lawyers of that day, did not know the value of money. He was proverbial for one thing, among many commendable traits of character: he was tenderly considerate of the feeling of the junior members of the bar who opposed him.

JAMES WICKERSHAM.

AMES WICKERSHAM, from South Bend, Ind., was a carpenter, and came to Memphis in that capacity, in 1837-8, and shortly after read law and was admitted to the Bar. Owing to an almost total absence of the gift of speech, and oratory, he had a long probation to serve, but he possessed in an eminent degree a fine discriminating judgment and that pertinacity of purpose which gives the tortoise the race in the long run over the active, sprightly hare. He was never married, was long enured to the most rigid economy, and looked on seven cents as a loss not to be tolerated in a settlement involving thousands. When his merits became fully known as a great land and chancery lawyer, a valuable clientage came in one continual stream until his death. He had a turn for profitable speculation, and generally "got in on the ground floor."

He was the first attorney for the Memphis and Little Rock railroad, which gave him the "inside track" in land speculations along that line, because he knew before hand where the road would ultimately be located, and thus virtually cut off competition during that era of land speculation.

The State of Arkansas, under the university school and swamp land donations of Congress, had an immense quantity of land, which was the basis of a large volume of land scrip issued by the State. This land scrip was receivable in payment for lands at $1.25 per acre. But the volume of scrip issued was in excess of the demand, and declined to thirty cents on the dollar. Wickersham took advantage of this opportunity, and located and patented a large quantity of lands in Arkansas, at the most eligi-

ble points along the projected line of road, and thus laid
the foundation of a large fortune for those days. The
scrip cost him 37½ cents per acre, and he sold at $10 and
$20 per acre. He projected and was the chief owner of
"The New Memphis Theater," located on the north side
of Jefferson, just east of Third street. He husbanded
and utilized many opportunities, and was a better financier than all of the local Bar together. I came in contact
with him in one of these small speculations, without in
the least originally designing it. Many parties away
back in the thirties had donated lands to the old "Memphis and LaGrange railroad," an enterprise that lan-
guished and fell through. These donated lands stood in
statu quo for many years, many of the original owners
had died and many had moved away.

The charter became forfeited for *non-usur* without any
proceeding by *quo warranto* or legislative declaration.

The purpose for which these donations had been made
having fallen through, the lands reverted to the donors
and their legal representatives, and Wickersham worked
this mine to great advantage by buying up these claims
for a song.

One day a gentleman from Illinois, son of one of these
donors to the railroad, called on me and told me that
his father, deceased, had donated two blocks in Fort
Pickering to the road, and that Wickersham had bought
one of the four heirs out, but had taken a deed to the
whole; that he wanted to sell the remaining three fourths
and would take $250. I told him that the property was
worth at least $5,000, and that the heirs could recover it
easily. There was a large, two-story dwelling on it, in
fine repair, which cost not less than $3,000. My client
was determined to sell. I did not want, and did not intend to interfere, but took my client around to Wickersham's office to give him the benefit of this trade, but instead of appreciating my courtesy he got mad, and while
not openly insulting, acted quite rude. I said, "Wick,

you will yet learn to appreciate the commercial value of courtesy, and I will be your teacher."

Returning to my office, I bought the property, and next day receipted the tenant for a few months' back rent, and put my own tenant in possession. Then I called on "Wick" for an accounting for back rents, my share of which amounted to five times more than the property cost me. Then I sold my interest in it to J. E. Merriman, the old jeweler, for $4,000 cash. Wick had a very valuable and talented partner in the person of Ed. Beecher, a nephew of Henry Ward Beecher. He was a profound lawyer, close reasoner, and had a masterly command of language. Wick prepared the cases and briefs, and Beecher argued them.

Judge McKinney, of the Supreme Bench, said that Beecher was the ablest lawyer of his age who had ever argued a case before him—a splendid compliment, and well deserved.

VAL. W. WYNNE.

VAL. W. WYNNE was born and raised in Sumner county, Tenn., within sight of my father's old homestead. His mother was the daughter of Gen. Winchester, the bosom friend of Gen. Jackson. Val. was a noble, chivalrous, handsome young man, full of life and high hopes. He married an heiress in Georgia, and settled in that State, but died in the flush and bloom of manhood.

GEORGE W. WINCHESTER.

EORGE W., the son of Gen. Winchester, came from Cragfont, the baronial seat of his father in Sumner county, Tenn. It was my boyish delight to go to Cragfont, the massive stone castle overlooking one of the most beautiful streams that ever leaped and poured its waters o'er rock and pebble through hills and gorge and laughed its way to the sea. Those waters have contributed many a gem to my boyish love, have poured a thousand floods of sunshine into my heart. The rustic bridge below Cragfont spanned a mossy islet May I draw the curtain back that hides the treasures of that youthful heart of "long ago"? Angling around that isle for treasure trove, a voice as sweet, a face as beautiful as a Peri's calls me to the rustic bridge, the chaperone released her vigil and angled the waters. That Peri with Grecian face as lovely as Juno, voice as gentle as a windswept harp, heart as pure as a sunbeam, unconsciously lit up an altar uncovered a throne in a rustic boy's heart as gorgeous as the orient, yet Josie Jamison never knew the magic she inspired in the soul of her boy lover. She was born and reared on an estate adjoining Cragfont, where she could look out upon that historic granite house. She became the bride of Dr. Gourley, one of Kentucky's noblest sons. A marble shaft marks the spot where the daisies and immortelles guards their rest.

George Winchester was my father's attorney. He was polished, refined, a chaste ideal of manhood; he represented his county in the legislature when able men aspired to that honor. He was a fine speaker, good citizen, "an honest man, the noblest work of God." After the war he settled and died in Memphis. A flood of lawyers from the North came in that migratory period succeeding the war, borne on that tidal wave that overrun every Southern State. Congress had closed the doors of Federal Courts to Southern sympathizers. Missouri with its infamous Drake Constitution struck down the clergy as well as the lawyers. The judicial machinery of every Southern State was in the hands of these men, with now and then a native apostate who lent his hand and raised his voice to strike down his mother in her desolation and voluntarily assumed the character of a political Iscariot, "that thrift might follow fawning," but these spots on the history, the chivalry of a noble people, were few. Many lawyers of noble and elevated sentiment came among us from the North. I do not mention, cannot recollect all of them grouped in this class, but remember H. Clay Conde, Gerald L. Griffin, Channing Richards, J. B. Woodward & Bro., L. B. Horrigan, John Bullock, Robt. Hutchinson, Irving Halsey, Chas. Cameron, E. L. Belcher, Judge Jas. O. Pierce, J. W. Westcott, Hosea Townshend, H. E. Hudson, and Geo. E. Stahl. These men, and many others, were eminently conservative, and were received with open hands.

DUDLEY M. DuBOSE.

DUDLEY M. DuBOSE, the son of Dr. DuBose, a weathly planter, was raised on Big creek, in Shelby county, Tenn. He was a man of fine physique, a tall, handsome blonde, and resembled the Grand Duke Alexis more than any man I ever met. He was liberally educated, was generous, and universally liked. He came to the Bar in 1854, and had a liberal patronage. Was married in the White House to the beautiful and accomplished daughter of Senator Tombs, of Georgia, President Buchanan giving the bride away. His residence was on East Court street, and I frequently dined

with him. He moved to Georgia, and was twice elected
to Congress from his illustrious father-in-law's district.

T. B. MICOU.

T. B. MICOU was *sui generis*, of Creole origin, with
an individuality that distinguished him from all
others of the earth and defied imitation, a good,
sober, industrious, conscientious man, but he entered upon all investigations at the other end of the line,
looked at things, and drew conclusions from a standpoint
wholly his own. He might arrive at the same conclusions
you did, but from an altogether different standpoint. He
was sensitive and courageous, upright and honest; but
when the Lord laid him down he rested his case and made
no more on that pattern, the divergence from primal
standards was too great to be pressed.

JOHN B. LUSTER.

JOHN B. LUSTER came in 1857 from Trousdale
county, Tenn., and went into partnership with
Hiram Vollentine and James Lee, the firm name
being Vollentine, Lee & Luster.
John was a fine specimen of manhood, well educated,
and well equipped, full of joyous life, effervescing with
buoyant hope, socially one of the most companionable
men, and enjoyed wit, humor, repartee, and the sunshine
of life as much as any man I ever knew. Everybody
liked John. It was an enjoyable treat to hear him act
and comment on Bret Harte's Heathen Chinee and the
Moneyless Man. Soon after he established himself he
went to Carthage, Tenn., and married the beautiful and
accomplished Bettie Moores, heiress and only daughter of
James B. Moores, an eminent lawyer. After the civil

war he never returned to Memphis, but continued in the harness to his death, which occurred suddenly at Dallas, Texas, in April, 1891, where he had gone on business from his Tennessee home. He was a good and brave Confederate soldier throughout the war—was my very warm personal friend from boyhood to the grave. We met only three or four days before his death.

GEN. JAMES R. CHALMERS.

BUN CHALMERS comes from a very distinguished Mississippi family. His father was an able lawyer, and represented his State in the Federal Senate. His brother, Ham, was a distinguished lawyer and jurist, and one of the Judges of the Supreme Court of Mississippi. "Bun," when a youth, was a very bright little college boy, and at an early period in his professional career took a prominent position at a Bar distinguished for able men. He was a gallant soldier in the Confederate army, where he won his spurs as General of Brigade, under Gen. Forrest. He has represented his State in Congress. After the surrender he moved to Memphis and was associated there with the author in the practice of law, which was, perhaps, another distinguished period of his life. "Bun" possesses very fine command of language, is eloquent, able, lucid, and on occasion profound—an entertaining speaker. In youth he was very small of stature, but has now added a bay window to the mansion, and covered it with gray thatched roof. "Bun" is his pet name, and his old friends refuse to surrender it.

JAMES MOORE.

AMES MOORE was a fine young man, morally and intellectually. He went to Friar's Point in 1858, and entered into partnership with General Alcorn. I had much business with that firm, growing out of levee contracts. Since the war I have never heard of him.

HON. CASEY YOUNG.

HON. CASEY YOUNG was born in Alabama, raised in Mississippi, and read law in Memphis under those sterling men of the early days, Judges E. W. M. King and Wm. T. Brown, and was admitted to the guild in 1858, and has remained in Memphis ever since, except when serving in the Confederate army. A Democrat of the old school, he has fought some hard Congressional battles for the party, made six races and won four. In his first race for Congress he was defeated by Barber Lewis. In the second race with Lewis in 1874 he was elected, and again in 1876 and 1878, defeating Wm. M. Randolph. In 1880 he was defeated by Wm. R. Moore. In 1882 he defeated Judge Wm. M. Smith. During his eight years' service in Congress he was a hard worker. Perhaps in nothing has the moral heroism of the man been exhibited in a stronger light than in the great yellow fever epidemic in 1878, when he remained in the city performing the offices of the good Samaritan when the appalling ravages of death decimated the city.

He was chairman of the National Bureau of Health, and prepared and secured the passage of the first bill establishing a National Board of Health. He also prepared and secured the passage of the bill providing for the erection of the Custom House building, and the construction of the bridge across the Mississippi river at Memphis, the bills creating the United States District Court for West Tennessee, and to protect the levee at Memphis.

War and politics divorced him from his profession for many years, but he has wooed and won his first love, and they are now happily reconciled, and he don't propose that there shall be any more estrangement. "Casey's" law sign hangs again from a busy office.

HON. WILLIAM T. AVERY.

HEN I was a boy this popular man was known as "Tom. Avery the draydriver." In early life he encountered all the disadvantages incident to poverty and daily toil, and drove a dray in Memphis, which fact, after he entered the political arena, became a popular slogan, a political war-cry, which tided him above the floods, and long made him invincible.

I was but nine years old when I first heard him speak in a canvass for the Legislature, in "the Mississippi hills," to a small audience. Small because of the sparsely settled country. He was followed by Thomas J. Turley, the father of Thomas B. Turley. He was twice elected to Congress—I think in 1856 and 1858. He was not profound by any means, but was eminently social and magnetic, a boon companion, who soon won the friendship and esteem of all who came in contact with him. He always kept the pleasant phases of his life in view, and his feelings green and fresh toward his fellow men, and threw the mantle of charity in broadest catholicity over their faults. He enjoyed an anecdote and hearty laugh with keen relish.

I knew him long and intimately, and loved him as a brother. He came home after the war to rebuild his fortune not in the least downcast or discouraged. But thousands had died, many removed, a new condition fronted us all.

One day Tom came to my office and said: "Come in the back room, I want to talk to you privately." After lighting our cigars, he said: "John, I once loved office for fun and glory, but that day has passed; now I want office for revenue. Do you think there is the slightest hope or chance for me?"

I said: "Yes, I think there are enough of the old boys left to put Tom. Avery, the 'Draydriver,' through. We will all pull together. Go and announce yourself as a candidate for the office of Clerk of the Criminal Court, and, my word for it, we will make the landing." And we did.

He went fishing with some of his friends to Black Fish bayou, in Arkansas, and fell out of the boat and was drowned some years ago.

HON. PHINEAS T. SCRUGGS.

PHINEAS, in early manhood, buckled on his armor and made a brilliant dash at the devil, armed and equipped with all the theological weapons to be found from Genesis to Revelations; but it required such constant effort to keep the old gent down that Phineas' ardor cooled to zero, and he abandoned the contest and the ministry, laid theology on the shelf, read profane law, and became Judge in the Holly Springs circuit in the commonwealth of Mississippi.

From there he came to Memphis in 1858, and was what the world calls a very good lawyer, earnest and zealous, but deficient in that compact logic and precision of statement which distinguishes men in the higher spheres of law. Ministers of the gospel very rarely pass the mediocre line when they come to the Bar. Having been trained in *ex parte* discussion, or rather declamation, against the devil and all his imps without question or contradiction, with an occasional grab at the schoolboy's eagle bird, they lose in early training that compact system of logic and reason lawyers are compelled to learn. They have been accustomed to loading a blunderbuss with anything and everything at hand, and firing away at the world, a corallary generally suits them as well as the text, and away they go like Ward's ducks. Men thus educated never become either careful lawyers or reasoners, and often get the starch knocked out of them.

Phineas was of large physique and commanding mien, and when he warmed up in the collar he opposed counsel very much as he did the devil when in a revival in his younger days, and would sometimes throw down the gaps and exclaim: "Lay on, Macduff!" I saw him once when leading a charge in the Macduff style go entirely out of his way to make a personal assault on opposing counsel, when his opponent had the close. "Stand from under!" "Ye gods!" "Somebody held while that man skinned!" His description of the apostate from the religion of the Nazarene for the lucre of the forum was lurid and appalling. We all occasionally jump a Roland who hands back an Oliver. The tenant of a glass house ought to protect it from hailstones. I mention this because it imparts a lesson. I have had many ministers advise with me about leaving the ministry for the Bar, and have universally discouraged them.

Judge Scruggs stood very fair in the profession, and made many friends at the Bar. I lost sight of him twenty-five years ago, but was told some years since that he went back to the ministry.

10

CALVIN F. VANCE.

VANCE was a distinguished lawyer when he came
from Mississippi to Memphis in 1853. His reputation preceded him, and he did not have to serve
the ordinary probation waiting for business. I
have known him since 1854, have heard him argue a great
number of cases, and he always had his forces marshaled
like a Marlborough, earnest, zealous, enthusiastic, confident, exhaustive, he had to be thoroughly thrashed and
twice whipped before he could be forced to believe his adversary was in it or had any rights. I am told now it is
dangerous to "monkey with him," if that classic coinage,
so American and so expressive, may be tolerated in print.

The first time I ever heard it was on the trial of a murder case in the Circuit Court, at Fort Smith, Ark., in
which I was only interested as a spectator, and was richly repaid for the time lost. A Mr. Beton was defending
in a murder trial. After getting through with the eagle
bird for the present, he threw both hands high up in the
air, declaimed on the martial bearing and courage of his
client, and came down, and brought the house down with
him, in the exclamation: "Gentlemen of the jury, it
won't do to monkey with my client; no, no, that's dangerous." That client went up. Perhaps too fond of the
comic phases of life, I yelled at the top of my voice. I
could no more have restrained it than I could have drank
the Mississippi river dry.

Pardon Calvin, there is not one word of this applicable
to you. I never know one word that I am going to write
until I pick up my pen, and then it winds off like a spool
of tangled thread, and I let it go. If something funny
pops up, down it goes. Vance was a foeman worthy of

polished steel, a close reasoner, strictly adhering to the ethics of the profession, strictly temperate and moral, universally esteemed, and very conservative until you began tearing his case to pieces. These were his idols. When you began to pick and break and tear them to pieces, Plutonian fire flashed from his eyes, and he would "pin up and come again."

He is quite absent minded, as shown by the following incident. On one occasion a number of lawyers, including mischievous George Gantt, were engaged in taking depositions with Vance in his front office. He brought a nice lunch for noon and placed it on the mantle in the back room. Gantt discovered and ate it up. Then placed the chicken bones back and wrapped them up nicely. Sometime after that, Vance said he would rest a little and eat his lunch. He untied it, found the bones, and was greatly astonished; then carried the bundle in the front room and said: "Boys, just look here. I brought a nice lunch, ate it up, and forgot all about it, and went back to eat it again. Here the bones are to show for themselves."

Calvin is as bad as that eminent jurist, Judge Eakin (deceased), of the Supreme Court of Arkansas. He once owned a valuable farm near Shelbyville, Tenn., and prided himself on fine stock. He would buy every fine horse offered in the market and send it out to the pasture. In an hour the boys would bring the same horse back to the Judge and he would buy him again, and has been known to buy the same animal four times in one day, giving his check on the bank every time.

THE OLD EDITORS OF MEMPHIS.

THE "old Memphis Appeal," the first newspaper I remember, and from which my father learned me the alphabet, was long edited by that old war horse of Democracy, John R. McClanahan, who handled a very racy, facile, and powerful pen, with which he smote the old Whig party "hip and thigh." John was a bachelor, never married. He was social, genial in an eminent degree, loved his friends, defied his enemies. Occasionally he would "take a lay-off," gather a coterie of friends around him to sample the best vintages of Europe, then ye gods, ye pagan shrines, came forth with "unbended bow" and tribute of wit, mirth, all aglow with the poesy of sunshine and life, without depth of excess.

John was my warm personal friend, and frequently spent much of his leisure hours with me, and often visited me at my residence, especially when my family was away. He was a noble man of the old school; honesty was crystallized in his nature, his character unimpeachable, his abilities as a writer of a high order.

The Appeal was moved south, and edited within the Confederate lines after the occupation of Memphis by the Federal army, and I never met John after that. Lewis I. DuPree, another able and facile writer, was long associated with McClanahan as associate editor of the Appeal, and he, too, went south with the paper, and never returned to the editorial staff of Memphis.

DuPree had much magnetism, was large, inclined to be corpulent—had a splendid physique, an address, a smile that was irresistible. He married a very charming and accomplished lady, the daughter of Gov. James C. Jones.

Jesse H. McMahon, the old editor of the Eagle and Enquirer, a whig organ from the early days of Memphis until the demise of that party, was a fine writer, brimful of the sunshine of life ; he could cover Court Square with a genial smile, and emphasize a laugh at times that would echo back from the western shores of the "inland sea." He had a mouth framed on broadgauge pattern, eminently constructed to give vehement expression to a good laugh at wit and humor.   He was broad in stature, and of physical height that confined him to a single story.

Lola Montez, in her charming, palmy days, away back in the forties, graced the Memphis footlights, and from her quiver sped an arrow that pierced and made tender Jesse's heart, and he never tired of the bonds when she was a terpsichorean star.   The flame became a delirious ecstacy and swooped him around the continent, over to Montreal in the queen's dominions.

Some wag wrote a book full of these exquisite travels, and Mac, "old Mac," as his friends called him, spent many ducats in buying and burning this exciting literature, which contained some magnetic photos of footlight and electric scenes.   But he shook off his dreams, mounted the tripod, and hurled many vollies of thunder at the Democratic party after that episode, and became a tower of strength to his party.   He went south after the occupation of Memphis, and I never met him again.

The Hon. M. C. Galloway, a native of Alabama, came to Memphis in 1857, an accomplished and polished writer, and established that sterling Democratic paper, "The Avalanche," a name typical in every sense of its editor and proprietor.   With a startling, robust individuality, wholly his own, he moved on an enemy like an avalanche clearing the Alps, and his motto was, "Lay on Macduff, and damned be he who first cries hold, enough."   When crushing an enemy he dipped his pen in the vats of the Inferno and wrote in characters as lurid as the belching flames of a volcano—truly "a cataract of fire."

When he chose he could, with the greatest facility and felicity of expression, indulge a smile of the gods, and cover the earth with a rainbow, and in the next paragraph sweep through the tropics like a cyclone shaking the Andes to their foundations.

"Mat," as all his familiar friends called him, in personnel is tall, and of splendid physique, and looks as gentle as the goddess of wisdom. To look at him no stranger would ever suppose that the slumbering fires of a volcano slept beneath his suave manner and magnetic smile, that he "Would not kneel to Jove for his thunder, Nor bow to Neptune for his trident."

He never did anything by halves in his life, with such a sanguine, enthusiastic life, it is impossible—his love is as strong and concentrated as his enmities. He had nothing too good for his friends, and nothing too bitter for his enemies.

When I glance over the career of this wonderful man I am astonished that he has reached the patriarchal age of seventy-five.

It is said that chivalrous men indulge the tenderest affections, and this is fully exemplified in Col. Galloway's life and that of his noble and accomplished wife, now deceased. They loved, and were endeared to each other through storm, and through sunshine, with a devotion that knew no change. When he was imprisoned for indulging in contempt, for a contemptible court, his noble wife mounted the editorial tripod of the Avalanche and wrote editorials as effective as a park of Gatling guns. I knew her well, and none knew her but to honor and admire her—her friends were legion.

Col. Galloway proved his devotion to the cause of the South by entering her armies. From the beginning to the close of the war he was on Gen. Forrest's staff, and with flashing saber rode with his gallant chief at the head of charging columns over many a bloody field. He is enjoying the sunset of a serene and happy old age.

JAMES LEE.

JIM LEE deserted the law and took to the river, and is the owner of many steamers plying on the Mississippi. He has a weakness for corner lots, steamboats, large rentals, and bank accounts—loves them all better than an Irishman does his grog, and enjoys yet a hilarious laugh; and the Lord has been with Jim these many years. Many competing boats have broken their owners trying to land him on a sandbar; but he "stays with them," and has always been "master of the situation."

Vollintine, Lee & Luster was the old law firm in antebellum days. I could load one of Jim's steamers with "good things" about him. The old firm had a large volume of business, but I never saw either one of them in their office too busy either to tell, or listen, to a "good thing." Jim could have made a fortune on the stage. In serio-comic he would have made a master; in the pulpit, a Sam. Jones.

I was standing some years ago on the bluff at Memphis when two of his many coast steamers came into port. The earnings of the trip were principally paid in silver, and it took four negroes to carry it to the bank in baskets. I was behind him unobserved. As the negroes moved by with the baskets, they grunted with fatigue. Jim's eyes —well, I will not say, but the water overflowed the corners of his mouth, and he said to himself, audibly: "Corner lots."

During Federal occupation, an old market farmer passed my residence one day. He wore what had once been a suit of clothes, the remnant was venerable in its quaint antiquity, and had evidently seen better days. He

wore rough, red brogan shoes to match, cracked at the
sides, run down at the heels, and rigorously stiff in their
expiring efforts to serve another term. His pants had
undergone the same campaign, and were rent in the effort
to reach down and meet his socks, which had given up
the ghost in the effort to stand, and had fallen down over
his shoe tops. His hat of ram's wool had lost its ancient
energy of brim, and had fallen down over his eyes. He
sat on the creaking, wabbling seat of a vehicle that was
not long for this world, to which was harnessed a lame
horse frame, and all were held together by ropes
and string. My wife said as he passed my residence:
"Yonder goes an old peddler, stop him and buy some butter and eggs."

I hailed the rural peasant, and called for the articles,
but when the venerable gentleman peeped out from under
the wool hat he was Jim Lee, and in surprise I said:
"What does this mean, Jim?" He roared with mirth,
and said: "I can beat Joe. Jefferson and give him all the
old 'Rip Van Winkle' he can muster. The fact is, John,
so far as appearances go, I don't intend to pass for any
more than I am worth with those yankee blue coats.
They seem bent on 'abandoned property' without respect
to non-combatants or neutrality; but I don't think they
will pick this outfit up as 'abandoned' property."

Every time I met him I called for butter and eggs and
sweitzer cheese. He then had his fine carriage horses hid
away in a dark cellar, and their feet well muffled with
rags.

To get even, Jim played on my virgin innocence, and
induced me to get in his ancient vehicle behind his venerable roadster and go to the suburbs on urgent business
which did not admit of delay to send for my own conveyance.

His long, solemn Methodist face and sepulchral voice
disarmed suspicion of evil intent, and I went on good intentions bent, to relieve suffering humanity told in pathet-

ic tenderness. Went? Yes, went; and urged the poor, hopping, skipping, spavined, remnant of a horse, and before I got back to the starting point, a dozen men at intervals hailed me as a peddler of butter, eggs, and sweitzer cheese. Jim posted them at intervals along the route. I will not repeat what either of us said after he remarked, "two can play at a game," because a minister of revealed religion might demur to the non-theological import of the dialogue. Jim and the improvised crowd of mutual friends reveled in mirth, but they voted refreshments to him, and it cost him as much as the price of a fine set of harness.

He is radiant in the sunshine of life, successful in all he undertakes, and is one of the very few lawyers who have developed fine financial and executive ability. If there are no navigable waters and competing lines of steamers and corner lots when he crosses the River, I am inclined to the opinion that he will quit the place. He was born at Dover, on the Cumberland river, but that classic stream was too small to accomodate his aspirations.

JAMES BRETT.

JAMES BRETT came in with a meteoric flash which surprised and delighted all, and the press went into ecstacies of praise over the maiden speech of this brilliant young man. He was of splendid physique, and looked every inch a royal prince. But like "Single-speech Hamilton" in the British Parliament, he was never induced to make another effort. He had reached the goal the first bound, and there was no round on which to perch if he made another spring.

But that speech was immense in immediate returns. That, with his good looks, won the hand and heart of the beautiful Miss Nelson, daughter of the banker. He had made his fortune in one speech, and generously left the field to less fortunate gleaners.

JAMES E. TEMPLE.

AMES E. TEMPLE was an old bachelor, quaint, curious, nearsighted; his laugh and look diverged at an angle of 45 degrees, and continued to recede from parallel lines, good-natured, highly moral, and of severe integrity, every man's friend, no man his enemy, but of that negative, passive character which neither grapples with emergencies nor creates them. He loved all mankind, but steered fearfully far from crinoline and all its complications. His education in that was neglected and he never tried to retrieve the misfortune. His individuality, though strikingly photographed on a singular background, presented difficult ethnological problems for the expert, and it was difficult to trace his national compound to any single, double, normal or mixed standards.

Saxon, Norman, and Celtic blood, with best crosses of Caucasian, made good-hearted Jim a wonderful man, and left it doubtful in the minds of many of his warm friends whether the lost tribes did not survive in him. *Sui generis* was the least but not the most that could be said of Jim.

His office for many years was over Ward's drug store, on Main street, "Bachelor's Inn." Passing along there one day I heard a furious uproar upstairs in the office department of the building—determined masculine and resolute feminine voices. Jim came running down stairs as though fleeing from an earthquake, bareheaded and eyes wild, as though thrust out by some terrible convulsion—he called loudly for help.

It was not his affair at all, but occurred in an office adjoining his. A Mr. H., of Mississippi, a gentleman of large fortune, spent several years at school in Paris, France, and there became involved in a love affair, which he could not shake off, and the stormy scene was between these two former lovers. "Hell knows no fury like a woman scorned." She had followed him around the world, and chased him from city to city, and continent to continent for years, and he got somewhat tired of it. Finally when he married one of the most charming daughters of Mississippi, this Parisienne broke in on him at the wedding feast and claimed to be wife No. 1. Gen. Chalmers knows the history of this case.

After the police quieted the parties down, Jim returned to his office as much agitated as the contestants, and said, "If I was engaged to be married I'd burst it up before night, and if I could not do that, I'd swim the ocean to get out of it. Boys, would you blame me?" Alas, poor Jim, we will never see the like of him again.

LADY YELVERTON.

IT will be remembered by most readers, twenty-five years ago, that Lord and Lady Yelverton had a divorce suit in the English Courts of much celebrity, about which much was written and published in the American and European press.

Lady Yelverton was not above the medium in physique. In the winter of 1868 a lecture, to be delivered by her, was extensively advertised, and the Greenlaw Opera House was filled with an immense auditory, including myself.

To my astonishment and chagrin an immense giantess, of cyclopic physique and stentorian voice that could pierce and shake the Alps to their foundations, ranted on the stage as the real, accomplished, and refined Lady Yelverton. Her dress and voice was as lurid as a cyclone

beating its way through the tropics—the rich brogue of
Erin, unshaded or modified, was exhibited in stormy
peals, and Lord Yelverton was pounded into smithereens.
Paddy from Cork, on his way to Donnybrook Fair, with
shilalah, and on blood intent, was not a circumstance.

I wrote a facetious criticism that night, it was beyond
effort at satire, which appeared in the Avalanche next
morning under the signature of "H."

All local Ireland was indignant and on chivalry bent.
A hasty conference was held with the Lady Yelverton,
who informed the chivalrous that a Mr. Hogan, a spy in
the pay of Lord Yelverton, was pursuing her from city
to city in the triumphal march through America, and that
he was the author of the criticism. A committee waited
on Mr. Hogan, and gave him thirty minutes to get out of
the city, and he went, "you bet," and involuntarily represented me in the hegira. Mr. Hogan carried with him
my sympathy and silence, but did not wait or call for assurances of either.

A STRANGE FRAUD.

 REMARKABLE fraud in the sale of a house
and lot in Memphis to me was once perpetrated.
I bought from Mrs. Georgiana E. K—, who produced a regular conveyance to Georgiana E. K—.
Eight years after the purchase I was informed that the
property was conveyed to her minor daughter, who was
named after her mother—that the daughter had married
a gentleman from Indiana, who would soon bring suit to
recover the property. The gentleman who imparted this
news told me that he was present when the deed was executed, and that he personally knew it was executed to
the child, but purchased with the mother's money.

I paid two thousand dollars cash for the lot—had often
loaned the mother money, without interest, to enable her

to conduct a restaurant. She always returned it, and I
had implicit confidence in her integrity. Her husband
was a cripple, and she had to support the family, and for
that reason had my sympathy. I immediately sent a carriage for the mother and daughter and son-in-law.

The mother confessed, and burst into tears, and asked
me how the wrong could be remedied. I told her that
her daughter and son-in-law could convey the lot to me,
and that would end the matter. The daughter was anxious, but her husband declined to execute the conveyance.

Then that little, imperious matron stamped the floor
like a princess, and told her husband to get out of her
sight, he was no longer the husband of Georgiana—that
brought him to terms, and the deed was executed.

KNIGHTS OF THE GOLDEN CIRCLE.

IN 1866 there was a secret organization in Shelby
county known as "Knights of the Golden Circle," which drew after it much attention and favorable consideration from many prominent men.
I never belonged to it, nor did I know anything of the
grips, signs, and secret work; but its design was to protect its members and society where the Order existed
from oppression and wrong during that excited and un-
settled condition of society immediately succeeding the
war. The authority it assumed to exercise in defiance of
established law was liable to great abuse if not guarded
by the greatest caution. Its membership consisted chiefly
if not entirely, of the rural population where my acquaintance embraced the entire population. The Order embraced many discreet farmers, and they caused me to be
chosen attorney for the Order, and a committee notified
me.

My position, this relation, and the discreet men who

conferred with me as to contemplated acts, enabled me to exert much influence over the Order, and to minimize its excesses, and I have no hesitation in emphasizing the assertion that no similar Society of six hundred men ever acted more discreetly.

Many superficial persons, whose zeal is much more fervid than their practical judgment, will condemn me for accepting such an office, giving such service to such an organization. But I have ever acted on my own judgment in such junctures, alone anxious to satisfy my own conscience regardless of what others might think. I knew the organization embraced many good and misguided men, many of them the friends of my boyhood, and I knew that if ever an association of men stood in need of well-considered advice, these men did. I had their confidence—to me more precious than all the gems of the Orient—I saw an opportunity to do much good, unmingled with a shadow of evil in so far as I was concerned.

Then why not stay the hand of a misguided friend before an irreparable evil was inflicted? Why "strain at a gnat and swallow a camel?" Everything including patriotism in time of war has its limitations and qualifications. Twenty-five men of this Order awoke me up at the dead hour of night and called me out in the street in front of my residence. They were on horseback, had one poor, trembling man pinioned with ropes and shackle. They wanted a consultation with me as to whether that man's life was forfeit or not. I invited the leader to dismount and come into my house and give me the details of the crime, to which I listened with the greatest anxiety and solicitude. I was on the judgment-seat—the nearest approach of man to his God—with no commission from man to guide, with no external responsibility to my fellow men to censure if I went wrong, but an awful responsibility to that accused man and to my God if I erred in judgment.

What was the crime? The wife of one of these Knights of the Golden Circle had been fearfully mistreated by a man in the absence of her husband. This pinioned man had been captured and accused of the crime, taken before the injured wife for identification. She said he greatly resembled the man, and believed he was the man, but that she could not swear that he was the identical man. His accusers believed he was the criminal, and certain circumstances strongly corroborated their belief. After hearing all the details I went out and stood on the steps leading down to the street, called the men close up around me so all could hear the low voice in which the surroundings compelled me to speak, and I said: "Gentlemen and friends, I have heard all the details, and if such a crime was committed against those dearest to me, and established beyond all doubt against a certain individual, I would take his life. But no such certainty exists in this man's case. By the laws of God and man he is entitled to the doubt. Were you to take his life, you would all be guilty of the greatest possible crime; and though man might never detect and punish you, your own conscience would lash you until time is no more. In the name of your own honor, in the name of our all-seeing God, I advise you to release and let him go."

The leader pulled out a bowieknife, and leaning over the saddle, handed it to me, saying: "John, we believe you are right; cut him loose." And I cut the cords that bound him. That poor, trembling man fell on his knees, hugged my limbs, and wept, and prayed God's benediction on me.

I will not attempt to describe my own feelings, no pen nor tongue can do it. I would not have erred on the wrong side in that supreme hour for ten such worlds as this. The man disappeared around the corner, and went southeast on Alabama street. From me no human has ever heard the name of one of these men. Ethics, law, and morals preclude it. The minds of troubled men

must have some place where they can unbosom and lay
bare the inward sufferings of the heart, repose the details of their life with the law's protection from exposure.   Three such depositories exist under our law: Confessions to the priesthood, details of disease to the physician, and communications to lawyers by their clients in
the line of employment.   The closets uncovered in a law
office and laid bare will never be known to the world.

BANK FAILURES—HEAVY LOSSES.

S. D. M'CLURE, THE BANKER.

THE history of this young man points a moral.   He
was born and raised in the vicinage of Memphis,
but a little my junior, the bright son of a widow
in humble, honest poverty.   He went to school
to me, and was one of the most studious and pleasant
boys.   During the early period of the war he was engaged
by bankers from Charleston to Cleveland in the exchange
of large quantities of currency which was tied up in both
sections.   His integrity at no period of his life was ever
questioned.   About the close of the war he bought the
brick building at the northwest corner of Jefferson and
Front streets, fitted it up at a cash cost of $40,000, bought
the old charter of the Franklin Insurance Company,
which conferred banking privileges, and opened up
a prosperous bank.   I was chosen attorney for the
bank and made it the custodian of all the funds I
owned and controlled.   Our attachment for each other
was strong and mutual.   The confidence and attachment
of the schoolroom strengthened with the advance of maturer years.

Dempsey, as I always called him, frequently came to
me and advised me when and in what way he thought it

advisable to speculate. I was not much disposed in that
direction, but on a few occasions gave him my check and
carte blanche to use the funds as his judgment dictated.
Twice only he invested in gold margins, and won, aggre-
gating in the two transactions, about $4,000. He urged
me in cotton, but I was fearful of that, not that it would
fall and inflict a loss, in the upward tendency and large
margin for profits I had the greatest confidence, but the
recent experience of my friend, Col. W. P. Grace, of Pine
Bluff, was a warning to me. He had embarked in cotton
in connection with a citizen of the State of New York,
and won $75,000, but when he went to settle with that
friend he was shown how criminal it would be to pay him
over his profits in derogation of a confiscating act of that
State. His partner was a praying, and conscientious
man, and could not be induced to violate the laws of New
York, where he lived. I was not afraid of Dempsey, but
of the other fellow at the New York end of the line. He
had but one deficiency, it crippled and ruined him as a
banker. He was too kind, and sympathetic, and too
easily induced to discount unprofitable paper. I learned
this when it was too late, had I known it ten days earlier
prudence would have dictated the withdrawal of my deposits and I would have been $27,000 better off. I had
noticed his care-worn visage for several days, but did not
think of attributing it to financial trouble. On the day
the bankrupt act of 1867 went into effect, he came to my
office after banking hours, and said he was "forced to
make an assignment." He handed me $1,000 of my own
money, and said, "There is but $45,000 in the bank, in-
cluding cash and convertible securities. I have paid my
clerks. I want to assign to you as trustee at once, and
before banking hours to-morrow. Let the assignment
embrace banking house and lot, that will increase the
available assets to about $100,000. I make you the first
preferred creditor." I was greatly astonished, but drew
the assignment to myself as trustee. When I arrived at

11

the bank to take charge I found two depositors there who were preferred after myself. They were wringing their hands, and one was crying like a baby. There was but $21,000 in cash in the vaults, the remainder of the immediately available assets was in acceptances and bills of exchange on New Orleans and New York. I postponed the preference in my favor and paid off the bewailing creditors. The Exchange was attached, and I never got the proceeds of that; in the hurry and press of business I had entirely overlooked the fact that the National bankrupt law took effect that day, which rendered the assignment void. Twenty-one thousand dollars of the deposits was in my own name, and belonged to me. Eight thousand dollars belonged to my debtors, who had put it there to pay me, but this unfortunate failure crippled them so they never paid, and the loss to me was total, complete, and final. I never received one cent except the $1,000 given me at my office that evening. McClure had let one merchant of limited means overcheck $80,000, which was afterwards paid in a bankrupt discharge. A successful banker is necessarily compelled to steel his heart against the influences of that Christian charity, so much commended by the Savior. There are a few noble exceptions, but they are rare. Before that I lost all my Confederate money, except that given to my brother, on his way from Camp Chase to be exchanged, and a very small amount spent. Poor McClure, the shock was great. Like an honest man, his failings attested a generous nature, and he gave up every dollar, but did not long survive. He did not possess those reserve forces and rallying powers which sustain men of greater nerve under greater difficulties. Thirty days after this failure the Gayoso Bank went to the wall, and buried in its wreck $3,000 of my deposits, for which I never received one dollar. John C. Lanier, another friend, went down with it to rise no more. Within a radius of eighteen months I lost $14,000 more, aggregating my losses to $44,000, not including my Confederate treasury notes. But I was in the full tide of success and no creditor, for I had none, was involved. My cash receipts from my office in 1867 were $30,000.

WILLIAM K. POSTON.

POSTON was a very prominent, able, and sound civil lawyer, and occupied a front seat when I came to the Bar, and had an extensive practice. He was upright in life, an exemplar in the performance of duty, pious, religious, a deacon in the Methodist church, a kind husband, indulgent father; the world was better in every sphere where he moved. Above the medium in size and height, fine physique, with hair inclined to the blonde type. He was dignified and reserved, and a little austere. I never heard him tell a joke or saw him in hilarious laughter.

In July, 1866, I was in Lebanon, Tenn., on my summer's vacation, when I was startled, astonished, sorrowed: the papers announced his sudden demise the previous day, the result of a congestive chill. Two fine sons took their father's place at the Bar.

JUDGE SYLVESTER BAILEY.

JUDGE BAILEY was quite an aged man when I first met him in 1853. He was among the first lawyers to locate at Memphis. His residence was two or three miles south of the city on the Hernando road. He was the synonym of honesty and purity of life. He was tall and slender, with long, flowing gray hair, and one leg shorter than the other, necessitating support with a cane in walking.

He died in the full fruition of ripe years, without one blemish on his pure life and character, and over his bier it was truly said: "Well done, thou good and faithful servant." "A patriarch in Israel gathered to his fathers." He was proverbially kind to all, harsh to none. His life seemed like the unruffled surface of a beautiful lake.

FREDERIC P. STANTON.

STANTON came to Memphis from Kentucky prior to 1840, and occupied one of the front pews in the guild until politics led him astray. He orated the first stump speech I ever heard, at Green Bottom, in 1840. I was but seven years old, but remember the occasion vividly. He was an able man, of fine physique and massive head that would have been a fine model for a sculptor. He represented the Memphis district in Congress for two terms, and was opposed in his second race by Edwin M. Yerger, the Whig candidate, and only defeated Yerger by one vote.

He was Governor of the Territory of Kansas under Buchanan's administration. I never heard him at the Bar only in a few cases. In these he maintained his reputation for ability.

JAMES T. LEATH.

LEATH had retired from the Bar prior to my advent. He was a large, well-proportioned man of elegant and refined manners, and universally esteemed. His mother was the founder and principal donor to the Leath Orphan Asylum near Memphis, and her son took great pride in promoting that noble charity.

CYRUS E. DICKEY.

YRUS E. DICKEY, the son of Judge Dickey, of the Supreme Court of Illinois, came to Memphis in 1858, a young and well-equipped lawyer, full of noble impulses, a gallant foe, a generous friend; had he lived long he would have achieved distinction. Both of us Douglas men in the campaign preceding Lincoln's election, and myself an active campaigner on the stump. He accompanied me.

We talked over the contest after armies were marching to the front. We looked in on each other's heart as through a mirror. He was preparing to go and join the army at home, and I to go into the Confederate army. Cyrus remained too long at Memphis. Col. L. D. McKissick was appointed Military Governor, and a warrant was issued for the arrest of Dickey. He was at my house awaiting an opportunity to get away. The soldier directed to make the arrest met me on the street, inquired of me after him, and I threw him off the track, secreted Cyrus, and arranged his safe passage through our lines.

Give up such a man, a friend, a gentleman, as he was, to a vigilance committee, the whirlwind inquisition of the revolutionary period? No; I'd suffer the pillory and inquisition first. War means many things, but does not embrace the base betrayal of a gentleman and friend under your own roof; and if it did, I would disregard it. He was of the staff of Gen. Banks, and was killed in the Red River campaign. When he came through Memphis he dined with me, and two brothers never met with more cordiality. He went to the Commanding General and did all possible in his power to mitigate the severities incident to my situation.

If I had been base enough to have qualmed my conscience and given him up to my Military Governor, what might have been with the tables turned?

CAPTAIN HAMILTON.

CAPTAIN HAMILTON, whose Christian name I forget, was a young man of fine address and splendidly equipped. He came to Memphis in 1859—entered the Confederate army under Gen. McCowan, as captain of artillery. The last time I ever met him was at Randolph, where he was in charge of a battery. No country the sun shines on ever gave her noble youth and glorious manhood with more lavish hand to the relentless demands of war than the South.

The bones of her chivalrous sons glorify a mausoleum, and fill an urn stretching from Gettysburg to the Rio Grande; and the heroic sons of the North sleep side by side with them awaiting the judgment day.

Their fame is the heritage of a common country.

ASA THOMAS.

THOMAS was a polished, educated gentleman, from Pennsylvania, a Professor. He spent several years in the mines of California, taught school in the Academy at Raleigh—read law under me, and was admitted to the Bar in 1857.

When war became inevitable, he went back to his native North to enter her armies, and was lost in the shoreless sea of blood. He fought a sham duel with Robert McCrary by moonlight near the tombstones of the village graveyard at Raleigh; at McCrary's fire he fell, a bottle of red ink was thrown on his white shirt, and Mc-Crary, who was not in the secret, walked up, bent over him, became alarmed, crossed the Mississippi river that night, and remained away for three months before he discovered that Thomas was still locomoting the earth.

WILLIAM MESSICK.

ESSICK, the son of a good, old carpenter, at Raleigh, read law in my office, and was admitted to the Bar in 1857. He moved to Memphis, and made quite a little fortune, the fees from one client, Boden Greenlaw, being the basal structure of this success in worldly holdings.

He was strictly moral and scrupulously neat in dress. From the schoolroom he went to my office, and was a laborious student. I dined with him at his residence not long before his death, and enjoyed the occasion greatly. Reminiscences of the old times long forgotten by me came again fresh from William's well stored memory, sandwiched with many a hearty laugh. Peace be to his ashes. God's blessings on his descendants.

SIDNEY Y. WATSON.

IDNEY Y. WATSON, he of the flaming red-head and nervo-sanguine temperament, looked upon the world as a stage and himself as a star performer, and was willing to undergo all the toil requisite to such achievement. Such men, like the Sculptor with his chisel and marble and hammer, carve out roads to the summit. He was a young man with exceptionaly good habits and extraordinary promise, but looked upon dollars and cents as idols to be worshiped, and was in danger from that standpoint, but never did anything to render his conduct obnoxious.

I greatly admired his talents and laborious efforts. The war between the States came on, and he was no more of Memphis; like thousands of others, the whirlpool carried him away from that mooring forever.

JUDGE HEATH.

JUDGE R. R. HEATH came in 1856 from North Carolina; he was an exemplary man, an able lawyer; but one of those quiet, negative characters, who have no aptitude either in seizing or making opportunities. It is a great mistake in such men in ever leaving a locality where they first obtained a foothold. He has a talented and worthy son now at the Memphis Bar.

COLONEL THORNTON.

COLONEL THORNTON was in the meridian of manhood when he came to Memphis, from his native Virginia. He was the author of a fine work on Conveyancing, and brought with him a well deserved reputation as an able lawyer, which he sustained to the end of his useful career. He was courteous, and dignified, and eminently moral and conservative until some sarcastic wit began to step on the toes of great Virginia to draw him out. That he could not and would not stand. The F. F. V. then rose in him to the altitude of the lofty peaks of Otter, and he would charge and discharge his Gatling guns until the enemy retreated or surrendered. He was too much absorbed in the dignity of human nature to indulge in hilarious wit and humor, so inviting to the sunny phases of life, and for that reason was frequently made the butt of a joke approached from serious standpoints. It was delicious to put him on the defense of Virginia. He would have made a grand old bishop in the church.

During the spring rise in the Mississippi river in 1860 Ed. Yerger, others, and myself were seining in the Bayou just below the bridge on the old Raleigh road. We caught a large number of fine game fish, and deposited them on a little grassy island in the Bayou, where they were floundering when Col. Thorton came by on horseback. He stopped, gazed admiringly on the beautiful fish, got down, tied his horse, and asked Yerger and myself to ferry him over to the island, where the boys were indulging in mint julep to drive off malaria and disease consequent on exposure in the water. Yerger was feeling like Tam O'Shanter felt after his first three drams on that stormy night when the warlocks got after him. How much malarial antidote I had taken I don't remember, and if I did, don't suppose I would freely disclose it. Four of us got in the boat to ferry Col. Thornton over. As we stepped in Yerger proposed that we accidentally overturn the boat when we reached the middle of the stream on the return trip. The boat was tilted to and fro, and all of us were trying to balance it, but over it turned, plunging the Colonel head foremost in water twenty feet deep. We rescued him, but those kid gloves and that white necktie were ruined. Yerger made profuse apologies for the accident, which was accepted by the Colonel, with the declaration that he only had himself to blame for trusting himself to the safe conduct of such sportsmen. We presented him with a royal string of fish, and sent them to his residence by one of our negro attendants. The Colonel never suspected the accident was designed, if he had thought that it was premeditated he would have thrashed the last one of the conspirators if it had taken him all summer. He belonged to that good old school of men who have left but few behind and few, if any, successors in the present generation.

LEROY POPE.

POPE was more distinguished as a gentleman of culture and refinement than as a lawyer, perhaps because he confined himself to commercial law, and was never a participant in those celebrated trials and contests which attract attention. His wife was distinguished for her polish, refinement and literary taste, and wrote poetry of merit for the periodicals of the day. He was brother to Col. John Pope, the planter, equally distinguished as a fine gentleman of the old school, whose farm was five miles from the city, on the Raleigh road. Dr. Pope, either the son of Colonel John, or brother, I forget which, was a surgeon in the United States Navy, and married a Spanish beauty in the West India Islands. They came from Georgia at an early day. Col. George L. Holmes was related to the Popes by marriage, and owned a large plantation adjoining Pope's, which he cultivated with slaves. He was equally distinguished for culture, and that broad hospitality so characteristic of the Southern planter. He came from Massachusetts, like Gen. Pike, Gen. Adams, and a host of others, who readily embraced and incorporated themselves with southern institutions.

JOHN G. FINNIE.

JOHN G. FINNIE came from New York, and for a time appeared to be succeeding as a commercial and collecting attorney. His Eastern connections and combinations were favorable, and he was a very fair lawyer. He went back to New York, and for a time practiced there. Becoming dissatisfied, he again returned to Memphis about 1867.

GENERAL PRESTON SMITH.

GENERAL PRESTON SMITH was a man of marked and strong individuality, mild, gentle, and courteous. He accorded everybody that respectful consideration to which he was entitled, but a more courageous and fearless man never lived. He was of the old era of the South, and was a typical representative of its true chivalry. He had retired from the Bar when I came on the stage, and I had no opportunity to judge of his legal attainments, but his ability warrants the assumption that he could have attained eminence in his profession if he had energetically pursued it. He long kept a fine pair of duelling pistols, made for him to order, the barrels were twelve inches long and carried an ounce ball. These pistols were at the service of all who recognized the code, and were often used on the field, and sometimes did deathly execution. He had two beautiful and accomplished daughters. The elder married Col. R. F. Looney, the younger married Joseph Sykes. a graduate of the literary and law departments of the University of Virginia, in the class of 1866. I first met Joe

Sykes and Thomas B. Turley at the University at the commencement of 1866, and took a great fancy for these boys then—we came together to Memphis. I may be pardoned in saying that with much interest I saw these young roosters when they first flew up on the fence and flopped their wings. They were both game little bantams and ready to tackle any old cock in the barnyard. Both were with me for a while when they first commenced the practice, and both married while in the office with me, and George Washington did likewise. Gen. Smith entered the Confederate army at the opening of the war and fell while gallantly leading his brigade at Chickamauga. No braver soldier ever drew a sword, or marched to death under the cannon's awful roar.

HIRAM VOLENTINE.

HIRAM VOLENTINE, the author of the digest bearing his name, was born in Stewart county, Tenn., of respectable but humble parentage, was apprentice to the saddler's trade, was ambitious, and rose to a useful and respectable position in the profession. His early life impressed lessons of economy; he took care of his accumulations and left an estate to his widow and children valued at $75,000. He was waspish and quick to resent an injury, but one of the most companionable of men. We were often together. "Vol," as his intimate friends called him, was one of the most genial and companionable of men, full of sunshine.

One, Moffitt, an Irish newspaper scribbler, became his enemy during the occupation of Memphis by the Federal army, in 1863, and exasperated him by penny-a-line squibs in the press, and "Vol," when they met in the City Council, of which both were members, raised a

small cane to strike him, and was shot through the thigh.
The ball severed the femoral artery and he bled to death
in a few minutes.   Moffitt was a Union man, and nothing was ever done with him.

KIT WILLIAMS.

KIT WILLIAMS, after whom the block at 43½ Madison street was named, was the son of a distin-
tinguished father, who represented his district in
West Tennessee in Congress.

Kit was a noble man, strictly temperate, laboriously
studious, ambitious, and animated by the highest sense of
honor.   Had he lived long, he would have attained and
honored the highest positions in the profession.   I greatly admired and thought him the peer of any man of his
age I ever met at the Bar.   Colonel of his regiment, he
fell at Shiloh gallantly leading it, and sleeps in the grave
of a hero.   He would have won distinction in any walk of
life.   Farewell, noble brother.   You pitched your bivouc
on " fame's eternal camping-ground."

B. A. MASSEY.

B. A. MASSEY was a man of far greater than average ability; a fine specimen of the physical man,
but became indolent and careless, and lost his
prestige and practice while in the meridian of
manhood.   If the driving wheel, that indispensable motor
to brain force and great achievement, had been larger, he
could have attained the highest rewards.

JOHN A. TAYLOR.

JOHN was a noble and chivalrous young man of fine ability, and of a family distinguished for its number of professional men of eminence. He married the accomplished daughter of R. K. Turnage, and was in partnership with him up to his lamented and tragic death on the duelling field, I think, in 1859, when he met his honorable and chivalrous death in conflict with Alonzo Greenlaw, both young and high strung. They were both my friends, but Greenlaw was not a lawyer.

JOHN M. CARMACK.

JOHN was a confirmed old bachelor, an "old-line Whig," wit, humorist, good lawyer, but too fond of luxurious ease to get down to the bed rocks. He rarely laughed, but was fond of perpetrating witticisms that caused others to laugh. He cared very little about forensic conflict, and rarely entered the arena as gladiator.

He was a great admirer of Gov. Harris, and after one of the Governor's successful campaigns, presented him with a fine hat, to which some of his Whig friends took exception. "What!" exclaimed John, "Can't a man cover the faults of his friends without incurring obloquy and criticism?"

E. De F. MORGAN.

ORGAN was a wasp, an impetuous little fellow, chiefly engaged in successfully spending the dowery of his wife. He always carried his little popgun and a chip on his head waiting for somebody to knock it off, and was frequently accommodated. I remember once when coming out of Schawb's, the Delmonico of that day, to have seen one, Mr. Brown, knock Morgan half across Adams street. He rose to his knees, and in that position fired at Brown, the ball passing through the fleshy part of both hips. Brown jumped three feet high, yelled like a Comanche Indian; and when he found that his locomotive powers were not destroyed, put every muscle into requisition, and "got a move on" down Adams street that would have shamed Nancy Hanks.

Morgan said that when his head was tested with that fist, " the Worsham House appeared to be on fire. I was taken by surprise—without a moment's warning. The fellow approached me so very politely, and said: 'This is Mr. Morgan, I believe.' I bowed the most approved courtesy, and admitted my identity. Then he said: 'This is Mr. Brown,' and launched out his fist. I never spoke to him before in my life, but I think he was a witness in a case I tried yesterday, and perhaps feels injured at my opinion of his veracity."

Poor Morgan, he had many good qualities mingled with his frailties, like most mortals. He died in 1868 from severe hemorrhage of the lungs, and Clara Craft, his beautiful wife, soon followed. They had no children.

WOODRUFF.

WOODRUFF, whose Christian name I have forgotten, was a bird of tropical plumage, with spicy, witty humor. He always looked on the happy side of life, and had a rainbow to throw over every social circle. He came from Marion, Ark., to Memphis, and was a very fair lawyer. Jurors never went to sleep when he addressed them. He dropped out and was lost to sight in "the mighty throng that forever heaves onward."

When asked why he left Arkansas to come to Memphis, he replied: "They whipped me at Marion twice a week for four years. I stood it until corns grew on my back before I thought of leaving."

SPECULATION.

CONFEDERATE MONEY, DRAY CHECKS, SALOON TICKETS,
EVERYBODY A BANKER—SUICIDAL ORDER OF
GEN. BEAUREGARD TO GIVE STABILITY
TO CONFEDERATE CURRENCY
AT THE POINT OF
THE BAYONET.

AS soon as the blockade to commerce at the confluence of the Ohio and Mississippi rivers was established, I saw that immense profits could be realized by speculation in pork. I had saved up some gold in anticipation of a worthless currency, and was prepared to speculate in a limited way. The upper

counties in West Tennessee, particularly Dyer county at
that time, raised a large surplus of hogs, many of which
were driven to Memphis on foot. I bought three droves
of very large hogs on foot, on which I realized a net
profit of $20,000 in less than sixty days, and if my mer-
chant had obeyed instructions and held the meat longer
on a rapidly rising market my profits would have been
double that amount. It may be an uncharitable conviction, but I then thought and have always thought that
no sales had been made when the merchant rendered an
account. I was astonished and protested, and the only
excuse for the early sale against my directions was that
he "thought it best to sell." The courts were closed
and I had no redress. A check was handed me on the
Bank of West Tennessee, and I was paid in Confederate
treasury notes, and compelled to receive them. General
Beauregard had a few days before issued a military ukase
making it a severe offense to refuse this trash.

This order of itself discredited the notes more than
all else. Strange that the President, and Secretary of
the Treasury, Memminger, could not see the immediate
effect of such a blow at the currency at the outset of the
war. That order did more to destroy the confidence of
the people, at that stage of the contest, in the currency
than the two hundred and fifty thousand soldiers of the
North who were advancing on our frontiers. I then saw
the mistake I had made in converting gold into promises,
which could never be redeemed only on the happening of
the remote contingency of ultimate success in establishing the independence of the seceding States, and in that
event history would repeat itself and settle to old continental values, like it did during and long after the revolutionary war. That military order was simply idiotic.

The circulating medium in the city soon expanded, like
the restless waters of a rising flood for an outlet, and
found it in brass dray checks, stamped with the name of
the merchants issuing them—"good for ten cents," "good

12

for twenty-five cents," "good for fifty cents." Saloon
men issued pasteboards in a similar way, merchants,
petty retail grocers, and anybody who wanted to issue
such promises, and these things circulated as money by
the ton in the city; and yet they possessed more intrinsic
value than Beauregard's tyrant backing of Confederate
treasury notes, the volume of which had no limit and "no
bottom," as the lead-heaver cries when he throws out the
sounding line. "Mark Twain" was never found.

Another ukase of equal wisdom soon followed. Col.
L. D. McKissick, Military Governor of Memphis, presumably acting under orders from the Department of War
at Richmond, issued an order commanding the destruction
of the vast surplus of sugar, molasses, and cotton which
had been accumulated at Memphis. Cotton had no present merchantable value, the first grades of molasses only
commanded 2½ cents per gallon, one dollar per barrel of
forty gallons; the best grade of brown sugar two cents
per pound. The vacant commons on the bluff in front of
the city was covered with molasses barrels; when the
heads of the barrels were knocked out floods ran out in
streams to the river like lava from a volcano. Cotton
estimated at three hundred thousand bales were hauled
to the suburbs and burned. Night was as lurid as
flames could make it, and the day as hazy with the
clouds of smoke as a fog on the river. These commodities would have been of vast utility to the population, the cotton alone commanded forty cents per
pound the 6th of June, 1863, the day the city was taken
by the Federals. The one hundred and forty millions of
pounds consumed in that patriotic fire would have brought
$54,000,000 to the city. The molasses and sugar destroyed
would have increased the revenue to $75,000,000, all of
which went up in smoke and ashes, on the idiotic idea that
its destruction would cripple the North far more than it
would injure the South.

The ports and commercial marts of the world were

open to the North, and all closed to the South. I condemned the policy then as much as I do now. There was some cotton secreted and saved, it was bought and paid for in gold. One of my friends who had been engaged in hauling and burning cotton for weeks secreted enough to bring him $30,000 in gold the first day the national forces occupied Memphis. When the destruction of property was in progress, before Federal occupation, everything had the appearance of a Sahara of misery for the people, desolation seemed crowned, and the future looked as dark as the smoke that ascended from the consuming flames. A fleet of trading boats followed in the wake of the iron-clad fleet of war, but the people of the city had but little to give in exchange. Some planters in the rural districts had saved some cotton which escaped the general conflagration. A portion of this cotton was long held back, not because the non-combatants desired to withhold it from market, but because straggling Confederate commands after the occupation of the city seized and burned all the cotton they found on the way to the city.

INCIDENTS OF THE WAR.

GEN. SHERMAN'S ORDER TO RESTORE STOLEN MONEY.

MRS. CURLIN, the mother of James and Amos Curlin, Confederate soldiers in Ballentine's troop of cavalry, to which I was once attached, lived on the old Raleigh road just beyond the picket lines. She had $2,000 in gold, which was taken from her by some of "Sherman's Bummers," as they were called. The old lady came to me next day in much excitement and distress. Gen. Sherman's headquarters were then in a tent in Fort Pickering. I called a carriage and took the old lady to the General, and told her to tell him her story in her own way. He listened patiently and treated us both with the utmost consideration. When the old lady concluded her story, he instructed his adjutant to issue an order at once, and at roll call in the evening have it read to all of his command.   In this order the robbery was described, and it was stated that if the money was not brought to the General's headquarters in twenty-four hours he would cause the arrest and execution of every man engaged in it, whether soldier or civilian.   He then said, "Call to-morrow, at noon madam, and I think I will have your money."   We called, and every dollar was restored.   For such services as this I never made a charge.   I always found Gen. Sherman courteous to civilians and easy of access.   After hearing complaints he was quick to decide, and never revised his decision so far as my observation extended without additional evidence, except in one case personal to myself. Dick Davis, the notorious guerilla, whose fate I relate in another connection, was then operating between the Federal and Confederate military lines of occupation, particularly on the line of the Charleston railroad.   He was a terror to the Federal army.   To prevent this, Gen. Sherman issued an order which can never be justified under the laws of civilized warfare.   The order was to place twenty citizens of Memphis on the trains, in the most exposed positions, so they might be shot by Davis when he fired on the trains.   I was included in one of these details. When the order came to me I drove immediately down to General Sherman's headquarters, and as vehemently as a civilian might, protested against the order, and told him the Roman Generals had acted thus with the Jews in their wars, and had left a stain on the splendor of the Roman arms which all the ages could never wipe out or remove, and that if death ensued to the helpless civilian who was thus made breastworks to defend arms that ought to recoil at such protection, it would be nothing more nor less than cold-blooded murder of non-combatants under the protection of Federal armies.   He exempted me, and in a few days rescinded the order. My recollection is that but three detachments of civilians went out on the trains under this order. What influence my protest had with him I never knew, but always thought that it set him to thinking, and influenced the rescision of this order against the defenceless. At least I felt under obligations to him for the courteous hearing he accorded me, and the personal exemption it secured. His soul was wrapped up in the war, and no man ever attributed to him mercenary motives in its prosecution. He was as dignified and polite to those deserving it as any commander I met during the war. But he had some of the meanest soldiers or vandals that ever disgraced the flag they served or arms they bore.

I stood on my porch one night and counted thirteen fires around the suburbs of the city, all charged to these soldiers. I paid $20 a night for a detail of two soldiers to guard my residence and protect it from incendiarism for three weeks, but made the arrangement with a subordinate in the army holding a captain's commission, and paid him directly. When these guards slept they occupied my parlor, and were fed with the best my table afforded. They appreciated the kindness, and treated my family with becoming courtesy, and had the emergency called for it I believe would have come fully up to the standard of true soldiers.

I PROMISED TO STOP THE BATTLE.

MRS. WALLACE, the sister-in-law of Major General Wallace, a kind hearted widow lady, and her daughter, occupied a residence adjoining mine. I knew that the naval battle was going to take place the morning it occurred, and was standing with my wife on my porch early that morning with Mrs.

Wallace and daughter, looking for the smoke from the Confederate fleet as an indication as to when the conflict would commence. The black smoke arose about sunrise, and I hurried down to the river front to witness the imposing spectacle. As I opened my gate Mrs. Wallace called to me and said: "Mr. Hallum, please hurry down there and stop it before somebody gets hurt." "Yes, madam, that is just what I am going down there for, but I expect it will take me an hour to do it."

Commodore Montgomery steamed up with his wooden fleet, just above the mouth of Wolf river, and opened fire on the ironclads, but I describe this battle in another connection.

THE SHOOTING OF A FEDERAL LIEUTENANT BY JOHN FORREST.

A FEW DAYS after the city was taken, a lieutenant on one of the Federal gunboats, anchored in front of the city, and John Forrest, a cripple, brother to General Bedford Forrest, of the Confederate army got on a "lark," and Forrest shot the lieutenant through the chest, under circumstances wholly unjustifiable. Forrest was taken on board of one of the gunboats, chained flat of his back over the boilers, sweated with exhaustive profusion as a punishment for the crime. His mother came to me in great distress, said she had been to many friends and places to obtain permission to go to the fleet and see her son, but without success, or even finding a citizen who would lend her aid, because they were afraid to incur any personal risk themselves. I readily assisted her, and had no trouble in procuring passes for both to the fleet, the only condition imposed was that I should hoist the United States flag on the craft employed in going to the fleet. I rendered this service to the mother often. The wound was of a very dangerous character,

and for some time the surgeons thought the lieutenant
would die, but he recovered, and as soon as he was out of
danger he petitioned the military authorities to discharge
Forrest, as both were intoxicated when the shot was
fired. This was noble and generous in the soldier, and
Forrest was released.

THE MOTHER OF GEN. BEDFORD FORREST.

THE mother of General Forrest was a lady of iron
nerve. She lived out near where the National
Cemetery has since been located, six miles from
the city. Some Federal soldiers went to her residence once, and very much displeased and angered the old
lady. She was justly proud of Bedford, as she called
her son, the General. He was disparagingly spoken of
by one of the soldiers. She rushed up to him with
clenched fist, rubbed it on the nose of the soldier, and
said, "Smell that, its the best secesh flesh you ever smelt.
If you ever face Bedford in battle you will bite the dust."
It was my fortune and pleasure to be of some service to
the noble old mother during the war period, as well as to
be of counsel to the General when he was indicted for
treason, but of this in another connection.

I never knew the General's father, but the doctrine of
maternal heredity was vindicated in him.

LIEUT. YATES, OF THE FEDERAL CAVALRY.

A NOVEL WAY TO COLLECT DEBTS.

LIEUT. YATES, brother to "the War Governor of Illinois," and presumably for that reason was tolerated in immunities and delinquencies not accorded to all in the field. He was as good a man as Tom Ochiltree or Beau Brummel, and admired the agricultural productions of the Rhine and Moselle, encouraged their importation and consumption, and did not believe that the saber and "hardtack" should always supercede these refinements. He believed that peace as well as war has its conquests, and "there is a time for all things." Col. Hatch, the head of his cavalry regiment, was cast in a different mold; with radical ideas in an opposite direction. He arrogated more importance than all the generals of the army. In fact he was the "dude" of the army, the "Captain Jenks of the Horse Marines;" but with all that, a brave soldier. With Lord Raglan's eye on him, he would have led the charge of "the Six Hundred" at Balaklava. His signature to the payroll was necessary, and for that purpose I went to his headquarters, in the woods near Germantown, and found as much charming ceremony connected with my retarded approach through three stratas of pickets as courtiers of low degree find in getting to the inner courts of an oriental prince. When I came to the outer guards of the court, my card was sent in by a detachment of three videttes, and I sat down on a log where I rested and recruited my strength and patience for half an hour, awaiting response from the woodland mogul. When they returned, it was simply to inform me that there was an informality in the address, and that my application would be considered after the correction. Another lesson of patience was administered. Three relays of orderlies finally deposited me some rods from the door of the inner court. His lordship in full uniform appeared at the door and gave me a military *salaam*, which I judged an improvement on the oriental article. I bowed in reverential awe, so low that my body was a parallellogram to the earth. An orderly in uniform passed up to his highness Lieut. Yates' payroll, and he put his august John Hancock to it, and I passed back and out of the same hole I went in.

The colonel and other officers of the regiment "set down on" Yates and punished him for more than a year by refusing to sign his payroll until the back pay due him amounted to $2,250. Yates had passed beyond the Ochiltree standard, and had reached the end of the Brummel precedents, when he came to me and offered to sell his claim for back pay for $1,125 cash, one half its face value. He was a gentleman of fine address and polish. I was much surprised—had never known or heard of such a case in all my experience with the army. Many thousand payrolls had been probated before me. Yates could not explain the difficulty any farther than to say that his captain and colonel had refused to sign the payroll. Why, he could not explain. His captain was in the city, and I sent for him immediately; and while the messenger was gone after him, I stepped around to the paymaster's office and ascertained that the amount due was correctly stated, and that he would be paid on presentation of the payroll properly signed and authenticated. When I returned to my office I found the captain there, and requested Yates to retire to the adjoining room while I conferred with the captain. The difficulty was solved in a moment. The captain had loaned him $150 early in the service, others had advanced him money, the liquidation of which had long been neglected. I paid these bills on the spot, went to the paymaster's office and had him make out the payroll, and Yates and the captain sign it, drove down to the depot, took the train for Germantown, secured the colonel's signature, and collected the money that day and kept $1,125 for my services. Here I may as well confess that I would not have charged a Confederate soldier anything more than actual expenses. Why? I was of the South; the enemy was in my country.

I was devoting a very large per centage of my income for the relief of my people. My life was at stake all the time. I took a thousand chances. As before stated, I devoted in a period of six months $65,000 of my earnings to the people of the South, both civilians and soldiers. I bought the oath of allegiance from Moses for a consideration, $500 in market overt, with a sub rosa awning. I had it to do or leave penniless, sick, and without a change of clothing for self or family. "To be or not to be" was the emergency, and I worked "to be" instead of "not to be." I played "Yankee Doodle" with the "doodle" left out, and paid the cash stipend demanded by the enemy for the right to do it. Load your blunderbuss, ye moralists, and shoot, and tell me whether the Savior was right or wrong when he advised tribute to be paid to Cæsar, the conqueror of Israel! Tell me how many would have played "not to be," and when you say all the world thus circumstanced ought to have played it, then tell me how many will believe, how many would have acted on it. Poor, whole-souled Yates. He lived but a few months after that. He went home on a furlough, and died a natural death.

THE NAVAL BATTLE IN FRONT OF MEM-
PHIS, JUNE 6, 1863.

ISLAND NO. 10 was taken by the Federals on the 7th of April, 1863, after a heavy bombardment by the ironclad fleet. Fort Pillow was soon evacuated, and it was evident that the occupation of Memphis could not long be retarded. Commodore Montgomery, of the Confederate navy, commanded a very inferior fleet of wooden vessels, the best being a gulf steamer with iron rails to protect the boilers in front: the next best was an old tugboat for, and used for piloting vessels to and from New Orleans; the remainder, old and inferior Mississippi steamers—I think six vessels in all. This burlesque on a war fleet lay anchored around President's Island for some weeks in the latter part of May, 1863. The formidable ironclad fleet of the Federal navy anchored above the city at Island 40. The smoke from this fleet could be seen at all times from the city. It had up steam and was ready for action at all times. The two fleets were about fifteen miles apart, the city being between them. On the 2d of June one of the ironclads advanced to " Paddy's Hen and Chickens," a collection of islands so named, and anchored in view of the city. On the evening of the fifth, Commodore Montgomery told a few friends that he would attack the Federal fleet next morning.

At sunrise on the sixth he moved his fleet up to a position about one mile above the upper limits of the city. The Federal fleet advanced to meet the enemy. The first fire being from the Confederates. I witnessed the engagement from the first to the last shot. After the first few shots, the Confederate fleet began slowly dropping down the river, the Federal advancing and firing all the time with accurate aim and destructive effect. Two small propellers, or dispatch boats, moved rapidly from the flag ship of the Federal fleet to the vessels engaged. One of the Confederate boats with sharpshooters moved up in gallant style to a position opposite the mouth of Wolf river, and within twenty rods of the advanced iron-clads, and fired volley after volley, killing but one man, however. The combat was too unequal to last more than thirty minutes. The Confederate soon sank near the Arkansas shore, and in a few minutes after another Confederate vessel sank almost touching the Arkansas shore. While this was going on, the Gulf steamer, the largest of the Confederate fleet, was disabled, and became unmanageable, and floated with broadside to the enemy, prow facing the Tennessee shore. It soon careened, turning toward the South. The white flag was hoisted, but firing on this vessel by the Federals did not cease until she sank beneath the flood in that deep water opposite Jackson Mound. My recollection is that five vessels were sunk in this engagement. The only one to escape was the smallest vessel in the fleet. Canon balls would strike the ironclads and glance off without doing any injury whatever. Both combatants fought with equal courage, but a more unequal contest could scarcely be conceived.

I was amused at one conspicuous figure on the bluff where the postoffice now stands. I knew the gentleman well, had heard him discourse eloquently about being able to capture the ironclads with "half a dozen skiffs and twenty men armed with cutlasses." From his heroic converse, I judged him to be as innocent of war as a fairy would be in charging a battery. He sat on a splendid charger, with French cockade hat and red plume, with sash and sword and gloves, showy, attractive and tidy, holsters and pistols in front. No general on dress parade ever showed to better advantage. His former magniloquent flirtation with war, artistic puff of the Havana, and exquisite twirl of the wineglass until the vintage passed the upper valves, to awaken melodramatic functions, presented a striking contrast to the awful solemnity of the other extreme which now decorated the visage of Brig.-Gen. M. Jeff Thompson. How easy circumstances control us; with what facility we pass from one extreme of the arc to the other, from joy to gravity. In the midst of the naval engagement, the tragedy on the river and the comedy on the bluff, equal entertainment was furnished. The difference between theory and practice was illustrated. When the firing ceased and the tragedy was closed, Gen. Thompson reminded his charger with vigorous touch of spur that the next objective point lay in the direction of Hernando, and so they passed out at the south end of Shelby street.

That was the last time I ever met the General. He was a brave soldier, and loved war for the sport that was in it. Vivacity, loquacity, chivalry, judgment, and courage were singularly blended in the General. He was entertaining, charming, loved, and enjoyed the sunny phases of life, and let it be said, no one ever had occasion to question his courage. Since writing the above I was told by Wm. M. Ransom, of Memphis, a highly respectible gentleman, that Jeff joined Gov. Womick and his negro henchmen in the hour of his country's distress, and I presume with skiffs and cutlasses.

THOMAS J. TURLEY.

URLEY came from Virginia as early as 1835, when quite a young man. He was of pleasing and commanding address, and of untiring application, methodical, logical, able, he soon wrought his way to the front. I never saw him but once—that in 1842, when he was canvassing for the legislature with Tom

Avery; young as I was, the personnel of the man was vividly photographed on my mind.   I do not know that he was a better man than his distinguished son, Thomas B. of the firm of Wright & Turley, but he was certainly a much handsomer man.

He died comparatively young, and left a handsome estate.   The people of the South were generous to poor, young men of merit.   It has often been said in the Northern press, and the idea has been stereotyped, that the slave oligarchy arrogated to itself a superior *caste* destructive to genius and men of limited means, not within that so-called exclusive class, but the assertion is utterly without foundation.   The Southern people were always great admirers of talent and oratory, and a more generous people in that respect have never contributed a page of renown or chapter to the history of the world.

They encouraged and lifted up such young men from the North as readily as those "to the manor born."

Sargent S. Prentiss, from Maine, was as much, yea, at one time, more admired than Jefferson Davis; they lived in the same county in Mississippi, opposed each other in a memorable contest for the legislature, and Prentiss was elected.

The same may be said of Pike and Adams, and thousands of others.   True, the Southern slave owner was exclusive in that sense which led him to despise a mean and sordid nature, and to spurn as an object of contamination, all men devoted to stratagem and spoil, whether private or public.   But it is a slander on them to say they weighed slaves and plantations and bank balances in the scale against genius and the lofty aspirations of noble youth. Young men like Turley were received with open arms by the wealthiest and most cultured planters.

I was born and reared among these people in a humble, but honorable home, have associated with their sons and daughters all my life, and ought to be a competent witness in my old age. I say this in no spirit of disparagement to the great mass of Northern people, nor to people of any of the States composing the greatest aggregation of commonwealths the world has ever known. In the Northern people I see and admire a thousand heroic virtues.

He who looks on such a mighty historic painting and confines his little narrow contracted vision to one small spot or corner, either for exclusive criticism or praise, without drinking in the vast panoramic whole, is an incompetent, discreditable witness, a dwarfed pessimist, who ought to be confined to the nursery and his mother's apron strings and "stall-fed on the history of his ancestors" until he either expands into nobler ideas or dies. The little penny-a-liner of any section of this great country who educates the people to sectional prejudice is an enemy to his country, a blasphemer of his God, in whose soul and heart the dry rot cankers as the mould on the ruins of Babylon.

HON. JOHN R. FLIPPIN.

HENRY HULBURT was Collector of the Port of Memphis under Buchanan's administration, and that prince of good fellows, now known as the Hon. John R. Flippin, was in his office as Clerk to the Customs, and I think transacted nearly all of the business of that office. John's pinfeathers were then emerging freely from their virgin roots, and his mustache was hestitating between the fuz of the gosling and the bristles of the man, his eyeteeth had not been cut, but his gums were swelling. A better boy than John never lived, none ever had a higher sense of honor, and none was ever truer to honest convictions. He honored every post of honor conferred on him. That of Mayor of a great city at a critical period in her history, and as Judge on the Bench.

I often visited him when we were not aged, long before
the frost of so many winters began to settle on our heads,
and enjoyed his mirth and wit and luxuriant humor.   If
he were not with us yet, I might add much more, but I
hope he may enjoy the sunny side of life as long as the
Triumvirate of Gantt, Sneed and Looney.   He is the same
John yet, witty, tropically pleasant to his old friends, to
all as for that, and it is hard to determine whether his
pleasant ways or mental balance is the greater factor in
his make-up.   He is the author of "Scenes in Mexico," a
charming volume, overflowing with chaste ornate periods
and the most powerful word painting.   John embarked
in mining and spent some unprofitable years in Mexico.
With a convoy of Greasers and $5,000 in silver bullion he
felt disastrously complacent in the canyons and mountain
passes of Mexico, but was captured by the pestilential
bandit and robbed—glad to escape with life.

He wore the gray from commencement to finish during
the late unpleasantness, and was as brave a soldier as
ever rallied around the Bonnie Blue flag.

THE SEARCEY'S, JOHN, BENNETT, GEORGE.

RICHARD, the elder, and Granville D., belonged to
a very distinguished family, but had all passed
off the stage before my time.   I have not access
to the material necessary to present these men as
their worth and character deserve.

Richard was very prominent in the judicial and political history of Arkansas as early as 1820 to 1832.   In another volume I have given a sketch of his life.   One of
the counties and a prominent seat of learning in Arkansas
is named after him, and it is not likely that this name
will perish for many generations.

ED. BURKE PICKETT.

ED. BURKE PICKETT came from Carthage, Tenn., a genius, full of talent, competent to have attained a high position; versatile, humorous, liberal. But he did not have those staying qualities which lift men to prominence and sustain them. He quit law and tried geology and the marlbeds, then came back to his first love to again divorce himself from the law. His versatility and the readiness with which he quit one to pick up another pursuit was a great disadvantage; good in all, great in none.

One day, in 1877, at the St. James Hotel, in Denver, Col., some one slapped me on the shoulder in the rotunda—turning around with some surprise, Ed. Burke greeted me. I was then spending some months there in attendance on the Federal Court, and Ed. had come in out of the mountains to spend the winter. He was then mining with flattering prospects. Ed. was an assayist, too; could do almost anything.

From poor Ed. I received a twenty-page letter not long ago from St. Louis: "Blind, John; my eyes were burnt out by the blast of a smelter some years ago, and I am now sitting and waiting patiently the final summons." Poor Ed. I shed tears over that pathetic letter, written in pencil, in irregular lines as a blind man does. We roomed together four months at Denver. A charming conversationalist, a joy in the social circle, sunshine in head and heart and always entertaining; a great reader, science, literature, history—a standard and exemplar in morals.

JOHN C. LANIER.

JOHN C. LANIER, the old Clerk and Master in Chancery, was never a success at the Bar. But in that reservoir of business he was a distinguished success, financially, and was one of the best of Clerks. He built a marble palace on Union avenue, and because the accoustics did not tap the tympanum precisely as he desired, he tore it down and rebuilt it; and he carried the same ideas of precision through every department of his office. No fastidious old maid was ever more particular than John in arranging her toilet or boudoir. When he retired from the Chancery office, he went to banking, and soon became hopelessly involved in trying to float the old Gayso Savings institution, which was bankrupted when he took hold of it.

Once I presented a check for $750 to his bank, but did not count the package of money handed to me there until I went to my residence that night. It was labeled $750, but when I counted it I found $1,000. Next morning I called at the bank to correct the mistake by restoring the excess of $250, but he would not receive it, and said: "Were I to establish that precedent it would break the bank in thirty days." Some time after the bank broke, and he was financially distressed, I returned the money to him, though not under any obligation to do so, as I had lost $3,000 by the failure and insolvency of the bank, for which I never got one dollar in return.

AYRES AND LOONEY.

T. S. AYRES and James Looney were associated as partners. They were commercial lawyers, and had an immense practice when I was admitted; but some years after retired with fortunes as the fruit of their professional labors. Looney went back to Columbia, Tenn.—"the garden spot of the world," as he loved to call it.

He was of large and commanding physique, dignified as a prince, a brother to the gigantic and irrepressible Bob, who is never satisfied unless he can get off a mirth-provoking joke on his best friend. Bob yet flourishes among the last roses of summer, as one of the old guard. I wish I had an arrow to throw at him. Perhaps I ought to say he is a deserter from the rank and file. He laid down his license "to give the Court to be informed" many years ago, for a broader opening to his genius for speculation.

Like George Gautt in one respect, he bids defiance to the ravages of time. His furlough seems to be indefinitely extended.

Ayres was a cripple, one leg was nearly perished, but he boiled and bubbled and overflowed with the sunshine of life. He was mirth provoking, genial, social; his heart was always full of sunbeams; at the comical and ludicrous he would go into convulsions of laughter; wit, humor, repartee, polished, keen, incisive was always at his finger's end.

If any friend was downcast, he could, and would, lift him out of it quicker than any man I ever knew. He was as scrupulously neat in his dress as Chesterfield or Beau Brummel, and avoided the barroom and the weed.

PAT MALVIHILL.

PAT MALVIHILL in many respects was a deserving and remarkable man. A bright little waif from Ireland in the streets of Philadelphia, he attracted the attention of a wealthy gentleman from Ohio, who took and classically educated him at Oberlin College. He went to Mississippi and was teaching school when the war commenced. He was enthused with the cause of the South, and early entered the Confederate army as a private, and remained in it to the end. He resumed his school a short time, and came to Memphis with letters of introduction to me, and desired to enter my office as a student of law, but I had two young men on hand at the time and did not receive him.

He found a place in Dixon & Avrey's office, and was afterward admitted to the Bar in Memphis. It was not long until he had quite a patronage from his countrymen, and maintained himself well. He had a fight with Gen. Forrest, and I separated them, taking the General's firearms from him.

Pat spent a week in my office once examining authorities with a view of bringing a damage suit against a railroad. He paced the floor as restless as a lion in a cage, and never sat to read. After he had finished the examination, I asked him what he found to support his view, to which he replied: "Nothing but an &c. in a Kentucky case, and that a mere dictum; but I intend to sail in like h—l on the &c." He did so, and obtained a judgment. His power of analysis and acute discrimination were well developed, and his energies untiring, but he made one great mistake in going to the Legislature, where he lost energetic love for law.

LEVIN H. COE.

COE was a prominent and distinguished lawyer from 1840 to 1848–49; a leader of resolved and deter-termined purpose, marked individuality and un-questioned physical courage, which finally cost him his life, under circumstances with which I have never been familiar, and will not undertake to relate, lest injustice might be ignorantly inflicted. He had passed off before I came on the stage, and I only speak the voice of tradition.

The Bar of Memphis once had a vast storehouse of men and names whose fame and memory ought to be pre-served. Much of it has perished, more is vanishing, and so far as I know, this little volume contains the only ef-fort to preserve the little that is left, until some kind brother finds time to sift and cull from it, with other col-lections and additions, and put it in a more attractive and permanent form. If such a volume had been preserved from the first day Gen. Jackson, Gen. Winchester, John C. McLemore, and Judge John Overton who laid out the city in 1826, it would be of priceless value, at least in a local sense. I suggest, and hope that her fine Bar of to-day, so ably and splendidly equipped, will make this an object and give it due attention in the future.

HENRY B. S. WILLIAMS.

WILLIAMS was one of the fossils of the "Old Bar" when I came upon the stage, but lived many years after. As his own client, he furnished himself with a harvest of litigation, and devoted himself exclusively to his private affairs. He was a land lawyer, and grew wealthy out of the opportunities his superior energy and knowledge gave him.

He uprooted and tore up, root and branch, more land titles than any ten men in West Tennessee. The vacant lands of Tennessee were never ceded to the United States, except where Indian titles were extinguished.

At an early day there was a law known as the "Occupant Entry Law," giving to actual settlers on the public domain priority of right of purchase at a nominal sum. The Legislature for quite a series of years, at every successive session, extended the time of payment by the occupant entry settlers, and in 1842, if I mistake not the date, there was a *cassus omissus* or *hiatus* in this legislation and a failure to extend the time of payment. This, unexpectedly, left the settlers at the mercy of the wideawake speculators.

Williams took advantage of this, and located an immense quantity of lands, and grew fat and rich; but it brought him a harvest of denunciation and much litigation. An old planter once bargained for a farm, and the usual warranty of title against all the world was embraced in the deed. The old man listened at the lawyer who drafted the instrument read it. When asked if it was sufficient, "No, indeed," said the farmer, "Henry B. S. Williams' name is not in it. I don't want the land unless there is a special warranty against him," and it had to be so drawn before he would part with his cash.

I often laughed at him about this, but it was a dry subject with Henry. The first large suit, or rather suits, I ever brought involving large values, was for two tracts of very valuable land lying in the vicinage of Memphis, against Williams, "The heirs of Bayliss against H. B. S. Williams." He had been attorney for the heirs in a suit involving the title to these lands, and bought them for a song from the heirs whilst their attorney, and took a decree afterward sustaining the title of the heirs. The suit was brought to cancel the conveyance to Williams, on flagrant grounds every lawyer will recognize, and his deed was cancelled.

Outside of these land transactions, he was hospitable, genial, and eminently social. He was always very sensitive over the reputation these land matters brought him, and in later life reformed in this, and died in a good, green old age with a large circle of friends to mourn his loss.

W. P. WILSON.

GLANCING again down the Roster of "The Old Guard," my eye falls on the name of Billy Wilson, and I have to pause and laugh and collect myself. If he was not yet in the active arena of old men, I could take some of the old boys, Judge Flippin, Bob Looney, or George Gantt, on a promenade around court square and tell much on Billy when he was young, punctilious with a Chesterfield carriage, and "felt his oats." I could commence by pointing to a dry goods store where Mr. Pope hung out his sign as dry goods merchant in the days of "Auld Lang Syne." In the run of business a claim against Pope was sent to Billy for collection, and he presented it. Pope said:

"Call again to-morrow, and I will pay it." And when next day came, he again said: "Call again to-morrow, and I will pay it." This was bordering on monotony, but Billy, though not feeling pleasant, retired and went again the next day, and Pope again said: "Call again to-morrow." This was trifling with the energetic lawyer beyond endurance, and he lowered the record by proceeding a few seconds in advance of forthwith to wipe the earth with Mr. Pope. He knocked him down, and when he got up, knocked him down again; and when he arose, Billy said: "I am calling again, and will continue the calls until you hand out the cash;" and Pope said: "Don't call anymore. I will pay it now," and did so.

After that no debtor ever asked Billy to "call again." It was understood that the term had acquired a potential significance. No frivolous excuses counted; if any existed, they had to be solid. Billy was famous for strict adherence to fixed principles, sturdy habits, and fidelity to clients.

Lest a wrong impression, I must add that Brother Wilson, since working off the effervescence of youth, has lived a strict Christian life, has ever been one of the best of citizens and men, was a brave Confederate soldier, and lost an arm in the terrible carnage in front of Atlanta. No truer man to clients ever fought their battles, and his name is an honor to the Roster.

J. E. R. RAY.

RAY was the law partner of Gov. Harris before that gentleman became the Chief Executive. He became Secretary of State under Gov. Harris. In physique he was rather tall and quite slender. He had a winning smile and pleasing address and was the charm of the social circle. I never heard either him or Gov. Harris in any case requiring depth of thought and elaboration before the courts. Harris was too much absorbed in politics to become distinguished at the Bar, though unquestionably an able man and profoundly earnest in all he undertook.

Law is a great stepping stone to politics, but when a lawyer abandons his office for political preferment for any considerable length of time, he rarely, if ever, gets back and wins either patronage or distinction at the Bar, many attempt it and fail. The lawyer who expects to win and retain prominence at the Bar ought to eschew every other pursuit.

D. M. LEATHERMAN.

D. M. LEATHERMAN was a wealthy bachelor and had abandoned the practice before my admission, and I was never able to form an accurate estimate of his legal attainments.

He came to my office once and asked my candid opinion of his aspiration for the Supreme Bench. He had been out of practice so long I was surprised and suggested that he would find it difficult to write an opinion coming up to the required standard, to which he replied that he could hire a clerk to do that, as though I referred to the mechanical execution of the penman.

I never heard any more of his aspiration for that office.

JUDGE S. VENABLE.

JUDGE VENABLE was advanced in years when he came to Memphis; did not succeed well during the eight or ten years he stayed with us. At the close of the war he moved to San Francisco.

HENRY D. SMALL.

HENRY D. SMALL was a native of Tipton county, Tenn. He was a good and faithful lawyer, a liberal-minded and high-toned gentleman of the old school, and was universally honored and respected —he was many years my senior. We last met when the civil war was bursting on the country with so many tragic farewells.

JAMES LAMB.

JAMES LAMB was a handsome man, well equipped in law, literature and the sciences; a Chesterfield, he had no fault to find with the world, and took every phase of life from the standpoint of a philosopher. He married a wealthy heiress at Winchester, Tenn., and abandoned the guild and the city.

JUDGES COULTER AND STUART.

IF Dickens had lived in western Arkansas, "near the Choctaw line," his creative genius would have been dead capital in a market where the realistic defies creative production. "Overproduction" of the natural and real would have driven the manufactured article out of market.

James Coulter, a Mississippian by birth, an Arkansan by adoption, came to the western border of Arkansas during the last years of territorial pupilage. Although a farmer by occupation, he had a commercial eye—a keen

(210)

relish for goods and chattels, and accumulated flocks, herds, and a baronial domain in the course of time.

He commanded the suffrage of his township, and was elected a justice of the peace, and by courtesy, yet common in Arkansas, was knighted "Judge." Inordinate acquisitiveness, many rare combinations of character, quaint and unique, marked him for local fame. The smallest and most trifling detail connected with the family history of all his acquaintances failed to escape his attention and memory. It was simply a matter of conjecture and wonder as to how he acquired such a vast storehouse of domestic knowledge, not one thread of which was ever broken or lost. He knew the names of every horse, cow, ox, dog, cat, and child, for fifty miles around, and the peculiar traits and habits of each, and as age advanced was delighted to find an auditor to hear him through with patience.

He was under contract of marriage in Mississippi before he left the State, but three days before the banns were to be celebrated the lady declined to proceed further, on the ground that she did not wish to bury her life in the wilds of Arkansas, and raise a family of children where there were no churches and schools.

He knew the Stuarts in Mississippi better than any one in that family, one of whom, born a short time after he left the State, moved to western Arkansas, and in time became Circuit Judge in the person of Hon. H. B. Stuart. Coulter had a number of important cases before him and was anxious to cultivate the good graces of the trial judge, and sought the kind offices of the Hon. Joe D. Conway to make the opportunity. Conway himself has a largely developed leaning to the comical and farsical phases of life, and when he tries can make a government mule laugh.

Court was in session at Center Point, in Howard county, and the opportunity occurred at the noon recess, in the parlor of the hotel. On the way from court to the hotel Conway said to Judge Stuart: "I will bet you one hundred dollars to ten that Coulter knows more about your own and your family history than you do." "Impossible," said the Judge, "because I never met or heard of Coulter before I came to Arkansas." "Very well," said Conway, "then you take the bet." "No, it don't become a Judge to bet with the officers of his court, and if it did, it would be betting on a certainty, and would violate the rules of respectable gambling."

Seated in the parlor, Coulter opened the ball.

"Judge, I knew your father and mother and your brothers, John and Bill, and sisters, Susan and Hannah. I remember well the oxen, Buck and Darb. Darb had but one horn, and Buck had but one eye. Buck was the off steer, and walked off the bridge and carried the wagon and Darb and your father into the bayou, and came near drowning him—lost the sugar and coffee and flour. Bad day that for your father. He was young and unmarried then, but I'll get to that after a while."

"I remember old Towser, your father's coon dog, with bobtail, and ears chewed off by the coons; he was a good one, I tell you, and coons were scarce where Towser ranged, and he would take a hand in a bear fight until he got too old to bite. When he died your father buried him in a coffin, and made his shroud of coonskins. And well do I remember your father's old brindle Thomas cat, he had lost an eye, too—as brave a cat as ever tackled a varmint. What became of your brothers, John and Bill, and did your sisters, Sue and Hannah, do well when they married? Sue was a beauty, and Hannah was a daisy. How many children did they have, and what are their names? And where did they settle, and did all of them get an education, and were their husbands kind to them?"

Without waiting for answers the loquacious Solomon ran on at a two-forty gait, while the hallway and room were being filled with eager auditors. "By the way,

Judge, did you know that your mother and I were engaged to be married—how well do I remember her. She rode a nick-tail gray mare to church—she pranced and cantered, the plume in your mother's hat waved and waved, and bobbed up and down, and old gray's nicked tail pointed upward, and then to the east and then to the west, and I was the proudest gallant you ever saw. Our engagement continued until three days of the time set for the parson to join us.

"Your mother broke off the engagement because she did not want to come to Arkansas. You see, Judge, that I came in three days of being your father."

The dinner gong rang and broke up the seance. Judge A. B. Williams, and Judge Rufus D. Hearne, were present, both of whom were afterwards judges of the same court. They did not adjourn to the diningroom, but to the lawn, where they rolled in the grass.

This was Conway's opportunity, he wanted to continue one of Coulter's important cases, and moved the court next day for a continuance on the obvious ground of the Judge's disqualification, being related to the suitor by the closest ties of affinity in a degree equally near as the closest relations of consanguinity.

The Judge was puzzled, and held up the motion for advisement until the next term. Mississippi is to be congratulated for her many valuable contributions to her sister commonwealth.

Among the many slaves Coulter owned prior to the emancipation was Scipio, who remained in the vicinage of his former master, a warm and devoted friend. Scipio was a thrifty farmer, and saved up eight thousand dollars to buy a farm.

One bright Sabbath morning Coulter visited Scipio, who was much flattered with this kind attention from his old master. Money, and the dangers to which it subjected those who were known to hoard it up in their houses, soon came in for discussion, and an artful alarm was soon planted in Scipio's mind and that of his aged wife, and he asked his old master to become the custodian of the treasure until he could invest it.

"Ah, no, Scipio, while I could do almost anything in the range of reasonable demand to serve you, I could not risk my own life to become your banker, it would but shift the danger from Scipio to James. These are terrible times, good men have been robbed and murdered for one hundred dollars; eight thousand, Scipio, would bring down half the murderers in the Indian Territory on me, and my life would not be worth a penny. I am sorry for you, it is often so much better to be poor than to be rich, poverty is protection, money breeds danger in every direction." The white of old Scipio's eyes rolled, his imagination depicted the robbers in sight, his aged wife was equally moved, and both joined in fervent supplication to "Mars James" to take the money and keep it. Scipio took out his old jackknife, ripped open the bed, and drew forth the treasure and laid it in "Mars James'" lap.

"You are a white man, and the robbers will fear to break in on you, but old nigger Scipio would give up de ghost wid de money." Mars James relented, and assured them that if they would not hold him responsible for the money, in the event of robbery, he would risk his life for them.

Several years passed, and Scipio wanted either his farm or the money but was too modest to mention his desires to his old master; an agony of suspense did not overcome this diffidence. But finally he ventured into a lawyer's office, in Locksburg, and unbosomed himself. The lawyer advised suit immediately as the only means to compel an accounting, and told Scipio that if he spoke to Coulter about it before he brought suit he would fall before his melodious tongue and loose his treasure. But Scipio would not agree to that; he had never mentioned his desire to his old master, and begged to give him just one chance anyway before action.

The lawyer then said, "Scipio, you will never bring
that suit—you will never come to this office unless you
live longer than your old master." Scipio cultivated his
nerves for courage to approach the trustee, and sat up all
night talking with his good old wife, who had followed
him with the plow and hoe and cotton basket, through
rain and storm and all the changing seasons for fifty years. Finally, after many of these domestic conventions, before a flickering faggot of wood in the fire-
place, it was determined that Scipio should approach him
on the next Sabbath morning, while the old master was
softened under divine influence.

The old gentleman, from some cause or source never
known, anticipated the business mission of his ex-slave,
and was prepared to satisfy or at least quiet the desire
and fears of Scipio.

The aged creditor, and his wife, Dinah, in their best
garb, were invited into the parlor, where the ex-master
and his aged consort, Sarah, sat, one with the Holy Bible,
the other with hymn book in hand. Two chapters from
Revelations were read, then the good old Methodist hymn
that stirs the foundations of the Christian's hope, "I
would not live alway," was sang by those two old
mothers in Israel with sweet, mellow, trembling voice,
that ran over and thrilled and trilled every nerve.

Scipio led in prayer, filled with humility of inspiration,
devoid of learning, but full of that Christian pathos
which lies at the foundation of inspired religion. The
god of mammon, and the God of Abraham and Isaac and
Jacob, father of the gentle Nazarine, were there united
in the same ceremonies.

Who can doubt, when the angelic hosts come through
the clouds, led by the martyr of calvary in the morn of
resurrection, the judgment when master and slave face
the throne?

When the sincere devotion of one, and the pious
mockery of the other, were ended, the aged women were

left, and the aged consorts walked out on the lawn, where the birds in wild coral were greeting the spring, thence through field and meadow to the family burial ground, talking of the "vanity of human wishes, and the penalty inflicted on Ananias and Sapphira, and of the chastisement of the moneychangers in the temple by the Savior. At last they reached the spot chosen by the master for the sepulchre of himself and wife. "Here, my dear Scipio, soon shall rest all that is mortal of your old master and his wife. I want you and Dinah to attend the funerals, and softly lay the clay over us, and plant a shrub here and a flower there, and when the springtime comes you come and sit on one grave, and Dinah on the other, and sing that good old hymn, 'I would not live alway.' Trouble yourself not about this world's goods, the thought of such matters ruins your soul."

Scipio burst into a flood of tears; he would not have mentioned the eight thousand dollars for all the world, and died without calling for it.

A ROLAND FOR AN OLIVER.

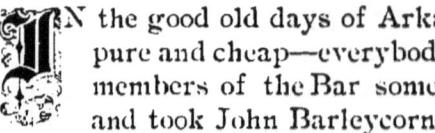 N the good old days of Arkansas, when whisky was pure and cheap—everybody had plenty of money—members of the Bar sometimes "unbent the bow" and took John Barleycorn into their confidence.

Robert L. Carigan and Gen. Grandisen D. Royston, eminent lawyers living at Washington, in the grand old county of Hempstead, never let up when they could get a good joke on a friend.

Hon. John R. Eakin, one of the ablest and most scholarly jurists who ever adorned the Supreme Bench of Arkansas, and Judge A. B. Williams, another very able lawyer and jurist, lived in the same town. Gen. Royston weighed two and a half hundred. He came from

Carter county, Tenn., in 1832; was president of one of the Constitutional Conventions, often in her legislative councils, and a prominent factor in the history of the State, as well as Judge Eakin, who came from Shelby-ville, Tenn.

All of them were eminent in the history of the State. Gen. Royston had an eye to business, and grew wealthy. His domain included Royston's Springs, in Pike county, where this quartette of brothers often repaired, like High-land chiefs, to recreate and enthuse the inner man. Car-rigan was a noted criminal lawyer, and had a client liv-ing near the springs who was always breveted on the Criminal Register of the court for promotion to honors he did not much like, and for ample cash fees Carigan saved him often—in fact, these oft-repeated acquittals got to be monotonous with the people of Pike, and to save any further trouble or expense to the State, they swung the fat client to a pine tree, there being no "sour apple tree" in the vicinity of the Springs.

A barbecued pig, roast turkey, boiled ham, and all that the culinary art and good larders could provide; negroes, teams and carriages, with the best and strongest of Bur-gundy and the Rhine vintage was provided by these gen-tlemen for an outing at the Springs, and to the favorite resort they repaired.

"Kings may be blessed, but they were glorious ;
O'er a' the ills of life, victorious."

Carigan wanted to see, must see, the tree from which his client departed this life for the good of the common-wealth, and all had to go with him to the hangman's tree. He was mellow, and grew eloquent and indignant by turns. He pronounced a panegyric over the lost, then poured out vials of wrath on the wretches who hastened his departure to the spirit world, then he became pathet-ic, and all stood with heads uncovered for some time. The tobacco juice unconsciously creeping down the fur-rowed rivulets of Royston's mouth. But he could not

14

hold in or bear up long, and all the attendants at this
sylvan funeral in the virgin wilds, except the funeral orator, burst, exploded, rolled over on the wild lawn, and
roared.

When Carigan's mind cleared up, he begged, implored,
pressed all hands to say nothing about it, and Judges
Eakin and Williams promised if he could induce Gen.
Royston to let up, to be silent; but the General was obdurate, wanted to even up old scores, and would not
promise.

The outing came to an end in eight or ten days, and
all started home—Gen. Royston and Carigan in the same
conveyance. After they had proceeded several miles,
Royston complained of the insects which had fastened
themselves all over his body from the crown of his head
to the soles of his feet, and proposed near a turn in the
road to stop until he stripped *cap a pie* even to his hoes
and shoes, so he could get rid of the insects, large and
small, which were tormenting him. The carriage
stopped, he dismounted, and weighed two and one half
net. The woods had been burnt off, leaving the undergrowth with only its outer branches burnt off, and it was
three hundred yards to a forest tree large enough to hide
one half of the General's rotund person, a contingency he
had neither thought of nor provided for. As soon as
he became engrossed in the business in hand, Carigan
drove up a few paces, and with a clear, pleasing voice
greeted several well-known ladies with a hearty salutation, and asked if they were going to the Springs, and informed them that he and Gen. Royston were just returning from a pleasant sojourn there.

The General was always a modest and gallant gentleman in the presence of ladies. He was horrified, picked
up his clothes, and started west through the burnt woods
like a fat quarter horse, and when his wind failed him,
squatted behind a pine tree, which only protected a part
of his person. Stooping low he peeped out toward the

road and carriage for ten minutes, saw no one but Carigan; then he realized that he had been badly sold, that Carigan had not seen any ladies.

His baywindow was badly torn up, blood was there. Slowly he came back, picking up a garment here and there, his body bloody and black. When he got to the carriage he told Carigan that it was beastly and shameful to treat an old man that way, and that he must fight regardless of consequences. By this time Judges Eakin and Williams drove up and patched up a truce, the terms of which were, they were to regard jokes as even for six months; but the little village of Washington soon had it all, and to this day the ancient "Athens of the State" has many a story around which a Scott or Hugo could weave a web of thrilling interest. Law is not always a dry subject.

WILLIAM CARR.

WILLIAM CARR was a native of Sumner county, Tenn., was enrolled in 1852; a brilliant, generous, erratic genius, with talents enough to have lifted him to exalted positions had he been true to himself. He was postmaster to the House of Representatives during Pierce's administration, and in Washington acquired habits which he could not afterward master. He married a very beautiful and refined lady, the daughter of a wealthy iron merchant of Pittsburg, and died in the meridian of his life.

His mother made a will leaving me her fortune, but when she told me what she had done I positively declined to accept the bequest and cut her two grandsons by William out, she became offended and never forgave me. The boys were splendid specimens of youth, their father was my warm friend. To take advantage of his misfortune and cut his children out of their just inheritance would have been scarcely less than legalized robbery in my estimation. The idea was abhorrent from every standpoint from which manhood could view it.

CAPT. CHARLEY TROUSDALE.

CHARLEY TROUSDALE, the son of Gov. Trousdale, was a prince, handsome as Adonis, with a smile peculiarly winning and attractive, a gallant knight with the grace of a Chesterfield, moral, and a perfect gentleman in the highest sense of the term. When the bugle sounded, he answered to roll-call, lost a leg in battle, married the wealthiest heiress in old Sumner, our native heath, and then deserted Blackstone.

JERE CLEMENTS.

EX-UNITED STATES Senator from Alabama, located in Memphis in 1858-9, in an office at the corner of Madison and Main streets, up the same flight of steps where my office was at that time. I saw much of him. His reputation as an orator was national. He was one of the most entertaining conversationalists I ever heard, and delighted to have an attentive listener, but he had been in politics so long he lost all taste for the law—the fate of two many lawyers who dabble in politics. He had written a novel just before coming to Memphis which struck the American public like " Childe Harold," and " The Lay of the Last Minstrel " did the English public. It was founded on southwestern life, and was entitled "Bernard Lyle." Many passages in it were of touching and exquisite beauty.

When the stirring events were transpiring which led up to the civil war, he left Memphis without having established a practice.

JUDGE HOWEL E. JACKSON.

JUDGE JACKSON often said to me, when young, that the acme of his hope and ambition was to sit on the Supreme Bench of Tennessee, a position he would have so eminently adorned, but by a combination in both State and National politics he was defeated before the convention for Justice of the Supreme Court of Tennessee, afterwards elected to the national Senate and then nominated by a Republican President for the Supreme Bench of the United States and confirmed. What strange junctures and combinations we meet in life.

Jackson was never a politician, had no taste for, made no effort in that direction. The bonded debt of Tennessee became a political issue on which parties divided. Many of the politicians were innocent of the legal relations the people sustained to these bonds, but they hooted assumed wisdom from the hustings as eagerly as an owl hoots his voice through the wilderness of night. Jackson had profoundly grasped the questions from the standpoint of an able lawyer. Listening to these political sages at Jackson, Tenn., where he then resided, he said to a friend: "The people ought to understand this bonded debt." This friend called him to the rostrum, and his explanation was so full, clear, complete, and exhaustive, that the Democrats forced him to run for the legislature, against his will, and elected him. There another rare juncture confronted that body, charged with the election of a Sen-

ator, and the swelling tide of fortune gave that prize to.
Jackson. All these things had their vital germ in that
explanation of the bonded debt. Without that speech,
in all probability, Jackson would never have been other
than an ornament, an example to private life. He merits
all these honors, and his old friends at the Bar rejoice at
his elevation because so well merited. It can truly be
said that the "Snollygoster in Politics" innocently
opened up the way to Judge Jackson's rapid promotion,
and for once performed a good service.

HENRY CRAFT, AND J. W. CLAPP.

HENRY CRAFT and J. W. Clapp came in the
early fifties from Holly Springs, Miss., and
brought with them from that classic suburb of
Memphis established reputations as able lawyers,
a fame which both sustained at one of the ablest Bars the
South could boast. They were men of eminent worth.

JUDGE B. M. ESTES.

JUDGE ESTES, when young, gave promise of
the fine lawyer and able jurist which have so
beautifully crowned a well spent life. He is
yet spared, and looks as young as he did twenty
years ago. He was tidy in dress, scrupulously courteous,
and painstaking in the preparation and argument of his
cases, and always had authorities on pivotal points.

JOHN P. HARLOW.

JOHN P. HARLOW, of whom mention has already been made, was in some respects a remarkable man, quick, sagacious, energetic, and a fine judge of men, a powerful factor in the career of a lawyer. A Russian, by the name of DeBar, had loaned a few hundred dollars to John Anderson, a prodigal spendthrift who had come into an inheritance worth $100,000. The shylook was nursing him with wine, to rob him ultimately' and sent for Harlow to draft a deed conveying a large amount of real estate from his victim to himself. Harlow took in the situation in a moment and wrote the deed. It was duly acknowledged, and put away by DeBar in his safe without being read over. The description of land conveyed was as follows: "Beginning at a stake in the northeast corner of hell, thence a thousand miles to another stake on the western line, thence nine hundred miles to Pluto's peachorchard, thence, with all the meanderings of a beautiful water course, to the beginning."

Harlow took Anderson to Mrs. Jennings, the wife of Captain Jennings, his sister, and thus rescued the victim. DeBar read over the deed the next day, and his agitation knew no bounds. He sent for Judge King, but there was no balm in Gilead.

Harlow took the gold fever in 1859, and went to Utah; thence to the mines in South America. Coming back to Utah he opened up valuable mines, and became wealthy. In 1876 we corresponded, since then I have not heard of him. A gamer bird than John never crowed in a barnyard; he could smile at his adversary or puff a Havana when placed in position on the duelling field.

DAVID M. CURRAN—"LITTLE RED."

CURRAN'S ancestry came in Ireland's pilgrim tide that has carried the name and fame of Erin and maintained her genius and heritage of renown and valor wherever letters are known and courage admired. His father was a near relative of one of the most gifted brains and eloquent tongues Ireland ever gave the world, John Philpot Curran. This pilgrim settled in Kentucky, where his son David was born, and grew to man's estate. At the same time a brother of this immigrant settled at Batesville, Ark., where his son, James M. Curran, was born, and became a very able and distinguished lawyer.

In the memorable campaign of 1844, Curran took a distinguished part as a Democratic orator, and met and curbed the overbearing Graves, who had killed Cilley in a duel. After this he came to Memphis where he practiced law till he died, a short time before the commencement of the civil war. I knew him well. He was my counsel in 1853, and successfully defended me when tried in the Circuit Court for getting in the second shot at Rogers, he having got the first and some leg bail, the details of which appear in another chapter.

Curran was a very able and distinguished lawyer, a man of lofty and heroic purpose. He was small of stature, stoopshouldered, and leaned forward and to the left in walking; his hair was red, from which he was known far and wide as "Little Red." He had a large and lucrative practice, but died in the meridian of life and splendid fame.

R. G. PAYNE.

HEN Payne came to Memphis, in 1856, from Columbia, Tenn., he was in the meridian of manhood and local fame as a jury lawyer. He cared nothing for, and was poorly equipped for arguing cold questions of law before a Chancellor or the Supreme Court. Before these tribunals he had many superiors; but give him a case turning on facts, I care not how complicated and conflicting, there he was master, a giant in the pathway of any adversary. The irony of Juvenal, the satire of Cervantes, the consuming fire of Dante, were all marshalled and hurled like an avalanche tearing down the Alps. Sometimes he was astonishingly ludicrous, but always effective.

Once, in one of his grand climaxes, he seized a bull whip, jumped on the table, and whirled and twirled and cracked the whip over his head to illustrate the manner in which his old farmer client had suffered at the hands of the prosecutor before taking the *lex talionis* in his own hands. Unusual, startling, without a parallel or precedent in a court room, yet it was very effective in lodging a feeling of indignation in the minds of the jury against the overbearing and tyranical prosecutor. That one moment's time fixed a verdict of "Not guilty," and stereotyped it on the minds of that jury so firmly that a thousand lawyers could never have removed it.

That a still greater, if possible, climax may be fully understood, some details must be given. It was the $50,000 damage suit for breach of promise of marriage brought by the beautiful and accomplished Miss Helbing, against that confirmed old bachelor, Philip R. Bowling, a youth of fifty summers. Philip for many years had a monopoly of the ice trade, and accumulated a fortune, but was cold from trade and habits, yet quite a "catch" in the vernacular of the present day. This was in 1855, before Payne moved to Memphis. Gov. Harris was Phillips' leading counsel, but after becoming Governor of the State he placed Phillips' defense in Payne's care. David M. Curran, the Little Giant, was leading counsel for Miss Helbing. During the pendency of the suit Miss Helbing married Mr. Handiworker, and the suit was revived in the name of Handiworker against Bowling, which put him on record as asking damages from Phillip because Phillip had not married his wife. An immense mass of evidence was laid before the trial court, then held in the old Exchange building, an immense hall, which was 148x75 feet. That hall was filled to its full capacity from day to day during the trial, wealth and beauty composed a large part of the auditory. Governor Harris left Nashville and came down to hear the trial. Poor Phillip knew all about dollars and cents, and large bank accounts, but nothing of the King's English. He could spell "Baker," and add columns of figures, and subtract less from greater numbers. He had broken off the engagement as many as three times after the day for the celebration of the banns had been agreed on and invitations extended. He wrote bushels of letters, adorned and ornamented with pictures procured from calico and other goods of the day, and pasted them on his love effusions. He also had a stock of very poor verses which he threw in with these ornamented letters, all of which indicated the distress of his saddened life, yet hopeful and youthful heart. In the liberality of his nature he bought many presents, including a very fine bedroom set, on which the lady and her liege lord reposed after their marriage. All these facts were in proof, and much more, but it was evident that the good lady had been compensated for all remote or hypothetical damages to her feelings in the youthful husband she obtained before the trial. Never were proofs better adapted to the peculiar and exalted genius of counsel for the defense, and never did a more eager auditory in Roman forum listen to oratory on which the fate of princes, armies and kingdoms depended. Payne was the cynosure of all eyes, the center sun around which the other legal planets revolved, and was in splendid trim. The most facile and powerful pen falls cold and lifeless in the effort to follow that magician, or to describe the waves and tides of admiration and passion which the orator inspired and controlled for five hours. At times he opened the floodgates of consuming irony, withering sarcasm, ridicule as poisonous as the fatal upas tree, holding Handiworker in front as the real plaintiff, asking, begging, beseeching a jury of *gentlemen* to award him $50,000 out of old Phillips' fortune because that old whiteheaded sinner had not taken his young, beautiful and accomplished bride to his arms.

In one of his many climaxes he described that fine set of bedroom furniture on which the plaintiffs reposed in transports of delirium, in the full fruition of God's first and best gift to man. Then with the hand and tongue of a master he drew back the curtain which veiled the bridal chamber, and led his auditory to the entrance and bade them look in on the gorgeous store of splendor and bliss. "There," he said, "look in on Handiworker and his bride in the delirious transports of that elysian hour, what mental agony and consuming torture must each be suffering because the old man who furnished that room was not the crowned, and Handiworker the deposed, neglected, overthrown, heartbroken and forsaken. Listen to the soft trill of that distressed heart, with uplifted silver stiletto to ruin the man who had abdicated such a throne for him. Mercenary to the last, he weighs the consolation of vulgar dollars against the holiest ties and affections God vouches to man; the commerce of avarice sweeps through his heart like the melody of the harp, rising note

on note higher and higher and stronger and stronger in
volume until it becomes ravishingly vocal with the solo,
Phillip R., Phillip R., Phillip R., until the furniture and
bed pick up the refrain: consolation, consolation, consolation, $50,000." This speech was like Niagara pouring
her majestic floods, resistless waters, sweeping on to the
sea. David M. Curran, though a great lawyer, was
simply overwhelmed and "lost in wonder and amazement at the strength and stretch of the human understanding." Verdict for defendant.

I have seen and heard men of exalted genius electrify
and lift and bear onward large auditories as on the current of a resistless river, but nothing to excel these efforts of Bob Payne's. Worthy of preservation in the Pantheon of our Southern literature; but no record was ever
made, and perhaps Gov. (now Senator) Harris and myself are the only men who recollect it. If I could, I
would preserve it and many others I have heard in dear,
old Memphis as long as a library is preserved, as long as
that "Mighty Inland Sea" by which she sits rolls on to
the ocean. Who even now, can tell us the author of the
term, "Mighty Inland Sea?" It was first uttered in
the same hall where this trial was had, by John C. Cal-
houn, in 1840, in a commercial convention he attended.
What a wealth of noble history and biography Memphis
has let pass down the relentless tide of oblivion! Sometime since I passed through the City and State Library
at Albany, N. Y. I was spending several weeks there,
and was presented with a ticket to each of these libraries. There I found a wealth of history, local to New
York—a history of almost every city and county in the
State, and biographies of her prominent men.

I loved "Bob Payne," as we called him in the sweet
privacy of social life. He was as gentle and kind as a
cultured woman, as free from vice. None knew him but
to love him. He was as free from art as a child, except
when animated in a trial; there he was the perfection of

art, and master of every noble passion that animates man. Columbia gave her jewels to Memphis when she gave her Payne, Gantt, and Walter Coleman—a powerful trio of talented and good men.

Payne was a widower, contemplated marriage, and his courtship was as free from romance as the preparation of an ordinary law suit. In that he was as artless and innocent as a child. One day he drove up in a carriage to my office, and said: "Hallum, come and go with me. You must not, you will not refuse me. I need a friend. I have much to confide to you. The heart must have something to lean on, something to bless, some storehouse where it can deposit its treasures." I was surprised, but dropped business and drove off with him, not knowing where we were going or the business in hand. He was a much older man than I. What was it? A middle-aged widow living in a beautiful suburban home four miles from the city was that evening to give him her final answer to his proposal of marriage, and he wanted me to go with him. When he told me this and the courtship, I took hold of the reins and stopped the team, and said to him: "I must return to the city; it is extraordinary; so much out of place. The act of taking me will of itself deter the lady."

"No," said he, "we are both advanced in years, and are practical, and I want you to console me on my return, for I have a presentiment that my suit will be rejected." I went and was introduced to the lady. I felt much embarrassed at the novelty of my situation, and soon attempted to excuse myself.

"No," both said, "you will be our mutual confidant." "You know the object of this call," said the lady, "and I am perfectly willing for you to remain seated." She then, in the kindest manner, said: "Mr. Payne, your suit grieves me far more than the result ought to grieve you. I am afflicted with cancer, and my physicians assure me that I cannot possibly survive long.

Under such circumstances marriage would be cruel to you.
I admire you as a man, respect you in the highest sense
that term implies. Your talent and standing at the Bar
challenge my admiration; but Providence has ordained an
irrevocable denial, and I must submit with humility and
resignation to the decree."

Payne was a man overflowing with kind impulses, tender of heart, and he felt very keenly his great disappointment. After we had driven through the beautiful lawn
to the public highway, he became composed and talked in
a strain of pathetic philosophy. Neither survived long.

Have I done right in relating this? My conscience is
animated by conflicting impulses. Surely I have related
nothing wrong, for I knew nothing but the inward suffering of two noble people.

He had one son, a talented member of the United States
Navy, a little wild when on furlough. Life is full of
shade and shadow; roses and thistles crowd the roadway
from birth to the grave.

JUDGE EPHRIAM W. M. KING.

JUDGE KING was a very prominent man in local
affairs from 1840 to 1860, but he had too many
irons in the fire to become great and eminent in
any department. In that flush and prosperous
decade between 1840 and 1850 he quit practice for some
years to become president of the Farmers and Merchants
Bank, which ultimately failed and entailed heavy losses.
It was said that the Judge did not put on the breakers
and curbed bits, but he never profited a dollar by the loss
—simply too confiding. A lawyer has no business assuming such responsibilities. Nearly all of us "live
easy and die poor." He was fond of politics, but did not
want office—when aroused was highly combative. I
never knew him to "take a back seat."

Volintine wrote a supplemental digest, which some-times gave the author trouble in the courts when trying to sustain propositions which were refuted by the digest. King cornered and floored him once. "I will appeal from Volintine drunk to Volintine sober." He had many noble qualities, and enjoyed communion with his brothers at the Bar. Great earnestness of purpose and a vigorous individuality distinguished him.

J. H. UNTHANK.

UNTHANK was a physical Hercules, the largest lawyer I ever met, but was thoughtful of his superiority in that, and never abused his powers. He was a perfect gentleman, an honored citizen, strictly moral, and eminently conservative. I never thought he made but one serious mistake, and that was in rating his mental, as superior to his physical, momentum.

Prof. Fowler, the scientist and phrenologist, in 1858 came to Memphis to sell phrenological charts, cranium surprises, cerebral wonders, and Brother Unthank bought a benefit. He had three stories to his head, the first and second rather crowded for room. Prof. Fowler was hardly justified in the scientific liberties he took. From the rostrum in Odd Fellows Hall, facing a large audience eager to catch all that fell from the philosopher's mouth, he said to Brother Unthank: "You have an immense mental force in the third story, which cannot be better illustrated than by comparison to an immense iron wheel, it needs much force to set it in motion; but when the momentum is once applied, Hercules himself could not block your pathway to fame."

The audible smiles which became contagious, could only be measured by the furlong, and none "smole a larger smile" than Brother Unthank, who refused to put any other than the strictest literal construction on the prophecy of the scientist.

He grew up a Democrat under Jackson's strict interpretation of constitutional powers, and never departed therefrom, especially in matters so pleasing and so much in accord with his own colossal judgment. It is not always dangerous to take liberties with the great, or to encourage violent presumptions.

W. L. SCOTT.

SCOTT came from East Tennessee in 1858, married the daughter of James Elder, the banker, was a very fine lawyer, and one of the most exemplary men. He was the author of a work on telegraphy, moved to St. Louis in 1872–73, and died there some years ago.

His life was austere and severe, all St. John, the evangelist, with him. He had no taste for wit and humor. The sparkling effervesence of life was as "sounding brass and a tinkling symbol" to him. I never saw him laugh.

GEN. W. Y. C. HUMES.

HUMES came with W. L. Scott from East Tennessee in 1858, and they were associated as partners until the war commenced. He was a sprightly, handsome man, a fine lawyer, popular and energetic, and the firm was not long in building up a good business. He, also, married a daughter of James Elder, the banker.

Humes came to me one day and asked if I knew where

he could make a good investment. "Yes, if you will do as I direct." He did so, and in ninety days sold for an advance of four thousand dollars. He was an enthusiastic supporter of the "Lost Cause," and entered the service as captain of artillery, and came home after Appomatox with a fine record as a soldier. He was social, genial, well liked, and stood high with his brothers at the Bar.

COL. LUKE W. FINLAY.

COL. LUKE W. FINLAY, from Hinds county, Miss., came to Memphis from Yale College saturated with absorptions from "the land of steady habits," and has never recovered from the severest code of morality: but he resented it afterward, and burnt a ton of powder at Shiloh, Kenesaw Mountain, Missionary Ridge, Chickamauga, and other places where differences of opinion and a slight coolness arose.

Luke is said to be very dry reading, but the Yankees pumped tons of fun out of him, and he "caught on," and pumped some, too, during the four years' relaxation he took from the severe demands of Chancery. He came home down cast and well thrashed, the only time I ever knew such an accident to befall him, since which he has been quietly disposed; but has never ceased troubling the courts with complaints, having made up his mind in 1865 that peace is more conducive to happiness than war.

Luke led a gallant charge on a park of artillery at Shiloh, and the boys in gray captured the guns. He mounted one of the cannons, waved his sword overhead, and shouted to the "Bonnie Blue Flag." No more glorious monument than a representation of that scene can mark the spot where the brave soldier will some day rest from his labors.

15

GEN. THOMAS H. LOGWOOD.

GEN. THOMAS H. LOGWOOD, he of the Lancers, was a social, genial, liberal hearted man, full of the sunshine of life, with malice for none and good will for all. He was not a severe student, the stimulant of necessity did not exist. When war came he recruited a company of Lancers, and equipped them as gaily as knights of chivalry going to a tournament. The last time I ever saw Tom he had his company of lancers on parade down Main street, with plumes waving and lances glittering, marching to the tune of Dixie's Land.

COL. O. P. LYLES.

COL. O. LYLES was a rare gem of the first water, a perfect gentleman in all the walks and relations of life. His resources in the field of wit and humor were as boundless as the waves of the sea, his native sense of honor keen, his perceptive faculties large, in his prime one of the best jury lawyers. His appreciation of humor bubbled and sparkled on all occasions and in all directions. He loved his friends, defied his enemies.

He settled at Marion, Arkansas, as early as 1851, and had a large following of clients. After the war he located in Memphis, was Colonel of the Second Regiment Arkansas Infantry, and as brave a soldier as ever led men in battle.

Pat Meath, one of the old celebrities of Memphis, was once party to a suit in the Federal Court, at Helena, before Judge Caldwell, with Col. Lyles as his counsel, and

Trieber opposing counsel, but Pat called him Mr. Fiber.
Col. Lyles had proceeded but a few moments with the argument when the court began to interpose objections,
which Pat regarded as fatal to his case, and addressing
the court said: "Will your Honor let me spake a word
to me counsel?" They retired, and he said: "Misther
Loiles, I see the court is retained against me, and it will
take but a few minutes for him and Misther Fiber to do
me up, sthop the case."

This was too good to be lost, and Col. Lyles immediately repeated it to the court.

Judge Caldwell roared with laughter, and adjourned
court until after dinner. The Colonel could produce
more convulsions of laughter than any member of the
Bar. He has left us. I presented the memorial resolutions touching his life and character to the Supreme
Court of Arkansas.

CHARLES KORTRECHT.

CHARLES KORTRECHT was an eminently successful lawyer, studious, laborious, and he strictly
adhered to the ethics of the profession, a severely
moral man in whom all reposed the utmost confidence. He had a tendency to speculation, and made some
profitable investments in real estate. He owned the old
Bank building on upper Main street, and sold it for con-
version into a synagogue.

I once saved his life at the risk of my own. He was
guardian of Clara Craft, an orphan adopted by a childless
couple, who educated her with much care and left her an
estate of thirty thousand dollars, and Kortrecht was her
guardian, than whom no better man could have been found
for the office.

She married E. De F. Morgan, whose name is on the
Roster. Morgan was a spendthrift, and was not long in

dissipating her little fortune. Kortrecht had invested the funds under order of the court, before Morgan's marriage, and the latter filed a bill to compel an accounting, and indulged in unwarranted strictures on the *bona fides* of Kortrecht's administration of the funds, which he resented in open court with uplifted chair.

I was present, and with others prevented a serious collision. The Hon. Geo. Dixon was presiding Chancellor.

Morgan always went armed, Kortrecht never. It was near the hour to adjourn, and I remained to prevent bloodshed, and kept within reach of Morgan after failing in my effort to get him to his office.

I knew a collision was inevitable if the parties were not obstructed. Morgan descended the stairway in advance of Kortrecht, and awaited his approach some minutes. When Kortrecht stepped on the pavement he started at Morgan instantly, and the latter drew his pistol. I jumped between them, and they seized and knocked each other over my head and shoulders, having me wedged between them.

Morgan held Kortrecht by the collar over my shoulder and Kortrecht held him with a similar grasp.

Then Morgan leaned to one side to prevent shooting me, and fired, cutting through my coat collar and tearing off the thumb of his own left hand, not injuring his adversary in the least. When the gun fired I threw Morgan in the gutter. By this time assistance came and the conflict ended. This occurred on South Court street, about seventy feet from Main, in 1860.

BOB LOONEY, he would not be recognized by any other name, and would feel astonished if addressed as the Hon. Robert. These old familiar abbreviations of names possess a charm, soft, radiant, beautiful; they throw wide open the doors, nestle in the brightest spots of the heart, exhibit the happiest phases of life and bring its rainbow colors to the surface, like the finishing touches of the artist to the canvass. Titles, decorations, place, power, position, retire to the background when these titles of boyhood bring in panoramic procession their golden urn of the fadeless beauties of "long ago," that "beautiful isle."

"Bob" yet lives to measure the earth in majestic stride, an emperor would feel abashed in his presence until he touched the key and "unbent the bow." As peerless as a Romanoff Prince, yet as gentle as a Troubadore with harp under the window of his love.

Not long ago I met him with a coterie of boys at the corner of Madison and Main, to one of whom he introduced me, with mischievous twinkle in the eye that heralded a "get off."

"It is currently reported that Hallum is one hundred and ten years old, but I will give him the benefit of all doubt and put it at one hundred and nine."

Bob simply got names mixed, he was thinking of "another Hallum who fought by his side at the battle of New Orleans on the 8th day of January, 1815, eighteen years preceding my advent."

He deserted the profession many years ago to indulge a broader field for finance and speculation and an easier life. Bob was always a "big Indian."

VACATION, SUMMER OUTING OF THE BAR.

HE Bench and Bar of Memphis, as long as I was there, maintained a convenient, a beautiful custom as part of the *lex non scripta* of the jurisdiction. The courts were suspended during the months of July and August, and every lawyer left to his vacation, his summer outing. The judges generally remained to hear applications for injunctions, receivers, and to transact such business as might come before them at Chambers.

In the summer of 1866 I made the tour of the Northern Lakes, down the Hudson with its joyous and magnificent scenery to New York, thence to Monticello, where Jefferson drew so much inspiration, uttered so many profound political truths, where he trimmed a lamp that will burn and shine as long as man walks the earth in the image of his God.

Thence to the University of Virginia, that Pantheon where so many Southern youths have laid deep the foundations of useful fame. There at the Commencement of that year I first met two of these young men, who had just completed the law course and were going home to enter upon the profession. We returned together. I was delighted with them, so modest, quiet, unassuming, accurate in judgment, polished, equipped.

This pair of boys, Thomas B. Turley and Joseph E. Sykes eminently illustrate the rich fruits which grow on the tree of toil and severe application, and never ripens on the uncultured tree of genius. The hare and tortoise. Turley entered the law office of Hallum & Chalmers, and the firm became Hallum, Chalmers & Turley. Turley's success is a matter of history, an open book where all can read. Now the partner of the able and brilliant Gen. Luke E. Wright.

Sykes had equal ability and culture, and in conversation was the more versatile. He was also associated with me after the dissolution of the above-named firm.

But Joe, as we familiarly called him when he left the University, relaxed that severe application so indispensable to high attainment, and has never taken that stand at the Bar his foundation and talents warrant.

HON. HENRY S. FOOTE.

FOOTE had been Governor of Mississippi, and had represented that State in the United States Senate. After his political sun had set in Mississippi, he came to Memphis and opened a law office, and was one of the many eminent counsel in the celebrated trial of Isaac L. Bolton for the murder of McMillan.

I heard him frequently, and always thought his forensic efforts more distinguished for classic beauty than legal strength. He was erratic and in many ways eccentric. He had a sublime conception of the dignity of Henry S. Foote, and in that yielded precedent to no man. The oscillation of the pendulum on which he swung never described an arc.

Like a brilliant comet making its first pathway in the political heavens, the periodicity of his orbital motions could not be calculated with precision. His calculations were always made with Foote as the central sun around which satellites revolved. His manner to the outside world was cold and reserved, to those not admitted to the inner circle of his life, he chose to exhibit the splendor of an arctic, rather than the warmth of a tropical sun.

In strange contrast to this dignified exaltation, I have

often heard that if a drayman challenged him to combat, he would have considered himself disgraced if he had refused the courtesy. Committed to the code, any adversary who chose to, might ask and receive accommodation. His courage was never questioned.

He fought a duel in Mississippi with the celebrated S. S. Prentiss, in which he was wounded, not dangerously, but seriously. As he lay stretched out on the ground in the hands of a surgeon, Prentiss came up in a spirit of reconciliation, they shook hands, bridged the chasm; then Prentiss said: "Foote, tell your good lady I meant no disrespect to her. The ball did not strike where I aimed. it."

In a question involving his chivalry or honor, Foote

"Would not kneel to Jove for his thunder,
Nor bow to Neptune for his trident."

A native of Virginia, the embodied crystallization of F. F. V.'s.

After losing his political foothold in Mississippi, he left the State and became an explorer of other fields without ever again becoming prominent.

THE CARPENTERS.

THE Carpenters were brothers from Kentucky. The elder was one of the able counsel who appeared in the trial of Matt. Ward, in Louisville, for the murder of Butler, the teacher. His argument in that case was extensively published at the time and ranked with the best efforts of the American Bar.

They came to Memphis in 1858, and occupied my office for a while, but did not succeed, presumably because Memphis then, as now, was abundantly supplied with very able lawyers. They became impatient at the long probation they saw before them, and left before the war period burst on the country.

W. C. FOWLKES, L. B. McFARLAND, LUKE E. WRIGHT, AND JAMES H. MALONE.

AMONG the young men of great promise, who were quite young when I left Memphis, twenty-five years ago, may be mentioned W. C. Fowlkes, the son-in-law of that distinguished jurist, Judge Archibald Wright. Fowlkes died young, but attained distinguished honors, President of the Bar Association and Justice of the Supreme Court of Tennessee. To these honors, so eloquent of his worth, a short sketch of his life like this can add nothing.

L. B. McFarland was full of hope and noble ambition for a seat in the front rank of the profession, of which he has since become a distinguished and honored member. He, too, has been President of the Bar Association of Tennessee, a very distinguished honor, and is still nursing his *alma mater* with great application and well merited success.

Gen. Luke E. Wright, the son of "Old Ironsides," who carved his way to the highest honors of the profession, Judge Archibald Wright, was a young man of brilliant prospects, and has, at every stage of progress for the last twenty-five years, fully justified every anticipation inspired since he left the college campus.

James H. Malone is another young man well deserving special mention. With firm resolve and great tenacity of purpose he has surmounted obstacle after obstacle in his aspiring and upward flight. There is an heroic and moral grandeur in such struggles, they ennoble and dignify man. Malone is now President of the Bar Association of Tennessee, which to-day stands in the front rank of such associations in the United States. If he never did anything more, his memory ought to be cherished for the successful efforts he inaugurated in preserving the memories of those departed brothers of the guild who have shed luster and renown on the profession in Tennessee. Of such young men as this quartette, the State builds her Doric columns for the temple.

ED. PICKETT.

E D. PICKETT, JR., cousin to Ed. Burke Pickett, was as peerless as a prince. For a while he mounted the tripod, and threw off brilliant editorials and many thunderbolts into the ranks of the old Whig party. Then he turned his attention to Blackstone and worked off many high pressure, polished forensics to the delight of his admirers.

HENRY A. ROGERS.

H ENRY A. ROGERS came from Haywood county after spending a cash patrimony of $10,000 on a trip to Europe. When he got to Queenstown, on his return, it took the last dollar to purchase a ticket to New York. When he arrived there he walked all the way to Brownsville, Tenn. I have this from Henry himself. He was a brilliant, erratic genius, and at times could dash like a comet through the constellations and exhibit brilliant flashes of eccentricities. After the war he went to Fort Smith, where he lives in tradition. Thence he moved to Hot Springs, where he died some years ago.

COL. A. J. KELLAR.

COL. ANDREW J. KELLAR came from Ohio, and taught school in the rural districts of Shelby, read law, and was admitted to the guild at Raleigh in 1856. He was kind, pacific, and social, and had a good clientage from the start. He espoused the cause of the Confederacy in its beginning, and I have heard him say, "I've watered my horse in every river from the Ohio to the Gulf." After peace he became associated with Col. Finlay in the practice of law. Tiring in that he bought an interest in the "Avalanche" and became involved in politics. From Memphis he retired to Kentucky and engaged in mining. He was a good man, well beloved by his friends, and they were many.

THE SEAY BROTHERS.

CHARLES AND WILLIAM A. SEAY came from Wilson county, Tenn., in 1857, each with a cash capital of $10,000. William was killed at the battle of Perryville. Charley married Octavia, the beautiful sister of L. O. Rives, and settled down on a plantation near Mason's depot, and was killed in a difficulty some years ago.

(243)

WHAT rapid revolutions a change of circumstances make in a mind not firmly fixed in basic principles. What a strange compound of frailty and greatness we sometimes meet with in men who are willing to profess anything that "thrift may follow fawning."

One change of the prism and exposure to other combinations of light and shade produces in such men a combination of character we perhaps never suspected. This man of the tribe of Benjamin lit on the world and struck out as a purist in Mississippi, an eloquent and fluent man of God. Scrupulosity was a shining text.

Tiring of that serenity of soul and the meek rewards reaped in the service of the Nazarene, he quit for the more exalted calling of politician, and became a member of Congress from that State. After this he came to Memphis, having a license to practice law. This about 1858.

He was pleasant, social, engaging in conversation without friction enough to arouse antagonism. Everybody seemed to like "Ben," and all knew him and called him by that name. No one ever thought he entertained thoughts hostile to the Confederacy, if he did, no such whisper ever reached the public ear—no one thought him capable of giving aid and comfort to a conquering army of occupation.

I witnessed the battle of the pigmies with the giants in the naval farce fought in front of Memphis.

Commodore Montgomery had announced at the Gayoso Hotel to a few select friends the night before the engagement that his fleet would make the attack the next morn-

ing. After the battle was over I walked up to Court
Square. When I got in sight of that gem of the city, I
saw a mongrel crowd gathered around Jackson's monument, and an individual delivering a stump speech with
animation, striking out from both shoulders.

I walked near enough to discover that Ben Nabors had
in that short space of time gathered a crowd and was
making a stiff Union speech, and denouncing the Southern
leaders. I have had my soul revolt at many spectacles,
but never more than at that man, electrocuting himself.
A lieutenant with the United States flag and a small squad
from the gunboats had been detailed to erect the flag in
the city, and it was flung to the breeze on streamers
above Jackson's monument, when and where Ben Nabors
constituted himself a committee of one to preach the funeral of the Confederacy, the glorious God-given land that
gave him birth. I stepped up beside the lieutenant, a
bright, intelligent man, and he asked me if the speaker
had been a pronounced or known Union man from the
start, and I told him he was not. Then he said, "He
may humbug others, but he can't inspire any confidence
in me."

Ben did the fawning, but the thrift did not follow. He
overshot the mark, the key in which he played "Yankee
Doodle" was too high.

I love the man who was true in that conflict to the soil
where he was born, whether under northern star or
southern sun, no matter where the tramp of armies
shook the earth or where the thunders rolled.

Tecumseh, the greatest of the Aboriginal tribes, spoke
with the inspiration of a hero when he called the earth
where he was born "My mother."

DUNCAN K. McRAE.

DUNCAN K. McREA was a native of the old North State; a fluent speaker and able lawyer. He was well advanced in years when he came to Memphis —had represented his State in Congress and the United States at the Court of Spain under Polk's administration, I think; but, like most men who divorce themselves so long from such an exacting profession, he lost the taste for its laborious phases, without which there cannot be many flowers gathered.

He was a pleasant, genial gentleman, and was sometimes easily embarrassed when an arrow struck him in debate, all the more because he was sensitive of his reputation as a great lawyer, a reputation hard to sustain after the possessor has been out of practice some years.

LUCIEN C. GAUSE.

LUCIEN C. GAUSE was raised on a farm near Cuba, in Shelby county, Tenn. In 1859 he came to me and solicited a position in my office. He was then a bright, fine looking young man. He did not remain in Memphis long, but went to Jackson Port, Ark.; was very popular and served but a short probation before clients poured in on him. He was elected to the Forty-third Congress but counted out. Was elected to the Forty-fourth Congress ('75 to '77) and served the term. He died of consumption about '82.

THE TRIAL OF EDWARD BARTLET, A UNION MAN, CHARGED WITH THE MURDER OF JAMES OBANION, A CONFEDERATE SOLDIER, "SO CALLED," 1865-66.

HE war gave rise to many strange combinations and embarrassing complications. The trial of Edward Bartlet, charged with the murder of James Obanion, was of much local celebrity at the time, 1865–66. Some of my best friends threatened to ostracise me if I undertook the defense of "that Union man for killing a Confederate soldier." Some knowledge of the details connected with this case is necessary to a clear understanding of the issues involved.

It was immediately succeeding the war, when the intense passions engendered by that contest were still at fever heat, and the defendant, the object of that malignity, to be tried by a jury selected from that class. So intense was this feeling, it threatened to sweep me away in the torrent, if I did not abandon the defense. I was reared in the midst of this people and had been the recipient of their unlimited patronage, and a great favorite with them. To discharge my duty, to stem that tide, to make it empty its flood in the lap of justice, was an undertaking of no ordinary character. To persist in that effort was my resolve if I perished in the ruins it threatened. Many of my personal friends, and hitherto warm supporters, held a meeting in the old courthouse at Raleigh and appointed W. H. Sneed, the father of my first wife, who was then living, a committee of one to inform me that although they held me in high esteem, they would abandon and ostracise me if I defended Bartlet. I wrote my reply in these words after the superscription:

"I greatly value the esteem of all good men, and particularly those with whom I have been so long and pleasantly associated; but as much as I value that, I cannot consent to disgrace myself and a noble profession to retain it. A lawyer who could thus be driven from the defense of a client, whose cause he believes to be just, is alone "fit for treason, stratagem and spoils," and ought to be shunned, condemned, and despised. I have ever regarded you all as good citizens, and yet so regard you, but permit me to say in all candor, that you have assumed a state of facts which does not exist. You are laboring under prejudices as deadly and pernicious as those which led the Savior to the crucifixion.

"An honest and a fair trial is all that Bartlet or his counsel asks. My life has been an open book to my fellow citizens, and ought to be an assurance that I will demand and insist on nothing but what I at least conceive to be right. With this assurance let me say that Edward Bartlet commands every energy of my nature, and that he waited and patiently suffered much longer than I would have done before killing Obanion, whose name is a disgrace to that of Confederate soldier. If you and those who co-operate with you will patiently and honestly, as good citizens ought to do, await the proofs, this will be demonstrated with as much certitude as a mathematical problem. But whatever be your course, duty fixes mine, you cannot fix the standard by which my obligations are to be measured."

If the restraining conditions then confronting society had been farther removed from the fearful lessons of the war, Bartlet would have been lynched. My response had some restraining influence. There were several conservative men, when acting under ordinary conditions, to whom it was read.

Bartlet was then in the old jail at Raleigh, and he depended on my judgment as to whether he should apply for bail. I decided that he should, and advised that if admitted to bail there would be no trouble about his bond, that I would go on it if necessary. Judge George W. Reeves, a citizen of the neighboring county of Fayette, was then Judge of the Circuit: a conservative Union man. I went to him at chambers that day, and presented application for bail accompanied with credible affidavits setting forth the facts attending the justifiable homicide, and bail was fixed at a reasonable amount.

I went with the sheriff to the jail after Bartlet, and he took my arm on the way to the courthouse, pale and fearfully agitated. The bond was made and he was released. Coercion was abandoned; the coolness of my friends was not of long duration. The more they discussed my determination, the more they felt like coming back to me. I gave out the facts on which the defense of the homicide was based, and reason was slowly awakened. The pivotal point was passed.

Now for the external surroundings. Bartlet was an honest, peacable, Union man, as the phrase obtained, and as a coincident, I may mention that he owned and lived on my father's old homestead in the northern part of the county; also the old homestead of Obanion's father, who was neighbor to my father from 1840 to 1844, both of which farms he conveyed to me in payment of my services for defending him. Obanion, the deceased, was left an orphan at an early age, and Bartlet and his good wife took him and raised him with the comforts and charity of their hospitable home, although he was not related to them in any way. He was sent to school and treated in every respect as the parents treated their own children. Obanion when quite young entered the Confederate army, and for a while was a good soldier; but he became dissipated and deserted the army, and became a marauder far below the degree of a guerrilla, for the latter did fight the enemy on his own account, whenever and wherever he chose. Armed warfare against the enemy was his occupation. Not so with Obanion. He did not war on the enemy, but subsisted on non-combatants, and in the light of the old common law, he became an enemy to mankind, whose life was forfeit to anybody who would take it, so clearly set forth by that ancient and able lawyer, Sir Joseph Jekyl, and others. Bartlet's political convictions were honest and sincere, and war and revolution did not, could not, emancipate or destroy them.

Obanion, in his downward debasement, became worse than any regicide that ever murdered his king, he conceived the base idea that it would be popular and lend a degree of importance to him to assassinate Bartlet, because he was a known and pronounced Union man, and proclaimed his intention publicly to do it. This was conveyed to Bartlet just in time to enable him to escape to the forest a few hours before the would-be assassin rode up to his residence with a chum to execute the design, in the presence of Bartlet's wife and children, the mother who had raised him and warmed him into life with her own, that mother in Israel who had lavished a kind heart on him and protected his helpless orphanage. Could the abandoned fiends of hell conceive of a greater enormity? Could any lawyer deserving the name desert such a client and skulk like a cowed spaniel before a torrent of misguided and debased public opinion?

Bartlet retired to the jungles of the forest with his trusty rifle, and lived like a wild beast pursued by wolves for three months. Obanion and his confederate, Roberts, made many visits to his residence, hunted him as an object of assassination. Bartlet would occasionally go home at the dead hour of night, and put his children out as pickets to watch and give the alarm when the assassins should approach. He did not do as I would have done under like circumstances. I would have treated Obanion as a wild beast, until the clear ringing crack of my rifle

echoed the death of a monster. But he did not think
public opinion, often the most dangerous of all tyrants,
would justify him, and he chose to live like a wild animal
in the caves, dens, and jungles of the forest, ever and
anon changing his resting abode for fear the sleuth
hounds would get on his track. It was then, and is yet,
a matter of wonder and amazement that human passion
and human frailty could go so far as to render it necessary to employ counsel to defend such a case, yet I have
never been called on during a long cycle of years at the
Bar, for more exertion than in the determination to save
Edward Bartlet.

The Hon. Thomas C. Mulligan, now of Gallatin,
Tenn., the junior member of my firm, one of Ireland's
gifted grafts on American soil, ably assisted me in the
trial of the case. One beautiful Sabbath, while the sun
was at its noon flood, Bartlet ventured out of the jungles
into the light of day with his trusted rifle. In passing
through a wild, woodland valley overhung with foliage,
he heard the sound of horsemen on the plateau above rapidly approaching. Startled, alarmed, he held his rifle
in readiness to defend himself against the, as yet, unseen
riders. Twenty yards away at the brow of the hill,
Obanion and his comrade, Roberts, came dashing toward
him like cavalry men on a charge, with pistols raised.
There was no time to flee to the old common-law wall.
Had he turned, had he lowered his gun he would have
been lost—assassinated. The decisive instant had arrived,
when to quail was to die. He turned that trusty rifle
loose with no uncertain aim, and Obanion "bit the dust"
in death, with his pistol in his hand and his saber at his
side. Roberts threw up his hands and begged like a
craven for his life, and Bartlet spared him. I would
have destroyed him for going to my house and harrass-
'ing my wife and children, and left no such false witness
against me. Bartlet was a better man than I claim
to be. But God took Roberts off, and did not leave him

to pollute courts with his presence. This occurred in the fall of 1863. Bartlet then fled to the Union lines, obtained employment as an engineer on the commercial marine of the river at a salary of $150 per month.

The first Grand Jury organized after the war indicted him, and charged him with murdering Obanion. His trial came on at the September term, 1865. To select a fair and impartial jury with such surroundings and from such a vicinage, the rural districts, approaches the impossible. The selection of the jury and trial occupied many days, and I was satisfied that I had the best jury that could be obtained. The evidence has already been stated.

At this distant day, after another generation has come on the stage, and public sentiment has advanced toward normal standards, it has the appearance of fiction, a wild legendary romance in the days of the Troubadores to be told that an enlightened people would condemn a man to death for defending himself against cold blooded assassination. Yet it will not appear so strange when we look back, even to England, but a few generations ago and survey the sacrifices these made on the political scaffold, and every country on the habitable globe is blackened with precedents, our own not accepted. There are more Cotton Mathers than one in our history. We have a lamentable example in the Chief Executive of the United States, who, animated by political cowardice, suffered an innocent woman's blood shed in the Capitol of the nation.

It looks like self-laudation to say I occupied seven hours in teaching that jury the alphabet of manhood, in urging them to rise from the ashes in which their minds were smouldering. That I succeeded, and that it was regarded as a triumph of no small magnitude at the time. It was an achievement. I stood in the smoking ruins of the mightiest revolution in modern times, when madness ruled the hour, and chaos was crowned, pleading for the life of a man who was regarded as the abettor of it all, and myself as a traitor to the hallowed associations of youth and the fruits of a riper age.

But my troubles and labors were not to end here in the defense of Bartlett. By a singular fortuity a mistrial was caused by one of the jurors running away before the rendition of the verdict of not guilty. The argument was concluded at a late hour in the night, and the jury as usual was placed in charge of a deputy until morning. One of the jurors was an old, honest farmer, my client and a warm personal friend. He was fearless as to personal danger, but was morbidly sensitive at the idea of being indicted and arraigned for trial in court. He was the second juror selected; his head was bandaged up with a bloody handkerchief—he had been engaged in a bloody fight the day before being taken on the jury. Many jurors were summoned—several hundred. Among these talesmen was one Isham Daniel, a constable, who asked to be excused on the grounds that he was an officer and had a warrant for the arrest of Roberts, my juror, as soon as he was discharged from jury service. This alarmed the juror, and incensed the judge, who imposed a fine on the indiscreet officer. Roberts sat the trial out, but when the sheriff took the jury in charge for the night he asked permission to step aside, which was granted, and he kept on stepping until he reached the interior of the wilds of Arkansas. Legs were regarded by him as of more intrinsic value than bail bonds and lawyers; but it was excessively foolish in him, as his offense was nothing more than a misdemeanor, and he was not the aggressor. The eleven remaining jurors were for acquital, and I had an array of authorities in support of the defendant's right to a discharge, but Judge Reeves overruled my motion to discharge the prisoner, entered a mistrial, and permitted the defendant to stand on his old bond. Many of the ablest members of the Bar held with me that the judge was wrong in not discharging Bartlett. The judge explained his ruling privately to me by stat-

ing, "You know I have almost exclusively to deal with
lawyers and suitors of opposing political sentiments.   I
am a Union man, and am very closely scrutinized by able
men, and for that reason desire to avoid criticism as far
as I can.   Under other circumstances I would not have
hesitated to discharge Bartlett.   If he is ever convicted
before me I will grant a new trial."   This was consoling,
but clearly indicated an absence of that courage of conviction which distinguishes higher manhood.

Before the second trial came on the legislature removed
the court to Memphis, and the trial was had in the old
Library building.   I no longer had any fears about the
acquital of Bartlett, but when the trial was called, was
engaged in the trial of a case of some interest in the
Chancery Court, and asked an old friend, as I thought,
to select the jury and detain the court until I could get
through the Chancery case.   The man whom I had often
favored, who undertook the selection of this jury, was
admitted to the Bar about the same time I was, but had
not succeeded.   I had not the remotest idea that he was
envious of the little patronage accorded me.   But this
infamous whelp put up a job for conviction on me.   There
are in large cities always a set of jobbers and hangers on,
willing to serve their master in the jury box, as well as
to rob a hen roost, and they convicted Bartlett.   I rose
immediately, moved for a new trial, and denounced the
jury, and before I took my seat Judge Reeves granted a
new trial.

This second trial illustrates the odious and dangerous
character of the low pettifogger who stoops to "pack a
jury."   Such a man is more dangerous to society than
a railroad wrecker or the higway marauder, who holds
up his victim; the pettifogger's injury to society is far
reaching and more injurious.

And it equally illustrates the damning influence of prejudice, which may sometimes embrace men otherwise
honest.   I had as soon talk by the hour to a monkey

perched on the shoulder of an Italian organgrinder, and expect to reach the remote recesses of his intellectual inspiration as to move twelve willful men in the jury box. Honest, fairminded men of average capacity can be reached, moved by reason, and led by logic.   The attractive speaker, the skilled logician, can arouse and play on the higher keys of humanity, and lift men like the rising tides of the sea, and bear them onward and they will feel delighted in the following.

When the third trial came on that able, logical, and eloquent lawyer, General James R. Chalmers, was associated with me as my law partner, and ably assisted in the defense.   He was a distinguished General in the Confederate army, has been a member of Congress, and enjoys much celebrity, and is yet with the few of the "Old Guard."   To the friends of his youth he was known as "Bun Chalmers," one of the pet names dearer to old men than all the titles won in later years, and I yet call him "Bun," simply "Bun," and nothing more.

We selected a jury of conservative men, grayheaded and considerate, and they did not go out of the box to consider their verdict, but as soon as they could bunch their heads together rendered a verdict of "not guilty."

I met "Bun" not long ago, and the first thing he said was, "John, have you forgotten the Bartlett trial?" "No, my dear 'Bun,' the mariner don't so easily forget the lighthouse in the stormy breakers."

DAVIDSON AND LINDSEY AND THEIR DUEL
IN 1853.

THESE gentlemen were law partners at Memphis in 1852, when I first met them. They came about 1846 from the South. They were large, portly, fine looking men. Davidson favored Toombs of Georgia very much. They were regarded as able men, but I never heard them argue a case.

They dissolved partnership in the spring of 1853, disagreed in the settlement of their mutual accounts—a challenge to the field passed and they made each a brave stand and shot six times, every shot missing the mark; their friends then demanded a cessation of the fight. "Uncle Dan Saffrans" was one of the seconds. I have in the long flight of years forgotten who the surgeons were and who acted as the other second. After the duel they left Memphis.

AN ADVENTURESS.

MARRIAGE OF MAY AND DECEMBER—PROFESSIONAL ADVICE AND ETHICS.

AN adventuress who called herself Annie White, possessed of remarkable beauty, thorough knowledge of the world, much literary attainment, and fine conversational powers, came to Memphis during military occupation by the Federal authorities and stopped at the Worsham House, then kept by A. J. Wheeler.

She was of English birth, had been a maid of honor to some of the nobility, and had traveled extensively in India and the East, and had become a thorough cosmopolitan.

When Wheeler discovered her real character he rather brusquely informed her that she must change her quarters. At the dinner hour, and in the dining room before all the guests, she belabored Wheeler with a rawhide. For this offense a military order was issued next day by Gen. Veach, Commandant of the Post, to send her north, out of the lines, within forty-eight hours.

She came to my office that morning and handed me $500 as a fee to procure a recision of the severe order. I had never seen nor heard of her until reading in the press of that morning the affair with Wheeler. I knew General Veach well—he was a kind hearted man, had many noble qualities, and was a lawyer of local repute at home in Indiana.

I told the fair and frail subject of her majesty that the best I could do was to give her an opportunity to plead her own cause with the Commander who had issued the order, and took a carriage and proceeded at once to Headquarters.

I introduced them, and jocularly told the General that the Federal army would yet find foemen worthy of its steel and martial occupation more in consonance with the objects of war than the fulmination of cruel bulls against defenseless women, and, said this lady can present her own cause and defend herself with eloquence surpassing yours or mine, and retired to the adjoining room. It was not twenty minutes until the order was cancelled. But this is prefatory to my object in referring to this woman.

There was a young, susceptible Hebrew from Cincinnati, who came to Memphis soon after Federal occupation, with a cash capital of $25,000 given him by his father as a "starter" in life. He met the adventuress and became overwhelmingly in love with her, proposed marriage and was accepted. He wrote hundreds of lovesick letters to the woman, all of which were carefully treasured as evidence to support her designs. The young man's father was finally apprised of his son's danger, and after much difficulty with the blind, obstinate son, succeeded in breaking off the engagement. This was the opportunity of the adventuress for spoliation and plunder. She brought these letters to my office, and told me her "well laid scheme," and desired an action for breach of marriage contract brought at once. A court called "The Civil Commission" had been established by military order at Memphis, following a precedent during the war with Mexico, which was sustained by the Supreme Court of the United States as an adjunct of the war power.

I cannot very accurately photograph my feelings when this woman offered me one half of the spoliation as a reward for espousing her cause and prosecuting this suit. I was indignant, with little will power to restrain its caustic manifestation, and said to her that the offer of such employment necessarily carried with it the presumption that I was a scoundrel and a disgrace to a noble profession. That if she had any claims to a higher type of noble womanhood, and had made a simple mistake, an error of judgment, I would deal with you gently, compassionately, deferentially, and advise you kindly as I would an erring child, but you have pursued a life of crime and have placed yourself beyond the pale of chivalrous consideration. You belong to that class of women so graphically described in the Bible, "whose ways lead down to hell." But she stood it unawed, unabashed, and said: "Judge —— will take my case." "Go to him, then; he may be seared and callous, but I don't believe it."

In a few days the same Judge brought her suit in the Civil Commission Court for breach of promise, the *ad-damnum* being laid at $50,000, and the mercantile establishment of the young man was attached as indemnity and closed up. In his distress he came to me to defend him, but ethics, public policy, sound morals, presented a barrier to this employment. I had been consulted, had seen the letters, knew the plan, the motives of the prosecution, but my lips were sealed.

The young man's father again came to Memphis, read these damaging letters—confessions of his son—and gave the Judge his draft for $5,000 for an acquittance.

This lawyer had been eminent in the profession, local politics, finance, but had long passed the meridian of life, and to a great extent survived his fame, but his monument in Elmwood speaks a charitable heraldry.

Another instance demanding nice distinctions and delicate considerations growing out of a combination of circumstances with which I was familiar came under my observation. Mr. B.'s first wife was one of those good, industrious housewives, honest, frugal, a loving mother, who had borne and nurtured with tender solicitude a large family of children, and aided her husband in amassing property of the value of $18,000, after which she died, her two eldest children in a flock of nine boys and girls, a son and daughter, had gone to school to me. The old man, of fifty and five, became enamored of a beautiful factory girl, who was then at the head of one of the departments in the cotton factory on Wolfe river, just north of the city. She claimed to be a niece of Gen. Winfield Scott, and was anxious to have the banns solemnized. The old man dressed up as fine as a Broadway dude, brought his flame to my office in his carriage, and asked me to draw up a conveyance vesting all of this property in her. I was shocked at the idea, a glance at her convinced me that she only wanted his property, and that she would "lead him a merry dance," and for no consideration would I be the passive instrument of so much injustice, either to him or his children, and prositively refused to draft such an instrument.

Both were greatly surprised, and asked me to assign a reason. I said to them, "Mr. B., I have for years been familiar with your family and social surroundings, no one contributed more than your departed wife to accumulate the property you have, charged with a holy and sacred duty to use it in promoting the interest and welfare of her half orphan children. You are now verging on three-score, and at best cannot long survive. If you will submit this settlement to my judgment I will draft an instrument doing equal justice to all as near as possible." "What would your judgment approve?" asked the blooming aspirant for matrimonial honors. "To convey not more than one fourth of this property to you, not one cent more. If you are actuated with that exalted devotion springing from affection, which alone can sanctify that relation, it will satisfy you, but if moved by mercenary considerations, a prostitution of the holiest relations of life, you ought not to have one dollar. You will both pardon me in the emphatic enunciation of my deepest convictions, the offices of an adviser are not always pleasant. Both of you return home and think well over this matter, give it your best thought, then return to me."

The next day the young woman drove up to my office in company with a much younger man, a man much devoted to the gayeties of social life, he was also a client of mine. This circumstance within itself pointed with index finger to the justice of my convictions, and convinced me of the folly of this marriage of May and December. She wanted a conference, the object of which was to soften the vigor of my judgment—the old man, foolish as he was, had been set to thinking, and had refused to consult a more pliant lawyer. She was thus forced either to abandon the scheme or to submit to terms. When she found me obdurate, she begged the favor of my silence. I told her that the highest ethics of my profession imposed that.

The old man came the second day alone, had a long conference, and finally came to my terms as the ultimatum, and on the third day they came together and I drafted the instrument giving her one fourth of his property, and it was formally executed. Lawyers are often called upon to steer between Charybdis and Cylla, and oftener in their consultation room than in court or elsewhere. It

was not six weeks until the flame of discord broke out in
this family, and the heart of the misguided old man became a raging volcano of jealousy founded on vehement
suspicions, and I became the unwilling depository of all
this trouble. They would come alone to my office and
unbosom their secrets, but neither ever knew the other
had consulted me. This wear and tear and constant
strain on the nervous organism soon wore the old man out
and he went to rest in Elmwood.

GEORGE GANTT.

EORGE GANTT, to the boys of the old Roster,
simply George and nothing more, a pet name as
dear to him as to the "Old Guard," as attractive as the thousand laurels he has won in the legal
forum. He of the silver tongue, whom Cicero would have
feared and respected had George broke a lance with him
in the trials of Roscius, Verres and Cataline. Prince
of good fellows, honored and loved by all. How easily
and gracefully he soars on tireless wing, how beautiful
and ravishing his ornate periods. How easily his polished
shafts leap from his inspired tongue and go to the heart.
Who asks me if I am a quailified witness? If fifty forensic
conflicts qualifies a well drubbed gentleman to take
the stand against George it is little I, and a straight,
creditable story shall be given to Court and Jury. Many
a thunderbolt he has hurled at me, many a quiver of Parthian arrows emptied, and when these failed, Ithuriel handed him his spear. He seems to lead a charmed life. Sometimes I have thought the devil had a hand in it, but never
could prove it. Forty years I have patiently waited before trusting either tongue or pen to this office, but he is
setting me to death—while I am growing old, he looks
younger than he did fifty years ago. I am near the river

and the ferryman is calling me, but George in appearance will not reach the ferry in the next century. You are a fraud and a burlesque on the ravages of time, George. After I have crossed the river and sleep under the daisies, I hope my immortal spirit will greet you when you throw your quiver and a sprig of myrtle on my grave and say "He was my friend." Give your arrows and lances to your boys and say to them: "Handle them as your father did, nor let them rust."

I once got even with George and paid up all old scores in the coin of the realm, and it was in a Chancery case, not one of those dry, profound, prosaic cases. George would never tolerate anything like that in any court. He rode a high horse, under whip and spur from the mount clear through the home stretch, and frequently would start before the bell tapped a send off. To get at bedrock facts we must understand the history of the case. And I may say the prologue is romantic and tragical.

The Rev. W. R. Slate and his brother Henry, were my boyish schoolmates in the old fashioned log school house in Middle Tennessee, before the advent of public schools, and our boyish attachments followed us through life. They are both dead now. After reaching man's estate we all came to West Tennessee, the brothers settling in Tipton, and I in Shelby county. They were good and prosperous men, and it was natural for me to fall heir to their legal business. Robert was the boy educated out of the fund "Uncle Billie Malone" raised to educate him and myself, related herein before.

Henry married a grass widow and became a frugal and prosperous farmer in Tipton County, but removed to Shelby and settled near the village of Cuba, where he was murdered by Holloway, his farm hand and his wife's paramour in illicit crime. The murder was conceived no doubt and planned by the two, but the proof was not positive as to the wife and she was not indicted. To this union two bright little boys were born. The estate of the deceased was valued from $7,000 to $10,000. At the suggestion of the widow 'Squire Massey was appointed administrator and took charge of the estate. Holloway was indicted and charged with murder in the first degree, and I was retained to prosecute him, and John Bullock was retained to defend him. It was one of the most remarkable trials I ever appeared in, remarkable for the almost transcendent ability displayed by the widow in the witness box in her efforts to save her reputation and the life of her paramour, to which was added the great ability and almost superhuman effort of Bro. Bullock.

Before the trial commenced, I felt that I would not be satisfied with anything short of a verdict of guilty, and a death sentence. But after the widow took the stand for the defense I saw that the work of a Hercules would be required to achieve that end. She commenced with consummate art, dramatic effect, by stating to the jury: '' I am the unfortunate victim of a combination of circumstances which will inevitably result in my social ruin, and fix a stain on the name of the innocent children born to him who was murdered, by whom, none but the all-seeing eye of the living God can tell. Society is so organized, and such are the infirmities of human nature, that the slander against me will be believed, though I am as innocent of the crime as the crucified Savior of mankind, in whose redeeming blood alone can I ever hope to find rest and protection. Ostracism will be the inevitable result of this foulest of all charges against me. Suspicion will do—it has done its work. Driven and spurned, heartbroken and crushed, from door to door, shunned, despised by all of my sex, death can alone be my best friend. Let a woman's virtue be once assailed, as mine is to-day, and the door of every asylum is forever closed against her, and her life becomes a living hell, though she be as pure in the sight of God as the Virgin Mary. Look at me, gentlemen, and pity a living corpse. You who have wives, mothers, daughters, and sisters whom you would defend until all that is chivalrous in man perishes."

Here she broke down and wept as only a woman can weep. Every eye in that courthouse was moistened, the depth of every heart was stirred. The Judge on the bench gave way and covered his face with his handkerchief, and I deeply regretted the duty my oath and office imposed. Could I have foreseen the temple of justice with so many tears, so much sympathy springing from all that is noble and chivalrous in man, "a living corpse," a soul "banished" from earth, appealing "alone to God for mercy and rest" and vindication, no sum of money would have been great enough to have retained my services. I have never been inclined to prosecution, have always thought that frail mortality had enough to contend with without any effort from me added to the sum of human sorrow; and now in my old age, when I look back over forty years of arduous labor at the Bar, I thank my God that I have been engaged in but very few prosecutions, ninety-eight out of every one hundred criminal cases I have been retained in, has been for the defense. I was then as convinced of that woman's guilt as at first, still I did not want to add to the weight of her sorrow. I have seen almost all the great masters of the stage in my day, but this woman from the common walks of life, in consummate art excelled them all. I thought when the curtain fell on the first scene that her powers were exhausted, and that when she was recalled the less exciting, direct examination would proceed in easier stages. But I was again as much mistaken as astonished at her tremendous resources. Raising her head from the table on which it had fallen, she wiped her eyes, brushed back her raven hair, and looked at the jury with the majesty of Juno, and the wisdom of Minerva, then turning to her two little boys, who were neatly dressed and pictures of rural health and beauty, she said: "For me, gentlemen, 'tis nothing to die. Waste no sentiment or pity on me, my race is run; but oh, in the name of the God who created us all, look on these bright, innocent little boys, and say to them under the sanction and power of the oath you have taken: 'Nay, nay, your mother is not guilty of drinking the blood of your father!' Say it in the name of God and heaven and all its hosts. They must walk the earth in sorrow, stripped of honorable lineage, debarred from aspiring to all that is honorable, noble, and great in man. To thus walk the earth is but a living tomb. For what? a mother's crime? No, a living slander that reviles and revels in blaspheming woman's virtue, supported by circumstances that an artless woman cannot explain." I thought I saw the fine hand of Bro. Bullock in training this extraordinary woman. He was a man of great ability, but I did not interpose any objection, any technical rule of law to stop the wonderful fertility of this woman's power and tragic genius. She gave away again to a flood of tears, and and when she recovered the examination proceeded.

After the witness was turned over to me for cross-examination, I held a consultation with my law partner, the Hon. Thomas C. Mulligan, now of Gallatin, Tenn., who appeared with me in the case and made a splendid opening for the prosecution. One of the most delicate duties a lawyer has to perform is to skillfully conduct the cross-examination of such a witness, and my conviction was that we had better refrain from cross-examination; but my Brother Mulligan differed with me, and insisted on a thorough cross-examination, and I gave way to him and held her under fire three hours. I commenced in very kind gentle and unimportant questions and soft modulation of voice so as to win her confidence, and remove the impression that I was unkindly disposed toward her, in this way she was gradually led up to the pivotal questions and points in the case. After reaching that point a rapid fire of gentle questions was put to prevent reflection, and catching the logical sequence and drift to

17

which they were leading. In this way some important and damaging admissions were obtained, but occasionally she would stop to reflect on object and result when led up to the points she had so artfully studied and guarded. Then she would exclaim in dramatic voice: "I told you that it is simply impossible to explain to your satisfaction all the circumstances connected with this murder, and I can neither add to nor take from what I have already said." But she again added: "Under the oath I have taken in the presence of God and these witnesses, I again repeat that Mr. Holloway is not guilty of this murder." The probative facts as to Holloway's guilt were overwhelming. Just before the murder they were all sitting by the fireside. Before Slate retired to bed he stepped out to look after his stock a few rods distant. In a few moments Holloway followed him and fired, a fierce scuffle ensued, extending over several rods of ground. Holloway came back to the house with blood on his clothes and clothes torn in the fierce conflict, and Slate lay dead about twenty yards from his own door. Circumstances and facts established the intimacy. Her efforts to save him confirmed it. Holloway was convicted of murder in the second degree, and sentenced to the penitentiary for eleven years. The case was carried to the Supreme Court, but I declined any further connection with the it after the first trial. It was reversed, and on the second trial he was sentenced to three years in the penitentiary.

But all this is prefatory to what I promised in the opening of the chapter. The Chancery suit growing out of this tragedy is where Brother Gnatt caught "Hail Columbia," and was paid in current coin for all he had perpetrated in and out of this answer, wherein he had snatched the schoolboy's eagle bird baldheaded in pronouncing "a eulogy" on me, attested by the oath and eloquence of the widow. George, with his little hatchet, had never before this trial in Chancery realized the force and truth of the prophet who tuned his lyre and sang to George's memory:

> Hark! from the tomb a doleful sound,
> My ears attend the cry;
> Ye mortal men, come view the ground
> Where you must shortly LIE!

After the criminal trial, W. R. Slate, the minister and surviving brother, a year after the murder of his brother, came to me and said: "John, I have been long hesitating and debating in my own mind as to whether I ought ever to open the skeleton closets in the house of my dead brother, I have prayed fervently over the matter and now feel that I am directed by divine power at least to lay the whole matter before you and submit myself to your advice and direction. Our relations since we first met on the schoolboy playground have been almost like that of brothers, and independently of the fact that you are a lawyer, I would have great confidence in your disinterested judgment. My brother left two very bright and promising little boys, for whom I feel great solicitude, and I fear their lives will be blasted, if I do not take them in charge and remove them from their present surroundings, all the details of which are perfectly familiar to you. I refer to their father's murder. I am a humble minister of the gospel, and would not knowingly do anything not justified by the strictest code of morals. My brother married a grass widow whose husband was living at the date of his marriage, neither party having obtained a divorce, and I understand that that fact renders the children illegitimate and entitles me and my two sisters to the estate. We do not want one dollar ourselves, but we do want those two little boys to have it entire. If we get it, it is our purpose to settle it on them. Now you have the facts, what do you advise us to do?"

"By all means protect the children. If the facts you have stated to me are true, the law casts the descent on the surviving brother and sisters."

"I am glad to hear you so decide, and so explicit. I am authorized by Mrs. Suddith and Mrs. Exum, my married sisters, whom you knew in their girlhood, and who are yet neighbors to your parents in Middle Tennessee, to see you and be governed entirely by your advice; so I want the suit brought immediately, the widow is squandering the property, the administrator is under her thumb."

"Well, my dear sir, I must know more of the proofs before risking my reputation in bringing a suit which we may not be able to sustain. Tell me more of the proofs you have at your command."

"To begin, my brother was deceived, he knew nothing of her living husband when he married this woman. It was five or six years after his marriage before whisperings came to his ears, and then he only unbosomed his troubles to me. She was the widow of a Mr. Harris whom she had married in Tipton county about 1850. I have examined the records at Covington and find a record of that marriage. She claims that he died in 1852, and was buried in a country churchyard, and she shows the grave where she says he was buried. But Mr. Harris has a cousin living in Tipton county, a Miss Reynolds, a very bright and intelligent woman. She says her cousin, Harris, for reasons satisfactory to himself, left his wife in 1851, and settled at Egg Point, Miss., and corresponded with her as late as the fall of 1854, two years after the marriage of his wife with my brother, in proof of which she exhibits to me a bundle of letters addressed by him to her, and says she is perfectly familiar with his handwriting. Since the fall of 1854 no member of the family has ever heard from him."

I told him that these facts were probative, but not within themselves sufficient to base a decree on, from the simple fact that Mr. Harris might have procured a divorce in some other jurisdiction before his wife's marriage and that I must take time and push the investigation further before commencing suit. He was much discouraged at this and seemed to think that the personal estate would be made away with if delay was interposed, and said: "John, I will assume all responsibility of completing the necessary proofs if you will bring the writ at once. It will not do to wait until the mischief is consumated."

Then I said, "I will prepare the bill to-night, and to-morrow seize on the corpus of the estate." Chancellor Wm. M. Smith was then on the Bench, and issued the necessary fiat, and I was appointed administrator and took charge of the estate. The widow hastened to Bro. Gantt, and he got off, shot off, and fired off some of the finest rhetoric ever penned by way of answer to a bill. He turned a brilliant lance at me, threw every arrow in a bundle of quivers at me *personally*. The charges against me were beautifully told, charmingly conceived, impudently written, as no other lawyer but George could do. He charged me with "slandering the living, traducing the dead, thus making innocent children worse than orphans." He said, he George Gantt, "would produce as witness the physician who attended Harris in his last illness, the old ladies who wrought the shroud, the grave digger, the coffin maker, the divine who preached the funeral, and the neighbors who threw the last cold sod on Harris' grave," and all before the widow married Slate. Ten pages of this poetic and pathetic abuse of me. I could have had all this stricken out on motion, but would rather have gone to jail than make such a motion. Bro. George had erected the gallows, and he must hang on it. I thought of what an old farmer said of Bailey Peyton in my boyhood. "It's a dangerous thing to spit tobacco in his eyes." A ton was thrown in mine, and I resolved to be avenged on him if it took $5,000 to get at the "bedrock" facts in that case. I sent J. S. Galloway, then a fine young lawyer, now Circuit Judge, to take Miss Reynold's deposition.

In the meantime I directed a letter to the postmaster at

Egg Point, Miss., and one to Harris himself at the same point, as a sort of forlorn hope to find Harris. The war had intervened since he was last heard from, and it was altogether problematical whether I would get on the track of Mr. Harris. Galloway came back with a masterly deposition from Miss Reynolds, with a dozen letters from Harris to her, as exhibits to and parts of the deposition, proof of handwriting, etc., and a vehement presumption that Bro. Gantt was the slanderer and not I. I intended to put Galloway on a steamer and send him to Egg Point to hunt up the long lost Harris, but to my "amazing grace" both of my letters to that place were answered. Mr. Harris wrote to me under his own "John Hancock" signature, stating that he had never married again, and never obtained a divorce, and that if I would send him a draft for $250 he would attend the trial in person. I sent him the draft by return mail with explicit instructions not to let his identity be known when he came to Memphis, and that I would advise him when he would be wanted. I sent Galloway to Bro. Gantt to fix an early day for the hearing of the cause, and it was set down for hearing early in the following week.

Miss Reynolds' deposition was the only one on file, and George knew that was not quite sufficient, although it was nearly so. Harris reached my office the day before the trial, and I carried him *incog* to my residence, and to the court room next morning. The widow was on hand, had sworn to all George had written in his answer. I told the attorneys in attendance to remain till after roll call, that they would be richly paid if they did so. I read the bill quietly and sedately. Bro. Gantt triumphantly, and with vehemence, read the answer. When he had gone through the ten pages of abuse hurled at me, I stepped up and gently tapped him on the shoulder and, asked him to suspend a moment, and then I motioned to Harris to come forward, and I said, "My dear Brother Gantt, your reputation for veracity has been great all your life, and I am sure you would not injure it for the first time in your old age. Let me introduce to you Mr. Harris, the man you have so eloquently buried." Harris extended his hand, but poor George, a thousand funerals would not have been half so appalling to him. His face was redder than a ton of vermillion. He dashed the answer with precipitate violence on the table and rushed out of the court room bareheaded, and the dumbfounded widow rushed after him. A more surprising scene was never enacted in a court room. Chancellor Smith said, "Take your decree, Mr. Hallum." As said of the charge of the Light Brigade at Balaklava, the answer of Bro. Gantt "was brilliant, but it was not war."

YOUR OX OR MINE.

THE HARDSHELL BAPTIST— BIG FEES AND NO FEES.

AN old farmer from north Mississippi stepped into my office during the war, while I was writing a bill of sale to a steamboat. The gentleman for whom it was written handed me my fee of $100. The old farmer was so astonished at the price he could not contain himself, and addressing the gentleman who paid the fee said: "Stranger, are you going to stand that without saying a word? I have pulled fodder many a day for fifty cents, and that man charges $100 for half an hour. I thought I wanted some writing done, but I don't. Bill Jones told me to come to this man, but I guess he made a mistake." The gentlemen, old steamboat captains, were greatly amused, and humored the joke. One of them said to the farmer, "This gentleman is a very cheap lawyer. I live in St. Louis. The lawyers there charge $250 for the same work. I spent a week there trying to get them down, but they stuck to their price. Then

I heard of this gentleman, who is cutting prices and working reasonable, so I just had my steamboat fired up and run down here and got this gentleman for $100, and saved $150 by it."

The farmer said, "It looks to me like the world has gone crazy. I can educate one of my children on less money than that to do that writin'. I came here to get a deed made to a piece of land, and I don't reckon this man would write it and take the land for pay." "Stranger," addressing me, "how long would it take you to do it, and what might you charge?"

"Ten minutes and ten dollars." "Do you charge a dollar a minute and expect to get to heaven? I have always heard it said that lawyers can't get there, and now I know it." "Well, my friend, you are getting very close to me, touching me upon a very tender point, and I begin to think I had better make some investments in that direction. If you will help me out I will begin right now and write your deed for nothing, and charge it up to the Lord. What church do you belong to?" "The Hardshell Baptist. We stand up to the fodder of the Lord, rain or shine, and we teach our boys and gals, the same, and we will do all we can to help you out, but I'm thinking its a going to be a hard job to pull you through, but we will try it." The river men could not contain themselves any longer. To a saloon we all went, where the old Hardshell took his first glass of champagne, and insisted on paying ten cents as his pro rata share of the $15 paid for three bottles consumed.

I wrote his deed. He stood up and took me by both hands and said, "Stranger, you have started off on the right foot, and if you will keep it up to the end of the row, its my belief you will get there yet." Some months after I received a letter from him in which he informed me that several special prayer meetings had been held in my interest in which some of the finest prayers he had ever heard had been offered up. He wanted to know how

I was getting along.   I wrote him that I had got the theory down finely, but was short on the practice; that I still charged a few people good paying prices for writing. After that he wrote again and informed me that he had been sending Tom, his son, to writing school, and had made him a good penman, and wanted me to "give him a job of writin' at them good prices."

THE KLEPTOMANIAC AND JEALOUS WIFE.

IN the summer of 1867 a retail merchant, by whom I was regularly retained, brought quite a large bill against a married lady living near Memphis to me for collection.   The lady was a wealthy kleptomaniac, and had from time to time stolen the goods.   I wrote a polite note to the husband requesting him to call at my office.   He did so, and paid the bill at once.   In the month of September of that year I was engaged in defending Wade Bolton and others on an indictment for murder, and during the progress of that trial some one entered my office and set fire to it.   Dr. Mitchell discovered the fire about 1 A. M., in time to extinguish it before much damage was done.   I was at a loss to conjecture who the miscreant was.   Fifteen years later a lady confidant of the kleptomaniac, who was then deceased, told me that the woman who committed the larceny from the merchant, dressed up in gentlemen's clothes and fired my office in revenge for the information I had imparted to her husband.

In the winter of 1867 the manager of one of the theaters in Memphis came to me to enjoin two beautiful actresses from playing at a rival theater, on the ground that they had broken a prior engagement with him.   I prepared the papers hurriedly and obtained the injunction from

Chancellor Smith about 6 P. M.   The actresses could not be found at that hour, and it was decided by the sheriff and myself that he must go to the rival theater and serve the injunction when the curtain rose.   I had associate counsel who had a beautiful, young and very jealous wife, but at that time I knew nothing of his wife's jealous disposition.   The couple took tea at my house that evening, and I related the story of the injunction, and requested my associate to go to the theater and see that the injunction was served.   He very readily complied, and came back earlier than usual with the information that the injunction had been served and obeyed, but his wife was not in the apartments assigned them, and could not then be found.

We were all astonished and alarmed, but my wife took me to one side and told me that the missing wife did not believe one word I had said about the injunction, but had interpreted it as an excuse for the husband to get off to the theater that night, and that she had hurriedly dressed up in men's clothes, and with my office boy had gone to the theater to watch her husband.   He was so alarmed at absence that I was compelled to break the *statu quo* gently to him.   He was greatly relieved, and I never knew one to enjoy a joke better than he did that.   He hid himself and caught his wife when she was trying to slip in the backway.

She went to the theater, saw the actresses taken off the stage, and her husband retire from the theater with the sheriff.   Who says law is a dry subject, stands on the outside.

GEN. ALBERT PIKE.

BORN of humble parentage in Boston, Mass., in 1809, raised in Newberry Port in the same State, classically educated by himself without the aid or degrees of college. In learning he surpassed any and all men I ever knew.

A profound jurist, poet of the highest order, philosopher, linguist, and philologist without a rival or peer in our history.

As ethnologist and oriental scholar no man in America has ever approached him. Some idea of the vast scope of his labors and attainments and magnitude of accomplishment may be gathered from his herculean labors during the last years of his life, and comments on the "Rig Veda" and "Zend Avesta" and other works of Aryan literature containing seventeen volumes. (Biographical and Pictorial History of Arkansas, by John Hallum, 233.)

He was a general in the Confederate army, and commanded an Indian brigade. After the war he located in Memphis, edited the Appeal a while, and then practiced law in partnership with Gen. Adams, their office being in the same building as that occupied by the Author. He has written three unpublished volumes on the "Latin Maxims of the Roman Law," and seventeen volumes on philology and ethnology commencing with the Sanskrit, the best preserved of all dead languages, and from linguistic monuments tracing with a master's hand the different races and languages of man. The field is intricate and vast, and no man but Pike could compass it.

He has also written and contributed more than any American author to Masonry, and was often consulted by the highest authorities in the Order in Europe.

Once he received a long communication from the Grand Master of the Order in Portugal, in the Portuguese language, which he had never studied. The communication referred to intricate questions of Masonic law. He procured a dictionary and grammar of the language, and in twenty-four hours wrote a lengthy reply in the Portuguese language. His capacity for brain work was simply enormous. His lyric poems are classed with the sweetest gems of our literature.

He published but a few copies in book form, some twenty. These he gave to a few intimate friends, the Author having one copy. He wrote for me a short Autobiography, the only one he ever gave or wrote for anyone. With his intimate friends he was the most social and charming of men. He died in Washington City in 1892, in his 83d year

LANDON C. HANES.

LANDON C. HANES, a native of East Tennessee, came to Memphis immediately after the close of the civil war with a reputation as an orator surpassed by none. His taste for beautiful, ornate language was cultivated to a high degree, and he was an entrancing speaker. He often prepared with studious care, striking and splendid passages in his forensic and other efforts, but as an impromptu speaker was excelled by many men.

He occupied an office in the same building where Pike & Adams, the Heiskells, and myself held forth, and I saw much of him to admire. He was as free from guile as any man I ever met, and won lasting friends wherever he went. I was frequently a guest at his hospitable home where he was surrounded by a charming family.

GEN. CHARLES W. ADAMS.

EN. CHARLES W. ADAMS was born in Boston, Mass., in 1817, and was descended from the Presidential family of that name. When only two years old his parents moved to Indiana, where educational facilities were of primitive character. He was a man of great energy, strong individuality, and much force of character—a self-educated and self-made man.

He settled at Helena, Ark., in 1835, was cashier of the old Real Estate bank, in 1839 he was admitted to the Bar, in 1852 elected Circuit Judge, a position he distinguished and adorned, a member of the Seceding Convention of Arkansas, a general in the Confederate army.

In 1865 he came to Memphis with the reputation of an able lawyer, which he maintained, being associated with Gen. Pike. He was laborious and thorough in the preparation of his cases; earnest, persuasive, convincing in argument; social, genial, magnetic; loved and admired by his associates.

Often after the labors of the day were over he would call me to the private rooms of Gen. Pike and himself, open a box of cigars and spread of fine pipes and choice preparation of the weed. We generally chose the latter. Then an attic hour, a genial feast of humor and flow of soul, the cream of the day, the nectar of the past. What capacity for intellectual enjoyment those men possessed— and happy the man on whom they shed their light.

THE DETECTIVE SYSTEM DURING THE OC-
CUPATION OF MEMPHIS BY THE
FEDERAL ARMY.

WHEN quite young and in mature age, I read and greatly admired the forensic efforts of that great master of the Irish Bar, John Philpot Curran, published in two volumes, now quite rare. The Crown prosecutions growing out of the revolution of '98 gave rise to some of the most brilliant defenses by Curran made in any country or age. The informer and the detective who belong to the sewerage strata of society scoured Ireland for objects of prosecution and persecution, and Curran's denunciation of the spoliation and plunder of the prowling detective and informer was as consuming as a world on fire. "They rise as they rot, like dead bodies thrown in the Ganges, and float on the surface an object of loathing and contamination."

The detective system at Memphis from June 1863 to the close of the war between the states justifies all that Curran or any other man could say or write in a century about the informer and detective. And all this holds equally true and applicable to those who conducted the "Abandoned Property Department," under Capt. Eddy. A commission from that department of the military government of the city was simply a license to rob the helpless.

The detective office was presided over by Capt. Frank, of Chicago. One of the first acts of the detectives was to throw Carr and Lissenberry into prison and seize and appropriate, or confiscate, their merchandise of the value, of $30,000. They were men of northern birth and Union convictions, doing business in the city long before the commencement of hostilities. There was not a scintilla of creditable evidence against either. I was their attorney; no written charges were ever preferred, and no trial was ever had.

Some excuse for confiscating their goods had to be manufactured out of whole cloth, and the detective agency was equal to the emergency. Letters were manufactured at Cairo, Evansville, Cincinnati, and St. Louis, and mailed to Carr and Lissenberry, giving orders to them to ship munitions of war to "Old Pappa Price," the ex-Governor of Missouri and Confederate general. When these forged letters reached the postoffice at Memphis, Capt. Frank's thieves seized them and pretended they were genuine letters.

I was three months in tracing up and proving the forgery of these letters by incontestible evidence. Carr and Lissenberry were denied bail and held in prison all this time, but their goods were shipped off within forty-eight hours after their seizure.

I presented the proofs of forgery and urged a trial, but it was denied, and the prisoners still held, and I never obtained their release, but a merchant did. One of the Lowensteins went to the prisoners and told them that for $1,000 he could secure their release in an hour. It was furnished, and they came forth into daylight within the time specified; but their goods were never restored, nor was restitution in any way made. Liberty was restitution enough, to breathe the air a boon.

Backed by the military arm, to whom it was useless to appeal, under Gen. Hurlburt's administration, these industrious and patriotic gentlemen made relentless war on helpless goods and chattels.

The office for the collection of "Abandoned Property" was another paradise of thieves. This institution was presided over by Capt. Eddy, as nice a gentleman "as ever cut a throat or scuttled a ship." A few illustrations will show the patriotic tide that adorned his career and shed luster on the flag he served. Loss Dale, of Mississippi, gave me, in part payment, for services rendered, a fine piano of the value of $1,000, then at a residence in the city where Capt. Eddy and wife boarded.

The captain asked me to lend him this instrument for the use of his wife for a few weeks. I complied with his request made in the name of his wife. When the time expired he asked for an extension of the loan, which was granted. When the extension expired, I applied for the instrument and was informed by the gentleman that the instrument had been confiscated under the "Abandoned Property Act" of Congress, and was now the property of the United States. I told him that as bailee of the property kindly loaned to him for the use of his wife, the larceny could not have been perpetrated without his active agency as the head of the Bureau, and he threatened me with the luxuries of a military prison if I further protested. That was the end of the matter. This was not all. I had accumulated a valuable law library of well-selected books, of the value of several thousand dollars, which was in my office. These knights of plunder and the abandoned garter broke open my office between two days and turned the library over to the "Abandoned Bureau" of invasion and occupation. It was several days before I found who were the patriotic gentlemen. I found my books boxed up and in charge of Capt. Eddy, who refused to restore them. My name was on the books. The library parted into divisions drifted up to law offices in the Northwest, where I often heard of them after the war. Many gentlemen up there wrote me about the books and made inquiry as to how they got out of my hands. I think that some of the gentlemen in possession of the treasure trove were running for office, but no restitution was ever made. It would have been disloyal to make a move in that direction. I was a loyal subject under their own rulings and views of patriotism when these larcenies occurred. I had paid a patriotic tax of $500 for a copy of the oath of allegiance, furnished me ready manufactured for that *quid pro quo* under the following circumstances:

As soon as the army of occupation took possession of the city an order was issued commanding all citizens within a prescribed time to take the oath of allegiance to the National Government, noncompliance meant banishment beyond the lines. This was gall and wormwood to all who had given their adhesion to the Confederate States. Rather than submit to its terms, I resolved to go South with my family, and teach school when my physical condition permitted. I was then suffering with an aggravated enlargement of the pleura of long standing, my system was much swollen and skin almost as white as cotton. In this condition I applied for a pass through the lines for my family and myself and household goods, clothing, etc., but was promptly informed I could not take any kind of property, not even a change of clothing. I had no national currency at the time, but fortunately John C. Lanier, the old Clerk and Master, a short time after called me into the Gayoso bank and paid me $1,500 in greenbacks, money due me. This was a God-send at the time.

A few days after I had applied for a pass through the lines, a strange gentleman came to me who said he was a "Moses" who could lead me out of the wilderness of my troubles, and I told him I was very much in need of just such a person. "How can you help me?" "You are an ex-Confederate soldier, and of course it's rough on you to be compelled to take the oath. That can be avoided and every object accomplished. I can bring the papers to you already made out, and all you will have to do is to sign your own name to them; no oath, whatever, required, you need not go to the office. I will bring them to you, but it costs money to secure these valuable privileges." "How much?" said I. "Five hundred dollars." "Well, my friend, call around in a day or two. I will think this matter over, and look into it, and if I find or become satisfied that your representations are true, I will invest and take stock in ' Moses.' "

No man could pursue any avocation, do any business, or purchase supplies without a permit based on the oath of allegiance, and specifying what he was permitted to purchase. I soon found that " Moses " knew what he was doing, and that a very lively cash trade had sprung up in the patriotic office where the oath was supposed to be *bona fide* administered. In fact was often administered there to those applying for and willing to take it. Two departments, Division Nos. 1 and 2. Two was the cash division, where *sub rosa* men presided, where " division and silence " was observed.

When " Moses " called again we " struck a trade." He took my height, color of hair and eyes, and the description *personne*, retired, and in an hour I was a loyal man, " paid the cash and took my choice," and swore to nothing.

" Moses " did an immense business, he was a shrewd trader. I afterward found that his scale of prices was graduated on adjustable scales, always fixed at standards suited to the customer's financial status. This scale ranged up and down from $10 down to $500 up. Unfortunately for me I struck the wrong end of the pole, but did not know it at the time " Moses tapped " me. Splendid trader, " Moses " was. His exchequer balances rapidly increased. There was much " silence " but little " division," and abundance of *sub rosa*. He was eminently practical, reduced everything to commercial standards, had a Bureau in every branch of the service, and an army at his beck and call. No man in sight, but Moses a subordinate; how he secured immunity was nobody's business.

Recalcitrants gave him no trouble. They understood that " an ounce of fear was worth more than a ton of love " when it came to kicking against the army of occu-

pation and its followers.   The army had great confidence
in " Moses."   He often out-generaled the Secretary of
War.   He was a good fellow.   Simon Cameron, the
first Secretary of War under President Lincoln, admired
him and "monkeyed" with him until he lost his place in
the Cabinet, but "Moses" did not "get a setback," but
took in more *sub rosa*.   "Shesus Krist,vat a kuntry dish
ish.   I fights mit Segel."   Cameron started the first
"Moses" in national contracts, it was charged; Simon
got out, "Moses" stayed.

I was as green and innocent as a gosling on a grassy
lawn when I first met "Moses" and his family, and did
not know the interpretation of that "bright lexicon" of
Yankee youth, where it speaks of being "on the make,"
and reduces soul and body to commercial standards, and
where "Eli" defied hell and all its imps to "get there."
An unwilling, a compulsory novitiate in the history of
war.   To stand aloof as a silent spectator was impossible—an actor I must be, no choice.   Society was in an
upheaval like Ætna in eruption, a cyclone like the French
Revolution was in progress, and I was a citizen of conquered territory, in hourly contact with my conquerors,
and forced to deal with them on their terms, not mine.

I now had the key to every fort a *citizen* could attack
in the walks of private life, a rudder to the steamship of
the revolution, a compass that enabled the helmsman to
glide through the breakers between Charybdis and Scilla.   And "to be or not to be" was the question of the
hour.

Go South with a penniless and helpless family without
food or clothing and a fearfully deranged physical system, or to *practically* ride the storm with the wings and
arms of "Moses" after renewing my health.   Although
every fiber, woof, and web of the heart and soul was in
deepest sympathy with my native South, I did not believe, nor ever did believe, from the crack of the first gun
in the revolution until the gray sun went down on Appo-

mattox, that the South had resources enough to achieve success. The spirit and valor and heroism of her sons and daughters were never questioned, but I always maintained that redress for her many grievances, if to be found anywhere was in and not out of the union of our fathers.

Hence I stood where Gen. Lee did, went with my people, whether they survived or perished. I am not offering an apology to any human being for what I did, I owe that alone to God, and to him alone will I give it.

I chose to stay with and protect my family if I could, to ride the storm if I could. Penny-whistlers have criticised my conduct, knowing as little of the circumstances which surrounded me, of the impulses which moved and impelled me as the Indian does of the diplomacy which obtains with civilized people.

A FIXED POLICY DETERMINED ON.

THE conditions confronting me, described in the last chapter, required profound consideration in determining a line of action to govern me. That I could be of much service to my fellow citizens was evident, as well as to myself. My position and relation to the actors in the exciting and frenzied revolution in progress, to the military and civilians on both sides of the contest, gave me much power and great opportunity for the accumulation of wealth if I chose to direct it in that dangerous channel—dangerous because of temptation to abuse power. All these things were vividly before me, and the fact that I was a citizen of the conquered country under 'the military government of the conquerer, wholly irresponsible for the corruption a horde of wealth seekers, that army had brought with it, powerless to achieve greatly desired objects without submission to the methods they introduced in the use of money as a factor, they offered themselves for sale, not in the market overt but through Moses the *sub rosa* go between. I say these considerations had much weight in determining my action. First, how far could I justify myself, as the conquered, in accepting the terms offered by the conqueror? I resolved that I would aid my suffering countrymen to the utmost of my power, and accept all the terms for their relief that the enemy voluntarily offered, let the consequences be what they might. The sequel will vividly disclose the result, and arm my enemies and friends alike with the same weapons. It was a crisis in my life when I had to act and determine in the vortex of a revolution then in its mad whirl. And here let me say that I did more for the Southern people in an almost incredible short space of time than any thousand soldiers of the rank and file the South ever put in the field.

I say this in defense of my name, and will state the facts on which I fearlessly base the assertion in chapter after chapter in the order in which they occurred. It will be readily seen from the volume of business daily, almost hourly pouring in on me, that it would require an enormous amount of time to go through the slow and formal process of a military court in trying these cases, and that if a more expeditious method was not found but little could be done. In addition to that my notarial business was voluminous sometimes, and often bringing me a revenue of $500 per day. Added to all this much time was devoted to consultations with merchants, traders and blockade runners. A corps of clerks were employed, everything systematized, and a large volume of business was dispatched every day with the greatest facility.

The business from the Bastile, the Irving Block, needs explanation, that has never before been given to the curious, superficial public, who can look on and grow as wise as a "Snolligoster Politician" or a flock of hooting owls in an Arkansas wilderness, at results without knowing anything of cause and effect. The Bastile was in charge of a young man of thirty, my own age at that time, whom I cannot better describe than by saying he was double-geared lightning, and continually propounded to himself "what am I hear for?" It devolved on him, this shrewdest of all the Moses family I ever came in contact with, to read the voluminous correspondence coming to me hourly from the Bastile. He saw every department, military and civil, in all of their ramifications, embracing every available opportunity to make money and caught the contagious fever, and determined to subordinate his opportunities to that end. Not knowing me, he at first tried to divert my business to an attorney from the North, who had followed along in the wake of the army, but he signally failed in that. Then he sought a private interview with me, not at either his or my office, but a secluded suit of rooms on the west side of Main street. He was excessively cautious, wise beyond his years, and I can pay no higher tribute to his genius than by saying the combination which he sought and formed with me never made a failure. He simply offered for a stipend graduated to a basis which my clients could pay to secure, their release and furnish, when desired, passes through the Federal military lines. Of my large volume of other business he knew nothing and had nothing whatever to do, and never knew the large amount of revenue I devoted from other sources of income to release a large number of penniless clients in the Bastile. I told him frankly that at least four fifths of that class of my clients were penniless, although every one without exception, in their letters to me, promised liberal fees, and that in these cases he must expect no compensation whatever. That I must be the sole judge of their ability to pay; that I had never charged but one Confederate soldier, John Rawlings, tried as a spy, and weeks consumed in the trial, and that I did not intend ever to charge another, no matter how arduous and difficult the service for them. That these conditions must be regarded and treated as imperative, and that he must be as vigilant and prompt with these poor men as with the wealthiest blockade runner. And it was further stipulated that I was to be entirely relieved from going to the Bastile to confer with my clients—that they must be sent when I demanded, to my office, under one or more of his guards on my order for them in writing sent by one of my clerks. This was all agreed to and promptly carried out, and on receiving a note from me if there was any impediment a sealed note to me explained the reason. We never had the slightest misunderstanding or disagreement. In six months I gave him $65,000, and he released for me many hundreds of Southern citizens and hundreds of Southern soldiers, and gave all who wanted them passes through the lines. Our, or rather my, business with the Bastile only lasted a period of six months, for reasons which will be fully detailed in its proper place. Moses scrupulously observed every engagement with me, and often assumed bold and desperate risks. Each of us risked and staked our lives at a thousand turns of the wheel, and the security of each, to a great extent, depended on rigid fidelity to the other, and neither made a single mistake. I will not give his name—he anticipated that some day I might indulge my pen in giving reminiscences of those times, and asked me, whether he was living or dead, to protect his name, and I keep my promise. I have not heard from him in twenty years, and do not now know whether he is alive or dead.

Man is a product of the times in which he lives, and no accurate judgment or estimate of his character can or will ever be made without taking into consideration all the circumstances surrounding him at the period we judge him, and that is often the most difficult of all human undertakings, because of the manifold combinations of light and shade operating to influence the actions of men.

BRIGADIER GENERAL VEACH.

EN. VEACH, of Indiana, was for quite a time Commander of the Post at Memphis, and I had much intercourse and important business with him. He was a cultured and courteous gentleman, educated and refined, a lawyer by profession, of prominence at his home. My first introduction to him ended in mutual esteem which, so far as I know, was never broken. One morning while at my breakfast table a file of twenty-five Federal soldiers marched into my dining room with muskets and bayonets. When I asked their leader "What is your pleasure?" he responded in the presence of my wife, children and friends present, "We have orders to arrest this John Hallum and place him in the local militia now being organized under Gen. John McDonald for the defense of Memphis." I said, "Very well, you can arrest a defenseless man, but there is no power great enough on this earth to make a Federal soldier of me." This file of soldiers carried me to Gen. Veach's headquarters, and I was at once ushered into his presence. I said, "This is Gen. Veach, I presume. I have been arrested to be conscripted into the brigade of Federal militia now being organized?" To which he replied in the affirmative. I then said, "I am an honorably discharged volunteer Confederate soldier. I was not forced into the army against my will. I went into it, not because I approved of the war, but as Gen. Lee went into it, because I could neither remain neutral nor take up arms against my native South. I was discharged because of long continued sickness and the consequent physical debility it brought. Now you have my explanation, let me say to you in all sincerity that having worn the gray, I will never wear the blue;

my honor is my own, it is the only inheritance I am striving to leave my children. I loathe and despise a traitor as I do the name of Benedict Arnold." He gave me a paper exempting me from such service, and said "That will protect you as long as I am in command of the Post, but my successor will not be bound by it." After the war was over he represented his district in Congress and held other important Federal offices. He was a gentleman in all the term implies. While he was Commander of the Post a blackeyed brunette, a Louisiana Creole, young and handsome, with a luxuriance of hair extending nearly to her feet, came into my office to engage my professional services in recovering 450 bales of cotton then on a steamboat under convoy of a gunboat anchored three miles below the city. The next day she brought her husband to my office, a young farmer named Smith, native of Tipton county, Tenn., but then living on his wife's plantation in Louisiana. Gen. Veach at once ordered the cotton held at the anchorage until he could investigate the claim. After he was satisfied, he ordered the cotton restored to the young Creole, and it was done without one dollar's cost to her, except that involved in making proof and my fee. She sold it in Memphis, the proceeds amounting to $101,250. My fee was $5,000. She was the most demonstrative and grateful little woman I ever met.

GOOD LUCK TO THE BOY THAT KICKED A TIN CAN.

MY office boy, whose name I now forget, as I changed them at that time frequently, a young man raised in Memphis, in crossing Shelby street in front of the Gayoso Hotel, struck his foot against an old tin can. Its weight attracted his attention and he picked it up. It was sealed and covered with

tar, and had a wire bale attached. He brought it to the
office, knocked the top off, and found $2,000 in gold in it.
There was no evidence as to ownership. Evidently some
one intending to convey it through the lines had disguised
it as a tar can and tied to a vehicle from which it fell and
was lost. The young man invested it in merchandise and
opened a little store in South Memphis. I advised him
to advertise it, find and restore it to the owner, and told
him that a good name for honesty might ultimately be of
infinitely more value to him, but he had been raised poor
and the temptation was too great. The owner never advertised for it, because the discovery of such a loss would
have exposed him.

JOHN RAWLINGS, THE SPY.

FTER purchasing five hundred dollars' worth
of patriotism from my friend Moses, I opened
a suite of offices on the ground floor on the
south side of Court Square, that being the
floor from which I expected to operate, in fact, the
only floor from which powerful arguments could be
formulated without the aid of libraries and a preponderance of facts, as long as Moses and his allies held the
fort.

But still I was a novitiate, my eye teeth not having
come yet.

The first case that engaged my serious attention was
that of John Rawlings, a Confederate soldier, son of Dr.
Rawlings, and nephew of J. J. Rawlings, the oldest patriarch of Memphis, who yet survives at an advanced age,
now the oldest of the early settlers in Memphis.

John was one of those good natured, rollicking, dare-
devil sort of boys, raised with a silver spoon in his mouth
by the best of parents. He came home from the Confederate army on a furlough to his father's plantation on

Hatchee river, ten or twelve miles north of the city; put on citizen's clothes and came into town and was taken into custody, and chained flat of his back in the basement of the Irving Block, charged with being a spy. Under the articles of war the facts developed a crime of the gravest nature, and gave me an amazing amount of trouble and solicitude.

A regular red tape military court was very slowly organized to try him, but I found the young men who composed it educated, refined gentlemen, and social with me. Their age and refinement were encouraging; they manifested perfect fairness, and I am sorry that I have lost the record and have forgotten their names.

They generously gave me every indulgence and opportunity I asked, and a fairer trial was never held in any court. It was pleasing to meet such men.

If it be possible, I want to do justice to all men as I pass through this upheaval of society; this tearing up of original foundations, and reorganization on an entirely new basis, and in this attempt to divest myself from the prejudices growing out of association and education, I recognize the common infirmities of human nature, and that it is the most difficult of all tasks.

John and his people were my friends from early manhood. I knew him when he was a schoolboy at Raleigh, happy, gay, thoughtless, and wholly ignorant of the stern realities involved in the great and troublesome problem of life, much less the demands of war. My solicitude was enhanced, not only from these associations and memories, but because his father and family and friends put far more confidence in me than I indulged in myself, and to this day they have never recognized the gravity of that trial. To lose such a case, such a life, under such surroundings, presented a momentous problem to me that rose infinitely higher than all the money consideration I received—the comparison is vulgar.

John had no more idea of taking maps and plans of the

fort, arsenals, position and strength of the Federal army than he had of trying to capture the ironclad fleet anchored in front of the city—he was not the daring and adventurous genius to execute enterprises of that gravity.

If I could lodge these facts in the minds of the chivalrous and true soldiers who tried him, he would be acquitted, if not, his life would pay the penalty. Fortunately for him, after much labor, time, and anxiety, I was successful in photographing the true facts on the minds of the court, and they acquitted him.

Those who have never had such anxieties and responsibilities, have no conception of the trouble and solicitude a lawyer feels; their observation is superficial, they see the flash in the last efforts of the final trial and conclude that success is an easy achievement, and many estimate the labors of such men as they do that of the common laborer.

John's acquittal was looked on by his relatives as a matter of course, a *pro forma* proceeding. While this case was in progress, the Bastile of the revolution, the Irving Block, was being filled from cellar to dome with prisoners, citizens, Confederate soldiers—the army in the field with its legitimate work, and the army of detectives, bent on spoil and plunder, made the Bastile almost a charnel house.

Letters poured on me in immense numbers, every man wanted assistance, from the blockade runner by water and land, to the impoverished citizen and destitute soldier. Sometimes one hundred of these letters came to me in one day. I was simply overwhelmed.

All these letters were read by officers in charge of the prison before they reached me. Hundreds of these distressed men in their great anxiety for relief promised large fees, when in fact they had nothing at command. These letters inspired Moses with visions of wealth, and greatly prolonged the period of confinement in many cases, influenced Moses to wait and see what there was

in it for him.   An effort was made to divert this practice
from me, but it did not make a ripple in my patronage,
none could supplant me, the Northern man who came as a
stranger could not take it from me.

DICK DAVIS, THE NOTORIOUS DESERTER
AND GUERILLA.

HE romantic and tragic career of this young man is
peculiarly interesting.   He was born and raised
in Hamilton county, Ohio, by intensely Union parents.   He was rather tall but of slender build, of
fine personal appearance, dark brown hair, large flashing
gray eyes, and had a slight, boyish mustache.

When he was put to death he was in his twenty-first
year of age.   At my request he wrote a very full account
of his life in the army and gave it to me for publication,
after his death, but in moving, the manuscript was lost,
and I never published anything of his before giving this
volume to the press.

He enlisted at eighteen years of age in an Ohio regiment, and went with it to the campaigns in Virginia
and was in many battles, the last of which he fought as
a Federal soldier was on the Chickahominy, under Mc-
Clellan, in the mighty conflict of the Seven Pines.   After
those battles he deserted and joined the Confederate
army at once, which division I have forgotten.

He deserted early in June, 1863, and joined a Confederate infantry regiment, but soon secured a transfer to
Gen. John Morgan's cavalry, because he liked the spirit
and dash of that brilliant officer.   The tragic romance of
war had a fascination for his brave and restless spirit—a
braver boy than Dick Davis never rode at the head of a
charging column of cavalry.   He was with Morgan in

his dashing campaign in Ohio, called by enemies incompetent to indulge impartial criticism, a "raid." He made his escape back into Kentucky after narrow escapes and thrilling adventures. He said that he well knew the fact of his leaving the Federal army would debar him from promotion in the regular service, that he was ambitious to lead and excel in all he undertook, and adopted what to him seemed the only avenue left open, that of an independent command of bold spirits without any commission as an officer.

Moving silently and cautiously in Kentucky where sentiment was divided, he organized an independent command of forty young men and secured arms and the best horses the State afforded. At a designated place they met in the mountains and elected their officers, he being unanimously chosen captain. Thoroughly equipped and mounted, he felt that he could cut or force his way wherever he wanted to go if not opposed by a largely outnumbering force. "My design was to operate on the rear, front, or flanks of the Federal army, and take them in detail whenever and wherever my own judgment dictated. The charge that I was moved by mercenary motives to plunder and spoil is as base a slander as was ever venomously hurled at a soldier's name. The charge that I ever injured a Confederate after firing my last gun on the Chickahominy in that awful rattle of musketry and roar of cannon is a base falsehood. Sometimes I commanded a hundred men, oftener less than fifty. I have played like the Hetman Platoff with his Cossacks, in the rear of Bonaparte's retreat from Russia, on a small scale it is true, but I have written my name with my saber in the blood of the men who have condemned me to die on the gallows, who deny me a soldier's death, a soldier's grave, and fight me with the basest weapons known to mankind, slander, and rear a mounment of odium to the name of him who fought them as a knight. My last hour, my last breath will be cheered by a soldier's consolation, that their bleaching bones on the field of conflict where the odds were theirs, will attest my courage and proclaim it to the world. Men can traduce and blacken memories in the minds of willing listeners; but there is a God above all whose throne will shine on truth as the sun on the bright saber of the soldier. Death I fear not. I have faced it on many a battlefield, but it is horrid to leave a blackened name to a noble mother and sister. That is the only uncompensated terror to me. Oh, could I have commanded and led victorious legions in this war, how different would have been the panorama of the short life on which I now gaze! How glorious it must have been to Marshal Ney when leading the charge at Waterloo!''

Thus spoke this almost beardless youth to me as his counsel after sentence of death. What a field marshal that youth would have made under auspicious suns! Youthful and misguided as he was, the flames of a lofty ambition lit his soul, and he craved opportunity to distinguish himself in arms. Two twenty-pound cannon balls were chained to his legs. He held the chains in one hand while he stood in the hallway in the Irving Block and talked to me with a soul that even under those circumstances pierced the astral depths and soared away to the stars.

The story would be but half told were I to drop it here, and its romantic interest would be lost in the sorrowful tragedy. No Confederate ever laid charge at his door. No unprotected mother, when marauding pillagers in uniform were abroad, ever appealed to Dick Davis for protection without the defense of his saber. When he wanted arms and munition he took them in conflict as lawful prize of war. He never made commerce out of prize of war, but gave it to the defenseless and needy. Seizure of abandoned property belonging to civilians, and confiscation of private property were terms and acts unknown and undefined in the chivalrous lexicon of this youth. No complaint, no cry ever arose against him except from those who wore the uniform of Federal soldiers.

He was finally captured near the Federal lines near Memphis, and chained flat of his back in the basement of Bastile with two twenty-pound cannon balls chained to his limbs, charged with being a guerilla. He had been of much service to the defenseless homes near the line of the Memphis and Charleston railroad from Memphis to Corinth, Miss. A few days after his capture that sterling matron of remarkable intelligence, Mrs. Stricklin, so often mentioned in this volume, came to my office and handed me $500, and said: "If you want a thousand more you can have it to defend Dick Davis." I told her that although not acquainted with him, I knew from the daily press the cloud under which he rested, and did not think it possible to save his life, and proposed to return the money.

"No," she said, "do the best you can for him, that money has been contributed by the wives and daughters of Confederate soldiers whose husbands and fathers are in the field, and I have been delegated to see and retain you, and you must keep the money and do all you can for him."

I soon held my first conference with the prisoner, and was astonished at his youthful appearance, noble countenance, and dauntless eye. He gave me the name of his parents and sister, Alice, and desired me to write and request a last interview. I dealt in the utmost candor with him, and told him that it would be a crime to hold out any hope of saving his life by the judgment of a military court. The parents and sister came immediately. Alice, the sister, was a spare-made beauty, of the blonde type, twenty years of age, and just graduated from school. The mother was a sedate matron of pleasing address and few words.

The father was of stern-knit visage and intense Union

sentiment, which embraced no charity for the Southern people, and was intensely anxious to hear the details of his son's history, about which he had read and suffered so much. Anxiety to see, embrace, and console her brother was the reigning passion in Alice's mind. The mother was by far the greatest sufferer, but quiet and undemonstrative; despair settled on her countenance, she abandoned her forlorn hope. The father promised me to utter no word, let no sentiment escape him in the presence of his son which would wound him, but did not keep his promise. I left the family in my office and went to the Bastile to arrange as pleasantly as the circumstances would permit for an interview with the son and brother. The offices at the prison were on the second floor, and we were all ushered into one of them to await the coming of the prisoner. Clank, clank went the chains, and thump, thump as the prisoner ascended the steps of two flights of stairs from the damp dungeon below. When these approaching sounds grated on the ears and cultured soul of Alice, she became as white as a corpse and as speechless as a statue for a few moments; the mother's face was the quiet picture of horror and despair; the father's stoically cold as marble. I suffered intense mental pain. The prisoner was halted in the hallway a few feet from the door, and I supported Alice to her brother. She fell on his neck and wept bitterly. The mother advanced with an embrace and kiss. All this time the father stood as immovable and speechless as a statue.

When he did speak, it was in censure like the eruption of Ætna; words more cruel than the knife of the executioner. The son tried to control his feelings, but the effort almost petrified him. The mother swooned away under sorrows she could no longer sustain, and was carried into the office, and thus spared at least a part of this cruel scene. Alice reeled under her afflictions, and covered her face with her hands; recovering, she embraced her brother whose face was much like her own.

19

I seized the father and shook him into silence, and directed the guard to remove him at once, which was done. Thus ended the most painful interview I ever witnessed.

I have seen wife, mother and father, sister and brother in the last embrace and farewell under the gallows, but nothing so horrid as the mistaken and misguided rage of that heartless father. I emphasized my demand that he leave the city on the next steamer, and he did so. The mother and Alice remained; the former two weeks, the latter till the end of the first scene in the tragedy. I obtained many interviews and concessions for them, but was never present at another meeting. Alice visited at my office daily, carried all the delicacies of the season to her brother, with pipe and tobacco. At first morose and downcast, but this gradually wore off, and she became cheerful and seemingly relieved from distress. She was a polished, entertaining, vivacious girl. At first I did not understand this, but at last became suspicious that she was the central and moving spirit in a conspiracy to release her brother, which would involve me in very serious trouble, as I was the lawyer in the case and would in all probability be held as the originator of any attempted rescue of my client, no matter who might execute it.

It would be so much more plausible to charge the offense on an experienced lawyer than on a girl just out of school. My anxiety was so great I unbosomed myself directly and plainly to Alice, and she innocently but unintentionally confirmed my suspicions. With a toss of her head she said: "All's well that ends well." She was a bright girl. "It would delight and surprise you, would it not, if a schoolgirl just out of her teens could out-manage and out-general an old lawyer. You can talk wisely and dispense law faster than an apothecary can compound his hateful medicines, but there might be more than you have dreamed of in your cold, methodical philosophy." I was astonished at the wisdom and intuitive perception of this girl, the sister of Dick Davis, who had equally astonished me.

This confirmation of my suspicions intensified my anxiety and uneasiness. She would not tell me any more, but bade me rest quiet and lend my energies in some other direction. Then she continued: "You seem to be supremely cautious. Let me say to you in all candor that you are innocent at least, and I feel that I am secure in trusting your honor in what you assume, suppose, guess to be a revelation, a confession. It is nothing of the sort, and ought not to be tortured into any such construction. But if it will be of any consolation to you, let me call Heaven to attest a girl's sincerity, a girl's faith, a girl's honor that if an ingenious combination of circumstances should require it, I would attest your innocence with as much loyalty to truth and justice as a martyr ever entered the flames. And let me add to that, if I could save my unfortunate brother by the jeopardy of many such lives as mine, I would have no hesitation in doing it, but would gladly embrace it. I will be loyal to you both, war, treason, or what not, never have I felt so strongly before Mr. Seward's proclamation to the world that 'There is a higher law than man can promulgate for the guidance of his fellow men.' I felt abashed, strengthened, exalted at the devotion that played and flashed in the soul of that Joan D'Arc in another role. Had Dick Davis led McDonald's awful charge when he broke the Austrian center at Wagram under the eye of his emperor, this little Northern girl would have been a worthy sister." In a few days the morning press announced in flaming headlines: "The escape of Dick Davis, the notorious guerilla."

Alice came tripping into my office that morning like a fairy, and said: "Now I am ready to answer all questions, relieve all curiosity, dispel all anxiety, and to go home with my heart overflowing with thanks to God. I put a little spring in the cake I carried to Brother Dick, he sawed off his shackles, I gave him a suit of citizen's clothes, $50, and a pass through the lines." That evening I accompanied her to the landing, she embarked for Cincinnati, and that was the last I ever saw or heard of Alice.

Davis rallied his command, but was again captured, in three weeks' time railroaded through, and executed on a gallows inside of Fort Pickering. I saw him at two hundred yards distance, but was looking through the bars of a prison in the fort, where I had been sent for resisting military oppression.

PRISONERS OF WAR—MY BROTHER—A CONVOY OF SIX THOUSAND "REBELS" ANCHOR SEVERAL DAYS IN FRONT OF THE CITY OF MEMPHIS—TOUCHING SCENES.

"But oh, what crowds in every land,
    All wretched and forlorn,
Thro' weary life this lesson learn,
    That man was made to mourn."

AFTER the cartel of exchange was agreed on, a convoy of six steamers, with six thousand Confederate soldiers, anchored in front of Memphis for three days on their way to Vicksburg to be exchanged. Many, if not all, of the prisoners were from Camp Chase, where my brother Henry, two years my junior, had been confined many months. The fleet was in charge of Captain LaSalle, of Indiana, who was a stranger and unknown to me. I could not obtain a permit from the authorities in the city to visit the fleet to search for my brother, because not within their jurisdic-

tion. I was distressed, had not seen my brother since the
opening of hostilities. He went with the first troops
from Tennessee to Virginia, and was in charge of a battery at Aquia Creek, on the Potomac, and was known as
one of the best artillery gunners in the army. He and
my twelve-year old brother, Bluford, stood side by side
in the hottest of the conflict through the battles of Mur-
freesboro, on the 31st of December, 1862, and the 1st of
January, 1863. Bluford, the kid, had run away from
home, thirty miles distant, to join his brother in that
battle. The Colonel of the regiment refused to let him
go into the battle, and started him back, but in a few
minutes he closed up and wedged his way in beside his
brother, and did a soldier's service. Fortunately, I accidentally found Captain LaSalle talking to a friend of
mine and an old schoolmate of his, who introduced us. I
found him one of the most courteous gentlemen I ever
met, but felt excessively oppressed when he informed me
that it was against orders to permit visitors on board the
steamers. I plead with him for a relaxation of the order,
as an excessively hard one in my case. He was a gentleman of refined sensibilities, cultured, and a true soldier.
He felt for me, and I continued to press my way to his
heart. He studied, and was silent a few moments, and
repeated, "Do unto others as ye would that they
should do unto you," then stepped to a desk and wrote
me a pass to any vessel in the fleet. I procured a light
craft and went from boat to boat, examined the prison
roster of each. When I reached the fourth steamer I
found my brother's name on the roster, and an obliging
soldier in charge, who immediately sent a sergeant after
my brother, and he appeared in a few moments. I will
leave those who have been nurtured into life by the same
mother to judge of the feelings I cannot describe. My
brother was in perfect health, but literally in rags, without enough to hide his person. Can a tear moisten a soldier's eye? Yes, and draw him nearer to his God. I

don't want a heart that can drive back and banish
them, it may be manly, but it is not the nature God
gave his children.   By this time Captain LaSalle came
on board and I implored the relaxation of another rule of
war, prohibiting aid and comfort to the enemy.   To feed
and clothe and succor, to "feed the hungry and clothe
the naked."   Brother had been confined six months without a change of garments, and other than the hard fare
of the soldier, he was bareheaded and with nothing but
strings hanging to his body.   The captain again relaxed
the rigors of war and permitted me to bring on board
a bountiful supply of provisions for my brother and his
mess.   I returned to Schawb's, the Delmonico of the city,
and obtained all his larder could afford, and servants to
send it, and repeated it as long as they stayed.   The
generous LaSalle permitted me to clothe the soldier *cap a
pie*, finally promised not to have me arrested if my gift
of Confederate currency did not exceed $500.   That was
an oasis in the Sahara of a soldier's life, one small island
in a monotonous ocean.

Benedictions, Captain LaSalle, laurels for your grave,
and blessings for your posterity.

CAPTAIN REUBEN BURROW, OF GEN. FOR-
REST'S COMMAND, A PRISONER OF
WAR, RELEASED, AND GIVEN
A PASS THROUGH
THE LINES.

APT. BURROW was a distinguished divine long
prior to hostilities, of a nervo-sanguine temperament, an original secessionist of pronounced type,
who believed war the only solution of the conflict
of ideas between the sections.   He was Captain of a company of cavalry in Gen. Forrest's command, was cap-

tured in 1864 and confined as a prisoner of war in the Bastile at Memphis. As soon as he was brought in, he sent for me, and manifested much nervousness and inordinate anxiety to be released. He belonged to that class against whom I made no charge for whatever services I could render, but for whom I felt none the less solicitous. He was also embraced in that class for whom Moses had stipulated with me to render active and available services, whenever he could without too much jeopardy to the contracting parties, of which he was the principal and primary judge. It was but a matter of small moment to discharge a private soldier who had made no noise, or at least not enough to distinguish and noise his name abroad. Captain Burrow was many degrees above the latter class. Finally all things were arranged, and a pass through the lines was secured by Moses for Mr. Wilson, who was cautiously put at business about the upper room, purposely to let him walk down and out at half past nine at night, when all was still and quiet. Clothing and the pass were held in readiness on the outside. The Captain, who personated Mr. Wilson, was as nervous as if he had St. Vitus' dance, but he came down and climbed on the plank fence just as some one with a lantern appeared in the hallway on the second floor, which threw a momentary light on him, and frightened him so he fell back on the inside instead of the outside, and he crept back to his prison quarters. Moses was much vexed at this play of the nervous Captain, and sent him under guard to my office next day for criticism and reproof, which I administered, as I shared in the vexation his useless fear had caused. It was three weeks before another opportunity was available, and then he acted promptly and fell on the outside and passed out to his command. I have had many a good laugh with Gen. Forrest about his nervous Captain. The General gave him credit for being a brave soldier, whom he would trust to lead any charge not led by himself.

MEMPHIS AFTER THE SURRENDER.

AFTER the surrender, thousands of ragged, destitute Confederate soldiers, on their way to their destitute homes and families and ruined fortunes, tarried in Memphis for aid and food. It was a sight to touch and quicken the heart of the stoutest and proudest conqueror. How much deeper down did it reach and stir the patriotic tide that flowed through the hearts of their dauntless sisters, brothers, fathers and mothers of their own Southland? They were the tattered remnants of broken legions, the survivors of heroic comrades whose lives had been given on a hundred battlefields, from Antietam to the Rio Grande, from Oak Hill to Mobile. They had walked the earth as a Colossus where the rattle of musketry and roar of cannon told that heroes and patriots of the same race and blood, equally brave, grandly great, were in conflict. The marshalled hosts on both sides were brothers, and their fame, their renown, is the heritage of the human race. The pension roll of the fallen is folded, laid away in the loving hearts for whom they struggled, and unborn millions as the ages come and go will see that the political harlot and tramp will not blot their burnished luster.

Equal glory to the Northman's shield. They are accorded equal credit for "rallying 'round the flag" and swearing that this greatest empire of States the world has known shall never be dissevered as long as its great inland arteries roll to the sea. The earth trembled, and the destinies of the world were changed, and a new book was opened up in the history of man. I loathe the narrow, contracted mind, who would diminish the splendor and cloud the achievements of either section. One of the brightest pages in all history holds Gen. Grant full high advanced above the bust of Cæsar, in the act of refusing the sword of the mighty chieftain he had conquered, and the name of Lee will forever brilliantly shine as a star of the first magnitude, and the Northman or Southron who is not proud of both cannot compass his country's greatness.

Those destitute soldiers were generously treated. Committees were appointed with which I acted. We collected ten thousand dollars in one afternoon for their relief, many of us filled our houses to overflowing, and dining rooms with bountiful comfort. The Wright and Chenault boys from my native county were my guests, my charge and care with others, and we all felt honored in their presence. Here let me gladly record the fact that merchants from the North contributed most liberally to this fund. I do not recollect being refused by one of them. Why can't we stand on a higher plane and embrace a broader charity for the errors of our fellow men? Are base politicians from either section going to forever lower the standard of man and chain him in subjection and hatred to his brother?

BLOCKADE RUNNING BY WATER AND LAND.
1863.

BLOCKADE running was one of the industries of the war period. The patriotism of the Northman succumbed to his cupidity and avarice, and they swarmed on the heels of the army like the locusts of Egypt. The contagion embraced every guild of traders, from the capitalists to the man limited to a few hundred dollars. The ease and security with which the capitalist could pass the contraband limit, induced and lent vehement presumption that the contagion extended to many high in the army. The Southron was driven by pinching necessity to assume in a small way all the risks incident to contraband trade, long deprived of the imported articles of commerce, as well as the vast volume of interstate trade with the Northern States, absolute want stalked abroad in the land behind the Confederate armies. The old woman of the household, long accustomed to her coffee, gladly embraced the opportunity to exchange one dollar for one pound of coffee; a piece of cheese, a calico gown, or a pair of shoes were luxuries. This trade was not confined to sex, age or previous condition. As soon as a city or town fell within the protection of the Federal army it was filled with competing merchants and large stocks of goods. A fleet of trading boats were anchored behind the ironclad flotilla weeks before the fall of Memphis, and they tied up at the landing before the emblem of National authority, the flag, reached the shore. Eager purchasers swarmed the decks of these boats. Vacant stores in the city were filled as soon as the merchandize could be conveyed and opened up. If a storehouse was found vacant, and four fifths were in that condition, the eager merchant did not wait to find the owner or his representive, but was put in possession under the "Abandoned Property Act" and the rents paid to that department. Residence property was subjected to the same confiscation. The rural population soon ventured in, and either bought or subscribed to the oath of allegiance, a condition precedent to the purchase of the limited supplies permitted under military regulation. Family medicines were in great demand, $10 to $15 being paid anywhere outside the Federal lines for an ounce of quinine. Whisky commanded from $10 to $15 per gallon beyond the lines. Cloth for uniforms commanded fabulous prices.

The negro was a favorite, and could command more in proportion to his means and necessities than the whites, being "a ward of the nation," and penalties were light on "Cuffie" when detected in the overt act; and I will say this for him, I never knew of one "giving his master away " when caught. Ingenuity exhausted itself in efforts to deceive the picket line of guards, and the small operator who did not "stand in with" the military had to be most ingenious.

After the occupation of the city, many dead animals had to be conveyed beyond the picket lines. Their stomachs were cut open and filled with goods, then sewed up and thus transported beyond the lines; dealers in quinine made large profits in this way before detection. The details of such operations, with Memphis as a base, would fill a large volume. Blockade runners from the North in quest of Eldorado, soon began to elbow each other. Both civilians and a few army officers were equally devoted to patriotism and commerce. This clash of pursuits and interests, soon filled prisons with patriotic civilians who were anxious to pay handsomely for relief. So many came and brought with them the means to gratify their love of gain by trading with the rebels, that a military order was necessary to check this hegira South, an order to seize and confiscate all moneys being brought into territories occupied by the Federal armies. Detectives with a large per cent of interest in their success were stationed on all steamers coming South after the order was issued. One of these blockade runners had $300,000 in Southern bank bills on his person, when a personal search was commenced. He was ignorant of the existence of the order when he took passage by steamer at Cairo. He escaped the discovery of his treasure, although searched personally fifteen minutes after he heard of the order. My cousin, James Owens, a Confederate soldier, was shot in the battle of Perryville, Ky., and his leg was amputated while in the Federal hospital. His mother, my father's sister, Mrs. Minerva Owens, had nursed him there for many weeks in Harrodsburgh, Ky. He was discharged when able to walk on crutches, and they were then on their way home in Morning Sun, Tenn. This wounded leg was much swollen and had bandages on it which gave it a size in appearance nearly equal to his body; it was off at the knee joint. When the detective began his search this man ran back to the ladies' cabin, hurriedly asked the mother and son into their stateroom, and threw into the mother's lap the $300,000 and asked her to put it around the wounded limb of her son as a substitute bandage, and "save it for him for God's sake." That good old mother did so, and the speculator underwent the examination with perfect security. My aunt gave him my name and address, and told him she would leave the money with me, which she did as soon as the steamer landed at Memphis.

The gentleman stopped at the Hardwicke House on Adams street, and the next morning I went in search of him, found him, but he denied all knowledge of the transaction, and of having any interest in the money. Here was a dilemma, which for the moment I did not comprehend: He was an utter stranger to me. I knew he was the right man and the lawful owner of the money. I was not charging or expecting a fee, it was not in the line of my professional employment. I was acting for his protection, wholly as a gratuity, and to preserve the integrity of my good old aunt, cousin, and self. I brooded over the matter several hours before I struck the key to his strange conduct. He simply wanted time to investigate my character, to ascertain whether it would be safe to trust himself in my power. He was a stranger in Memphis, and had to move cautiously, he thought, even in this very simple and easy investigation. I was burdened. I dare not keep my own money in my safe or a bank. My own was in large bills sewed up in my wife's corset. Thieves, detectives, and robbers were abroad. It was dangerous even to secrete that amount in my residence. I wrapped it up in an oilcloth, took it to the south end of Main street to a deep culvert and put it under a log and left it there. Next day I went to the gentleman and he still denied ownership of the money.

The fifth day afterward he came to me and said he was satisfied to acknowledge the ownership and receive his money. In the meantime a very heavy rain had fallen and water and sand had wet and covered the treasure. We went together, recovered it, and carried it to an upper story in the hotel and counted the wet but uninjured bills, and he said every dollar was there, and thanked and receipted me, and gave me a $100 Bank of Tennessee bill to hand to the maimed soldier, and I never met or heard of him again.

The ingenuity of the blockade-runner was simply great, Napoleonic. After the publication of the military order to confiscate money coming into the Federal lines going South, one of these men had a large double-sheeted iron pan filled with $50,000 in gold coin securely riveted to the bottom of a steamboat where the confiscating detectives would not be likely to investigate. When the steamer landed at Memphis the Captain of the craft rose largely in his price, and the owner of the coin came to me to aid him in recovering it. I told him: " Yes, I can recover it for a fee less than the Captain demands. One thousand dollars will satisfy me. I think we can turn the tables on the Captain, and leave it to your discretion whether you pay him anything or not; but I advise that you pay him the original fee agreed, less the $1,000 you pay me, that would be honest."

This agreed on, I went with him to the steamer, and said: "Captain, that little treasure you have nailed to the bottom of the steamer to avoid military orders, renders both the coin and the steamer liable to confiscation, and I advise an arrangement between you gentlemen on terms honorable and safe to both."

" Why, certainly, there is not the least bit of trouble about that, just as soon as the steamer is lightened we can run up into the mouth of Wolf river and get it." That was done, and in an hour's time my fee was earned and paid. Nothing difficult about that, an "eye-open-er" is sometimes a good thing to impart conscientious inspiration when that commodity becomes a little insipid. When both the bull and the bear find themselves in equal danger they become generous and accommodating, and the lion and the lamb lie down together. These gentlemen of the blockade guild were not always fortunate. I must relate one serio-comic adventure of one of the citizens of Memphis, whose name I withhold because of his relatives and descendants who yet live there.

He ventured into my office one day and told me he had a "Mulberry Sellers" scheme on foot by which he could accumulate a fortune rapidly if I would aid him. He said: "I can buy whisky by the barrel cheap and make five hundred per cent clear on the investment if I can get it through the lines. I can convey twenty barrels at a time in a flat up Wolf river if you can secure protection. Can you do it?" I told him I knew the Colonel of the regiment stationed at Wolf river bridge, two miles north of the city, in charge of the water picket line. He is a good fellow, accommodating, but you must "take him in" to the scheme, and then it will work like a charm. I wrote a sealed note to the Colonel and asked him to call at my office. He did so, and the arrangement was made between the citizen and Colonel. Several days after, they came to my office and informed me they had abandoned the scheme. I knew they had not, or believed it. It afterwards developed that the arrangement between them was to be consummated on a certain night, and twenty barrels were put on the flat and cordelled to the bridge. But the Colonel who was to protect its passage through the lines was ordered late that evening to move his regiment, which was replaced by another Ohio regiment, the commanding and subaltern officers of which were ignorant of the cargo and promised protection. When Mr. G. got to the lines he was arrested and his cargo was confiscated. He was placed on a barrel of whisky next day and driven through the streets of Memphis and banished the city.

Dick Gaither, a discharged cavalry soldier, who had served under Capt. Ballentine with me before I was transferred to Gen. Pillow's staff, came home to Memphis after being wounded and disabled. Dick was like most of the boys, without a job and without a cent to venture in any enterprise. In this condition he appealed to me. I bought a fine horse and spring wagon and loaded it up with quinine at a cost of $2,500. He went through the lines out on the Macon road and across to White's Station on the Charleston road. To his consternation when he arrived within two hundred yards of the station he beheld thousands of Gen. Sherman's troops on the march, but no scouts coming North toward him. After catching his breath he changed his mind and course from due South to due North, and when down a declivity out of sight he tested the speed of that roadster, and kept it up until under cover of the maiden cane and dense chapparal in Wolf river bottom. After the army passed, Dick went through by starlight into Confederate lines. He was only to return to me the cash I invested in an old comrade without interest. He returned a month afterward and reported: "All confiscated by the Confederates." My desire and effort to aid him was at least gratified.

THE CITIZENS OF MEMPHIS CONSCRIPTED INTO MILITIA DUTY AND DEFENSE OF THE FEDERAL ARMY, AND MY CONNECTION WITH ITS DISCHARGE.

I N 1864 a detachment of Forrest's cavalry command fought their way in open day into the heart of Memphis, and many dismounted at the Gayoso Hotel and purchased cigars and tobacco. At another time a detachment from the same command had a lively skirmish with Federal soldiers in the southeastern suburbs of the city, near the State Female College, in which the Confederates used a small piece of flying artillery, and one or more cannon balls penetrated the College walls.

The fright and stampede of both citizens and soldiers on the first occasion was only equalled by that of Bull Run—Calf Run is more appropriate. I was in the city on both occasions and the stampede was in range of my vision. A false alarm a night or two afterwards struck appalling terror to the hearts of some Federal soldiers, and it was said that Gen. Washburn, the commander of the post of Memphis at the time, fled in his nightgown, ran under the house to escape when no one pursued. An old grayheaded negro man who waited on my office told me next day that he was at the General's headquarters at the time and witnessed it, and the old darkey indulged in hilarious laughter. Whether true or false, it was dramatized by a strolling troop of players at the time, and acted on the stage in Memphis. Personally General Washburn was a most affable and courteous gentleman.

I met none more so either in or out of the army, nor did I ever hear his courage as a soldier, or conduct as a gentleman questioned. A stampede at night under the circumstances, when the imagination was inflamed with expectation, and the soldier was away from his supporting arms, is no disgrace.

These attacks gave rise to a military order to conscript and mobilize a brigade of three thousand citizens of Memphis for its defense, and the order was carried into effect by Gen. John McDonald, later of whisky fame and penitentiary polish. The pretense was to make non-combatant citizens defend themselves against their kindred and friends; in other words to defend themselves against themselves. To conscript the non-combatants of a conquered State is a shame and disgrace to any commander, authority or country from which it emanates, and must forever stand in the estimation of mankind as wholly defenseless, under any and all circumstances when the conscript is forced to act as a soldier against his own country.

Such an order is as defenseless as an order to conscript prisoners of war and force them into battle against their late comrades in arms. At least such were the deepseated convictions upon which I acted at the time in causing that brigade of conscript citizens to be discharged. These Southern men felt the outrage keenly, many of them were discharged Confederate soldiers. All were placed under the command of that able-bodied General, who invented the phonetic cipher. "The goose hangs altetudelum," which being interpreted meant "My grand larceny of the government whisky revenue is active, lively, large," all of which was proved by the government in the prosecutions in the Federal Court in St. Louis in 1875, which resulted in his conviction. McDonald, without the costly intervention of the services of a Moses, came directly to me, and for a per capita consideration of $100 offered to dis-

20

charge the conscripts. I told him that there were some in comparatively comfortable circumstances who could and would gladly pay it, but that a very large majority were poor men, out of employment, and unable to pay anything, however greatly they desired to get rid of the odium imposed by the service, and that I would not under any consideration impose an exaction on any of those men for my services or benefit, and that the fifty per cent which he proposed as my compensation would be deducted from the charge and not demanded or collected from the conscript. That, he said, would be left entirely with me. I further demanded or required that he bring the muster roll to me, or furnish me with a copy so that I could form an approximate estimate of the tax he proposed as a basis of discharge. He did so, and my estimate was that I could pay him $7,500 to discharge the whole brigade, and he accepted that proposition and brought the discharges to my office, all properly signed by him. His handwriting was as well known as the steamboat landing. In about five days I collected the $7,500 and paid it over to him, and "The Brigade of Enrolled Militia" was no more. Not one dollar of that did I keep; the man or men who say I did are falsifiers of truth. But suppose I did, what of it? Who did I injure? What principle of law, military, civil, or moral, did I subvert? A correct solution of these questions will determine the degree of dereliction, if any. I maintain there was none. It is self-evident that I did not injure the three thousand conscript citizens of the conquered territory, by relieving them from the odium of conscript treason against their homes, firesides, and fellow citizens.

Nor can it be said that I injured the Federal Government by using the only means its officer would acknowledge as effective in inducing it to rescind and abandon a shameful order. Did I injure John McDonald by bribing him? Bribery consists in paying, buying, or by other considerations influencing an officer, judge, witness or other person to do an unlawful act. Was it unlawful to influence a military tyrant to desist from further infliction of injury to his country and fellow man? Not possible when judged in the light of existing facts and surrounding circumstances. If so, it was the bribery, the seduction of the wrongdoer to the standard of justice.

It would be just as justifiable to charge a virtuous woman with bribery or seduction who pays money to the despoiler of virtue to protect her innocence. Just as justifiable to charge bribery against the friend of the conscript slave who buys and restores his freedom. Must all of three thousand men remain in odious military bondage because the tyrant master and usurper will not relieve them without a money consideration? These conscripts did not create the situation for which money was paid to relieve them. We were under the military government of the enemy. We complied with the terms they imposed when we were powerless to demand or enforce any other, and if there was odium attached to the transaction it was all theirs. But I am not hypercritical, not captious, do not stickle on technicalities, and scorn to invoke them. I was a true Southron. I gladly embraced every opportunity to serve *my friends*, and under like circumstances would repeat the act to-day, to-morrow, and forever, and accept cheerfully all the consequences flowing from that act. The man who says, or insinuates that I was influenced by mercenary motives, slanders and falsifies truth. I have fully explained elsewhere in this volume that I paid sixty-five thousand dollars of my own money in other ways for the relief of Southern men, both civilians and soldiers. Whatever may be my faults, avarice has never been charged as one of the infirmities. I took a thousand chances, embraced a thousand opportunities, to shield and protect my people as far as possible against the oppressions and shameful exactions of a debased military government, when all the responsibility, and all the power, and all the terms were theirs and not mine; and I employed money to reach their vulnerable vitals, just as the soldier in the field applied the saber and the musket. "If that is treason make the most of it." I have stated facts. I was a confessed Southern sympathizer, everywhere and under all circumstances, and it was publicly known to every Commander of the army stationed at Memphis, my name as such, with 270 others was printed on heavy pasteboard, and hung on the wall in every military office in Memphis. I deceived nobody, deception has never been charged as one of my faults. I have never been a saint, but have chastised many who have tried to make me a devil, John McDonald included in the latter inventory. I have enjoyed the warmest attachments, and suffered the bitterest enmities, have always been devotedly attached to my friends and openly defiant to my enemies. A negative, passive character, that wires and worms its way, was never admired nor imitated by me. The act of disbanding the three thousand conscripts, and breaking up their camp in the city of Memphis, in the midst of active war, was *ipso facto* notorious, and could no more be concealed than the sun could be covered with a nosegay. The fact that Brigadier General John McDonald was in market overt, on a conspicuous stall, with an itching palm, was very soon after the sale and purchase of the militia equally notorious, and the public eye and gaze was focalized on little John Mc, as a thrifty soldier in the commerce of war. The remote recesses of his nature remained undiscovered until the gaze of the public focalized on him; but he rallied and tried to rise, with the declaration to the public, that citizen Hallum had forged the discharges, and of his own motion had discharged the enrolled militia of Memphis, to the great injury of the public service for which he, McDonald, was in no way responsible. Perhaps I ought to have laughed at it in the derisive scorn the citizen public did, but my Irish got the better of me, and I forthwith went to his office, pulled down the railing behind which he was fenced off, knocked him down, jumped on the warrior dude, and laid on Macduff until a file of soldiers rushed up stairs with bayonets presented and persuaded me "to let up." Little Me was carried off for repairs, but did not call up the enrolled militia of Memphis. Next day I published the facts in the local press and my vindication under my name. This was in 1864, when we were under the rottenest military government of modern times. The people were forced and coerced to submit to exactions and extortions, and do a thousand things which could never have been possible under an honest government, either civil or military. I took many dangerous risks for my myself and people, and executed with the only practicable means available. I did not then, nor will I ever, regret the little I did to aid a suffering and distressed people, and I submit to the candid judgment of my fellow citizens. There were many great and honorable exceptions to this rotten military administration by subalterns, Generals Grant, Sherman, Washburn, and Veach, but Major General Hurlburt was the shield of these cormorants. When they could get in his shadow they were safe; how they obtained his protection is a matter of conjecture. He was longer in Memphis than any other general of equal rank, and had better opportunities to know what was going on than any other in chief authority. His normal sensibilities were to a great extent obliterated by excessive drink, and that may have been the cause of the apparent ease with which his subalternates managed him. Captain Eddy at the command of "The Abandoned Property" brigade, and Captain Frank at the head of the "Detective" brigade and John McDonald at the head of the "Conscript" brigade were favorites at his headquarters, and it was useless to lodge any complaint against either of them there. A ton of proofs after the most flagrant outrages, like that of the robbery of Carr and Lissenberry, was of no practical avail when presented to Gen. Hurlburt, if subalterns opposed. Whether

he was deadened to all sense of justice by the vintage so
freely supplied, or more costly influences was not known,
because Moses always stood between him and the injured
citizen.

SENT TO PRISON FOR SIXTY DAYS, AND A FINE OF ONE THOUSAND DOLLARS IMPOSED BY A MAUDLING GENERAL WITHOUT CHARGE OR SPECIFICATION OR TRIAL.

THREE weeks after the affair with John McDonald,
and the publication of my severe criticism of the
corrupt military government, Major General Hurlburt, without charge, specification or trial, even
before a drumhead courtmartial, and without ever hearing any proof or statement from me, issued a military
order in which he stated that "Memphis needs an example, and Mr. Hallum furnishes the subject. He is
therefore ordered to be confined for sixty days in the blockhouse at Fort Pickering, and to pay a fine of one thousand dollars." Why not prefer charges? Simply because
I could prove by overwhelming testimony everything I
had said, and run a den of thieves into Major General
Hurlburt's office. When freebooters and robbers run to
a fortress, the presumption is they know what they are
doing, especially when they find the desired protection
and immunity from punishment or accountability in any
way. Why did Major General Hurlburt not examine
into the public charges, specifications and proofs against
his pet, John McDonald? That was the least and last
of all things desired at his headquarters. Why did he
permit the unblushing robbery of private citizens, when
the proof of that robbery was lying knee deep on his

table? Why did an order for the discharge of Carr and Lissenberry come from his office within thirty minutes after a thousand dollars were handed in there for that object? Echo answers, and vehement presumption points with index finger. If the conscript militia was discharged on my forged discharges, why recognize and let it stand? If Memphis needed an example, why not investigate his own household and lay the ax at the root of the rotten tree? I positively refused to pay any fine, but W. L. Shipp, a merchant and friend, did it without consulting me, upon the advice of friends that I would be released if it was paid. I knew nothing of its having been paid until I was released at the expiration of the sixty days.

A meeting of the Bar of Memphis, a majority of them being Northern gentlemen, was immediately held and resolutions indorsing me, and urging my release were adopted.

I shall ever feel grateful to all of them, and especially to those Northern gentlemen who protested against the outrage. In this connection I will state another fact which may or may not bear on the causes leading to my imprisonment. If not, it presents at least a singular coincidence. A very short time before the difficulty with McDonald, Captain Williams of the regular army, who was then, and for many months prior, Chief of the Provost Marshall's office, came to my office and sought a private interview in my back room. The door was closed and he began to speak about the abundant chances to make money, and the large number of letters coming to me daily through that office from prisoners, both civilians and soldiers, of the Confederate army, and stated that my influence in that direction would be worth $250 per diem. I interpreted it as an offer to enlist me in spoliation and plunder, and with language more forcible than elegant, told him so, in the broadest ancient Saxon. The presumption in my mind was that he knew the Moses who had been discharging both citizens and soldiers for me, for the stipends demanded and received, but I did not allude to that. Captain Williams then appeared much disappointed and disconcerted, and remained quiet for some moments, perhaps three minutes, in a sort of bewildered meditation, thumping his fingers on my desk, then he rose up and passed out of my office, saying in measured accents as he left, "Perhaps you will think on this matter in a different light some day." To which I replied, "Not before hell usurps the jurisdiction of heaven will I aid in the oppression of any man to inspire him with willingness to give up his money or property."

It was not long until "the winter of my discontent" came. I was confined in Fort Pickering blockhouse, 36x75 feet, with bunks from ceiling to floor, arranged like shelving in stores. In this narrow charnel house three hundred prisoners were confined. Vermin by the quadrillions invaded everything. Smallpox victims were there. Two stricken with this dreadful disease occupied bunks adjoining the one assigned me—one died before the ambulance for the pest house arrived. The sanitary equipment—there was none. The odor would have sickened a mule. There was no bedding wooden boxes. One kettle served as washing and cooking vessel. Coffee was made in it. Clothes swarming with vermin were washed in it. Potatoes and pork boiled in it. It was the death caldron for vermin, where millions perished, and yet hungry human beings crowded like pigs for the food that was cooked in it. The prisoners were drawn up in line and crackers were emptied in front of them on the ground, in the dirt and mud. I was not permitted to take one dollar in the prison, nor to furnish my own food, nor were any of my friends permitted to visit me. For four days I did not taste food. Finally I obtained an interview with the "trusty" who went into the city every day for commissary supplies. I touched his heart with an order for one hundred dollars and he brought me my first food, and for another one hundred dollars continued to smuggle it

in, with a daily paper occasionally. For the first ten
days no surgeon came. My nervo-sanguine temperament,
with easily aroused capacity for suffering, as well as enjoyment, invited prolonged indigestion and insomnia.

One day I opened the paper and caught its startling
head lines, "Fort Pillow captured by Gen. Forrest."
All the soul stirring animation of that most glorious of
all national airs, "Dixie," came like a torrent, and I
jumped out of that bunk and shouted for the "Boys in
Gray," strained my vision up the river and hummed in my
soul.

"The patriotic tide that flowed through Wallace's dauntless heart."

For a consideration of $200 I obtained permission to visit
my family once. These Federal guards were always anxious to be ruined.

The last scene I remember in that prison was, I suppose, a lucid interval, when I opened my eyes on the face
of a gray haired Scotch physician, who was bending over
me with anxiety and sympathy depicted vividly in his
kind face. When consciousness again returned, I was
dazed with almost vacant mind, and was told I was in a
hospital, and had been there ten days. Humanity asserted itself in this establishment, everything was neat,
everybody courteous. I was permitted to buy everything
I wanted, and when, able to walk was discharged, my
time being out.

MONEY MADE FOR BOTH SIDES IN A LAW SUIT.

CAPT. CHEEK was one of the noted ancient land-
marks about Memphis, a man of the strongest
convictions and very decided individuality. He
relished with keenest zest the excitement of litigation. As evidence of this he told me that $100,000 would
not cover the fees he had paid to lawyers. I was never

his attorney until after the occupation of Memphis by the Federal army, and then very reluctantly assumed that relation to the old man. He owned the ferry which plied between Memphis and Mound City, five miles up the river on the Arkansas side, out of which much litigation was evolved to his final success.

The first professional visit he paid me was in the winter of 1863–64. He brought quite a batch of claims against the government which I declined to take, because he was excessively fond of discussing his cases with counsel, which if indulged to the extent he desired, occupied more time than the fees were worth. He came back again with like result, and to my surprise he came the third time, at a moment when I had some leisure, and I said: "Mr. Cheek, upon one condition I will put your claims in proper shape for presentation at Washington, and no other. When I get through you must not ask me to continue the discussion of the merits, nor come to my office until you hear from Washington, nor then unless more business is to be done at this end of the line. I am too busy to listen to a rehearsal of matters after I am through."

He promised and kept his word. Some time after, he came back and said: "Those papers were in red-tape trim. I received my money due on those claims, and a complimentary letter for having given the department no trouble in referring the matter back for further proofs. Now I have a serious matter which you must attend to, which will pay you better."

"Well," I said, "I'm too busy now to think of other matters. You must get some other attorney." "What? A steamboat is involved in this matter, and I guess that is big enough." "No matter," I replied, but could not shut him off so easily, he would proceed with his story as follows:

"I gave Capt. Malone, my son-in-law, one half of the steamer 'Mark R. Cheek,' and he has had her in possession six months, and now refuses to give her up to me. I did not give him any writing, and in law he cannot keep her. He is not treating me right, and I intend to nip him in the bud."

"Well, Captain, if that is what you wish done, I am certain not to attend to your business; and if I did, I would charge you $2,500 cash to begin with. I happen to know that your son-in-law is an honest man and an upright gentleman, also that the steamer was in bad repair when you turned her over to him, and that he has just brought her from the docks at Evansville, Ind., where he expended $10,000 in repairing her."

He said: "Great God! I never heard of such an exorbitant, unreasonable fee in my life, and I have been in the hands of lawyers all my life. I have paid out more than $100,000 to lawyers, and not one of them ever thought of making such a charge."

The truth is, I was doing all I could to discourage him, there was no affinity between us, and I did not want his business. The old man left grumbling, in a sour humor; but to my surprise came back the next day and said that he had thought the matter over and had concluded to pay my price. I told him that I had also been thinking it over, and had concluded not to touch the case for less than $5,000, and not even at that fee, unless he would sign a paper empowering me to manage his interest in the steamer for twelve months as I pleased; also, to do what I conceived to be justice between him and his son-in-law. This I felt sure would end the interview, and drive him to some other office. He declared he would as soon see the steamer sunk or burned up as to submit to such terms. The fact was, he was very angry with Malone without justifiable cause, and felt more interest in gratifying his feelings than he did in the money involved. He left the office.

I knew where I could charter the steamer to very wealthy blockade-runners without any risk of seizure or confiscation of the boat. Such boats were in great demand and commanded high prices. A charter party contract with these men would yield more than they could reasonably expect to earn with the boat in any view. But I did not intend that Malone should suffer.

The second day after the last interview, to my great surprise, Capt. Check came back and said: "Draw up those papers, Malone will leave port this evening; get the boat as soon as you can."

It was the trimmest craft that plowed the waves, and defiantly crossed and recrossed military lines. I drew the papers and he executed them. There was at that time a Court in the city, established by military orders, and called the "Civil Commission," presided over by Judges Williams and Lewis. The precedent for this was a similar Court organized in Mexico during the invasion of that country in 1846 by the United States, which was held to be valid and Constitutional by the Supreme Court of the United States. From this Court I obtained the necessary order of seizure, and took charge of the boat after steam had been raised and the bell tapped to leave port. Then in the cabin of the steamer I told Capt. Malone that I had full charge of his father-in-law's interest, and a plenary commission to settle all matters between them on terms I deemed equitable and just, and that I would make no war on his interest whatever, but protect him to the extent of equity and justice. I also told him that I could at once charter the boat for $30,-000 for twelve months, with insurance and repairs to be paid by the merchants to whom I proposed to charter the boat, with his consent and co-operation. I also pointed out to him the freedom from seizure and confiscation. The result was his delight and hearty co-operation. Next day the charter was duly executed. I adjusted the differences between them on an entirely satisfactory basis and made more money for the owners than the boat would have sold for the day of seizure.

Paradoxical as it may appear to the lawyer of the present time, I was forced to accept a large fee from a client I tried to repel, and legitimately managed both sides of the case, something I never did before nor since.

A MEMBER OF GEN. E. KIRBY-SMITH'S STAFF IN MY OFFICE IN DISGUISE.

ONE day a large gentleman of fine address but effeminate voice came into my office for the ostensible purpose of selling me a very fast trotting horse. I told him I had a pair and did not wish to invest. He insisted that I go with him to the stables and look at the horse anyway, but I declined and dismissed him.

He took a seat in the front office and sat there for some time. I was very busy and paid no more attention to him and did not even learn his name that day.

The next day he came again, took a seat in the reception room, and I began to think I had a bore on hand, but still paid no attention to him, my office was full of gentlemen on business, and I had no time to devote to him. He remained until the noon hour, when I generally had a little recess while the people were at their meals. To my surprise he requested me to dine with him. I declined, but he insisted so graciously, saying that perhaps we were related by affinity, I accepted. While our orders were being filled, he said:

"Capt. E. E. Dismukes, of Arkansas, married your cousin, Jane Hallum. My name is Joseph Dismukes, and I am first cousin to the Captain." I then made myself more agreeable, asked him many questions about my Arkansas relatives, and his knowledge of them was accu-

rate. He told me that my old gray-headed uncle, George
Hallum, was badly wounded at the battle of Oak Hill,
but had recovered, was discharged, and had returned
home. That Capt. Dismukes was in the Confederate
army. I told him that my gray-headed father, the senior
of Uncle George, was also in the Confederate army; that
my brother, Henry, was reputed to be one of the best
gunners in the Army of Virginia; that all of my people
old and young, able to bear arms, were in the Confederate army.

His address was pleasant and that of a gentleman to
every appearance. I put the direct question to him:
"Have you been in the Confederate army?" He replied
in the negative, and said he was a Tennessean by birth,
but had long been a citizen of Arkansas.

The meal over I hastened to my office.

The succeeding day he came again, and sat quite a
while. I had but little time to devote to social converse.

These daily visits were repeated for a week. He had
quite a number of horses, and several men in charge, had
made some sales. I regarded him solely in the light of a
trader and gentleman of ease and leisure, and that he fre-
quented my office to while away the time in reading.

Finally he asked me to close the door to my back office
and give him a private interview. I did so, and he said:
"Perhaps my frequent visits to your office appear a little singular to you. I am a stranger in the city, and on
business of the highest importance. I heard much of you
before I came, and have been closely investigating to find
a gentleman in whose confidence I could repose my life,
and have selected you."

I said: "Great God! my friend, while I would not betray your blood, I have too many such responsibilities
resting on me now, and they are increasing daily, their
multiplicity endangers none more than my own life. We
are in the midst of war, and under military government,
and the world seems to have gone mad; no risk seems too

appalling to deter men from assuming them.   You are a
fool to jeopardise your life!   I will not assume such responsibility.''

I threw open the door and walked in the front room,
where several gentlemen awaited me, and went home that
night to my family without knowing what Capt. Dismukes wished to do, disclose, or make known to me.

At nine o'clock that night there came a knock at my
door.   The servant handed me the Captain's card, and I
directed that he be seated in the reception room.   He
came in a carriage and dismissed it when invited in, indicating a desire to remain as my guest, and stay with me
that night.

After talking a short time, he handed me a paper and
asked me to read it.   Although accustomed to surprises,
which were of hourly occurrence in the new world which
active war had brought to the city, and changes like the
combinations of light and shade in the tube of a kaleidoscope as the prisms fall, this was the greatest surprise.
It was a four-page document under the signature of Gen.
E. Kirby-Smith, Headquarters of his army on Red River,
offering safe conduct to as many as five steamers to be
loaded with clothing and supplies for his army, to be paid
for in cotton on Red River, pledging the faith of the army
in the execution of the contract, and safe conduct for the
transports back into the Federal lines.

"There, now," he said, "my life is in your keeping.
I am a true Southron, and if necessary am willing to die
for my country.   I was charged by my General to take
this risk for the benefit and support of his army, your
army, my army, the army in the field fighting for every
man, woman, and child in the Confederacy.   As for my
life, I am not the least fearful that you will expose it;
but I fully realize the gravity, the responsibility, the
danger I ask you to incur in aiding me, or in making the
negotiation, or in attempting it.   Others will necessarily
have to be approached and informed, and induced to take

the risk. If you cannot do it, I know not where else to go. You have a large ramification of business and must know where to apply. I do not. But let me say to you as compensation for the risk I am authorized to give $50,-000 for the service."

I told him I was sorry he had approached and confided this matter to me; that as a Southern man, an ex-Confederate soldier, I would not charge my distressed country, that was bleeding at every pore in the unequal struggle, one dollar for such service, even if I could render it; but if I did undertake it I would reserve the right to charge the other party or parties to the contract such fee as I might in my own judgment determine.

Many of the large contractors and blockade-runners were known to me personally—that is, those living and doing business in Memphis. They did not openly confess these things to me, but I knew they commanded safe conduct whenever and wherever they wanted it, and from these facts, presumptions were vehement as to the source of their power. A very short time before that seven hundred cavalry was placed at the disposal of one of those speculators and myself, to go into the interior, thirty miles east of Memphis, to enable safe transportation of cotton purchased from farmers to the city; and I was furnished with $150,000 for the purpose. I told the Captain that I knew some men who would invade hell itself in the pursuit of such a prospect.

We smoked several cigars and talked late into the night, and he retired in my house, at least encouraged and hopeful.

Next morning I put that paper from Gen. E. Kirby-Smith in my side pocket, drove up to Front Row, between Adams and Jefferson streets, went back into the counting-room with two of the three partners, showed all, and before ten thirty A.M. had the arrangement consummated, and a promised fee of $50,000 from the firm.

I took Capt. Dismukes to them and left them to ar-

range the details.   Afterwards he told me that the contract had been honestly executed by both parties, but the
firm refused to pay my fees, and as the contract was in
contravention of both civil and military laws there was
no compulsory process.   Had they been of the chivalric
mold which distinguished Southern gentlemen of that
day, their simple promise would have been treated as of
primal obligation.   But I did not put much faith in their
promise, nor assume the risk for the money consideration,
but would have accepted it as an incident to the transaction, and was entitled to it, measured by the war standards which then obtained.

In that "War between the States" I loved my native
land and her chivalrous people better than any the sun
ever shone on, and I owed allegiance to no power, no authority on this footstool that could force me to war, or
act against those people, however much I differed with
the leaders on both sides in precipitating that political
war.

Patriotism in such a crisis as that, applied to the
Northern States from a Southern standpoint, has its limitations and qualifications which, at least with me, rose to
the attitude of inalienable rights, as taught and acted
upon by the Pilgrim fathers of New England, as well as
the Cavaliers who settled on the James, and the noble descendants of both who were led by Washington, until the
last roar of the cannon at Yorktown announced to the
world the noblest achievement of man.

He of the North and he of the South will defend or
criticise these actions from opposite standpoints.   The
little hypercritical, cross-eyed moralist, whose contracted
vision is bounded by the light which sweeps within a few
inches of his nose, will adjust his "specs," balance himself on a pinnacle, and spout wisdom by the ton, without
knowing any more about practical methods in the great
emergencies of war, than a jaybird knows of Plutarch's
Lives: "Shoot, Bub," from the portholes in your casemated

21

shield, a thousand of you from both sides of the warline
have shot.

The last I heard of Capt. Joseph Dismukes he was living the life of a hermit in a little shanty on the banks of
the Poteau river, a tributary of the Arkansas, uniting
their waters at Fort Smith. He rarely came into the
city, although living in sight, but was a constant reader
of the papers, and kept up with the current literature of
the day. Occasionally he visited me during the two
years I lived in that city, and our meetings were always
cordial and joyous.

AN UNPLEASANT EPISODE.

THE war and reconstruction period threw to the surface many men who were caricatures of all that is
noble and elevated in man. Many of them came
to the surface in the Southern States because of
pausity of available material professing allegiance to the
dominant party. Ninty-eight per cent of the educated,
worthy population of the Southern States were disfranchised because of their participation in, or sympathy with,
their native soil in the war between the States. Many of
these men who were thus elevated to high official position had no more conception of true manhood than a Digger Indian has of basic rocks found in the Silurian period
of Geology. There were some noble exceptions, but I
class them as such, and not as the rule.

I had incurred the malice and hatred of one of these
spots on the administration of justice during the war, because I had kicked him for intermeddling officiously in
business matters which did not concern him, in a tender spot, when and where his manhood denied the usual
redress.

After the close of the war this man held Brownlow's commission as Judge of the County and Probate Courts of Shelby, a jurisdiction concurrent with that of the Circuit and Chancery Courts in the partition and sale of lands belonging to the estates of decedents, and as this Court was much more expeditious with its twelve terms per annum than the others with their three terms, I resorted to it with an immense volume of this, and other business. This man now held a judicial club over my head, and forthwith proceeded to glut his appetite for that revenge his manhood denied, by refusing to decide on my case, holding up the simplest *pro forma* matters for advisement, as he falsely termed it.

If I wanted an administrator or guardian appointed, or the settlements of these fiduciaries passed on, or the appointment of commissioners, it went into the long advisory mill, while the business of similar character conducted by other attorneys, went along smoothly and with dispatch.

I took hundreds of such instances of intentional wrong with the patience of an afflicted Job, and with him, beat my own record in the line of patience. But the outward form of respect for such a Judge, even when you despise the man, will ultimately give way to the fury of a cyclone. Finally, I sold under a decretal order of Leonard's Court quite a lot of valuable real estate belonging to the firm of Brooks & Suggs, for the sum of $28,700, all of which was collected by me and paid out to creditors as ordered by the Court. I made my report, filled all my vouchers as directed, and asked for a confirmation of the sale, and that the title be vested in the purchasers. Leonard "took it under advisement" from term to term, to the grave annoyance of the purchasers and myself, the latter being the sole object that influenced him to soil judicial obligation and injure my practice as an attorney.

I still "held up," disliking to come into personal collision with the Court. If he had acted on the report unfavorably, I had my remedy to appeal; but he would not act. Lawyers ought always to strive to maintain the respect and dignity of the Court, if their personal integrity is not unjustly involved. When that becomes an issue, then to the winds with judicial impunity or sanctity.

Finally, the purchasers of this land came in a body to my office, and told me that Judge Leonard had expressed to them grave doubts as to whether he would ever confirm the sale, although their money had been accepted and paid out, every dollar, to the creditors of Brooks & Suggs on his order of record. Then I said to these purchasers, one and all, to "meet me the next day in Court, and if their titles were not confirmed they could assist in removing a corpse from the Courthouse." There was no flaw or even dispute of title, no objection from any source on earth to the confirmation of the titles.

We all met in the court room, and as soon as I could, I called up the case, and asked for a confirmation, and Tom Leonard replied: "I am not satisfied yet, I must hold up the case longer for advisement."

I then advanced to his desk, told him of his base motives, soil of the judicial ermine he disgraced, and said: "Decide in one minute! If you refuse, one of us must die now." He turned to the Clerk and ordered the confirmation and decree entered of record at once. I then said: "If you say contempt to me, I will cut your ears off."

Gen. Albert Pike was in the court room. He threw his arm on my shoulder, and said: "I have been from ocean to ocean, but never saw a decree entered that way. Do you think it will stick?"

"Yes," I replied, "this Court will impute to it absolute verity, and entertain profound respect for it." And there the matter ended forever.

Gen. Pike and myself occupied offices in the same building, and were warm friends, but this episode intensified his friendship for me. He came to the wilds of Arkansas from Massachusetts as early as 1832, was a front-

iersman, knew what a gentleman ought to take and what
he ought to resent. He had been on the field and fought
a duel with Gov. Roan, with a lighted cigar in his mouth,
was possessed of as much true courage as any mortal
man. This noble old Roman justified me, and I am con-
tent.

WOMEN IN MILITARY PRISONS.

A HEROINE.

" Full many a gem of purest ray serene,
The dark unfathomed caves of ocean bear."

THE annals of literature, the mythical creations of
romance in the age of chivalry, when the Trouba-
dors tuned the lyre and sang to woman's praise:
the stories of legendary lore; all the recorded
creations of fancy, do not surpass the sublime and heroic
devotion, the exalted patriotism of our Southern women
during the war period.

Women, in all ages, gentle as their natures are, have
loved the true soldier.

When Memphis was occupied by twenty-five thousand
of the army of occupation, sometimes more, sometimes
less, the city was under military government, and a cor-
don of bayonets guarded its approach day and night.

Citizens occupying the adjacent territory, mostly
women and children and aged or crippled men unfit for
military service, were compelled to resort to the city for
supplies which could be obtained nowhere else. Smug-
gling contraband goods through the lines, it must be admitted, was one of the industries in which many of the
ladies were engaged, because they were necessarily the
chief purchasers, but only in small quantities and for
special purposes. Inspection at the station of exit for
many months did not reach those articles which could be
readily concealed in woman's dress. Uniforms for Con-

federate soldiers, and the material to make them, were contraband, and very scarce.

The affianced of a young Confederate officer, living near Collierville (whose name now escapes me, because my record in which it was kept was long since lost) came to Memphis and purchased from a large dry goods firm, cloth and trimmings to make the dashing young officer a uniform. To obtain this favor she pledged her honor, that in case of detection she would not disclose the name of the merchants.

It was in the winter of 1863-4. She wrapped the cloth around her person and proceeded out on the Germantown road to the exit through the lines. On that day for the first time, tents had been erected, and ladies put in charge, to search the wearing apparel and persons of all their sex passing out of the line, and our little heroine, who belonged to the middle classes, was the first caught at that station. She was handed over to the guards and conveyed to the "Irving Block," that Bastile of the revolution, situated on Second street opposite the northeast corner of Court Square.

Ladies confined there were always placed in the upper story, without fire in the most inclement weather, and no bedding whatever, except a mass of straw thrown loosely on the bare floor, and without a chair, table, box, or anything on which to sit.

For a cultured and refined lady this was hard, as was the prison fare of coffee, cold potatoes, salt pork, and hard crackers. To a gentleman who loved to honor and preserve untarnished the uniform and arms of the country he bore, it was simply revolting, especially so because in the heart of a city overflowing with all the luxuries the arts and commerce of the age commanded.

This young lady, whose innocent and pure, yet exalted love was her death, sent for me. I found her in that cold and cheerless room alone, sitting in the corner on a bed of loose straw, cold and shivering in the pitiless air; her large blue eyes swimming in tears, which stirred up the fountains of my own.

She told me the details above stated, the merchant from whom she purchased the cloth, after my solemn assurance that I would not betray them. She manifested the greatest solicitude about that, and declared she would rather die than betray them. The detectives had been to see her many times before her message had been allowed to reach me, and they offered her immunity and freedom, if she would tell them from whom she obtained the contraband goods, consisting of ten yards of gray cloth, some buttons, thread, and gold lace trimming. But she was as immovable as the basal rocks of mountain ranges. A young girl, thus situated, cut off from friends, with her heart overflowing with keenest sorrow, to thus firmly resist and scorn freedom at such a price, rises to the loftiest summits to which God permits the children of men to reach.

The merchants who trusted her had a stock of goods worth two hundred thousand dollars, which would have been confiscated had that suffering girl told them where she obtained the goods. This girl was in the incipient stages of consumption, aggravated greatly by exposure in that cold, damp, fireless and bedless room. Already the arrows and seeds of death gave voice to their presence.

After a confinement of three weeks in that Bastile, she was sent to the Alton prison, where she died keeping her faith.

> " But oh, what crowds in every land
> All wretched and forlorn ;
> Thro' weary life this lesson learn
> That man was made to mourn."

Mrs. Stricklin, the accomplished wife of a wealthy planter, then living near Collierville, was arrested and confined in the same room, on the same bed of straw, because she refused to give information to Federal scouts of the movements of Confederate soldiers ; a truer, nobler woman never lived. I visited her frequently in that dismal prison, where she remained some weeks before I secured her release. She was an unusually brilliant lady, and was of much value to the cause she loved.

I have seen large numbers of ladies of refined, polished manners, driving ox teams, bringing cotton to the city to sell and purchase supplies for their families, and happy were they who had produce to exchange for supplies. Ox teams were used because all the valuable horses and mules were impressed into the service of either one or the other contending armies.

THE VICISSITUDES OF LIFE.

AN ABLE LAWYER IN A ROCK QUARRY WITH BALL AND CHAIN—A BRUTAL JUDGE TAKEN DOWN—PAT BURNS THE BRAVEST CLIENT I EVER HAD—DEC. 1870, JAN. 1871.

FOR obvious reasons I withhold the name of that brilliant and accomplished young lawyer, from Alabama, who was admitted to the Supreme Court of the United States in 1859 on the motion of Wm. H. Seward, and distinguished himself in an oral argument before that court. He stopped in Memphis several months and made my office his headquarters, but was not practicing law there. In December, 1870 I moved to St. Louis, and before my library was arranged, one of those fortuitous circumstances which sometimes rise up in our pathway, threw me into an immediate practice. I received a card from this lawyer urging me to come to the city workhouse. A deep snow lay on the ground; to my sorrow and astonishment I found him with chain and ball locked to his leg, working in a stone quarry to pay a fine of $500 at seventy-five cents per day. Like a great many unfortunate men, he had contracted the habit of drink in the Confederate army. He did not resume the practice of law, but drifted North after the war and became passenger Conductor on a train running from St. Louis to Chicago. When "laying off" he got on a spree in St. Louis, spent all his money, and was arrested as a vagrant—was advised to plead guilty to every crime defined in the nine sections of that ordinance in which "pimps for bawdy houses, bunco steerers for gamblers" and other vile crimes are defined. He was not a vagrant in any sense of the term, but was spending a vacation. He never read the ordinance, was assured he would be given a stay of execution, and released if he would plead guilty. He accepted the terms and resumed his position on the Alton road. When the next vacation came, he went into St. Louis and was seized in execution, and put in the rock quarry. The ordinance was unconstitutional, and had been so held by the Supreme Court of Missouri, on the ground that a police justice could not impose such an exorbitant fine without the finding of a jury. I prepared and presented a petition for a writ of *habeas corpus* to Judge Wilson Prim, of the Criminal Court, a bestial tyrant, who had lost all sense of honor or shame. I saw him the day before that treat two young attorneys of unquestionable repute, so shamefully, they sat down and wept. As I had just been admitted to all the Courts of the State, and was a stranger, I expected the tyrant would make a break at me, and was resolutely determined if he did, to resist and repel him, and was hence forewarned and forearmed for whatever might take place. To defend my honor was a grant from God. If he did make a contest with me, it would be a pivotal crisis at the start there, and I would either rise or fall on the result of my first case in that city. I appeared in open court in the afternoon, and at a convenient moment asked the Court to hear the application, but the Judge said he would read it at night and pass on it the next morning.

I took my seat in court next morning, expecting to argue any question on which the Court might differ with me. The large court room was densely packed with auditors, and the reporters of the city press were present. He refused to either let me read the petition or argue the case, but consumed half an hour in a personal assault on me. Joseph G. Lodge, since eminent at that Bar, was present and rose and told the Court, when he commenced that assault that he was in no sense justified in it, and that he had no hesitation in saying that Mr. Hallum is an honorable gentleman, and entitled to every courtesy as such from the Court. I thanked Brother Lodge, but said, "let him alone, I will get the floor when he gets through," and the brutal judge, who had never seen me before in his life, continued his brutal tirade under the assumption that his office as judge would be his shield of protection. He went on to say that my client was confessedly guilty of all the vile crimes enumerated in the ordinance; that these vile criminals appeared to have no trouble in securing sympathetic counsel, who did not look on a whorehouse pimp and an associate of thieves, as belonging to an unworthy class, who would soon overrun the city if not effectually discouraged; that it was his duty to protect society against their aiders and abettors, and the sooner strangers learned this policy, the better it would be for them and society. That as to the alleged unconstitutionality of the ordinance, it was but a dream, that he was as familiar with the constitution as the alphabet; then threw the petition down, refused the writ, and denied me the right to be heard. And when I arose to speak peremptorily ordered me to sit down. When I refused he repeated the order the second time. Here was a clean cut issue, as base a slander from the Bench as ever uttered by a man who disgraced the ermine; and I would have repelled it then and there, if the twelve Apostles had been on the Bench. I refused to be seated in obedience to the third command. I told him that I would perish before I would obey him, that he had not only slandered me, but had falsified every material allegation in the petition, and had cast unwarranted reproaches on my client, which I would defend and denounce as false and cruel ; that my client, although unfortunate in contracting the habit of drinking, was not more unfortunate than the Court in that respect; that he had occupied an infinitely higher social and intellectual position than he had ever aspired to. This paralyzed him at the start, and he never opened his mouth again except when I commented on the unconstitutionality of the ordinance, and the decision of the Suprem Court so construing it. I told him that he had read a garbled extract from that opinion, and I read the whole opinion and proved it. Then I said Daniel Webster, and Story, and Marshall, and Taney, who ranked with our greatest expounders of organic law, would have hung their heads in shame, rather than announce, either on or off the Bench, that they were as familiar with organic principles as the alphabet; but that the Court had demonstrated one thing more forcibly than it had ever done before, that is, the law is a progressive science. That I had been called on but few times in my life to distinguish between that profound respect due to a Court and the man who happens to preside in it; that my client stood as far above a hog as the eagle does above the carrion crow. I never felt more indignation in all my life. The Hon. Mr. Cole, Mayor of the City, was present, and of his own motion immediately went to his office and issued a pardon discharging my client. The city press commended my attitude and said, "Judge Prim had at last met with a man who would not down at his bidding." A Mr. King, high in the Masonic Order, was in Court, and followed me to my office and paid me a large retainer to represent Hiram A. Pryor in a criminal case then pending in the Supreme Court of Missouri. Fees came fast after that tilt with the Court.

PAT BURNS, THE BRAVEST CLIENT I EVER HAD.

Prim nursed his wrath for me "to keep it warm." The petty judicial tyrant, who prostitutes his office to avenge the malice his manhood denies, invites derision and contempt and reaps the harvest in the end, like Haman—they swing on their own gallows and fall in the grave they dig for others. Pat Burns, a hero in humble life had been tried in Prim's Court. He was an uneducated Irishman, had been convicted of murder, and sentenced to be hung, and the day of execution named, then about three weeks off. An appeal had been taken to the Supreme Court, but that Court had refused a stay of execution until the appeal could be heard. An Irish friend of Pat's heard the tilt with Prim, and conceived the idea that I could be of some service to friend Pat, in leading a forlorn effort to save his life, all others having failed, his former lawyers had given it up as hopeless. Without consulting me, or even making himself known, he rushed out of the court room, like a generous hearted, impulsive son of Erin, to the telegraph office, and sent a message to the operatives of a factory in Rhode Island asking them to raise as soon as possible $250 for their former co-worker, Pat Burns, and to send it immediately by express to me. Next day he came to my office, told me what he had done, and begged me to take "poor Pat's case," a case I had never heard of before. The earnestness, solicitude, interest and profound friendship he manifested for Pat touched me, and I felt with Tennyson, that

"Kind friends are more than coronets."

and undertook the case, stepped over to the Supreme Court, a division then being held in St. Louis, got the record without more being said about a fee—generous Mike had fixed that in his own mind—and although I put little faith in it, determined to render any assistance I could. In that record I found a romance for the pen of some master, capable of being dramatized into a world-

wide fame, which I cannot stop to develop further than
to condense the simple facts found in the record.   John
Duffy, the principal, and Pat Burns, accessory, were
jointly indicted for the murder of the cold-blooded seducer
of Jennie, the niece of Duffy, under the promise of marriage.   Jennie had weighed the world as a feather against
her lover, who, after accomplishing her ruin, mocked her
sorrow and laughed at her shame.   I would have staked
my life on clearing him before an impartial jury of chivalrous Southern men, but he was tried before Prim and a
jury of Dutch, sandwiched with other foreign elements,
convicted and executed.   They severed in their trial, and
Burns was awaiting execution.   Neither had been ably
defended; this was the condition of the case when I took
it.   Jennie, the daughter of Duffy's deceased brother,
was left an orphan at a tender age.   She was bright and
of comely appearance.

Her uncle, who died on the scaffold for resenting her
injuries, adopted her, and lavished all the wealth of his
heart and purse on her.   He was a private soldier in the
regular army of the United States.   Severely economical
with his small wages, which he saved up and expended
in the support and education of Jennie, she obtained a
good education at the Catholic institutions in St. Louis,
developed into attractive womanhood, and engaged herself
to marry a man who proved himself the basest of mankind.   Duffy was with the army on the frontier when he
heard the distressing fate of his idol.   Long months
passed before he could get a furlough to visit her.
Coming to St. Louis, he met Pat Burns by chance for the
first time, and they joined each other in several social
glasses.   By chance they entered the room where the seducer sat.   Duffy was not armed, and whether he was
searching for the seducer or not will never be known; but
the fact that he was not armed raises a strong presumption that he was not hunting for him then.   Duffy
grabbed a smoothing iron and struck the seducer a blow

on the head, which resulted in his death, and for which he was executed as above stated. Burns always vehemently denied knowing anything about the seduction, or of Duffy's intent at the time of the killing. The seducer was also a stranger to him. The record developed nothing more. The *venue* was not proved, and there was not a *scintilla* to support it, except that the homicide was committed on Mullanphy street. Whether that street was in St. Louis, Chicago, London or Paris or elsewhere did not appear. On that point I prepared as able a brief as I ever wrote. B. Gratz Brown, the Governor of Missouri at the time, was a near neighbor to me, and I took the record to him, with an application for pardon, and alternative prayer for a commutation of the sentence, if he could not grant a complete pardon. He commuted the sentence to ten years' imprisonment. Pat's life was at least saved, and I had what I regarded as more than a fair chance to reverse the case in the Supreme Court. I advanced thus far in less than forty-eight hours after I took the case. Pat had many friends in the city, of his class and station in life, and, although uneducated, had a high sense of honor. This news awakened the sympathy and enthusiasm of his friends and their generous impulses towards me, which found expression in little, humble incidents, the haughty and great would rather avoid, but to me they were of touching and tender interest. Cicero has wisely said " an orator ought to know everything." A lawyer ought to be able to move with facility from cottage to throne, and understand all the springs of human action that move all grades and classes of men. A dozen or more of the Irish gentry and ladies, with poor, ruined Jennie, paid me the honor of a visit to my office to give expression to their kind feelings and gratitude for what I had done. A penny pitcher of beer—several pitchers for that—were brought in, and my good health drank from deeper fountains of the heart than I have ever seen in the banquet

halls of the great. A tear for poor, bashful Jennie.
Reader, did you ever have the fountains of your heart
stirred by those great master kings of our literature,
Goldsmith's Vicar of Wakefield, and Scott's Heart of
Midlothian, where with immortal sweep of genius and
pen, they take subjects from the humble walks of life,
and rear a monument to human sympathy and virtue
higher, infinitely loftier than the spires over the palaces,
or shafts above the mausoleum of kings? If virtue and
aspiring poverty are necessary elements in the development of such sympathies for our fellow mortals, bless the
Creator for the impress of that signet, no matter on
whose brow. With reverential feelings of filial gratitude in my old age, I look down the vista of departed
years and again sit on my father's knee, while he reads
those pathetic gems, with ever and anon a tear, which
told that the fountains of his better nature were at the
flood, and the love he had for virtue. Then a kindred
poem from the sweetest lyric Caledonia ever gave to the
world,

"From such scenes as these old Scotia's grandeur rises."

I filed the Governor's commutation of sentence in the
Criminal Court, called the attention of the Judge to
it, asked that the proper entry be made on the record,
and left, thinking, as any lawyer would have thought,
that that was all that was necessary, and all that could
legally be done in that Court at that time; but Prim
caused Pat McGrath, then Clerk of his Court, to write
across the back of the Governor's pardon, "In consideration of the within commutation of sentence I hereby agree
to serve ten years in the penitentiary of Missouri," and
announced from the Bench that he would execute Pat
Burns if he did not sign it. I was never more surprised,
but knew the venom of the adder was directed at me, defiantly denounced it in open Court, and advised Burns to
refuse to sign any such order or agreement. Here is
where Pat showed his Irish nerve. He said: " Be Jasus,

yer Honor, it's not what you want I'll be afther doing, you have already gone farther than suits an honest man like meself. Be Jasus, an' it was hanging me you were afther, an' me lawyer has put a sthop to all that foolishness, an' its him I'm going to mind, you may stick a pin there." The operatives in the Rhode Island factory sent me $250 in a surprisingly short time, like the widow casting their mite into the treasury. The peasantry of all countries is the greatest foundation of State.

> "Ill fares the land, to hastening ills a prey,
> Where wealth accumulates and men decay."

Surprises were now the order of the Court, they came like meterioric showers. Pat's neck or my scalp, nothing less, one had to dangle at his belt. His *honor* was on the war path, and blood was on the moon. The Court was then held in the old court house, on the square south of the Planter's Hotel, and the jail was a two-story rock building, about two squares northwest of the court house. Prim had McGrath make out a death warrant, about the size of a newspaper, with broad black border, held a night session, and had Pat brought into court with both wrists shackled together. He stood him up in front, while McGrath in sepulchral voice read the portentous document to Pat. Prim informed him that he would execute him if he did not sign the indorsement. He took a contemptible advantage of my absence, and an unusual hour, to intimidate that brave Irishman, whose request to send for me was refused. But Pat was equal to the emergency, and defiantly refused to sign. Prim plead with him, and told him that his ignorant, backwoods, country lawyer would cause him to loose his life. "Be jabers, I'm thinking he knows more than you do, and that you are running a bluff. Me lawyer tould me so, and he's the mon I'm afther sthicking to. You may bet your bottom dollar on that. Pat Burns is not the mon to go back on a friend, sthick a pin there, Judge. You may be a good mon, and all that, but you've an unfortinate way of showing it." The bailiff came to my office early the next morning, roaring with laughter, and repeated all that occurred in Court. He had a keen sense of the melo-dramatic, and a sovereign contempt for the judicial clown who was playing that maudlin role.

I went to see Pat immediately, carried him some comfort, so much appreciated by the hardy sons of Erin, found him in as good condition as the master of ceremonies at Donny Brooke Fair, game to the last, and as confident in his counsel as in the Pope. He was again brought out in my absence to gaze on his death warrant; but he was as firm as adamant; was begged again to sign the promise to serve ten years in the penitentiary as a condition precedent to the Governor's pardon. Idiocy crowned in the temple, a maudlin owl on the throne, bloated with the idea that his hoot would be taken for the roar of the lion or the defiant scream of the eagle. Foiled again. The next step was a burlesque on low comedy, as long as Pat stood by his counsel. The brilliant jurist next caused the sheriff to erect a tall gallows in the jail-yard, coming up to the window facing Pat's cell, where he could look on the awful reality in which he was to play the chief role in the tragedy. Pat and I looked on the scaffold as the carpenter intently pegged away at beam and trap door, with derisive contempt. Two whole days with the dark nights thrown in, were given Pat for awful meditation before being brought into court again to look on the lion on the bench, the death warrant in front, the gallows in the rear, as persuaders to induce his signature. By this time the local press was teeming with exciting articles on the gravity of the situation, in which Pat's counsel did not figure to much advantage. To prevent, if necessary, an undue influence on Pat, I had a boy to watch the jail and tell me when he was brought out, so I could accompany him to the Court, and I slept at my office to be near the call. I was master of the situation as long as Pat stood firm and obeyed me instead of the Court.

My watch was vigilant and faithful. When Pat was brought the third time I was on hand and vehemently denounced the scaffold farce, and told the Court that Pat would ascend the scaffold with a firmer tread than he dared execute it. That he would not execute it, every man but an idiot knew, and Pat endorsed what I said and still refused to obey the mandate of the Court.

The papers then said, While it was believed I was right in judgment, it was evident that I was given over to stubbornness and stiffness of neck, which would result in the death of my client, if we did not yield to the demands of the Court. I made no reply to these harmless squibs; to hold Pat firm was all I desired. The death warrant and the gallows did not move Pat in the least. But there was another move which gave me much concern. Pat was a good Catholic, and the influence of the Priesthood is always great over the professors of that faith.

The Catholic Priesthood was now brought into requisition, supported by the powerful appeals of the Sisters of Charity, who visited Pat in large numbers, and persuaded him to abandon his Protestant lawyer, and argued that he could not afford in the hour of his evident approaching death to disregard the advice of the Priesthood, and the simple requirement of the Judge to sign his name. They told him that his counsel was probably right as to the mere question of law involved, but that he could not afford to give his life to test it. I confess that this pressure gave me great uneasiness, to measure my strength and influence against the whole body of the Priesthood with one of their own faith, when life was the issue presented a serious problem. It was the pivotal point in the effort of that debased Judge to break me down, by means as unlawful as disgraceful. Some envious lawyers lent him their aid in that direction. While this was going on a ponderous article of two columns in the shape of an editorial in the old Democrat, then edited by McKee—of whisky fame afterwards—in which I was

berated and denounced as a backwoods ignoramous, willing to sacrifice the life of a client, rather than to obey a
simple order of the Court. I felt sure that I knew the
ear marks of Pat McGrath, the clerk of the Criminal
Court, under Prim, but it came with editorial responsibility, and the first step was to settle with the editor,
harpoon that fish before casting a net for shad in the
drift. Pat still stood firm as the rock of ages and as true
as steel. The moment to stop that slander had come, forbearance had ceased to be a virtue. I was as before stated
a stranger, and knew but few in the city, but in that
number was a lawyer, Col. J. C. Schoup, who had served
in the artillery arm of the Confederate service, a chivalrous gentleman, on whom I could rely. His office was
near by. I armed myself and sent for Col. Schoup, and
we went to the editorial rooms of the responsible Democrat, where we found McKee, the editor, of whom I demanded the author and responsible party in courteous and
respectable terms, and he brusquely refused. Then I
said, "The responsibility is yours. I intend no advantage, one of us must die if you refuse to accede to my just
demands. They are imperative and shall be obeyed. I
have more power in this arm than any slandering editor
in the universe," and he sang out, "Pat McGrath wrote
it." "Then why did you not say so at first, like a man,
instead of crouching like a cur?" Col. Schoup proceeded
with me immediately to McGrath's office, but he was *non
est inventus*. It was the third morning after the offensive
editorial before we found him. When we did, he wrote
out with his own hand a respectful apology for the article.
On hangman's day I stayed with Pat all day and he stayed
by me as truly courageous as any man I ever saw, not
one moment did he ever waver. The Priesthood did not
one moment cause him to hesitate in his loyalty to the
backwoods Protestant lawyer. Late in the afternoon of
that day Prim ordered him brought into court again
and piteously asked Pat, "Won't you sign the paper?

The last hour has approached." A clearer, more resolute voice never responded to a tyrant. "No," said
Pat, firmly and resolutely. The death warrant was then
being held in his face. A more crest-fallen, bluff-player
never sat on the judgment seat. Prim then hung his
head, and in a subdued voice gave up the ghost, and told
the sheriff to take Pat back to jail, and that was the end
of the disgraceful farce. Next day Prim was placarded
and cartooned in the city. The cartoon represented him
with fishing pole, leaning forward in a brisk walk, under
which was printed, " Judge Prim going fishing." I argued Burns' appeal in the Supreme court, and Judge
Waggoner, an intense radical, with no charity for Southern men, stood on tiptoe in his opinion, and held that, *the
venue was proved by presumption* in a matter involving
human life. All hail to the brave Burns. I would rather
stand in his shoes than those of the prejudiced Judge who
murdered the law to give a sleuth vent to his prejudice.
Burns was thus compelled to serve the ten years in
prison.

LANDED LITIGATION.

A PANDORA'S BOX OF COMPLICATIONS IN THE LANDED SYSTEM OF THE UNITED STATES—1870, 1874.

VIRGINIA, that grand and patriotic old mother of
commonwealths, at the termination of the war of
Independence, owned by far the largest part of
vacant lands ceded by the Crown in the treaty of
peace. All of the Northwestern Territory was hers, her
arms and valor had conquered it. Gen. George Rogers
Clarke, commanded the old " Virginia Continental Line "
of soldiers in the northwest, under whose arms the territory was conquered from the British and Indian Allies.
To pay the soldiers of the " Continental Line " the colony
of Virginia, and afterwards the State of Virginia, issued

landed scrip, under quite a number of acts, which was located in the Northwest Territory, and became incipient foundations to titles. These titles were imperfect when Virginia ceded the Territory to the United States, and were uncertain and imperfect obligations. Lands were cheap, and the primitive settlers did not perfect their titles, nor take steps to do so. The fee under the deed of cession vested in the United States against which the Statutes of Limitations do not run, " no time runs against the King." A similar condition as to titles existed in the sparsely settled, yet vast Louisiana Territory. Of the many thousand incipient titles under the Spanish and French Crowns but ten were perfect when we acquired the territory in 1803. The obligation of the United States to protect and perfect these incipient titles, under the treaties of St. Ildefonso and Paris was undefined, and there was no fixed standard, no way to coerce the sovereign will. Appeal to the magnanimity of the Government through the legislative department being the only remedy. The carelessness of the primitive settlers, both as to boundaries and preservation of evidence once in existence, added to the further fact that but very few lawyers knew much about the landed system of Spain and France, added chaos to confusion. Forty different acts of Congress, extending through a period of seventy-five years, from 1804 to 1875, touching these incipient titles, are on the Statutes at large. Scarcely any two of these acts are framed in the same language. Every backwoodsman who represented his district in Congress was expected to do something for his constituents in settling these land titles, and he went to work with more energy than skill, to do something in that direction. The result was to plant uncertainty in these titles and impose an immense labor on the courts.

When I went to St. Louis I found a large volume of this litigation, and went to work to codify, digest, arrange, simplify and reduce these laws to something like a system for my own convenience, a labor requiring much patient research. Justice Catron, from Tennessee, was the ablest land jurist on the Supreme Bench of the United States, and rendered more aid in settling western titles than any other Federal Judge. A Federal Commission was appointed as early as 1804 to take evidence and report to Congress on claims to lands in the Louisiana Territory. These Reports were published in five large volumes of "The American State Papers," which ultimately became of great value to lawyers and the courts. These State Papers were very scarce and costly. I paid $300 for the five volumes. The original volumes of the Reports of the Supreme Court of the United States were of great value also, because they contained the Briefs of Counsel in these cases, and they were scarce and hard to obtain. I paid $600 for them. The impeachment of Judge Peck, in 1825, had its origin in the discussion of these claims. A large volume of this litigation soon engaged my attention after I went to St. Louis.

Gen. Jonathan Crews, of Vincennes, Indiana, employed me in a large number of cases, involving at least half a million of dollars. Many of these lands were in the valley of the Wabash river, the incipient titles to which emanated from Virginia. Others lay in the American Bottom, near St. Louis, the incipient titles to which originated under the laws of France. I went to Washington and obtained patents to all these lands. The pivotal questions in these titles involved the rights of the grantees, measured against the rights of the "squatter," who had located on these lands, without any semblance of title in those claiming under him, and the Statute of Limitations. After the decision of Gibson *vs.* Chotean, reported in 13th Wallace, where the Supreme Court of the United States held that the Statute of Limitations do not run until the *fee* passes from the Government. It was thought by the ablest land lawyers in the West that my patents conveyed a perfect title. The only fear expressed was that the doctrine of Gibson *vs.* Choteau, although unquestionably sound, was so far reaching in uprooting so many titles that the Court would recede from it, and substitute *expediency* for law.

I feared that, yet it was with the greatest reluctance I indulged a doubt so derogatory to that greatest Judicial tribunal in the world. That the days of Taney and Marshall had past, that the Pagan Jurist before the Christian era in picturing Justice blindfolded, had reached a summit in human greatness, attained a higher standard of Judicial obligation than our own great tribunal. The idea was painful, compared with which the interest of my client was worthless, insignificant. But I remembered what the great body of the Northern people had done in traducing that tribunal, when it stood firm as the rockbound shores resisting the waves of the sea, in the Dred Scott case, when giants of intellect and of virtue adorned that Bench. Then came the sweep of the revolution, and the awful charge, believed by the many yet that "that great tribunal had been packed to decide currency questions in favor of the political bias of the appointing and confirming power." That *expediency* could fawn its way into that tribunal, and rob it of its only jewel, presented more horrors to me than the civil war. Were the transcendent achievements of the sons and daughters of the revolution to be thrown in the dice box? Were the six hundred years of decay in the Roman Empire to be repeated in one?

To test everything involved, I brought suit in the Federal Court at Springfield, Ill., against Judge Law, to recover a valuable tract of land on the Wabash, opposite Vincennes. The Judge and his son were good lawyers. The case is that of Langdeau *vs.* Hanes, reported in 22 Wallace, I believe. After ripe investigation, Law & Son, whose title was an unadulterated squatter's title, and the fee had been only recently passed to the legal representatives of the old "Continental Soldier" from the United

States, to whom it passed under the cession of the Northwest Territory—and if by any circuity of sporadic or fallacious logic it did not pass to the United States under the
cession, it remained in the State of Virginia, and was as
effective there to cut off the Statute of Limitations as if
in the United States—a military warrant of itself never
passes the fee, a patent, a grant, must follow the location.   This was Hornbook law, and the pith of every decision on the question.   Judge Law thought so, and offered $10,000, one half the value of the land, to compro-
mise, but as it was a test case, and thoroughly prepared,
it was refused.

The issue was simple and clean cut.   If I won the test
case my fees would aggregate a million dollars, for I represented many other very large interests involving the
same question.   "The incalculable mischief the rebel
lawyer from the South would accomplish in uprooting titles in Illinois" was a unique argument, derogatory to
the tribunals to which it was addressed, because it carried assumptions a Pagan jurist would despise.

But read the spacious, special pleading of Justice Field
and see how he distorted the "doctrine of relation" he
had so ably refuted in the Choteau case, and how he conscripted it as substitute to destroy what he had so ably
established and illustrated in the doctrine, "No time runs
against the King," how he picked up his own empty shell
and exploded what he had established in the ablest opinion
he ever wrote.   He delivered both opinions, they cannot
stand together, they represent opposites, "One foot on
the land, and one on the sea, Aggie up and Aggie down."
The Law Journals took it up at the time, some plucked
and some smoothed the feathers down.   The discussion
proceeded some time before the under dog in the fight
took a hand.   The impulsive Jurist winced, and the Attorney of the United States, Williams, came to his rescue and took a hand in the free fight under cover of a *nom
de plume* in which he attacked Mr. Hallum's *ignorance*

for saying "The American State Papers touching the public lands, *import absolute verity*." He opened a park gatling guns on me. He hooted and tooted on his best key from his masked battery under cover of his *nom de plume*. He was a Goliath, and beat the Old Virginia plantation melody. "He stamped his foot and jarred the ground a mile all around." *Ignorance* when it intruded in such high place swith the temerity of criticism became, a crime in George's opinion. The editor when called on removed the mask, and "gave George away," notwithstanding he had earned the princely title of "Landaulet Williams" because of his fondness for inexpensive carriages. George was referred to two decisions of the Supreme Court of the United States, in which that Court held: that "The American State Papers import absolute verity," and was asked who "fought with the jawbone of an ass?" He or I? But he has not yet determined the question.

THE ROMANCE OF A TYROLESE PRIEST.

HIS DESCENDANTS CONNECTED WITH THE MOST DANGER-
OUS RISKS OF MY LIFE—A TENNESSEAN SAVES
ME FROM THE FURY OF A MOB ON THE
FRONTIER—PURCHASE OF A MEXI-
CAN LAND GRANT—FRONTIER
LIFE AND CONDITIONS,
1872 TO 1876.

IN 1790 there lived in the valley of the Italian Tyrol, not far from the Plains of Lombardy, an Italian priest whose biography would fill a volume, more entertaining than the romance of the best writings in the realm of fiction. Father Leitensdorfer, Christian, Mohammedan, Turkish Mufti, Prince of the Harem, American Physician.

His bones rest in Carondelet, on the inland sea, the lullaby of whose turbid waters chant his requiem as they flow on to the ocean.

His biography was once the inspiration of my untutored pen, when all the material in tropical profusion was at my command from his own cultured pen; but inexorable demands divorced that desire from fruition, and the tyro novice in the guild of letters was prevented entrance through that gate.

Dr. Leitensdorfer was a man of much ability, strong individuality, great energy, and much force of character. Reared under a soft Italian sun, a land rich in the sensuous literature of romance and song for ages. Luxuriant in the sensations of an emotional nature, he was not strong enough to consistently wear the iron toga of the Christian priesthood.

His descendants in America are closely connected through professional channels with some of the most exciting and dangerous episodes of my life. After the conquest of Italy by Citizen Bonaparte, he expatriated himself from his native land and religion and settled for a time in Algiers, when the United States was at war with Tripoli and the Barbary Powers, because of piratical depredations on American commerce. The reigning Bey had been deposed and banished to the Desert of Sahara. Dr. Leitensdorfer was as politic as wise, and his loyalty to the Government of Tripoli was measured by the same adjustible standard by which he scaled his religion. He was in close communion with the commander of the American squadron off the coast. He was familiar with the politics and internal affairs of Tripoli, and was ambitious to advance his own interests; and but for him the United States, with her little squadron off the coast, could not have suppressed the Barbary Powers so easily, and put an end so quickly to depredations and enforced levies of tributes on our commerce. These inside facts are not recorded in our history. I get them from a three-hundred-page manuscript written by Dr. Lietensdorfer himself, and left with his children. Personally, I never knew him.

As a stroke of policy equally beneficial to the United States and the promotion of the schemes of the ambitious Priest, it became necessary to send an envoy hundreds of miles distant into the sands of the Sahara, and bring back the deposed Bey upon condition that he would advantageously treat with the American Government, and in reality become our ally. This scheme constituted a Triumvirate, with the Priest as its originator and chief, and its successful execution by him alone, and without arms in the midst of a semi-civilized and hostile people, attests a genius like that of Cardinal Mazarin. He assumed the office and dress of a Turkish Mufti, went hundreds of miles into the Desert, found the Bey, disguised, and brought him to the American squadron, with the aid of which he was restored to power, and with whom the treaty for Tripoli and the other Barbary Powers was made.

The greatest favorite at Court, he embraced Mohammedanism, substituting the Koran for the Christian Bible, and was fast advanced to the high office of Chief Mufti, and became Judge and Lord of the Faith, with a princely income, and a palace and Harem of beauties. When the Bey, sometimes called "Basha," died, his powers waned, and he came to the United States in 1812, abandoning the Priesthood of Islam as he had that of Christ. He married wife No. 12 in Carondelet, and imparted to his children, Thomas and Eugene Leitensdorfer, much of his own erratic and romantic nature.

Thomas, for many years an employee of The American Fur Company, roamed the Western wilds from the Missouri to the Pacific, and British America to the heart of Mexico, contracting morganatic relations without reference to the inhibition of creeds.

Eugene, long before the conquest of Mexico by the

United States, settled at Taos, New Mexico, and at one
time was a merchant prince. He was intimately associated with Vighil (pronounced Veheel) and St. Vrain and
Gov. Bent; was the originator of the celebrated Las Animas Land Grant, on which is located the town site of
Trinidad, Las Animas county, Col., and a block of the
finest coal beds on the American continent; 16,000 acres
to which I became the successor and owner in 1872, and
heir to the suits, expenditures, mobs, and dangers which
I am now going to relate in brevity. In 1844, the Governor and political chief of New Mexico, a territory of
Old Mexico, with Santa Fe as the capital, granted to
Vighil and St. Vrain a tract of land embracing 2,000,-
000 of acres, known as the "Las Animas Grant."

Leitensdorfer was the originator of the claim, but as
both himself and Bent were American citizens and aliens
to Mexico, they could not take as grantees, hence the
grant was made to the citizens named. All of them being equally interested, they divided the grant *inter partes*,
and Leitensdorfer, whom I succeeded, became owner of
the undivided one fourth, and it is with this interest
alone I am dealing. The conveyances to American citizens
were void under Mexican law, but after the conquest and
acquisition of the territory, Congress cut the grant down
to 100,000 acres and confirmed the conveyances made by
the original grantees to the extent of the lands confirmed,
and provided in the Acts of Confirmation that the first .
grantee should have priority, and the next *seriatim*, until the quantum confirmation was exhausted, and that
these grantees were at liberty to locate their respective
claims anywhere within the exterior limits of the original
grant. I succeeded the first grantee, and was entitled to
priority under the Acts of Confirmation. The exterior
limits of the grant on the eastern boundary, extended
from the waters of the upper Arkansas, at a point South
of Pueblo more than one hundred miles with the Arkansas river as the boundary on the east, thence west more

than one hundred miles to a monument on the Raton Peak of the Rocky Mountains. The western and northern boundary lines are immaterial to the elucidation of all I want to say in this connection. The original grant was a principality within itself, and embraced the Chucharas, Huerfano and Las Animas rivers, and the western bottom lands of the Arkansas river for more than one hundred miles. Also the towns of Trinidad, Chucharas, Las Animas, El Moro, La Veta, and many others which have since sprung up with the advent of railroads and the ever increasing population.

Leitensdorfer's claim was located on the 16,000-acre block of coal lands near Trinidad, Col., and it embraced that town, which was the county seat of Las Animas county, and at my succession, contained a population of 1,500, the larger part of whom were Mexicans. Squatter sovereignty obtained in the territory, and every man located his claim, assuming that the United States owned the land, and that he would have no other party to deal with in perfecting his incipient squatter rights. To determine the priorities under the original grantees, Vighil and St. Vrain; Congress, in the Act of Confirmation, constituted the Register and Receiver of the local land office, a special Commission to hear proofs and determine these priorities. The Acts of Confirmation did not provide for an appeal on the face of the Acts from the decisions of this special Commission; but an Act of general application, as early as 1836, did provide for appeals in all such cases, and amply covered the ground, but the Local Register and Receiver were innocent of the general law; hence they came to the conclusion that their decisions would be final, and any fraud or outrage they might perpetrate could not be corrected on appeal or otherwise. Being afflicted with moral and judicial "dry rot," they adopted "division and silence," and one half of the claims confirmed as the rule by which they would be guided in the exercise of their administrative and judicial functions.

And herein they opened a Pandora's box, and here I first came in direct contact and conflict with Gen. Benjamin F. Butler, who displayed more ingenuity in avoiding the direct and real issues than any man I ever met. But it is not with that branch of the case I am now dealing. Enough for the full comprehension of what I do relate is all that is proposed.

Trinidad at that time, 1872, and for a decade preceding was one of the most lawless places on the frontier. To the Mexican greaser element, with all of its treachery and perfidy of character, was added those lawless spirits which have made the frontier their rendezvous in every period of our history. The better and more conservative element of the population was in a hopeless minority, and for that reason unable to protect themselves, and afraid to complain and inform against the vicious. But this so-called conservative element were not free from moral taint themselves. In this, they gave way to their own interests and inclinations, and asserted the rights of a squatter against law, with as much vehemence as other grades of the same class, but without resorting to murder and mob law as a protection to the fiats and assumptions of the squatter. If they did not wink, they did not protest. So the law-abiding citizen, who claimed those lands, and dared venture among them, was an idiot, if he expected them to protect or attempt to protect him from mob law. I so found it, as the sequel will demonstrate, and came near losing my life by acts of as base perfidy as man in his lowest state is capable. My knowledge of human nature then, as it has ever done since I was twenty-one years old, protected and saved me without a requisition on my legs.

The citizens of Trinidad appointed a Committee in the fall of 1872 to confer with me, having in view the perfecting of their assumed squatter titles to improved property in the town. This Committee consisted of Pat McBride, a wild but easily tamed Irishman, whose morality

and integrity was measured by the lowest scale of frontier standards. He was County and Probate Judge at
the time. George W. Thompson, then Sheriff of the
county was also on the Committee. His standards were
also measured by the necessities and opportunities of the
hour, be them what they might; and when danger loomed
up, his instincts were measured by the *non est inventus*
tapeline. John W. Terry was another member of the
Committee. He was a banker, and endeavored to come
up to the standard of his obligations implied in his letters
to me as Secretary of the Committee of conference. Mr.
Swallow, whose Christian name now I do not remember,
was another member of the Committee, and I am more
than glad to say that Mr. Swallow did nothing to impair
his manhood in the discharge of these duties. Swallow
and Terry of this Committee were bankers there at the
time. I had a large package of letters from this Committee, urging me to come to Trinidad and settle the titles
to the town site, on a plan to be discussed and agreed
upon. I was not near so solicitous about the town lots as
I was about the coal lands, and was perfectly willing to
make any reasonable concession as to the improved town
property, but was not willing, and did not intend in any
event to concede the vacant lots and my coal fields. With
assurances from the Committee, that they were the authorized representatives of all the citizens of the town
who desired, if nothing more, an amicable discussion.
I went alone in December, 1872. I had bought the
Overland Hotel, a large, two-story building in the
town, for $10,000, and was the lawful owner. One
George Boyles, a shyster from Pennsylvania, by the
most fraudulent means, set up a claim to this property.
His countenance was an insult to a gentleman. After
my promise to visit the town, he secretly set to work
to inflame the mob spirit against me, and succeeded
to his entire satisfaction. Thompson, the Sheriff, knew
about it, and ran away before I arrived. Pat McBride,

the Judge, knew all about it, but acted with the Committee, ostensibly in the role of an honest man, but secretly in that of a coadjutator with Boyles as a murderer. I have always been satisfied that Swallow and Terry knew nothing about it. Their anxiety when the mob tried to get in its foul murder, proved to me that they had been deceived and were not a party to it.

I started from Pueblo, one hundred and ten miles distant, one cold, December morning in an overland stage. My friends there urged me to abandon the trip, and said that if I went I would be mobbed. I told them I did not think it possible for such baseness, and did not share in their convictions; that my business called me there, and that I had never abandoned the performance of my duty from any cause, much less from fear of personal injury.

The stage left at sunrise with but one passenger beside myself, a very pleasant young lady from Iowa, who was on her way to Silver City, seven hundred miles distant, to wed a miner. We passed a pleasant day, and I never felt more innocent of impending danger. The coach halted directly in front of the Overland Hotel at 1 o'clock in the morning in the midst of a large crowd of men. Late, cold, and an unusual hour, but I attributed it to curiosity, or a mere desire to see the man who claimed so much of that territory, and felt no more alarm than if I had been entering a church. Terry and Swallow and McBride rushed up to the door of the coach hurriedly and excitedly, and rushed me upstairs into the hotel, I thought very hastily. They ushered me into a front room and hurriedly ran down stairs, saying they would return in a few moments. Call me a fool, or anything else, when I say that I was still perfectly unconscious of danger. But that happy feeling was dispelled in a moment. The Committee had scarcely landed on the pavement before the crowd began hallooing "hang him! damn him, hang him!" Then I knew that I had reached the "happy hunting ground," and in a moment had out my large Colt's revolver and trusty bowie knife, and took my stand at the head of the stairway, up which the crowd was preparing to come. I had very greatly the advantage of positions. I determined to await the filling of the stairway, then pour the six shots I had into them, and in the recoiling confusion certain to follow, jump into the crowd with my bowie knife and if possible cut my way out. But it seems that God has been on my side in a thousand dangers. Just as the front of the crowd reached the pavement, six men sprang in front of the stairway armed with Henry rifles pointed toward the crowd, and the leader in the voice of a hero, with unmistakable ring of iron nerves, said: "That man is doing nothing but appealing to the laws of his country for what he honestly believes to be his rights. I dare one of you to molest him."

I rushed down to those wholly unknown friends, not one of whom had I ever seen, with my pistol in one hand and my knife in the other, and that crowd obeyed, simply obeyed, the imperative order to move on in an instant or be fired on, and they moved on. Set it down as a fact without exception in the history of the human race, that no truly brave man since Adam left paradise has ever joined a mob to take the life of a man under such circumstances as those that surrounded me. Knaves and cowards and caricatures on manhood can easily be rallied to do it, and much easier to run like curs when danger opposes their progress. And set it down as axiomatic fact, that bullies are arrant cowards, and when they do get scared are the worst scared men on earth. They will take every advantage, join a gang of cowards, and inflict all kinds of injury and insult, but the moment their object gets on equal terms and shows resolution to make them desist or die, they become paralyzed with fear, and as helpless as a flock of goats, and will gladly eat all the crow offered them. I have seen that medicine tried many times, and it always took the premium over "Radway's

23

Ready Relief," and it is a great mistake to suppose that the medicine is less effective on the frontier or in the Rocky Mountains than in any other locality; it's a universal remedy and applies to all localities.

Who were my friends? Whose imperious voice penetrated the heart of that mob? rang out on the air and warmed the snow under their feet? chilled and froze every purpose on hell intent? made them wondrous kind? softened their stony hearts when told the undertaker was ready? That the requisition embraced more than one funeral. That they must be conscripted into the service of death, too.

My native soil, my loved Tennessee, whose chivalrous sons have commanded respect wherever they have pressed their pilgrim feet, a son of that good, old commonwealth, founded by the "Commonwealth Builder," John Sevier, was there to defend a Tennessean with six guns, to crack and rattle and roar through gorge and glen if necessary; six guns there to make two hundred obey.

The Hon. William S. Garner, formerly a member of the State Senate, of our native State, lived forty miles from Trinidad, down on the Las Animas river, on his cattle ranch. He had taken five of his cowboys and brought a herd of beeves to town that day, and was invited by George Boyles to remain over that night and "see some fun in hanging Hallum, the land pirate." He accepted the invitation quietly for himself and cowboys, coolly and pleasantly, excited no suspicion, but at a convenient time posted those boys, "picked their flints, and kept their powder dry." Garner knew of my standing at home, and that was all he wanted to know. We had never met.

I remained there until the next north-bound stage came, and returned to Pueblo. There were some men looking on who passed for good men, negative, passive characters, who would not have interfered nor participated in the ball, and yet when properly handled by a

JOHN HALLUM AND WIFE.

leader, capable of much good, and I subordinated those qualities one year later to make that lawless town know that the reign of mob law had ceased.

AUDACITY WON.

IN 1873, Judge Knight, of St. Louis appointed me *amicus curea* to examine witnesses in a default divorce suit. I was very busy, and begged him to excuse me, but he refused to recall the appointment. I then said if possible I will go to the bottom of this suit and turn up some bedrocks if the trial consumes the day. Fridays are devoted to the trials of divorce suits in the five divisions of that Court, and the cases are generally railroaded through in a few minutes in that great rival city of Chicago. My object was to consume time and deter the Judge from ever again appointing me to that office.

I neither knew, nor had ever before heard of the parties. After reading some depositions, the complaining husband was put on the stand. He was a florid-faced, pert, little dude, dressed as finely as those Broadway brothers of his who follow pug-nose dogs about by a chain. He was evidently pleased with some great expectation, and enjoyed the high social distinction of the rank to which he belonged.

He said he was quite wealthy, and that his young wife who he married in Philadelphia, where both were raised, was also handsomely endowed, that he was much devoted to her, and she reciprocated the attachment. That his only unbearable distress was too much mother-in-law, whose baneful influence induced his wife to remain in Philadelphia, while he was doomed to the horrors of bachelorhood in St. Louis. That he had never neglected anything calculated to promote the happiness of himself or wife, for whom he had generously purchased avairies of parrots and birds, and the most choice selection of lap and pug dogs, for all of which they had a congenial taste.

I did not embrace, or take kindly to half of this story, and thought I discovered the undercurrent of another woman in the case, on which line I cross-examined him quite rigidly. He vehemently denied the soft impeachment, and manifested the only resentment I ever knew a dude to pull himself up to. It drew the coloring to his face, and a few tell-tale flushes told the treason he was struggling to hide. A package of letters protruded from his side pocket, and it occurred to me they might possibly contain a disclosure, so I stepped up to him, and before he knew my motive, had possession of the letters. He was confounded, amazed at the audacity of the movement, but entered no protest. I returned to my seat and began reading the letters. The first one was but three days of age, and was headed "Philadelphia, Pa.," addressed to him by a woman, who urged him to press his divorce suit, that they might consummate their marriage engagement. I read this letter aloud to the Court, while the dude hung his head in shame, and his non-protesting counsel writhed in confusion.

The court refused the divorce, and scathingly rebuked the little plaintiff, and sent him back to his bride and pug-nose kennel.

COL. SAMUEL W. WILLIAMS, OF LITTLE ROCK.

COL. SAM. W. WILLIAMS, one of the ablest lawyers the piney woods of Arkansas ever turned loose
on the Bar, has many striking peculiarities, a distinguishing individuality of character peculiarly
his own, one of which in the group is, he cannot write a
legible hand, and a century of expert training would not
improve his chiography.

Chaldean symbols, when her shepherds were star-gazers, the Cueniform inscriptions of remote Assyria and Per-
sia, the hieroglyphics of prehistoric Egypt, the rude symbols of the extinct Aztec, the Sauscrit that represents the
cradle of letters and civilization, are insignificant and
easy of interpretation compared to Col. Sam's waste of
ink and ruin of paper. But the strangest assumption by
him is that it is as plain as Roman capitals, and stranger
still, it irritates him to fighting heat to even question its
perfect legibility.

Before I had learned to descipher a few words and guess
at the remainder of his excellent bills in Chancery, I
spent ten days in perplexing, laborious effort, and gave it
up in despair, and resorted to the only remedy known to
the law, a motion to compel counsel to file his complaint
in a legible hand. I was as innocent as a child in this,
and had no more idea of insulting, than of shooting him.

But when I read the motion he knocked over chairs and
walked over benches, and it took the Sheriff and two deputies to hold him. Although since, often in contact and
forensic conflict with Col. Sam, I have never repeated the
motion, but have spent money and hired professional ex-
perts to help me guess at what he honestly tried to write.

The Colonel sometimes turns loose a ton of sarcasm, and woe to the litigant or hapless witness against whom he hurls thunderbolts. He is concise and powerful in logical argument.

On one occasion during a night session of Court, so often held by that upright and thoughtful Judge, Joseph W. Martin, when he was on the bench, I had the concluding argument in answer to Col. Sam in a hotly contested case, involving only a question of Corporation Law. A Convention, or Association, of Baptist ministers was then in session, and soon after I commenced the argument fifteen or twenty of those ministers took seats in the court room.

I felt humorous, and embraced the opportunity to touch up Col. Sam for all he could possibly bear in criticism. He rose to his feet several times to inflict argument more forcible than elegant, but the presence of the ministers restrained him. I crowded him until the expectation of trouble was painfully manifest all over the court room. Then I said: "Now let us turn the other side of the picture and look calmly and dispassionately at the bright and brilliant side. It affords me the greatets pleasure to say to Judge and Jury, that there are tons of the milk of human kindness, and all the elements of the Christian gentleman away down beneath all I have said in the bosom and noble nature of Col. Sam." When the play I had made was thus disclosed, the Colonel rose to his feet, slapped his thighs, and said: "That's so, John." And those preachers all went to bed laughing.

No man known to the history of the State could have better served her on the Supreme Bench. Had he been on that Bench since the close of the Civil War, judicial legislation, disregard of positive and plain statutes, and favoritism to corporations, would not have marred the judicial history of the State without his dissenting opinion and vehement protest.

INTERRUPTION OF COURT BY A BEAR.

IN 1843, Judge John T. Jones was holding Court at Osceola, on the Mississippi, in open air, the prisoners were tied to a tree, the Jury sat on a log, and the bystanders and Bar on any convenience they could improvise. The Judge was furnished with a chair, and leaned back against a monarch of the forest.

A number of deer and bear dogs had followed the attendants to Court. After the dogs had several fights, and the Jurors had been excused to part them, the dogs retired to a neighboring canebrake and jumped a huge bear, which made for the river and came within fifty yards of the Court. Several of the Jurors, without permission, jumped up and joined in the chase. The Judge told the Sheriff to bring back the Jurors, and the Clerk to enter a fine of $50 each against them, to which one of them responded in language more forcible than eloquent: "Go to Hades. I am going to follow the dogs and bear in spite of h—l or high water, and Judge Jones thrown in."

The Judge is yet with us, and is a distinguished citizen of eminent worth and of national fame. Ex-President of the National Grange, and father of the able, distinguished, and eloquent Paul Jones, of Texarkana, Ark.

THE COURT'S RESPECT FOR A POKER GAME.

THE Hon. Joe D. Conway, of Washington, Ark., himself, *sui generis*, *a rara avis* of marked and distinguished personality wholly his own, of whom the Creator has never made a counterpart, or anything approaching his duplicate, except in ability as a criminal lawyer, integrity, and high standing, tells on his uncle, Judge George Conway, an episode illustrating frontier conditions.

In 1845, the Judge was holding a term of the Lafayette Circuit Court on the western border of Arkansas. A murder trial was in progress, and one of the witnesses did not respond when called. The Judge asked the Sheriff if he knew where the witness was and what he was doing. The Sheriff said: "Yes, he is across the street engaged in a big game of poker." He called one of the members of the Bar, and said; "I do not wish to disturb that game, can't you go and play his hand until he can be examined?" The attorney went and played the hand, and the Court and game progressed.

A SUMMER VACATION, 1869.

WE shift, move, roll, whirl, like grains of sand in the circling eddies. In moving from place to place, the indulgence of passion for travel, the American people excel the ancients and lead the modern world for many reasons : facilities being greater, we have a vast landscape, more rivers, lakes, mountains, cities, people. The custom to travel has become a deep-seated national trait.

How pleasant, delightful, exhilarating when the season and arduous labors approach the annual vacation. How the joys of this season are heightened when we have a companion, who can with delicate mould of heart and touch of sentiment, awaken in rough man the inspiration of flowers ; who can point out to him a pearly dewdrop sitting in the lap of a rose, drinking and radiating all the prismatic colors of the rainbow, a tiny ocean, a delicacy to be uplifted by a sunbeam.

When rough and toiling man can escape the mad whirl of business with his wife, who can call into active being and inspire in him a love for the beauties and gems of nature, he may well feel proud that man is the oak around which the laurel twines. A companion who can wondrously, lovingly gaze on the mountain,

"That swells the vale and midway leaves the storm,"
and from its storm and snow-capped head, read a thousand sermons—who can sit the deck of a storm-driven ship, and read from the foam-crested billows, hymns of the creation—who can glance on the rolling clouds that speak as plainly as the law from Sinai, and proclaim that ceaseless change is the primal law.

One who looks in the tube of a telescope and aggregates

in a few sentences the accumulated wisdom of astronomical ages, and tells us that ten thousand times ten thousand worlds rolling through the universe proclaim the
immutable laws of ceaseless change as plainly and as eloquently as the rose that blooms to-day and dies to-morrow; who reads man's creation and fall in the rainbow
arching the heavens, and rapturously gazes on sunset
tint and cloud, as it drinks the gorgeous gold of the sun
sinking behind western hills and landscapes beyond the
reach of night and shadow.

Then laborious man realizes the beneficient beauties
embodied in God's first proclamation after the creation,
" It is not good for man to be alone."

In the summer of 1869 we made the tour of the northern
lakes and cities, stopping longer at Niagara than elsewhere, because of its superior natural scenery and historic associations.

In the " Cave of the Winds " under the American falls,
under the falls on the Canadian side, behind, buried in a
falling sea, yet protected by " the rock of ages."   Around
the island, that gem dividing the falling river, over rustic
bridges to the Baby Isles, against which the mad waves
dash and spend their fury.   Up the Niagara, watching

"Wave by wave as the tide heaves onward."

Then to the top of that tall tower on the Canadian side, on
the field of Lundy's Lane, on the fifty-fifth anniversary of
that battle, fought and won by American valor on the
25th of July, 1814.   Field glass in hand, a splendid prospect, frontier of two mighty empires, battlefield after
battlefield in view, where

" The patriotic tide poured through dauntless hearts "

at Chippewa, Fort Erie, Toronto, Lundy's Lane, and
the naval battles of Lake Erie, where Commodore Perry
stood on the deck of his gallant ship and wrote, " we
have met the enemy and they are ours."   All American
victories in the war of 1812.

Turning to the East, we beheld the marble shaft herald-
ing the heroic deeds of Gen. Brock, on the border line of

two mighty peoples. He fought one, and died for the other.

> The boast of heraldy, the pomp of power;
>   All that wealth, all that beauty e're gave,
> Await alike the inevitable hour."

What a theme, what a field, what a place for meditation. How sorrowful, how pathetic we felt, when we threw the glass on Toronto, where the heroic young Zebulon M. Pike fell at the moment of victory, where the snow drank his blood, where fame claimed the heritage of his name. Thence we went to the mouth of Niagara, where it delivers its raging floods to Ontario; then on board of one of those fine Canadian navigation steamers, that rode the rising and falling billows "like a thing of life" to Toronto. After a rest with our British cousins, one hundred and fifty miles on the unrippled bosom of Ontario in repose, a glorious sight, full of sweet memories, a Pentecostal feast of mind and soul, yet fresh and green and beautiful as the flowers that fringe the "Beautiful Isle of Long Ago," which Bayard Taylor sang with so much charm of soul in the fields of Lapland and in the gorgeous tropics.

How charming it is to be charming. to others. I love those splendid touches of "Old Scotia's immortal Bard," and those Scotch Airs, wife's artistic touch of key, with vocal accompaniment, on the silver sea of Ontario, "A Mile from Edinburg Town," floated out until I could hear the music roll and swell and fall in beautiful cadence until the hills, valleys and mountains of Caledonia handed it back to the crystal riplets of Bonnie Doone.

A Scotch lord and lady were there, and their souls reveled as the nightingales in the moon-kissed bower.

To Charlotte and Rochester and Albany, down the historic Hudson, with its world of memories, past the Catskill mountains, where Irving made old Rip Van Winkle as immortal as our literature. Such a vacation, a rest for the fray of the forum, to be whipped by George Gantt on return, or thrashed by some other equally as heartless a Brother.

Touch not, stand back ye gods of fate, ye remorseless vandals of time. Touch not these paintings that hang in the gallery of the soul, they are grants of immortality and belong to God and I; they are beyond the treacherous vicissitudes of time, and the reach of death, and as fadeless as the beautiful life of the martyred Nazarene.

RECOLLECTIONS OF GEN. BUTLER.

GEN. BENJAMIN F. BUTLER, in many respects one of the most remarkable men I ever knew, a cross between Celt and Puritan, he inherited the talents and energies of both races. Educated for the Baptist ministry, he was cosmopolitical as to creeds, and an evolutionist in politics; as Junius says of the Duke of Grafton, he traveled through every sign of the political zodiac. A great lawyer, possessed of an enormous memory with powers of condensation rarely equaled, never excelled.

A prolific genius, impelled with a momentum of character that led the aggressive in all he undertook.

Charitable, humane, sympathetic with the poor, an orphan at birth, his father having died on a West Indiaman when he was a few months old. His mother, an Irish woman of great worth and energy, a boarding house keeper for the factory operatives at Lowell, where the boy early developed the sympathetic phase of his nature. I was brought into contact with him in the landed litigation of the West, saw much of him, and after the matter was adjusted was with him much in his office in Washington and New York.

He had offices in Lowel, Boston, New York, and Washington, and made the circuit of these offices as his

vast business demanded. With him the telegraph super-
ceded the post letter. He could systematise and dispatch more business than any man I ever knew. I have
known fifty clients in a day to consult him, including
many importing merchants. One to five minutes was all
the time he could devote to any one, after once getting
the history of the case.

The client, admitted to his inner room, he would
question, the answers to which were taken down by a short-
hand reporter, and he would say: "That is all I wanted
with you." The client would say: "General, I wanted
to say many other things to you, and have been here several days awaiting this interview, and have not said one
word I came to say." "Yes, you have given all the information I want now. When I need you, I will wire
you;" and the usher would be directed to call the next
name. I sat for weeks in his office, astonished at the ease
and facility with which he dispatched such a volume of
business.

While I was in his office an importing merchant from
Philadelphia came in, and asked him to write an article
foreshadowing the policy of the United States, as indicated by commercial treaties since 1812. I left the office at
9 o'clock that night; next morning he handed me the article to read, and I regarded it as one of the ablest docu-
ments I ever read. It would have required weeks of investigation for others to have written such a paper.

The better phases of his nature were to me very forcibly illustrated in many instances. One morning a poorly
clad lady came into his office crying, and said:

"Gen. Butler, I am the widow of a rebel Colonel, with
three boys to educate. I have an estate at Arlington involved in litigation. Mr. ——, of this city, is my attorney. I have disposed of all I had to pay him $1,500; the
trial comes on to-day, and he says he will abandon my
case if I do not pay him $1,000 more—that is impossible.
Can you, will you take my case?"

"Certainly, Madam."

He instantly ordered his carriage, and went with the distressed widow to the Court, told the Court what the widow said, had the name of the attorney stricken from the case, and his own substituted, and the cause continued. On my next visit to Washington, he informed me that he had won the case, and found the little widow one of the most grateful women he ever met. She authorized him to sell the land and retain his fee. "My dear madam, your gratitude is a rich fee to me. Educate those promising boys—that is all the reward I ask."

At another time he handed me a long telegram from a man in jail in Boston, begging for the loan of $500, and told O. D. Barret, his local partner, to fill out a check for the amount and mail it to him, and reply by wire. "This man," he said, "is the dissolute, degenerate son of a noble sire, who was my friend in youth. He has spent a large fortune in dissipation, and is a worthless wreck, but I cannot forget his father."

I had made a special study of Mexican and Spanish land titles, which are the initial basis of title to vast tracts of land acquired under the treaty of Guadaloupe Hidalgo and the Louisiana Purchase, which attracted the attention of Gen. Butler, and caused him, in his desire to serve me, to seek my appointment as Territorial Judge for Arizona without having conferred with me. His Democratic friends in New England, he said, at his suggestion, had the matter ripe for consummation. I was much astonished and told him I would not accept the office under any consideration; that my business engagements prohibited it; that it was only for a period of four years, changing with the political fortunes of administrations; that it would whet my appetite in all probability for office without the ability to gratify it, and make me one of those pitiful political tramps who throng the capital, and end in loss of business and the misery of my family. He was equally astonished, and for a few days was quite angry with me.

After that, he said: "I can secure you, perhaps, permanent employment in Washington by starting you on the French spoliation claims."

"That," I said, "would at least be as permanent as my life, for those claims have troubled every Congress since 1812, with as little assurance of settlement now as then."

"Then how can I serve you, and get you out of Arkansas?"

"No way I can think of now."

He had great love and admiration for Gen. Roger A. Pryor, who settled in New York in the practice of his profession after the Civil War, and is now (1894) one of the Judges in that city.

On one of my visits to Washington to see him, I found a telegram in his office awaiting and urging me to come to the Fifth Avenue Hotel, in New York, as it was impossible for him to leave, a cause then being heard. I found him and Gen. Pryor together in a will case involving $10,000,000. They had superceded Roscoe Conklin in the case, and had five volumes of evidence printed in book form, each volume containing one thousand pages.

I was told by a gentleman, that an eminent phrenologist took the chart of his head in early and later life, and that his frontal brain had grown one half inch in forty years.

I wore a broad-brim felt hat. One morning he asked me what size hat I wore. In a short time his servant entered the office with a derby: "Take that and wear it while you are in the East. You will be taken for a cow-driver with that Stetson."

At times he indulged in refined taste for repartee and wit. He could close the valve and shut off thought, and pick up another thread quicker than any man I ever knew; could deliver a political speech, and in a few minutes engage in profound legal argument before the Supreme Court. I know no parallel in our history. He had a sovereign dislike for Conklin's pretensions to the abilities of a jurist. "No man," said he, "can be engaged in politics twenty years and be more than a case lawyer."

I told him that my cousin, Charles Hallum, was weak enough to embrace all of his political heresies and vote for him, and threatened to disinherit his sons if they did not do likewise. "That is the worst sort of coercion. Tell those sons to rise up in rebellion." He sent a fine portrait of himself to my cousin, Charles.

MORE TROUBLE, 1875.

AFTER the defeat of the second demonstration in Trinidad against my life "peace reigned in Warsaw," and I was lulled into a sense of perfect security. I had the warmest friends and the bitterest enemies. I went any and everywhere unattended, fishing, hunting, and on any other business that called me away from the town, which was very frequent. The Lodge of Pythians had boldly proclaimed that if I was harmed, either clandestinely or openly the members of the mob, and particularly its ring leaders, should pay the penalty of death. I believe that their cowardice was my protection. One Sunday evening George Thompson, that delectable sheriff, who could smile in your face and ape manhood while encouraging a mob to take your life, came to my residence and gravely told me that three assassins had been induced to come up from the mountains of New Mexico to kill me, and urged me to leave under cover of night, if I valued existence. He said they had already arrived, and would execute the job next morning, and that he would be powerless to protect me. I said, "I know you, you took an active part in inducing me to come here in December, 1872, both as sheriff of the county and as a member of the committee appointed to confer with me. You knew then that a mob intended to murder me,

and you were a cowardly party to their plans; you had it
in your power to summons every man in the county to
prevent it, you did not do it. You ran away that the
mob might have no hindrance in executing me. If nothing else, you could have telegraphed me, or rode out and
met me and warned me, you did neither. When I call on
you or your clan of murderers for protection I will get
it, but it will be at the muzzle of my own gun or the point
of my own knife. When I take to my heels and flee under
cover of night as long as I can drive a knife or pull a
trigger, I will want my name spit on and forgotten.
Go." And he got on his horse and rode up the Las Animas river, three miles to his home, knowingly leaving
these three assassins at the hotel, hirelings of George
Boyles and company for blood money. I did not go out
that night, but put "old Betsy" in good order, sixteen
blue whistlers in each barrel, saw that my revolver was
in speaking order, and knife in tune, and did not call
any of my Pythian brothers because I thought I could
handle that case myself, as I would have daylight to
move in. My office was in Hubbard's building adjoining
the bank of Swallow & Terry. I did not put implicit
faith in what Thompson said, because I knew him to be
a deceiver and a liar, and thought it was probable he was
"running a bluff," but got ready for "the ball." Next
morning, after breakfast, I walked up to my office without "old Betsy" in hand. A few minutes after I opened
my office I looked anglingly across the street, in front of
the store of Jaffa Brothers, and saw the three armed
gents standing on the pavement. I then started back to
my residence to get my shotgun, realizing that I had
made a mistake in not taking it with me to my office when
I first went there. One of these would-be-assassins approached me and asked where I was going. I told him
"deer hunting in the foot hills," and politely asked him
to go with me, and he accepted the invitation. I told
him that I would be back in a few minutes and we would
24

then start. This threw him off his guard, until I
could get my gun. I returned to the corner fronting
Jaffa Brothers, and stopped. In a few moments the
three came in a bunch to his door and I threw my gun on
them, but they jumped back in the door before I could
fire and did not come to the front. I stood there fronting
that door half an hour waiting for them to come out, but
they had retreated to the rear end of the building and did
not come. The overland stage from the South at this
juncture drove up, and Fine Ernest, one of the cattle
kings of New Mexico, got off. During all this time there
was no passing along the streets, everybody appeared to
know what was up and kept in doors. As soon as Ernest
learned what was up he went into where the corralled
assassins were, and in a few minutes came towards me.
I had but a very slight acquaintance with him at that
time, and warned him to stand back. He did so, and
again went into the store where the assassins were, and
in a few moments approached me again, saying, "Hallum,
I am your friend, these men have asked me to say to you
that since coming to town they have found you are not
the man represented to them, and they have abandoned
all idea of harming you in any way, and will leave if you
will not molest them." I said, "Tell them to get on
their horses and leave now, so that I may see them execute their promise, that I will not molest them if they will
do that in good faith." They submitted to the terms,
and in a few moments got on their horses and rode off.
One Sam Doss was the leader of these would-be-assassins,
himself a refugee from justice from the State of Texas,
whose only claim to the slightest consideration was a
bunch of cattle and a ranch, the other two I never knew.
Doss had a remnant of conscience left, enough to make
him despise himself and commit suicide some years afterwards, but what route the others took I never learned,
they were in the wake of "Ward's Ducks" when I last
saw them. I afterwards met Fine Ernest often at Trin-

idad, Pueblo, Denver, and other places, and found him to
be a conservative, well behaved gentleman. He went
from Missouri to New Mexico twenty years prior to that
time as convoy to a prairie schooner, a poor boy, but by
industry and integrity, mixed with good judgment, became the wealthiest cattle king in New Mexico. At his
request, and the permission of the family, I introduced
him to the daughter of Gov. John Q. A. King, whom he
addressed with serious intentions.

Fine and myself have had many a laugh over what he
called my "hold up" in Trinidad. All new arrivals on
the frontier, in virtue of their supposed innocence and
simplicity, are called by the expressive name of "tender
foot." That fall I was employed by a large number of
the most influential cattle men of Colfax county, New
Mexico, then known as the "Kingdom of Elkins," after
the renowned Stephen B., to go to Elizabethtown to defend them. They were political opponents of Elkins, and
for that reason were regarded as malefactors. They
were charged with arson in the burning of a petty school
house, of which they were as innocent as Queen Victoria
and as far above such a crime. My fee for all of these
cases was $3,000, but when I arrived in the northern
county of the "kingdom" the judicial luminary who presided in the Territorial Court, ruled that I could not practice at that Bar because I was not a citizen of the "kingdom" of New Mexico. My clients charged that they
were indicted simply because they were not loyal to "King
Steve," and after the election of delegate to Congress
the cases were *nolle prosed.* Steve was the unique Phœnix of political birds, and his history on the way to, and
on the throne, represents a rectangular quadrelateral,
broader than long. After serving in the Confederate
army he migrated from Missouri, took passage on a
prairie schooner, served in the double capacity of convoy
and passenger, and when he got to Santa Fe, he disem-
barked at that ancient burg. He soon picked up enough

knowledge of greaser idiom to communicate ideas. Steve was a lawyer and soon adopted a coat of arms which has been his polar star ever since : "Get There Steve." This talisman has led him all the way from a Mexican Alcalde's Court to the War Office at Washington. The Catholic Priesthood of New Mexico are as absolute as a Persian satrap. To control them, was to hold the province in absolute subjection and "Get There Steve" knew how to do it. That knowledge was the Alpha and Omega of his power in New Mexico, when he first started on the road to wealth. It was afterwards powerfully supplemented by a big bank account.

MOVE TO TRINIDAD.

ANOTHER MOB—PYTHIANISM ILLUSTRATED—A TRUE FRIEND—1874-'75.

THE unexpected has always loomed up in my pathway. In April, 1874, my family physician asked me for a private interview in the library. "What is it, Doctor?" "Your two-year-old daughter, Mattie, cannot survive long in any climate; and if you do not remove your wife, she will soon follow. Take her to Southern Colorado, California, or New Mexico. Pulmonary trouble has set in."

We had laid one bright, little boy to rest in Bellefountaine Cemetary.

> "Ye tiny elves, that guiltless sport
> Like linnets in the bush;
> Ye little know the ills ye court,
> When manhood is your wish."

I went down town with a mournful heart, and ordered my residence sold. Went to see some brother lawyers, and arranged with them to take charge of my business; and when I came home in the evening, struggled to drive my troubles out of my face, and counterfeited a happy disposition.

My wife, at all events, must not be burdened with the idea that her misfortune had thrown such a cloud over my prospects and hopes. She already had a store of anxiety.

Laura was a babe at the breast. In twenty days I was on the way to Trinidad. That was the climate, and I had interests there to look after. As for the mob, I was now possessed of full knowledge, was forearmed, and felt competent to control it. I arrived there on the 20th of May, 1874, with my wife and two little girls. Dr. Le-Carpenter, an elegant gentleman, had preceded me a few months, and he became a warm, confidential friend, through whom I could, and did, accomplish much without either he or anybody knowing my design. Through him I organized a Pythian Lodge of twenty-five members, composed of the best material of the town. My object was to be ready for the mob if it came, and with my Pythian Brothers to strike it and smite it, and put down the lawless desperadoes; but if my real object had been known, no Lodge, with myself as a member, could have been formed. I kept in the back ground, with my friend, Dr. LeCarpenter, leading. When the Charter members had been secured, I gave each one a deed to the improved lot he occupied, and told them to say, whenever occasion required, that I was not wanting or asking for one dollar's worth of improvement put on my land. This had its effect. The Lodge was organized, and I was chosen Chancellor Commander, but resigned, and took a subordinate position. I cared nothing for the ostensible, if I could be the real power. If I had been the open leader, it would have defeated my object. Dr. Cushing, from Mississippi, was the head. He was an impulsive man, and loved to work in the lead, and was chosen Chancellor Commander of the Lodge, and when backed, would charge on the breastworks of the devil—the right man in the right place. When George Boyles, the knave, saw how rapidly I was gaining the respect of the better element, he again aroused the mob element, and they threatened to burn the Lodge up, the worst possible of all things they could have done to fire the Pythians. I let my Brothers do the outside talking. All I had to do was to be in reach of a few of them when the ball opened.

I recollect some of the names of the old Charter members of Trinidad Lodge, No. 3, and am sorry I do not remember the names of all of them. Dr. E. N. Cushing, Webster Brown, William Baldwin, Ted Baldwin, Frank Dunton, Horatio Dunton, Stephen Penny, Louis Kriger, James Burton, Pat Drennan, Archibald Baldwin, John Hallum, Dr. LeCarpenter. Dr. Michael Beshoar, and many others, afterward became members. The Charter members numbered twenty-five.

A Pythian banquet was given soon after the organization, and the lawless bullies attempted to break it up, but was glad to throw up the job.

At that time I occupied an abode building on the West side of Commercial street. My front gate being but thirty feet from my front door, with an ell easily barricaded, and it would have taken a six-pound cannon ball to penetrate the walls.

The January term (1875) of the Territorial District Court was in session—I mean at the time the brave mob came. I had argued cases against the wild Irishman, Pat McBride and George Boyles, and had taken the "woof and warp" out of them. Jefferson Luellen, of whom I will have much to say hereafter, an old soldier under Gen. Albert Sydney Johnston, a frontiersman, and one of the truest and bravest men the world ever knew, whose wife was a Hallum descendant, a distant Cousin, was rooming at the Overland Hotel. On the evening of the 12th of January, 1875, at dark, Lu, as he was called, came to my house bringing his buffalo robe, rifle, and pistols, and told me that for four nights he had overheard the conspirators, the leaders of the mob, who met late at night in a room adjoining his, to discuss the plan and details of my execution, that there was nothing but a thin plank partition wall between his room and theirs, and he could hear every word they said. "Between forty and fifty men will come here to-night at 1 o'clock to mob and execute you. Get your wife and children out of the way. I have come to stay with you to the end. It is going to be bloody work." He continued: "First, barricade the ell room. Lay mattresses down and put your wife and babies on the floor, so if that part of the building is fired on, the balls will pass over them. I know you will not trust them out of your sight this cold night, and that you have no safe place to take them."

God bless that brave man's memory! When he told me this he did not know that I had paid detectives, spies, on their track, and that I knew the details and was prepared for the bloodiest tragedy that town ever saw. Lu lived forty miles distant on the Trinchera, a beautiful mountain stream in Northern New Mexico, and was at Trinidad attending Court, and did not know of the Pythian Lodge or my precaution. And the fact that he did not, enhances his friendship and heroic courage. His noble resolve to defend, and if necessary die with a man who was to be attacked by forty or fifty men. George Boyles, Pat McBride, Al. Sopris, and Watt Riffenberg were the consulting moguls, the agitators, but neither of them would ever have been at the blood letting, if their scalps were in the least danger, but they could hiss others on. We barricaded the windows with the furniture in the house, so we could remove and adjust as emergencies might require, and maintain a raking cross-fire when necessary.

In less than an hour after Lu came, seventeen Pythians well armed, came to await and take a hand in the tragedy. Dr. Cushing, the Chancellor Commander, being with them. Web Brown, smoking his pipe as coolly as he would have done if sitting in his office. Jim Burton, the dare-devil Confederate, who had heard it thunder at Chickamauga, Missionary Ridge, Kennesaw Mountain, and many other fields of blood, a native Tennessean, stood side by side with the Duntons, from Maine, and the Baldwins, from the British Isles, Pat Drennan, from Ireland, Louis Kregar, a descendant of Fatherland, Luellan, from Pennsylvania, Stephen Penny, from Ohio, Dr. LeCarpenter, a descendant of the Huguenots, who worshipped the name of Bonaparte as an idol, Dr. Cushing, from Mississippi, and others. All as cool as if at a matinee.

The mob gathered at a large livery stable on Commercial street, about eighty yards from my residence. Our doors were shut and room darkened. The moon and stars occasionally peeped through floating rifts in the clouds, down on the silent, pale earth wrapped in her mantel of snow. My wife made coffee and handed it around, and put a small pistol in her pocket, a wee bit of mortality, careless of danger as the sleeping children.

I regretted, deplored the necessity to shed blood, but could not give up mine in such a cause as that. To kill every man that entered my yard was the resolve of the nineteen men who had collected to write in blood, if necessary, proofs of their loyalty to the vows of a noble Brotherhood. That an awful tragedy was soon to take place, we were all sure, not a doubt was entertained, and we felt equally as sure that we would be the survivors. I took charge of one squad, who were to fire from the window on the left; Lu of the other window to the right. No voice, but low whisperings. No light. No sound reached the street. All was still and dark. I cautioned, begged for one promise not to fire a gun until the crowd came on the inside of my yard. The street was a public highway, and serious legal complications might arise if we piled them up in the street.

At half-past ten Dr. Cushing detailed Baldwin and Burton to reconnoiter the enemy, and we silently let them out at the back door, with directions to creep up to the rear of the livery stable where the mob were in rendezvous. They executed the order and reported forty men there with white masks and side arms. Within twenty minutes after they reported a light tap came on my door. Had the mob come sooner than the appointed time and stole a march on us from the back way unobserved? I answered, "In a moment I will open the door." The light was turned up and the guns held in readiness to fire, I threw open the door, and there stood a man named Orton, a spy from the mob. He involuntarily threw up his hands and reeled back and to one side. I asked, "What do you want?" He said, "I came to consult you on some law business, but will come again." He appeared astonished to see me ready to receive company. I caught him by the collar, jerked him into the room, shut the door, then lowered our light and said to him, "You are a dirty spy, and I am persuaded to cut your throat." At that my friends were eager to kill him on the spot. But I said, "No, he has a family, and is nothing more than a contemptible tool." He was very much frightened, and confessed that he was sent to my house to see whether I had protection, and said forty-two men were masked in the stable, and were coming at one o'clock to mob me, but he changed his ideas, and begged to be allowed to lead us to the stable and fire the first gun on them himself. We held him a prisoner, and the fact that he did not return, and could not be found, alarmed them and disconcerted their plans. I felt then that the backbone of the mob was broken, and that not one of them would enter my yard until they found out more about Orton's fate. But at one o'clock they came to my front gate and stood there seemingly irresolute, disconcerted, without spirit or leader. Sopris and Boyles, McBride and Riffenberg, the arch instigators, were not "in it." We were ready for them, but they were as spiritless as sheep in the shambles, and if one shot had

been fired would have scattered like a covey of quail.
The excitable Cushing wanted to fire, and so did several
of the other men, but Lu, Brown, and Penny, were more
cautious. To restrain them during the ten minutes those
cravens stood there, required a great effort on my part.
I told them our object was to put down, not to convert
ourselves into a mob. That we must wait for the overt
act, let them open the gate and start in, then we will not
leave one to tell the tale—that the majority of those misguided men had wives and children—that they were in
the public street we knew for an illegal purpose, but true
Pythianism would be greatly injured if we were hasty,
wait a moment, we are not in the least danger until
they come in." A flock of school girls would not have
been easier handled than that mob, without a resolute
leader. I appreciated the noble men, and generous impulses that made me so secure, but the responsibility was
mine, to protect them as well as myself, to think for them
as well as for myself, to save us all from that all consuming remorse that would attend the widow's weeds,
and the orphan's cry, the stain of blood so easily avoided.
That mob, with masked faces, stood and peeped, and
gazed on the silent walls of my residence, whispered one
to another, but what was said will never be known; but
their conclusion was eminently wise, they marched off
the way they came and dispersed. My friends remained
all night. Next day the town was astonished at the
idea, that there was no job for the coroner when so many
men had undertaken to give him one. "The talk of the
town." Yes, but who of those citizens came even to
warn the intended victim of the intended murder in their
midst? Echo of human infirmity answers, None, except
the Order and Lu, the psalm singer at church was in
town and the moral coward. The intent of that mob was
as notorious as pigs tracks around a barnyard. I could
have taken ten brave men and run them all into the mountains. I stood toward the "braves" of that community

like the Yankee to whom I once gave permission to exhibit paintings in my schoolroom. He told the children
when he came to a picture of Daniel in the lion's den, with
wand in hand: "Now we come to this splendid representation of Daniel in the lion's den, observe it closely and you
will see that Daniel don't care a damn for the lions, and
the lions don't care a damn for Daniel." How fast the
prisms change their combinations, how quick the curtains
fall, the scenes shift in the comedy the little man plays in
his brief hour on the stage of life!

I said, "Lu, you knew four days ago that this mob
was coming last night, why did you not tell me sooner?
Why wait until dark on the night I was to be mobbed?"
"Because you were busy in court, and I did not wish to
disturb and disqualify you for that, I intended to be on
hand." So responded the brave Lu.

I was busy. I had stood up before a mixed jury of
whites and Mexican Greasers three hours that day, speaking one sentence at a time, and then waiting till an interpreter could translate it into Mexican, and then another
sentence, alternating with the interpreter.

Lu said, "Three of those jurors were with those men
in the mob last night."

"Yes, I suppose they were sworn to enforce the law.
Tell me, Lu, I am always bluffing up against freaks of
nature, I have made it the closest study of my life. Jurors in closely contested cases are generally apt to go
with the lawyer for whom they entertain the highest regard. I tried two pretty close cases for you before that
jury and won them both, and that indicates a paradox I
don't understand, they decide for me, and join a mob to
execute me in a few hours afterwards, strange junctures
to me. But I don't know much about a Mexican—have
been told they are treacherous devils—worse than the
low bred Italian with his stiletto. I don't see into it.
Lu, can you tell me?"

"Oh, yes, I know enough on some of those Mexicans to

hang them, and they know I know it. It was fear of me
and not respect for you."

"No, Lu, 'they were sworn to execute the law.'"

THE BULLY OF THE CHUCHARAS.

ANOTHER TRAP SET FOR ME, AND I INNOCENTLY WALK
INTO IT—THE WAY OUT—DECEMBER, 1874.

MY leniency to my enemies emboldened them, check-
mating brought them no penalties, hence they
persisted. In December, 1874, Thos. Stephens,
the wealthiest man of Trinidad, came to my
office and wanted my professional services in a case of
emergency. He had never been in my office before.
George Boyles was his attorney. He had not taken an
active part with my enemies, but was altogether in sympathy with them. If he had known that the most flagrant outrage was going to be perpetrated against me,
he would not have put me on my guard. He was largely
engaged in merchandising, had been on the frontier
nearly all his life, was once the partner of Gov. Carney.

He had established a branch house in Huerfano County,
on the Chucharas river, forty miles distant from Trinidad, on the Pueblo road, and had put W. Y. Suydam in
charge of $20,000 worth of goods. Suydam had graduated
in the "Kansas Jayhawking school," was as fine looking
specimen of the physical man as "ever cut a throat or
scuttled a ship," and ran largely on his reputation as a
bully. Tom did not sufficiently investigate him, and it
was not long until things went crooked with the ledger
balances, the tracks all went Suydam's way, and he was
"The Bully of the Chucharas." Stephens was conservative, and his attorney, Boyles, was more so. This con-
servatism was all Suydam wanted, all he cared for, as

long as he could keep it developed with his "reputation."
He was "getting away" with the goods, he had the cash
and Tom the "experience." Tom was afraid to go, and
his attorney would not go until the bovine had been las-
soed. In short, he wanted me to go down that night on
the Overland stage, attach and close up the house. I
supposed it an easy matter, and that Suydam would not
know who was after "Billy Patterson" until the sheriff
tapped him on the shoulder and took charge of the assets.
Tom gave me his check for $250, and thought it large.
The coach came along a little after dark and I got in, a
solitary passenger for the Chucharas, a stage stand two
miles from Walsenburg, the county seat. The village
was composed of a store house, some stables, Mexican
"hackells," and the stage stand, a log cabin with dirt
floor, and two rooms. I got out, at eleven at night, and
entered the stand. A deep snow was on the ground and
it was cold. A huge log fire afforded fine entertainment.
I stood up before it, and turned about and around, with
one foot at a time held out to the fire. I had scarcely
thawed out before Suydam and a young man entered,
with side arms buckled on, and with an oath, backed by
his "reputation," said, "You have come here to attach
my store, and find your grave." This was a revelation
in which I read the cowardly hand of George Boyles.
There was a dim light burning in the small back room,
and I saw a double-barrelled shotgun in the corner. I
asked the landlord if I could have that room, and he
gave his assent. I entered it immediately, closed the
door, picked up the gun and found it was loaded. I had
my pistol and knife in my belt. I cocked the gun, threw
open the door, and said to Suydam, "You and your
pard, disarm yourselves instantly, and throw your arms
here at my feet, or I will drop you both in your tracks."
They obeyed, and the trouble with "The Bully of the
Chucharas" was over. A Mayday girl on the lawn
never behaved nicer. "Now sit down by the fire, both

of you, till daylight, and if your outside pals, if you
have any, make a move, I will drop you and take my
chances with them. Be pleasant and agreeable. I have
only come to close the store and take charge, nothing
more. I did not come to get hurt, nor to hurt you, unless
you make another break, its all with you."

I sat there all night, and they sat too, and after the
dash wore off we chatted and whiled away the time.
After daylight I took the key to the store and let them
go. I sent for the sheriff, he took charge and I returned
to Trinidad.

George Boyles had sent a letter down to Snydam by
the same stage I went on, giving him full information as
to my purposes and advising him "to get away with
Hallum, I will stand by you." Snydam showed me the
letter. That was a miserable episode, foreign to my raising and every impulse of my nature; but let the practical
man, who knows something of the world and "the wild
West" say how I could have accomplished my mission
and saved myself from harm without doing as I did. As
to taming the Bully, that was the easiest of all things,
and I disclaim any credit for it. They all quail when on
an equal footing with resolute men. What I despised
was having such a disagreeable necessity forced on me.

A SUMMER OUTING IN THE ROCKIES, 1875.

IN the summer of 1875, I went with my wife and two
little daughters, Miss Addie Winters and two
other families, to the source of the Las Animas
river in the Rocky mountains, forty miles from
Trinidad, on a fishing and recreating excursion. Our
route was up the banks of that river, which came roaring
and pouring, dashing and leaping over rock and pebble,
through wild gorge and woodland glen, from the snow-

capped peaks of the mountains.   A more attractive landscape, romantic scenery of nature in her picturesque
grandeur, cannot be found in that mighty range of mountains.   Of the thousands of miles I have traveled in those
mountains I have never seen a rarer collection of nature's
beauties crowded into more compact compass, from the
tiniest wild flower to the sublimest toss of mountain head
above the clouds.   Under the base of these snow-capped
sentinels lay Stonewall Park, a garden gem of the gods,
with its wilderness of wild flowers, and wild forest lawns,
through which the roaring river, with its crystal foam
caps chants an everlasting lullaby.   The facile pen stag-
gers and fails in the effort to paint it.   A stone wall,
hundreds of feet in height and many miles long, fence off
the Park from the mountains, with colossal masonry and
blocks of stone, from one to a thousand tons, like the accurately designed work of masons.   A narrow opening
in this wall affords a gateway to the floods from the
mountains above.

Here in the Park we pitched our tents, late one evening
as the sun was sinking behind the mountains, to rise
again with its golden treasures and delicate, luxurious
pencilings on field and flood.   We had an outfit of angling supplies, and the waters swarmed with that most
beautiful and delicate of all fish, the brook or mountain
trout, the rarest sport that ever rewarded a disciple of
old Izaak Walton.   The catch was great, the beauties
reflected all the colors of the rainbow, and weighed from
one half to three and a half pounds.   But how fast we
passed from a sense of security to that of alarm.   After
a lengthy stay I left my friends in the Park and proceeded
with my family down the river to its junction with its
North and South forks.

In that gorge of mountains we were suddenly surrounded by several hundred Ute Indians, only a few days
after they had been on the war path, all around our home
at Trinidad, and had been driven off by an armed force,

after killing many ranchmen and stealing many cattle and horses. I had a gallon of alcohol, for use in cooking purposes, which they smelled and wanted, but succeeded in emptying it before they could get it. The men looked angry at me, and the squaws looked angry at my wife. We were thirty miles from Trinidad, the only place from which we could expect support. An Indian is as treacherous as the imps of hades, and with all the boasted civilization he has never lost his impulse for scalps when he can get them with any degree of impunity to himself. My wife and children were in their power, as for myself I cared nothing. I have seen the Indians of many tribes, have seen them on the hunt and on the warpath, and in their wild scalp dances, have been in their power on the plains, and in the mountains, have faced danger from many sources, and many times, but have never felt alarmed like I did on this occasion. But they left without doing any harm, to our intense gratification.

INVESTMENTS IN SAN JUAN MINES.

TRIP THROUGH THE MOUNTAINS, 1876.

THE San Juan mines were then attracting much attention. I purchased twenty-five Mexican boros, and loaded them down with supplies and mining outfit, and sent two young men into the mines, in the spring of 1875. They located on the Uncompogere river, near Mineral Point, which was on the plateau above. The boys reported great success, and sent me ores that assayed a $1,000 to the ton. In July, 1876, Jefferson Luellen, who defended me against the mob, went with me to San Juan. We had a splendid team and outfit for camping out, and a pair of extra fine horses. Previous to starting I had sent my wife and children to my father's, in Middle Tennessee, their health having been fully restored. I furnished my wife with a list of all the post offices on the route, so that I could get letters, papers, and magazines, from her at every post office.

Our custom was to write every day, when convenient. We started on the 10th of July, and drove fifty miles, to the Aryahtoyah Peaks, so named by the Ute Indians, from their resemblance to a lady's breast, but called by Americans the Spanish Peaks, where we went into our first camp. The next day we met with a bad accident, in running one of our horses against a seasoned bush, which passed literally through the shoulder of the fine animal, which we had to leave at a ranch until our return, so one of our extra animals was soon brought into requisition. The next day we drove fifty miles, to LaVeta, at the foot of the main eastern range of the Rocky mountains. In that high, pure atmosphere, both animals and men can stand much more fatigue than in a lower atmosphere; there I have frequently driven a fine horse one hundred miles between the rising and the setting of the sun. The next day we ascended to the summit of the mountains, at an altitude of about twelve thousand feet. Here, with field glass in hand, vast range of vision, and clear atmosphere, we beheld a wilderness of mountain peaks, piled like "Pelion upon Ossa," with rolling clouds far below their crests, and to the east vast plains stretching away for hundreds of miles, sinking into the blue outlines of the horizon, with its lowing herds, which we could plainly discern with our field glass. To the west at our feet lay San Louis valley, in the lowland lap of the mountains, one hundred and twenty miles long by sixty broad, literally covered with herds of cattle, while through the valley ran the silver thread of the Rio Grande or Grand River of the North winding its serpentine way. Across that lovely valley a thousand snowcapped peaks greeted the eye, towering in mighty and awful majesty in their sublime solitude. What a splen-

25

did panorama. It is said that Jefferson's brain forces were expanded by the lofty impulses the mountains imparted to head and heart. I believe it. To be in touch with greatness and grandeur is to embrace the ideas they invite in greater or less degree. Out on the San Louis Valley we beheld a white village and a lofty pole, from which streamed and fluttered the National ensign of our greatness. It floated over Fort Garland, where I would get my next relay of letters and papers from home, having received my first package at LaVeta. While making coffee on the summit, one of those sudden cloud-bursts, with flash after flash of lightning, and peal after peal of thunder, and heavy down pour of rain came, to be gone in thirty minutes and replaced with sun and clear sky. The larch forests so tall, profuse and beautiful, that never grows at an altitude below ten thousand feet, wrapped and festooned these mountain elevations in a wilderness of beauty. Yonder a herd of elks, the noblest of American game, and yonder on another mountain, away up in the cliffs, the wild mountain sheep, and in the crags, around the summit, the eagle on tireless wing wildly screams. As we go down and down Wagon Wheel Gap, a herd of black-tailed deer scampered away. Down in the valley the trilling rivulets expand into streams of crystal waters, filled with brook trout. Here, across this perennial stream, dam after dam, and pool after pool tell us of a colony of beaver, settled here, perhaps, centuries ago. The most ingenius little engineer known to the animal kingdom. In the foot hills on the western slope, we drive on and come to a deserted placer mining camp, and there find on the roadside an old "Forty-Niner" settled there still, almost a hermit in the solitude. We "pull up" and ask for shelter, assuring him that we had plenty of provisions and bedding. With a generous welcome we are invited in, a huge fire and a garrulous old man, glad to escape the dreary solitude of twenty and six years, glad for a willing listener in me. He tells many a weird story of mountain and plain in the years gone by, after Lu, the silent, was wrapped in sleep. Lu was not "much on the talk," but great in action and execution. I absorbed enough at that hermit's fireside to fill a volume of romance and legend. Next day we entered the monotonous plains, the outer skirts of the San Louis valley, and drove through sage brush, grease weed and cactus; jack-rabbits here and there and everywhere, and here and there a herd of antelope, there a flock of sheep, and yonder a herd of cattle, and miles and miles in front the old flag fluttered and kissed the breeze. That night we camped on a beautiful stream, where we found luxurious grasses, and larieted our horses, and found sound sleep beneath the stars. At noon we reached Fort Garland, where I found another package of three letters, from my wife; not the small sheet and one-paged letter, but ten-page letters, which photographed all that was going on around the fireside at home. These letters were treasures, and came like sunbeams. The papers and magazines told of all that was going on in the outer world. We rested here a couple of days. I wrote many letters and found much entertainment in reading. Sixty miles pull to Del Norte, through deep sands and across a peat bog, where the earth would shake and tremble under us as though it were going to swallow us up, where we saw the bleached bones of hundreds of animals, cattle and others, that had perished in the bog. And I cried, "The bones, see the bones!" Next night, on the banks of the Rio Grande, and the marshes bordering its banks, where we saw tens of thousands of fowls, every variety and size of snipe, from the smallest to the plover and curlew, the mallard and wild goose; there we replenished our larder. The next day a long, tiresome drive through the hot and deep parching sand to Del Norte, where we remained several days in that prosperous, pretentious town, the gateway to the Western mountains, the gateway to the valley, the miner's mart and rendez-

vous, the mecca of the Rockies, where prince and pauper
elbow each other and mingle on a common level. Here
another package of three letters from home. Here I
witnessed a transaction typical of mining life. Two
brothers-in-law, with their wives and children, had been
roving and tramping the mountains for years, often half
clad and half fed, in search of gold. Finally they made
a valuable discovery, and sold to New York capitalists
for a hundred thousand dollars cash, and next day
"pulled out for the States." Our road from Del Norte
led up the Rio Grande, one hundred and ten miles to its
source on "the dome of the Continent," wild and picturesque scenery every mile of the way, the crystal waters
roaring and foaming like a cataract through deep, wild
mountain gorge and glen. Sometimes our road was cut
out of the mountain sides, a thousand feet above the
stream below. When we reached "the Half Way
House," fifty miles up the river, it was noon. At that
log cabin a fisherman made his living by selling mountain
trout, the only fish that can live in the cataracts. Here
we halted for our noon meal, and while Lu was arranging for that, I strolled up to the cabin and bought two
three pound beauties for fifty cents, and while Lu was
frying them I walked around a mound, a few yards off,
and there my face was lit up in wonder and admiration.
I saw fifty trout floundering on the bluegrass lawn.
This scene surpassed anything recorded by Old Izaak in
his classic Angler. A sugar-loaf tent was near, and by
it stood a middle-aged man and several servants. He
advanced with pleasant smile ; my admiration of the fish
was evidently pleasing to him ; he was the favored sport
who had made the splendid catch. He said, "My friend,
let me present you with at least half of those fish you so
much admire." I bowed an Oriental salaam of profound
acknowledgment. He was a cultured, refined genius.
He could play the courtier in the mountains more gracefully than any man I had met there. We sat down on a

stone and divided time in trying to entertain each other.
He succeeded to my heart's delight. At this juncture of
the pleasing episode, Lu peeped around the mound and
summoned me to our repast. I invited the stranger to
join us, but he had just finished his and declined. I
urged him to at least take a cup of fine coffee, we had
the best, and he accepted. I told Lu that I had found a
prize where least expected, and that we would camp
there until next day. I returned to the tent with the
stranger, neither as yet knowing who he had found. He
was one of the owners and editors of the London Times,
in England, and I was who? It is the reader's province
to find out and determine for himself. I saw a larch pole,
thirty feet long, lying on the ground, and a line of equal
length attached. Grasshopper bait for the beauties could
be caught by the thousands. A throw of the hand on
the grass would fill the palm. I took that, and in a very
short time landed thirteen of the finest trout I ever saw,
three of them weighed five pounds each. The English
servant made a "fine spread" beneath the moon and
stars, and mine host and I talked the night more than
half to death. Next day we drove on, and killed a pair
of pheasants, and a wild turkey, and had a larder that
would appease an epicure's appetite. Ours were robust.
We spread our buffalo robes under the stars, lay down
and threw our eyes to the snowy peaks, as they looked
up in Luna's face, while she rode through a shifting sky
and threw her silver sheen on a mist of falling snow on
the mountain tops. There we beheld Luna's rainbow,
more beautiful and delicate than the finished pencilings
of Angelo or Raphael. Who could look on that splendor
spread in the sky and fail to read the presence of an om-
nipotent God, whether he had ever read or heard of Rig
Veda, Zendevesta, Koran, Bible or of Christ? God's
proclamation to His children is as full and broad and deep
and wide as the infinite universe. It is as plain to be
read and seen in the dewdrop as in the ocean, as legible

in the delicate tints of the lily as in the burnished rays of
the mighty sun, as legible in the pebble that rolls at the
touch of the waters as in great Jupiter that rolls around
the sun at the same infinite touch.

Next day we met two caravans of seventy-five boros,
laden with silver bullion, coming from the San Juan
smelters. Those hardy little animals subsist like the
goat, by brousing on the mountain shrub, and they carry
each from one hundred and twenty-five to two hundred
and fifty pounds of bullion, according to the age of the
animal. We also met hundreds of disappointed pros-
pectors returning from San Juan. Next night we went
into camp on the banks of the river, and were soon honored with the presence of a caravan of Navajo Indians,
who had come eight hundred miles, with grapes and
peaches laden on the boro, and were going into the San
Juan to sell to the miners. And here I saw an amusing
romance of coquetry and courtship, between a white man
and a Navajo Indian girl, who favored the courtship, but
whose father spurned and despised the white man. But
the space allotted in this volume does not admit of that
interesting romance.

The next day's journey brought us to Wagon Wheel
Gap, one of those gems in the mountains that impresses
and clings to the memory. Here two streams form a
junction at one of those small parks so renowned for romantic beauty. We found a hotel here with fine accommodations, and a post office, where I received another
package of letters and papers. But the weather was so
beautiful and the company on the banks of the stream so
attractive we camped there. Three large wagons and
several camp fires were to be seen, but when we drove up
there was no one present in camp, though in a short time
a gentleman came in with a fine catch of fish and presented me with four fine specimens. Next came several
gentlemen with a large deer, and gave me a hind quarter
of the venison, from which we cut royal steaks, and

broiled them and the fish on a bank of coals we found
already there. These gentlemen were polished, educated
Philadelphians, then enjoying one of those delightful out-
ings in the mountains. I found them very entertaining
and sat up with them long, around the camp fire. The
next drive brought us to Antelope Springs early in the
evening, where we found an excellent hostelry kept by a
curious, thrifty pair from the Swiss Alps. They had an
immense hay field of native luxuriant blue grass, which
they sold at eighty dollars per ton. A post office and
stage stand were adjuncts. Here another relay of letters, papers and magazines from my wife, always a joy.
Here the road for the Lower San Juan bore off to the left
and up the Rio Grande, the main road leading on to Lake
Village over the main range of the mountain seventy-five
miles. Here I varied the monotony of camp life by reg-
istering and taking a room, where I remained all next day
writing letters and reading; but Lu occupied the camp
from choice. Those springs are the gateway to Antelope Park, one of those ravishingly beautiful gardens in
the mountains, as lovely as a tropical isle, in area, containing about five thousand acres, oval shaped, hedged in
by perpendicular walls of rock a thousand feet high in
places. Through this Park the Rio Grande flowed. A
drive of four miles brought us to the center of this enchanting landscape, where we found good hotel accommodations and entertainment at whist and euchre by two accomplished young ladies from Ohio, sisters of the landlord; but my greatest enjoyment was in angling for that
prince of the crystal waters the two days we spent here.
The catch was equal to the Englishman's at the Half
Way House.

Stand back, ye tyro anglers of the lakes and lagoons of
the lowlands! hold your peace, you peasant pot fishermen
in the presence of the royal angler! Shades of Izaak Walton! "spirits of the just made perfect," come and take
a message to old Ike, invite him to the head waters of the

Rio Grande. I know he will ask for a furlough, and for time to revise "The Fresh Water Fish of England." I shall never regret the many wholesome thrashings my mother gave me for running away to the purling streams of old Middle Tennessee, to enjoy my first lessons in angling, but I am glad she did not succeed in whipping it out of me, and I thank my father for giving me a copy of old Ike's book.

We left our carriage here in the park as it was the terminal point of such navigation, then packed our camp equipage on horses and took the saddle; we were nearing the dome of the mountains and the goal of our pilgrimage, but sixty miles distant, yet that meant much. The first day brought a panoramic flood of delightful scenes, a large herd of that majestic monarch of animal beauty, the elk, with head and mighty antlers erect and tossed as proudly as the plume of a prince. I threw my gun on the prince of the herd, cut him down, and a steak. Vandal, I was, shame to betray his confidence and take his life. Yonder high upon the cliffs where the eagle plants its eyrie, a herd of wild sheep, whose name vandalizes its beauty of motion. No Arabian courser at tap of drum ever raised limb with more ease and grace. Yonder deep down in glen and gorge springs a herd of deer, there a flock of pheasants whir the air and perch high up in the plumage of the pine. Hush, a startling sound, with boulder of a thousand tons leaps from its seat at the dawn of the ages, crashes through the opposing forest, grinding tree by tree to powder as it leaps and re-leaps and bounds to the valley below, where it half buried itself within thirty yards of Lu and I. "Stand from under" is good advice. Again high up, we hear a rumbling sound as of distant thunder, and see millions of tons of loose, detached shale moving down the mountain with accelerated momentum to the valley below. The freezing of the winters of the ages and the expanding thaws of as many returning suns, finally disintegrated the rock and imparted ertia to inertia and play to the laws of gravitation. Incident to this dissolving sport of the giants and elements, was the terror-stricken deer and a pair of grizzly bears it startled and alarmed; how many if any perished, we did not investigate. A grizzly is hard to frighten, but when alarm does reach him, he simply "means business" and "gets a move on" in the superlative degree. I laughed until I had to dismount and lay down on the grass. All this in one day. With what facility the mind passes through the extremes of the arc. That night we camped at a beautiful fount of gushing water at the foot of the cliffs that hedged in the river. A dense pine forest covered the mountains above, a brisk wind was rushing through the foliage, and it made a mournful dirge; a thousand trains of cars would not equal either the momentum or volume of the sound. To me it was appallingly distressing, to Lu as charming as the lullaby of a mother wooing her babe to sleep. How different are brain forces, how different the same note to different ears. What infinity of combination embraced in the works of our Creator. Where one finds a pearl, another picks up a thistle. Infinity was a primal fiat, an active germ in the breath that spoke creative forces into action. We were now at the foot of Cunningham Pass, where I would soon stand on the "Dome," and plant my perishing footsteps above the clouds in the lap of eternal snow, where that little "harp of a thousand strings" would sing Aeloian whispers to the soul, and bring it in nearer touch with God. There are moments of sublime pathos when the soul is enthralled in the presence and majesty of the Creator, when the voice is powerless to give expression to emotions, when the soul plumes itself on astral wings, cleaves away from this tenement of clay and lights at the foot of the throne. That hallowed hour came to me that day and planted its signet, which I hope will be the guide when this little tenement for an hour, dissolves and sleeps

in the valley. To stand there in that majestic grandeur
of scenery, far above the rolling clouds, where the world
was turned into mountain peaks, all pointing divinely
heavenward, was to feel and revel in all that is divine in
man, and realize the splendors his Father holds in trust
for him. I climbed that mountain with the devotion of a
pilgrim, when nearing the shrine and my Father breathed
on my soul, and gave it a new covenant of immortality.
Stay yet a little while, pilgrim, the toils and troubles
and sufferings and heartachings of this transitory sphere
are but burnishing irons to the soul to brighten and
cleanse it for its immortal flight. The astral gates and
starry way will never close on it. It was created for
that flight and my Father's designs never fail of execution. His wisdom, power and glory are infinite. Away!
ye wrangling sophists and narrow creedsmen. "Get behind me Satan," you shall not compress my mind into the
details of trifles and confine it there, you teach more
blasphemy than religion.

On top of this mountain is a wonderful display of nature, two flat rocks lying parallel within six feet of each
other, twenty feet long by twelve in width, in the longi-
tudinal center of each, a chasm ten inches in width, from
which a crystal fount of water boils up, one the source of
the Rio Grande, the other of the San Juan river. I know
of no parallel in the world. The narrow space between
these rocks is "The Dome," "The Divide," "The
Water-shed." I drank from both of these founts on the
26th day of August, '76, and there plucked some beautiful snow flowers from their arctic bed, and like a knight of
the days of the Troubadores, gave them as a memorial
offering to my wife who has them yet. While standing
there on the summit a wild snow storm hurried along
over the peaks, but was soon gone.

THE SAN JUAN.

IN ascending Cunningham Pass, my well trained mountain horse was so near a perpendicular, I had to get off and pull up by the animal's tail. In descending, the extremes of the perpendicular changed ends, and my horse sat down on his haunches, and slid down with judgment, no instinct about it. Late in the afternoon we reached Howardsville, in the heart of the San Juan. In the exploration of new fields, I have always enjoyed the gratification of curiosity. In the matter of dress my outfit was unique. I thought it would be effective in disguising my identity, and for once I would be *incog*, something I had never enjoyed in my life. A Navajo Indian had made my dress out of polished buckskin, with all the trimmings which indicate a chief of the first class. This was a very convenient dress, and I did not know but that I would have to play "the chief" if captured by the roving Indians of the mountains. My boots were made with special reference to mountain service, and came to a heighth where further progress upward was vetoed, and were lariated to my body above. A belt of mountain wampum held a brace of "persuaders" and a knife, to relieve them from duty when empty. I abandoned tonsorial polish, and my make-up would have been an eminent success, if I had finished out *a la* Davy Crockett, with coonskin cap and tail appendage, but as it was "The White Chief," as the Indians called me, was highly respectable in their estimation. Some young Ute bucks sent me two whole prairie dogs, cooked, as a token of respect; and old Capitan, an ancient

Ute Chief, offered to give me his oldest and ugliest squaw
as a starter for the harem, he supposed I was ready to
establish. A Comanche Chief invited me on a buffalo
hunt, and offered me the distinguished honors of son-in-
law, and Navajo girls attached to the fruit caravan, in
the courtly dress of wristlets and anklets of bone and
tooth and shell, pirouetted around my camp in marriageable
coquetry. Altogether I "stood in" very well with every
tribe of Indians I met. They all spoke Spanish or rather
Greaser lingo, called Spanish, and Lu, who was familiar
with the language, interpreted for me. He rarely
laughed, but some of these scenes were so comic he could
not resist their tendency to cultivate a vein of hilarity.
My answer to all these propositions was that "I have
plenty squaw at home."

When we got to Howardsville we lariated our animals
in a pine grove, and I said to Lu, "we will go to the hotel
and order the best 'spread' the village can turn out." A
rough pine board nailed to a tree, with primitive representation of hand, drawn in charcoal, with index finger
pointing Northwest, under which was written in the same
character "hotel," with a small h, indicating a small
log cabin as the hostelry. We entered, the floor was of
native earth, covered with a fine Brussels carpet. A
well-dressed lady, with fine Caucassian appearance and
dress, presided over the establishment with the dignity
of a queen. I gave a princely order for everything the
mountains afforded for the table, and especially some
fresh butter. With a quizzical smile and proud toss of
the head, the landlady assured me that she had butter,
but that it was not young; it was old enough to walk,
but that age had imparted dignity and respect to the article, and that it was only brought out on rare occasions.
"Shall it appear before you?" To which I replied, "No,
madam, I am not prepared to entertain it." This was a
"take off" for San Juan. Bless that good landlady, she
has made me laugh at intervals for sixteen years. I sat

down on a log, above which hung a fine mirror. On the opposite side, sat another gentleman on another log, under a beefsteak. He did not try to contain himself, nor I to restain myself. Lu did not consider himself the object of Parthian arrows, but monopolized all the gravity and dignity "in sight." The hot suns on the plains had bronzed me, and it was difficult to determine from my exterior, whether I was Indian, Mexican, of mixed race, or a stray Mongolian, but I was none the less the victim of native audacity, and the satirical wit of the queen of San Juan. He under the beefsteak was in European costume, but it was venerable with antiquity, and evidently not long for this world. An old silk hat, with the silk gone, covered his faults. Good soul, what cared he? He had evidently read much, seen much, knew much, and perhaps had traveled too much, but why stare at and smile and scrutinize me? His very eyes laughed. But I was *incog*, and as for me he was too. After the queen's sporadic wit and mirth had settled down, and the aroma from the viands in preparation excited other inspirations, I settled to a counterfeit austerity. But he under the beefsteak did not vibrate to the other end of the arc so readily. Despairing of efforts to force me to recognize him, he said, to my surprise, "John, come down, old boy, out of that disguise, your voice and laugh has betrayed you." Here was another turn in the wheel of surprises. I did not know him, and said, "Pardon, my friend, indulge me in saying, you look like the Lay of the Last Minstrel, but like the Dying Swan, your last notes are the sweetest, pray disclose yourself. I am John, who are you?" He lay down on the carpet and yelled and rolled and rested and yelled again. There was a ton of the sunshine of human nature in him, of which no disaster or change in fortune could rob him. A lawyer, and a good one, too. A Mr. Howard, whom I had met at court in a Western town, and in those impromptu levees at night, where a "feast of soul and flow of reason" relieve from toil and

fringe and ennoble the guild. He dined with me, and
wined with Lu. All the guild of toilers who wire and
worm and elbow for money, place and power, never enjoyed that philosophic wealth of head and heart, that man
had. Misfortune did not sour his nature, nor avarice cor-
rode his heart; his character is typical of that of the vast
majority of good lawyers. There is an inspiration in our
profession, and a teaching to those who ascend the higher
rounds of the ladder, which opens and expands the better
elements of man's nature, and lifts him to higher planes
of manhood. "Most of them live well and die poor."
How many fly away from the roses of life to flitter it
away in thorn and thistle hedges.

The Uncompoggere, where my boys were, was but
twelve miles from Howardsville, but the passage was
slow and tedious, the first six miles led through the deep
and narrow canyon called Cunningham's Gulch; then
across "The Divide," a high mountain plateau which di-
vides the waters of the Gunnison river from those that
flow into the San Juan river. We led our horses, Indian
file, through the gulch, myself in the advance. Half way
up the gulch we found a log cabin, a whisky shop, and
several rough miners in front, by whom stood W. Y.
Suydam, the Chucharas bully, who had dropped out of
my sight for more than a year since the episode with him
on the Chucharas. I was within forty feet, and we
looked each other intently and squarely in the face, and
neither spoke. When I first discovered him I halted and
told Lu, and we tied our horses. The chances were that
Suydam, with his crowd of drinking miners, might try
to "even up" with me, and my best way to prevent it
was to be ready for anything that might transpire. Lu
was a thoroughbred, "True Blue," and could be depended
on in any emergency. We tied our horses, not a word
having been spoken by Suydam to either of us, but he
talked in a low voice to the crowd around him. I whispered the situation to Lu, so that he might be on his guard,

and we advanced to the door of the saloon, ready to welcome either peace or war. Suydam, with a pleasant smile, advanced and extended his hand, and I shook the olive branch in the same spirit it was offered. He "set them up," as the Western phrase goes, but I politely declined on the ground of my teetotalism, but Lu took a "tip." Cigars came next, and I accepted them as a relish. Suydam was a humorous, witty fellow, and enjoyed a joke. Turning to the miners he said, "Boys, this is the only man I ever feared in my life; he is a stem-winder when he starts in, but never opens the ball himself, he lets the other fellow do that. I was fool enough to give him a starter on the Chucharas once, and in less than two minutes was glad to get out by throwing my guns at his feet." He was so open and frank in what he said it embarrassed me; a kind word always disarms me, and I said, "Suydam is like President Lincoln, he can put up a good joke and a good story on all occasions; it is my time to 'set 'em up' now, if you will allow me to light another cigar and smoke in place of drinking to your good health." All took "a bumper," and Lu and I moved on up the gulch, at the head of which we found a flourishing mining camp and good hotel accommodations. The sun was bright in the forenoon, but the clouds in the afternoon harbored much darkness, followed by a precipitation of rain. It can rain on shorter notice, and with less judgment, at this season of the year in the mountains than any place I ever saw. The rain drove us into the hotel, where we stopped for the night, having made six miles through the gulch that day. I repeated the order for the best "lay out" the hotel could afford, and was assured by a neat, tidy, handsome, vivacious landlady that she could give us the best of coffee, bread, and every variety of canned goods, with some fine venison steak, but that she had no eggs nor young butter. There was a bright, sweet little girl, of ten summers, the pride and pet of the camp, standing by. I have ever been a great lover of

children, have kissed and caressed many thousands, and
feel when I have them around me like they feel when
gathering flowers.   It had been long since I had caressed
such a treasure.   I soon won the confidence of the little
maiden, and she sat on my lap and kissed me, typical of
her innocent little heart and soul.   "Suffer little children
to come unto Me, and forbid them not, for of such is the
kingdom of heaven," preached the Savior to mankind.
What a thrill of joy that child unconsciously poured into
a rude heart that had been shaken by many storms, since
it bade farewell to childhood, to enter on the stern realities of a life it knew not of.   But there is always a gem
and a flower near us, if we only know how to find it.
Life is to a great extent what we make it, the grand
total of its treasures is but an aggregation of small
things.   The mother and father of the child looked on
approvingly, while the little maiden gave me her confidence and told of all that had transpired about the camp,
and who of the hundred miners she liked best, and I almost knew the history of that camp before I sat down to
the table.   The father eyed me closely, but did not say
much, the mother with more vivacity and searching scru-
tiny interjected many queries, but I was *incog*, and to
them just a little stoical, because of the superior attrac-
tions of the child.   That I was recognized was a remote
improbability to me.   I certainly did not recognize them.
But to my astonishment, the wife with emphasis and
pleasant smile finally said: "Mr. Hallum, I have tried
my best for half an hour to make you recognize me, but
you seem determined not to do it, don't you know my husband and me?"   I plead innocent ignorance as graciously
as I could, and she said, "Why don't you recollect Mrs.
Webber, of St. Louis?   I have sold your wife many a
sheet of music and conversed with you both many times.
We then owned the Webber Music Store in St. Louis."   I
made a pretense then of recollecting the bright, little,
vivacious brunette, but did not.   I found that matron one

in ten thousand, "a gem of purest ray serene," from
whom the silken things of cities might learn to shed a
healthy radiance on the world. "Why are you here,
Mrs. Webber, and how do you enjoy life in the mountains?" This inquiry drew forth pearls and diamonds
from head and heart, rarely found in the guild of the Four
Hundred, and still rarer around thrones. She replied,
"Since marriage all the wealth and happiness of life with
me have been centered in my husband and child. I would
not exchange the comforts of home, however humble it
may be, barter the happiness which centers there for all
that wealth ever gave, for all the empty honors of what
we call society. My happiness is interwoven with theirs
and that of the home circle and domestic fireside, with
me rises transcendently higher than all other pursuits.
My husband's interests lie here in the mines, where his
presence is indispensable to success, and my heart follows
him." Society women will do for empty-headed young
men to flirt with, but when sensible young men assume
the fearful responsibilities involved in the marriage relation, they want to perpetuate a race of men and seek
women of the Webber pattern. Look down the vista of
the ages, explore the history of the world, make a roster
of its great men, those motor powers which have made
and controlled its destiny, accomplished its glorious
achievements, then tell me how many society women have
given birth to giants? Point the "butter-flies" out on
another roster and I will show you more of them who are
mothers of dudes who are led by pug-nosed dogs. They
are not mothers of the Grachii who advised their sons
when they spoke of their short words, "you have but
one more step forward to reach the enemy, my sons." It
was but six miles to my camp from this point, Mineral
Point, a large mining town lay on the route, across "The
Divide." Here I found a large package of letters, papers
and magazines from my wife and another large install-
ment of that happiness which springs eternal from the

26

happy domestic fireside, the first received since leaving
Antelope Springs, on the other side of the Rockies. Then
two miles down the crystal Uncompoggere as it leaps
from its virgin beds of snow to my own camp in the deepest of mountain glens, where the sun dips but an hour at
its noon tide.   Here we were met with a hearty greeting
by the boys, and the best "camp spread" the most pretentious larder the mountains coul dafford.   The boys
knew we were coming and were anxiously awaiting our
arrival with a hospitality that sparkled like diamonds.
The boys had erected a comfortable cabin on the banks
of the romantic stream where its beautiful waters
chanted in wild rhythm to the echo of the glens
and mountains, an inspiration that touched many
chords of the heart and called up many a story of romance and song.   A thousand pounds of bacon, two
barrels of cut sugar, canned meats and fruits and a
dozen old Burgundy, and as much brandy from the vintages of France made that a pleasant hermitage.   Books,
papers, literature up to date, pens, ink and stationery,
table and seat under the dense foliage were special accommodations prepared for me by the boys.   Horatio
Dunton, who had, with other Pythians, bade the mob defiance at Trinidad when it sought my life, was chief and
head of the camp, his Brotherhood for me had been
crowned and crystalized in Pythian beauties.   Hundreds
of pages were written to my wife on that rustic table in
the mountain glen, and this trip to the San Juan is copied
from those letters.   Every mail bore away messages
home, and every mail brought messages from home.
There were no domestic animals around the camp, but
that prettiest of little busy-bodies, the chip-munk, made
themselves familiar and numerous.   They would steal
into camp and help themselves before your eyes, burglar-
ize your pockets at night if you had therein a nut or delicacy, and take what they desired, and when admonished
would scamper up a tree a few feet and look down at you

with a sense of perfect security. They were nearly as gentle as house cats and afforded us much amusement, and in exchange we did not harm one of them. Then there was a bird of blue and white plumage about the size of the blue Jay of the States, a pretty bird, called the "thief" from its disposition to help itself on all occasions. It would dash down on the table from a tree while we were eating, and when scolded, it would mock you from the tree to which it returned. How much entertainment we can find when resources become so limited. I spent many hours alone in that camp while the boys were out at their work in the mines, and necessity drove me to communion with the chip-munks and birds; I stayed there six weeks. But even here in the heart of these mountains where solitude seemed crowned, surprises unlooked for did not desert me, fate, freedom from this was not even here to be respited long. A few days after my arrival, an old German whose name I could not pronounce even if I could recollect and spell it, asked the loan of my saddle horse to ride down to Silverton, thirteen miles off, and I readily accommodated him. Some hours after he left, the boys told me he was a murderer, a thief, and regarded as the most desperate character in San Juan, and that I would never see my horse and saddle again, that he would return and report the animal as stolen. This was very unpleasant news, and I foresaw some trouble if their prediction proved true. I did not intend to tamely give up my horse thus stolen on the assumption that I was a "tenderfoot" and would submit because of his tender reputation to back the larceny. I resolved to recover my horse, peaceably if I could, forcibly if I must. A "tenderfoot" is generally the object of such depredations, and it was evident that this man was presuming on that. Three days after, the old rascal came and reported that his prolonged absence was caused by delay in hunting for my horse which had been stolen from him. I then said: "Hand me two hundred and

fifty dollars, the value of the horse, and save both of us
some trouble." This he defiantly refused to do and "run
a bluff" from "the jump." I was at that moment as
gentle with him as a girl on a May day, and only said,
"we will look further into this matter to-morrow." It
was then about dark, and too late to accomplish all the
work that lay before me. I wanted daylight to operate
in. His camp was about one-fourth of a mile from mine,
and on the route from my camp to the Post Office at Mineral Point. He had two stout men working in his mines,
and a veritable witch of Endor who passed as his wife.
Next morning I asked some of the boys to go with me to
his camp, but to my surprise they refused, evidently inspired with fears growing out of his savory reputation. Dunton had gone off to the mines and was not
present, had he been there he would have gone with me.
The only successful way in such cases is always to take
the "bull by the horns" at the first dash. You alarm
and startle him, and he crouches like a spaniel, but if you
stop to parley with him a moment, he bristles up in defiance and you bring on the trouble you wish to avoid. I
have never known this to fail, take hold of him resolutely
at the start and he becomes penitent. At this juncture
Lu stepped up and said: "John, put on your gaffs, I'll
go with you." When we arrived at the camp we found
the three men sitting down on the ground about twenty
feet apart, each with his Henry rifle leaning against the
tree by which he sat. The trees represented a triangle.

The old witch of Endor was cooking breakfast at a log
fire. It was agreed by Lu and myself that I should
cover the thief while he took a supporting position and
covered the other two men. We did not take the old
woman into account. We executed the plan in an instant,
and told them that we would drop the first man that
moved. I then told the old German that I intended then
and there to have my horse and saddle, their value or his
life, and that I would leave the choice with him. I said

to the two strangers, "I have no designs whatever against either of you, unless you attempt to aid or rescue this thief; sit still and you will be in no danger." They assured me that they were simple laborers for hire and would take no part in the trouble, and acted in accord with their declarations. I then said, "pass up your guns, one at a time." The old German handed me his, and I stepped backward while he sat on the ground. Lu was in the act of receiving a gun from one of the men. At this juncture the old woman seized a gun and fired at me. Lu knocked it up, and the charge lodged in a tree over my head. If he had not been as quick as a flash of lightning, I would have been a dead man from a source that I was not guarding against. We then broke all the guns and pistols in camp belonging to the old German's outfit, and were then master of the situation. The old witch of Endor was the only one who had any "sand," if I may use that classical coinage of the West. The thief confessed and said that my horse was lariated out on the Mesa, a plateau near two miles distant. We tied the thief on the horse, and led him to Mineral Point, where after the curiosity of the crowd was satisfied, we released him and told him that if night caught him anywhere about the Uncompoggere we would execute him. He acted on the advice and was never heard of any more in the San Juan while we were there. We went to Mineral Point every day after our mail, and no man in the San Juan had warmer friends than those rude miners were to Lu and I. They did not know that Lu had graduated in the Rocky Mountains and that I had been conscripted in some service before that. Romance was idealized in this retreat. The Uncompoggere with its dashing cascades, circling pools of clear water, miniature parks of lawn and forest, as beautiful as the garden of the Gods. Smoke from the rustic cabin curled in festoons as it slowly wired and rose through branch and foliage of the stately pines, until lost in the clouds around

the peaks. To those summits I must go, move through
the forest, climb above "timber line," survey the crags
and mount to the peaks, hard work, but gems for the
toil, a pearl for the soul, grandeur enthroned, sublimity
crowned. Alone at sunrise, on the 10th of September,
1876, I cast my eyes to the clouds through which I must
climb, and set out on the journey, first through an irregular field of boulders that had, through the slow disinte-
grating process of ages, slipped from their moorings on
the summit and piled up on one another like "Pelion
upon Ossa" at the base. Two thousand feet brought
me to a field of shale rock, which retarded my progress
and increased my fatigue, but far upward were the crags
and firmer base. Zig-zag with upward angle till the
"timber line" was passed and the eyrie of the eagle
reached where solitude reigns sublime. Finally the snow
capped crown, and the first foot-print of man since the
creation was planted there. The sun poured its golden
floods where I stood. To the Northwest and far below,
an angry cloud with lightning flash and thunder's roar
proclaimed the war of the elements. There I sat,
wrapped in contemplation that swept every key of the
soul with new impulses. I thought of the peasant harp-
ist who lyered his way through Europe, climbed the
Swiss Alps and drank inspiration that will touch kindred
spirits as long as our literature is preserved:

> " Like some tall cliff that lifts its awful form,
> Swells the vale and midway leaves the storm,
> Although around its head rolling clouds are spread,
> Eternal sunshine settles on its head."

My father, so fond of Goldsmith, Burns and Scott,
taught me these lines in my childhood. His selections
were but few, but from the masters. On that summit I
was once more in my father's lap, listening to him repeat

> "Sweet Auburn, loveliest village of the plain."

"As the twig is bent so it will grow." Mountain
peaks at that great elevation towered all around me. To

the East a few rods from where I sat, a yawning precipice; two thousand feet below its rim I saw a beautiful park, a flock of deer and herd of mountain sheep. I had just shot a snow hen, one of those snow white birds with red eyes, so gentle and devoid of fear. Curiosity, and a desire to survey this park and the game it held, impelled me to advance toward the rim of its outward wall, without any thought of the impending danger of such a step. The peak from where I sat sloped at an angle of about thirty degress toward the canyon. I threw my bird down, leaned my gun against the rock on which I sat, and advanced toward the rim, not more than fifty feet distant. The shale rock began to move under my feet and pour over into the canyon below, and I tried to retrieve my steps, but the shale moved under my feet and I stood tramping like an ox on a tread-mill, until exertion caused profuse perspiration. I now realized that I was lost where probably no trace of me would ever be found. I then turned facing the rim where I saw a small shrubby bush a little to the left of me. My strength was fast giving way, and I threw myself on my stomach and reached out for the shrub as I slid towards it. My left hand came within reach and I seized it, and it saved me from instant death. Fortunately my position was so near the summit that the momentum of the shale was not sufficient to sweep me and the shrub away. I worked the toes of my boots and moved the shale until it ceased sliding down, and thus provided a retreat. "A divinity hedges in the destiny of man." And there is none other than God. I have been shot at many times by resolute men at short range, have escaped many close "calls," but this shale rock gave me the closest.

Business at Lake Village, on the Gunnison river, thirty miles away, and across one of those high mountain plateaus, called me there the first of October. We were compelled to get out of the mountains or be closed in by snow until the next summer. Lu and the boys

went to Antelope Springs by way of Cunningham Pass,
and I took the Overland stage at Lake Village to be re-
united with them at the Springs. One of those beautiful October mornings when the sun bursts in gorgeous
splendor on the Rocky Mountains, I took the stage which
was drawn by four as fine roadsters as ever wore harness. A journey by stage of seventy-five miles over the
lofty range lay before me. But one passenger to accompany me, a stranger, a lady in all the term implies. I
have always been a social animal, fond of communion
with my fellow creatures, accustomed to the society of
refined ladies, but my plumage already described was
now very embarrassing. The lady was splendidly
dressed and occupied the back seat and I the front, facing each other, and there we sat for half an hour as
speechless as two statues. Her appearance indicated the
refined and cultured lady, and etiquette required her to
lead in breaking the silence. I was afraid to transcend
the limits by doing it myself, and held my tongue until
monotony became more distressing than my courtly dress.
Was I to sit there like Poe's raven perched on the bust of
Pallas, and let the transcendent beauties of that day perish, simply because dressed like an Indian Chief, and so
far removed from the "400?" Won't the lady speak
and break the awful silence? It seemed; "Nevermore!"

"But with mien of lord or lady, perched above my chamber door,
Perched on a bust of Pallas, just above my chamber door—
Perched and sat, and nothing more.
And the silken, sad, uncertain rustling of each purple curtain,
Thrilled me—filled me with fantastic terrors never felt before
Merely this and nothing more."

Must that glorious day, so full of splendid possibilities
become as silent and mournful as the Catacombs? Evidently the lady did not intend to throw out a rainbow.
She sat like one of the "400" of Ward McCallister's exclusive set. Some New York bankers were in the village
where we took passage. I thought perhaps she was the
wife of one of them fleeing, in time to avoid the coming

snow, if so we were on parallel lines, at least to that extent. I wished the coach would overturn and create a
necessity to speak. The ice must be broken, I could not
stand it any longer, even on the ragged edge of the
"400" exclusion; it was evident that she did not intend
to speak, and I said: "Pardon one word, madam, my
embarrassment is great because of my uncouth dress
here in the mountains, but I have been accustomed to the
society of refined ladies all my life, and do not yield prec-
edence to any gentleman in chivalrous devotion to them.
This is a day that neither you nor I can ever forget, and
the thought occurs to me, that social converse might possibly enhance its charms. Again begging your pardon
for the intrusion and suggestion, let me say that I recognize your perfect right to decline the advance." She
said: "My dear sir, your ideas and the manner in which
expressed find sympathetic touch in my own, and I must
thank you for awakening them. My husband told me of
having met a gentleman yesterday answering to your
description, with whom he was pleased, and I am sure if
you can entertain him, you will be equally as gracious to
his wife." The veil was lifted and the raven had flown
from the bust of Pallas. In all the years that I have
spent in a long life, I have never met a more entertaining
stranger, a more facinating conversationalist. When we
arrived at the summit, we got out and had the driver join
us in a pleasant lunch above the rolling clouds. She
was the wife of a Mr. C., a banker of New York, with
whom I had conversed the day before. I found the boys
and Lu awaiting me at Antelope Springs, and another
batch of letters and papers from my wife. Thence to
Trinidad, thence to my father's in Middle Tennessee,
where I found my wife and children in perfect health
after a separation of six months.

TRIAL OF TURNER FOR MURDER.

IN 1888 two young farmers of good repute in the vicinage, Benjamin Turner, and Oscar Gay, were persistent rivals for the hand of a beautiful young lady, her choice falling on Gay. This exasperated Turner against his rival, and in the impetuosity of youth he said things good judgment could not approve.

They were members of a debating society, which held its sessions at night in Mt. Zion church, Lonoke county, Arkansas. Both attended meeting on the night of the 14th of April, 1888. After hitching their horses they met in the shadowy foliage fronting the church, and after a few words between them, the purport of which was differently interpreted by different witnesses, they engaged in a conflict, and Gay was mortally wounded with a knife, and died a few hours after.

I was retained by the State to prosecute Turner on a charge of murder in the first degree, and the Hon. Thos. C. Trimble appeared for the defense. The trial came off at the fall term of Court, and attracted much local interest, a large volume of testimony going through all the antecedent relations of the parties was laid before the trial Court; the young betrothed maiden, as usual, being the center of attraction. A night session was held in the capacious court house, which accommodated a large auditory, who had come to hear the closing argument which devolved on me, and there was a large attendance of ladies, including Mrs. Trimble, the best of wives, neighbors, and Christians, but I did not know of her presence, else I might have "let up" on "Tom," her good husband, who had cast many stones and shot many arrows wide of logical game. In a long argument, I have always found it a relief to the jury and a palliative against the ennui of monotony to opportunely introduce a little spice and pleasantry. In pursuing this method judiciously, counsel is sure of the undivided attention of the tribunal he addresses, whether on the hustings, before the Senate, or a jury of ordinary men.

In answer to many untenable assumptions of my Bro. Trimble, after pointing them out in sharp contrast, I said, "His argument contradicts and defeats itself, and reminds me of a scene I have often witnessed, and as often laughed at; a little frisky dog in a field of high oats, when he jumps a rabbit and in a moment loses sight of the game, then springs up above the oats, with head careened from side to side, an anxious flirt of the tail and forlorn yelp, looking to see which way the rabbit jumped and how he got away. A bench-legged member of the kennel guild never caught a rabbit in high oats, nor did a superb greyhound ever catch one in rye or barley field, and brother Trimble is shaming himself and wasting time by personating and burlesquing these noble sporting animals, in trying to succeed where they have failed. An ambitious terrier has better sense, when he can neither thrust his nose, nor shove, nor push, nor paw dirt beyond the stretch of his tail, he quits the chase."

Trimble and I were the best of friends, and he enjoyed the extravaganza, but his good wife's religious foundations were stirred to the bottom, and she told "Hubby" that if he did not thrash me she would thrash him; the idea of being laughed at by such an audience, and compared to a dog.

MOBS IN YELL COUNTY, ARKANSAS—REMARKABLE SCENES.

JAMES BRUCE, son of Dr. Bruce, of Smith county, Tenn., descendent in the male line of Robt. Bruce, of Scotland, was a bright and promising boy, of classically educated parentage, and moved in the highest circles of society. He enlisted in the Confederate army, and became addicted to periodical indulgence in the foaming bowl. The fortune of his father, Dr. Bruce, a gentleman of rare culture and attainments, suffered the common wreck of the war, and the son, after its close, drifted into Yell county, Ark., settled in the spur hills of the Pettijean mountains, taught school, married there, and added farming to his occupation. In 1881, he came to Dardanelle with cotton and produce, and bought a jug of distilled poison. Driving out some three miles from town that night, he camped in a pine grove in the Chicala Hills, with others, and one White, who had but a short time before led his bride to the altar.

White and Bruce were joyful, and the best of friends, and hugged and kissed each other as they drove off from town.

The moon, after nightfall, rode through a cloudless sky and peeped down through the interstices and foliage on the camp, where all were wrapped in slumber. Two young men camped a few rods distant. Just after midnight they went to Bruce's camp, and there beheld an appalling sight in the flickering shadows of the moon, pale, ghastly, dead, lay White, with Bruce across the breast of the corpse asleep. A barlow knife was sticking in the heart of White, and Bruce's shirt-bosom was saturated with the blood from the wound. These were all the facts. Bruce was brought into Dardanelle, the venue of the crime, the next day. He recollected nothing, knew nothing. The excited populace were for lynching him, but Robert E. Cole was a resolute sheriff, and prevented it.

Bruce's relations in Smith county, Tennessee, employed Judge Bowles and myself to defend him. After indictment found, I went to Dardanelle and found every step in the prosecution bristling with error. A dense crowd listened to my argument exposing these errors, and concluded in advance of any ruling of the Court that Bruce would escape. Just before sunset the crowd dispersed, to prepare to mob Bruce that night.

The town is on the Arkansas river. The Hon. Arch McKennon, the prosecuting attorney for the State, got wind of the purpose of the mob, and had Bruce put in a skiff and conveyed to the opposite shore of the river. The craft had barely reached the middle of the stream when the mob galloped up on horseback, defeated in their present purpose, and Bruce was conveyed to the jail at Ozark, in Franklin county, where he remained some months.

Yell county, at that time, had two county seats, Dardanelle, and Danville, on the Pettijean river, and but one jail, which was at Danville, the old county seat, twenty miles distant from Dardanelle. After the excitement was thought to have died out, Bruce was carried to Dardanelle for trial, and confined in a small log house.

One night a large mob gathered in front of this prison to hang Bruce, but the sheriff's brother, Mr. Cole, whose Christian name now escapes me, and one other guard, had the noble courage to step in front of that mob and say to the men composing it, "We have a high and important duty assigned to us by the law, and that duty we intend to discharge at all hazards. We suppose every man under those masks knows us, now let us say to you in all kindness, if you attempt to execute your design, Bruce will not be the first man to die; we will kill the first man who dismounts." The mob parlied, wavered, dispersed, and was gone. This proves what I have often seen demonstrated, that a few resolute men can *drive*, *make*, *force* a brigade of irresolute men when they are in the wrong. "Thrice is he armed whose cause is just." Bruce was then conveyed to the Danville jail, and his friends of the Pettijean hills and valleys swore that the mob from Dardanelle should "die some too," if they got Bruce, and for many weeks kept guard over the approaches to the jail, where he was confined, and no demonstration against the Danville jail was made. Farmers cannot be on the watch all the time. It was again thought by many that the passion and excitement had died out. Judge Bowles and myself were both of this opinion. When the next term of Court at Danville came on I attended it. Bruce sent for me. I found him chained to another prisoner, a Mr. Wilson, who was also indicted for murder. Wilson was a quiet, peaceable citizen, credulous, and easily imposed on. Out of mischief he had been told that a warrant for his arrest was in the hands of an officer, charging him with carrying concealed weapons, and that he would be fined $200 and put in jail, and would be taken dead or alive when found. This was a myth, but it frightened Wilson, and he took to the woods to avoid arrest. Some days after, these mischievous fellows learned that Wilson was in a skirt of woods, and resolved to charge on and frighten him. They proceeded on horseback, and when within a short distance charged at full speed on him. He dodged behind a tree, and by the light of the moon fired and killed one of these mischief-making men, and was indicted.

When I arrived at the jail, Bruce wanted me to record what he said, and to take down a message to his sister, Mrs. General Payne, of Chattanooga, Tenn., a noble, cultured woman, whose lovable and beautiful life was only equaled by that of her noble husband, an ex-Confederate Captain and able lawyer.

I took down the message in my note-book, and as requested, kept without delivering it, until time proved whether his confirmed presentment of death at the hands of the mob was true or not.

Bruce, as before said, was educated, polished, and there was nothing of the ruffian about him or his life, and nought against him except his occasional sprees. He was a gentleman by birth and association, and often for six months at a time did not imbibe. After recording the tender message to his sister and relatives, in which he assured them of the conviction that he would yet be the victim of the mob; he then turned to me, with keen piercing eyes, full of animation, yet a mournful and pensive expression, which foretold the deepest conviction, and said: " Mr. Hallum, I know you and Judge Bowles and all of my friends who have so long known and tenderly watched over my life, are convinced that I am no longer in danger of the mob. I do not reproach them now, nor do I insist that the guard shall be kept up; they are farmers, most of them poor men, have families to support, and cannot afford to lose more time. I feel profoundly grateful to them, and am proud of the tender spot my life has given me in their hearts. The name that will survive me in their good opinion is all that I have to leave as a heritage to my little children, who will soon be orphans. I do not fear to die an honorable death. I have charged where musketry rattled, and cannon roared, and feared not a chivalrous death. No descendant of the heroic Bruce, who shares the fadeless glories of Bannockburn, ever feared to die an honorable death. But it is simply horrid to die, manacled and shackled, at the hands of a brutal, cowardly mob, where a Bruce cannot strike the foe, and mark the spot where he dies."

My soul was stirred. I had profoundly studied every phase, every detail of his case, and had an abiding confidence that " not guilty " would be the verdict if ever I got to a jury of impartial men, and that would have been the verdict; but if I had failed in securing that verdict, the terms of two Confederate Governors of Arkansas embraced the period of these troubles. Gen. Thomas J. Churchill, and the Hon. James H. Berry, now United States Senator, and either would have pardoned him; so in any event he would have gone forth a free man. His trial at Dardanelle was coming off within two weeks from this time, and he, with Wilson, were conveyed to Dardanelle for trial. But the brutal mob dashed in there at an unguarded moment and hung both, just as Bruce said it would be.

JUDGE AND JURY AND BYSTANDERS TAKE ME FOR A FOOL.

IN 1878, in the Circuit Court at Lonoke, Ark., I defended Ford Breedlove, on a charge of murder in the first degree, for killing John Floy, and he was guilty under every legal aspect in which his case could be viewed, and I resorted to an extraordinary method to free him. The circumstances were these:

The deceased was accused of stealing cotton from the defendant, and he went to his house with an officer and arrested him without a warrant. On the way to the Committal Justice, they passed through a lane, the fence on either side being very high and staked and ridered. The defendant had a rifle gun on his shoulder. The accused, when passing through the lane, stooped down and put his hands on a very large rail, one end of which was under the fence and could not be moved. When he stooped down the defendant struck him over the head with the gun barrel and knocked his brains out.

That was all the evidence in the case. Under no rule of law could the murder be justified or mitigated. I did not ask a question, or introduce a witness, and declined to address the jury. The Court insisted that I should address the jury, but I firmly declined. The man's wife and daughter were in court and when I refused to address the jury, screamed out, kicked over the bench they occupied and fainted, all of which produced the wildest excitement in court. Judge Joseph E. Martin was on the bench, a religious, conscientious man, whose sympathies were easily touched, was almost dumb-founded at my course. The jury returned a verdict of murder in the second degree and sentenced the prisoner to the penitentiary for five years. They could not do less. No one in the court but the prisoner understood my conduct or motive. In the first place, there was no legitimate argument to be made —the more light turned on the plainer the offense would appear. In the second place, I felt sure that every man in the court house would sign a petition to the Governor to pardon him, without my solicitation, because of his having what all conceived to be no defense at all.

The Judge started the petition, and it was signed by Prosecuting Attorney, jury and every bystander, and the Judge went up to Little Rock that night, called on the Governor with the petition for pardon, the main reason being the unexplained abandonment of the case by his counsel. Everything else was lost sight of, and the pardon was granted to repair the injury I had inflicted on my client. I was the condemned, my client the pardoned martyr. If I had argued the case and provoked that argumentative criticism, which could not have been avoided, the defendant would have been convicted of murder in the first degree and sentenced to be hung and left without any chance for pardon.

A NOBLE WOMAN.

IN 1881, I filed a bill in the Circuit Court of Lonoke county, Arkansas, to enforce a lien for the erection of a fine residence. The defendant, now deceased, had a noble and spited wife, the daughter of a once celebrated Minister of the Gospel in Memphis. The court house was a two-story building and court was held in the upper story.

The end of the term was approaching, and Judge Martin held night sessions. A Church meeting was also in progress, and the wife of the defendant passed the court house going to and coming from Church.

The statute of limitations was interposed, and much irritable matter crept in with a liberal supply of doubtful and reckless evidence to defeat the lien. Caustic criticism and vehement enthusiasm was contagious and extended to the auditors. I always thought it bad generalship in Counsel to thus throw open the gates of his fortress, when he had to stand behind empty guns to resist the last charge.

The wife, on her return from Church, stopped under the windows of the court room and heard me in the closing argument, her presence below not being known to me.

In discussing the statute of limitations I said. "These laws are necessary to the repose of society, but are often invoked as a protection to legalize robbery—that the husband who would screen himself behind such a defense, and resign the proud position of the oak around which the laurel twines, to shelter his wife from wind and storm, and the rude blasts of winter, by deceiving the creditor who had finished the house, was unworthy the hand of the noble woman who had been equally deceived at the altar." Much more caustic criticism was pro-

voked—limitation was a side show, an abortive plea.
Judgment was for my client. Next day at the noon recess of the court the husband followed me out of the
court house and said: "You owe me an apology," with
his hand in his hip pocket. I declined such humiliation,
but had no arms except a small walking cane. He gave
me the alternative of an apology or death. I advanced
on him and struck several blows with my stick, touching
only the rim of his hat. He was active and sprung backward, drew his pistol and fired; to my gratification the
ball had more respect for me than he had, and did not
perform the work designed. Bystanders interfered and
stopped the fight.

After this episode, I learned that the wife, as a condition to further conjugal relations had imposed this be-
ligerent duty on her husband.

When I heard this, I expressed admiration for the noble
wife. She is truly a noble woman and lives now in
Memphis in her widowhood.

Village gossip soon conveyed my remark to her, and she
said to her husband: "Bob, go and make friends with
Mr. Hallum." He did so, and when they moved to Memphis, both joined in a cordial invitation to me to dine with
them, and I was never more hospitably entertained.

Enthusiasm sometimes supplants good judgment in
the defense of a bad cause, and the attorney is frequently
more to blame than the client.

THE CONSTITUTIONAL CENTENNIAL OF 1887 AT PHILADELPHIA.

THERE were a few specially invited guests by the United States from each State to the Constitutional Centennial of 1887, at Philadelphia, and I was one of the favored from Arkansas.

For some time before it came off, I was at Albany, N. Y., correcting proof sheet, and was too busily engaged to keep up with special details before the Celebration came off, further than to know where to find the various committees, and any information desired. I went from Albany via New York, expecting to arrive in time to attend the banquet given in honor of the Justices of the Supreme Court of the United States, and would, if I had escaped the attention of one of those energetic Authoresses from New England, who had more vim and determination than any lady I ever met in the South. She was bent on the same mission, intending to attend that night some banquet. Her Saratoga was checked and piled up in a mountain of baggage. My assistance was requested in recovering the baggage, and accorded. We arrived at the "City of Friends" late in the evening and elbowed our way through a vast sea of humanity, with much difficulty, to be informed that three days would be required to find the Saratoga—give it up?—no, indeed, that lady, with vim enough to drive an engine over the mountains, said: "My wardrobe for the banquet is in that Saratoga, and I don't intend to leave until it is forthcoming."

After being detained an hour, she generously released me and continued the enterprise alone. I proceeded to the Continental to find the committee rooms closed for the evening, and the impossibility of finding hotel accommodation. An hour afterward I met the Authoress for a moment, and she, with an air of triumph, announced success. The proprietor of the Continental, after I had made a drive to all the hotels of the city, gave me a card to the Madam of a boarding house, and weary, I directed my pilgrimage hither. She met me in the vestibule with courtesies enough to run the Court of St. James a month: the refusal was deliciously charming, the disappointment cold as a glacier. The burden was so great I felt like turning some of it loose, and asked the good lady if she would indulge me a moment. "Certainly." "I am an invited guest of the Nation," handing her my invitation. "Here I am now begging from door to door, like a street tramp, begging a cellar or garret for shelter. I have cash enough to feed on when the hash houses open up to-morrow, but fear my appetite will be consumed in tramping the street before the delicious aroma of those resorts for the common herd are open. Here we stand beneath the shadows of "Old Independence Hall," where liberty first lit her trans-Atlantic torch. Madam, did you ever stop long enough to think about Captain Smith and Pocahontas and the charming romance fame has woven around their names, and have you forgotten those beautiful lessons of childhood wherein every child in America was imposed upon by the false teaching which led them to believe that the 'City of Penn.' of Quaker brothers and sisters, of friendship and broad hospitality, is only a myth, 'a tinkling symbol and sounding brass?' My delusion, dear Madam, was perfect; long have I nursed and enjoyed it with the love of a mother for her first born, and now it is with deepest regret, in my old age this bright little spot must be torn up by the roots." While this little episode was going on, a dozen couples gathered in the adjoining parlors, and I hastened away with my footman. I had not gone far when some gentleman slapped me on the shoulder and startled me; my first impulse was that it was ominous of a visit to the guard house, a mistake of some alert guardian of the city, anxious for its prosperity.

The gentleman, rather excitedly, said: "You will please return with me to the mansion you have just left. We all heard what you said to the landlady. I am deputed at the unanimous request of all those whom you may have observed, to bring you back, with the assurance that every exertion will be made for your comfort. I am the owner of the mansion, the lady to whom you spoke is simply my tenent. I live in Trenton, am one of the largest shoe manufacturers in the United States. My name is Atwood." "My dear sir, I am greatly obliged, and through you, say to those generous guests, I feel profoundly grateful for their kind consideration, but, must decline, because I cannot humiliate myself by appealing to the landlady again."

"My dear sir, we cannot stand that. You must return as the guest of Mrs. Atwood and myself—she requested me to say to you that the best apartment in the mansion is at your command."

I returned, and after due preparation was conducted to the Saloon and introduced to all the guests; and Mrs. Atwood—charming lady—took my arm and accompanied me and a dozen couples to many noted places in the city, after which Mr. Atwood accompanied me to the Art Gallery, where Gov. Beavers was holding a reception extended to the Governors of the United States. I found Mr. Atwood a gentleman of much culture and refinement, and am indebted to his equally cultured and refined lady, for one of the most enjoyable occasions of my life. Next morning I hastened to the committee rooms to find the hostelry where the Arkansas delegation were entertained, and found the Aldine, where Gov. Hughes, Col. Sam W. Williams, Gen. Tappan, and others, were quartered, and a command to serve on the Governor's staff, but they were out, and I never met with any of them. When I returned, Mrs. Atwood per-emptorily ordered the servant to return my baggage to my room, and declared they could take care of me as well as the Aldine, and that they would serve on my staff during my stay in the city, which embraced several days.

Mr. Atwood had an immense arch spanning the street, fronting the Continental Hotel, where we repaired to witness the immense procession, which passed beneath, commencing at 9 A. M., and had not ended at 4 P. M., when we left the arch. Next day I wandered, with a sea of emotions, through that greatest of the world's Pantheons: Independence Hall, where immortality inspired the hearts and kindled the souls of men, whose voices will ring and echo around the world as long as civilized men inhabit it. I stopped in New York several days on my return to Albany, where I had been many times before, but had not been up in that glorious inspiration of Bartholdi, the Statute of Liberty, on Bedloe's Island.

I went early on the crowded steamer to the Island, and hurried up the supporting masonry to the base of the statue, where I found a soldier, with bayonet fixed, marching the circuit of the basement to prevent ascension. I gave him a silver dollar, provided he would descend to the basement and eat large Baltimore oysters with a bottle of wine. He laughed, and accepted the proposition, and long before he returned to duty I was standing in the hand of the statue, enjoying one of the most splendid prospects land or ocean affords, with libraries revolving in my mind. None other of the many hundreds who went for the same purpose made the ascension.

Next, I hurried to Central Park, and sat for hours before that Needle of the Nile, presented by the Khedive of Egypt to the United States, representing a civilization that was old when Moses slept in the bulrushes. Thence to the Museum, where the Needle builders slept in Mummy shrouds four thousand years, awaiting the Judgment day. There, too, the Roman conquerer was asleep in the Sarcophagus, no longer rallying his victorious legions to empire and conquest.

There, too, the Syrian, Assyrian, Chaldean, Babylonian, Grecian, hero and sage—the carved bulls with the nomenclature of Senacchareb's time, from the ruins of Ninevah—the Cueniform inscriptions from the ruins of Babylon's tower. Mutations of time, prisms of the ages, changing in the little kaleidoscope of time, chrysalis of the worm to-day, the butterfly to-morrow, onward and upward through the gates across the river.

MOB INTIMIDATIONS IN ARKANSAS.
1882.

IN September, 1882, while arguing a case, I received a telegram from Jake Chapline, calling me immediately to Clarendon, in Monroe County, Ark., to take charge of a contested election case for the office of County and Probate Judge, against T. W. Hooper, the democratic candidate, to whom the certificate of election had been wrongfully issued. As soon as the argument was finished, I handed the telegram to the Judge and asked that my cases on the docket be continued for the term, and I discharged from further attendance, which was granted. Chapline was a republican, and had been represented by Rice and Benjamin, two very able attorneys of the same political faith. I thought it a little strange that my services were required, as I was a democrat of orthodox faith, but took the next train, as Jake was good pay. When arrived on the scene, I found a state of war existing between the political factions, which threatened blood-shed, each side was determined to press the issue at all hazards.

Rice and Benjamin had retired from the case, leaving Jake without counsel until my arrival. The Hooperites threw out a line of pickets by night, extending two miles out to Chapline's farm where I stayed with my client.

Jake had a hundred or more followers from the hills who looked after his interests. The Circuit Court, before which the case was to be tried, was to convene the next week, and the taking of testimony by depositions devolved on me. I proceeded first to Holly Grove and took the testimony exclusively of democrats, proving beyond all doubt that Chapline's interest at that polling precinct had been fraudulently dealt with. Next, I proceeded to Clarendon, to prove the poll books from Indian Bayou had been tampered with, erasures had been made, and thirteen Hooper votes substituted where Chapline's votes had been erased. The court house and yard were crowded with excited Hooperites, but I elbowed my way through the crowd and made the proof of erasure to their consternation. Chapline was not with me on either of these trips. The next day a committee of one came out to see me, and told me that I was in great danger of losing my life, if I remained in the building with Chapline at his residence—said that they did not want to hurt me, but if I remained by my client's side the sacrifice of my life might become a necessity. I told him to say to the gentlemen who sent him, that I appreciated their kindness, but knew no politics in the discharge of professional duty; that I never had abondoned a client, and would prefer death to the odium which would attach to my name, if I abandoned a righteous cause, that come what might, I would stand by my client and sleep by him, or anywhere I chose. I then gave notice that I would proceed next day to Mr. Tugwell's, on Indian Bayou, and take his and other depositions in the cause. Tugwell was one of the judges of the election and had possession of a duplicate poll book, which had not been tampered with, which furnished the proof of erasure and made it as strong as holy writ. A grave felony had been committed, and the perpetrators had fled to the woods. Something more than a right to a petty office was now involved. Chapline's wife and children were from home, and at his request, I occupied the same bed he did. Next morning when we got up, we found a coffin at the door, labeled thus: "Thus we treat all d——d rascals."

The fresh morning dew on the ground rendered it easy to track the vehicle, and there was a peculiar track made by one of the horses, which drew the vehicle in which the coffin was brought out, and stealthily deposited at the door where we slept. I ordered this vehicle tracked to its cover. The owner of the horse which made this peculiar track was known, and all were found in his lot. He was a lawyer and a prominent speculator from Ohio, by name Parker C. Ewing; whether he knew anything of the service rendered by his team and vehicle, I never knew, nor did I then, nor do I now care. He was a rampant democrat, and in sympathy with Chapline's enemies. One thing I do know—the designed intimidation did not work. It was twenty miles from there to Tugwell's, and I went there after seeing that coffin, the work of men who feared the day, and stole under cover of darkness to do what gentlemen would scorn to do. I drove down to Tugwell's by myself, getting there early in the afternoon preceding the day the depositions were to be taken. Several prominent gentlemen of the vicinage came to talk with me about the case, and to learn whether I intended to proceed with the evidence, and were informed that I did.

Within an hour after they left, an old negro woman came to Tugwell's and said something was up, she did not know what, that there were mysterious movements on foot—twenty-five white men had congregated in the woods not far off; she thought murder was in the air.

This convinced me that an attempt would be made that night to take the duplicate poll book, before I could use it as evidence. To thwart this design, I immediately caused a duplicate of this poll book to be made, carefully compared and sworn to by five witnesses. This copy I took charge of myself. There were at Tugwell's a young lawyer teaching school, a Doctor Daugherty, a young man, Tugwell and wife and myself. The young lawyer and myself occupied one room, Tugwell and wife an adjoining room, the Doctor and young man occupied separate rooms.

I was unwell from a long ride in the hot sun, and the physician gave me a sedative which caused sound sleep. At one in the morning I was awaked from this sound slumber, to find Mrs. Tugwell in my room in her sleeping robe, half crazed with fright; she had escaped to the rear yard to find it filled with armed men. The front yard was also filled with gallant knights, four of whom had guns pointed to the windows of the rooms occupied by Tugwell and myself, and were demanding the instant surrender of the poll book on pain of death. The game, but indiscreet Kanawah, the young lawyer, was in the act of firing at the mob with a pepper box through the window. I had barely time to seize his pistol and prevent its discharge. In the meantime the brave Tugwell said to the mob, that he would not deliver the poll book, unless I advised him to do so. He seemed to have forgotten the object for which I had taken the sworn copy. I handed the mob the poll book, saying to them, that they had made a bad job, infinitely worse than if they had not thus gotten possession of it. They immediately retired through the front yard without further ado.

A Mr. Smith, from Alabama, was the Justice before whom I proceeded next day to take the evidence of Tugwell, Kanawah and others, as to the contents of the poll book taken by the mob, and the correct copy which I produced and had attached to the depositions; which were taken in a log school house in the woods, in the presence of a dozen men, who I felt sure were in the mob of the preceding night, and they were dumb-founded when I produced the copy of the poll book. The next attempt I feared would be to capture these depositions, and to throw them off their guard, I told them I had three copies of the poll book sent off by messenger before day. I also had the Justice, after these men had left, to appoint me a Special Commissioner to convey the depositions to the Court, and had Mrs. Tugwell rip open my buggy seat and sew the depositions up in it. That night I drove twenty miles to Chapline's and next morning delivered the evidence to the Clerk of the Court.

George M. Chapline, a lawyer and brother to Jake, came down that day, to pursuade his brother to abandon the contest. George and Jake were both "dead game," and Jake swore he had rather die than be driven from the contest.

That night a platoon of horsemen from the town, loped hurriedly through the lane leading by Jake's residence; George and myself proceeded through a cotton field to see if a collision would take place in the edge of the timber, where Jake's men were stationed. As we passed a cotton pen, six guns were instantly cocked, and the owners were in the act of firing on us when George told them we were Jake's friends. Our lives were thus preserved at the last moment of time. When Jake asked me what I thought of George's advice to withdraw from the contest, I declined to advise him, because I had become innocently involved in it, and my advice to withdraw might have been construed into fear, and involved me in serious trouble. But Jake finally, and very reluctantly gave way to his brother and abandoned the contest. The court house was densely packed when I rose to withdraw my client from the contest. I denounced the mob, and said to the Court that I was convinced many of them were listening to me. Judge Cypert asked me why I did not apply for a bench warrant to arrest the mob. "Simply," said I, "because cyclones cannot be arrested by puny straws, and I cannot be guilty of the folly implied in that impracticable mode of procedure. Many of these proceedings are published in the Congressional

Globe, and were called to the attention of Congress by the Hon. Wm. R. Moore, then representing the Memphis District in Congress. Hooper usurped the office when he knew he was not elected to it, an act a gentleman would have scorned. He was elected the second term—forged Treasury warrants and finished his career in the penitentiary where he died. Another preacher stepped aside from his calling—seduced by the "Snolligoster Politician," who is to-day the most dangerous animal, the most dangerous parasite infecting the body-politic—he can be found from the American Senate to the back-woods cross-roads.

JUDGE GEORGE W. McCOWAN.

McCOWAN has a many-sided life, which eminently illustrates the painful vicissitudes through which men of eminent abilities may pass, when not firmly grounded in basic, unchangeable principles. His life "points a moral and adorns a tale." He came fresh from the University, in 1854, and settled in Raleigh, and opened a law office adjoining mine, and I don't suppose there is a lawyer now in Tennessee who remembers that scrupulously neat, blonde, handsome young man, who was possessed of abilities and attainments far above those of the average young lawyer. Like most of them, his mental pictures of patronage, fame, and advancement, were drawn in rainbow colors.

A native of the old North State, that well advanced and finished up country, from which he had imbibed ideas far in advance of frontier conditions. He had an exalted estimate of the dignity of man, and was a little mistaken in supposing that exaltation and dignity, could and did, in his case, precede those achievements, which are basic elements of renown. George was too *ne plus ultra* for the average man of affairs; there was an apparent stiffness and *hauteur* about him that did not attract a client-age. The average business man don't take kindly to su-perlative gentry, who have the appearance of haughtiness.

George was a brother to that sterling old Confederate soldier, General McCowan.

He did not mix with the people, scarcely communed with any one but myself. It was a matter of aston-ishment to him to see men succeeding where he was failing. He remained one year without having a client, then swore he would shake the dust from his feet and go West, and did so. He never wrote back, and I lost sight of him for many years. He settled at Paraclifta, in Se-vier county, Arkansas, near the Choctaw line, and finally began to patronize the vintage. When the civil war burst on the country he was a secessionist *perse*, and en-tered the army. Coming back after the war he vibrated to the opposite extreme of the arc, evoluted in politics and principle that "thrift might follow fawning." Al-ways a sorrowful sight to the true Southron, to see his brother bartering his fame for a mess of potage.

He joined Powel Clayton's reconstruction clan, and made war on "rebels," became a member of the legisla-ture, and an active supporter of the worst government in the South. As a reward for services rendered, he was appointed Judge of the Ninth Judicial Circuit of Arkan-sas from July, 1868, to October, 1874, when the people got control of their own affairs. His career on the Bench is what concerns us most; it is unique, roseate, mel-low, rich, rare, and stands out in solitude. He was ut-terly devoid of that true dignity which so much adorns the Bench. His chief inspiration was a well-filled bottle or jug. He carried his bottle in his side pocket, with a six-inch quill inserted through the cork, and when he wanted a drink would pull the lapel of his coat over his face and suck from the quill until satisfied, but never interrupted a trial to "take a drink."

J. S. Dollarhide, of Sevier, one of the Western tier of

counties adjoining the Choctaw Nation, had been Sheriff
and Probate Judge of his county; he always kept the best
article of the "overjoyful." He lived in the valley of the
beautiful Cossatot, which meanders through the hills
and valleys, over rocky and pebbled bed, with laughing
waters, so famous in that section.

He was a great friend and admirer of Judge McCowan
and at times "a fellow feeling made them wondrous
kind," and as the Judge had a week's vacation at that
end of the Circuit, he generally put it in with his friend,
Dollarhide. After awhile, this friend of hilarious and
spiritual tendencies, presented himself in open Court for
admission to the Bar: feeling that the ordeal would not
be pushed to extremes, and that he would not be required
to tell half he knew about Ferne on Contingent Remainders, or Coke upon Lytleton, and such light literature.

"Take your seat in front, Brother Dollarhide," said
the Judge.

"Silence, gentlemen. There are many things of which
the Court may take judicial notice by calling to its aid
things difficult of proof, and I will not require Brother
Dollarhide on this occasion to produce the usual certificate of good character because the Court is satisfied on
that point, and would not take any man by surprise. I
have known Brother Dollarhide in the privacy of social
life ; we have long been hail fellows well met.

"This is one of those joyful occasions in life which
rises up like a beautiful oasis in a Sahara of strife and
turmoil, to relieve the common place monotony, and I
gladly embrace it to confer a valuable franchise of honor,
trust, station, and dignity, on one of the best of men. In
fact I may say that no judicial act of mine in all the coming years, will shine with more luster than the patent of
nobility I am about to confer. I remember vividly one
occasion after the adjournment of the summer term, he
took me home. Sister Dollarhide, the best of wives,
with the children, had gone on their summer outing,

thus enlarging our opportunities to embrace the happiest phases of life, without those embarrassing social restrictions which frequently restrain the best of men. It is not always a king would have his queen looking in on his courtiers when they unbend the bow. So it was with Brother Dollarhide and myself. From a given 'state of fact, the law supplies many things by presumption. In a few days we found it wise to cool off in the beautiful Cossatot, whose crystal waters as they leap from rock to rock, chant a lullaby to forest and field. Hither, Brother Dollarhide and I hied ourselves, and laved in the inviting waters. A neighborhood road led down the valley, and it was not long before we heard many voices approaching, to our nude consternation, rapid transit was the only protection from exposure. Brother Dollarhide was quicker than myself, he threw on his shirt and left in rapid flight. Just as he turned around the root of a fallen tree, a huge rattlesnake fastened its fangs in his shirt tail. I am familiar with the memorable inspiration which swept the harp of poesy and song, and immortalized John Gilpin's ride, and Tam O'Shanter's race, that dark and stormy night through the hills and glens of Caledonia, to escape from goblins damned. I have seen the antelope majestically racing for life over the plains, and the wild deer of our native forests running for life to escape pursuing hounds. Yes, I have seen the Arabian courser, with panting lungs and feet as fleet as the winds, but my brothers of the Bar, I have yet to see anything approach Brother Dollarhide's race with that snake hanging to his shirt tail. Had I not been possessed with that felicity of genius which can equally entertain fear and overflowing mirth at the same time, I would have lost a splendid opportunity to entertain both passions. I followed along in his wake, and at the end of half a mile, found that he had broken down from sheer exhaustion, and that the snake was dead, dead, dead, with every bone in its body broken in that stormy flight."

" After Brother Dollarhide recovered his wind, he stood up and said, 'Judge, look at that yellow stream of virus on my legs.'

" This little episode in his eventful life demonstrated to me that he possesses one of the prime factors to success in the professional life upon which he is now about to enter. He knows when to run and when to stand. Swear him, Mr. Clerk."

George W. McCowan had the learning and ability to have succeeded anywhere, if he had only been possessed of those staying qualities so necessary to success, particularly with lawyers, the great majority of whom have long probations to serve. He had an exhaustless fund of humor, wit, irony, and sarcasm, which bubbled up in almost every trial before him. Under other suns and happier surroundings, he would have become eminent and useful. He died many years ago, with the measure of hope and aspiration unfilled, himself his worst enemy.

James R. Page, a prominent lawyer of Washington, Arkansas, before and during the reconstruction period, was not on good terms with Judge McCowan, and it was said the latter did not extend to him that courtesy to which he was entitled. The Judge one day rendered a decision against Page, which he thought a great outrage. He was trending towards Bacchus, and in his anger walked up and down the Court room, gritting his teeth, and repeating unconsciously to himself, in an audible tone heard all over the room, "I am a whale." McCowan drunk, as usual, took great offense at the attitude and expression of Page, and said: "Mr. Sheriff, adjourn Court for five minutes, I have been wanting to harpoon a whale for some time." The Sheriff adjourned Court. The Judge opened his pocket knife and made for Page, but Judge Eakin and others caught him and prevented a bloody scene in Court. Page stood firm as a rock awaiting the onslaught and ready to repel it.

On another occasion, in the same Court, Judge Eakin

28

was profoundly arguing an application for a mandamus
to restrain the illegal issue of County Scrip, a procedure
so common in those days that it bankrupted nearly every
County in Arkansas.   Judge A. B. Williams was opposing counsel, and both were very able lawyers.   McCowan
went to sleep for a half hour on the Bench, while Judge
Eakin was arguing the case; so intently engaged that he
did not discover the Judge was asleep until the jurors,
lawyers, and bystanders were laughing all over the Court
room at both of them.   But Judge Eakin, not to be out-
done, stopped arguing the case, and sang "The Last
Rose of Summer," quoted Shakespeare, and learnedly
commented on the author's great genius.   Then he pronounced a eulogy on Sir Walter Scott and his 'Lay of
the   Last Minstrel,' and quoted Burns' Tam O'Shanter:

> ' O Tam ! hadst thou been sae wise
> As ta'en thy ain wife Katie's advice,
> She tould thee weel thou was a skellam,
> A bletherin, blustering, drunken bellam."

At this juncture the Judge, whose head had been reel-
ing from side to side as he slept, awaked, straightened up
in his seat, and Judge Eakin said, "As I was proceeding
to say, your Honor, when you lost the thread of my argument—" "Stop there, Judge," said Judge McCowan, "I
have been greatly entertained in listening to your profound argument.   You have stated your case well, and
argued it as well, if not better, than Story or Marshall
could have done, and have fortified yourself with able ad-
judications, but I will not grant this mandamus, if I do,
God damn us."   Eakin was shocked, incensed, and started
over the seats to pull him off of the Bench, but the
lawyers interfered and prevented him.   McCowan said,
"Turn him loose, gentlemen.   He will be glad to get
away.   He can't make me grant that mandamus, if he
does, God damn us."   Judge Eaken was a profound lawyer and scholar.   He was born in Shelbyville, Bedford
county, Tenn., of Scotch-Irish descent.   He inherited a

large fortune. His lineage is traced back two centuries to the Highlanders of Scotland, and the name is purely Highland Scotch. He was afterward Associate Judge of the Supreme Court of Arkansas, where he distinguished himself as the most scholarly Judge who ever sat on that Bench. It was my fortune to know him long and intimately.

THE KNOW NOTHING PARTY—KNOCK DOWN IN COURT.

DURING the Know Nothing craze of 1856, composed chiefly of the old Whig party, political excitement was at flood tide. I was an orthodox Democrat of the Jeffersonian–Jackson school, and all my relatives, both of the lineal and collateral lines were of the same faith without exception. Born in the shadows of the Hermitage, to impute treason to party affiliations and associations, was an offense that must be atoned.

There was an enthusiastic lodge of Know Nothings at Raleigh, and some of the zealots and political fanatics caused John White, an industrious Irishman, to be indicted, charged with the larceny of a fine gray horse. The criminative facts were circumstantial, and when analyzed and probed to the bottom had no real foundation. Excitement ran high, as usual, in political prosecutions. I defended White, Jesse L. Harris prosecuted. Harris and myself were not on the best of terms, and it was not a difficult matter to produce emphasized collision.

In opening the defense I crowded with caustic' severity the political phase of the prosecution, and the Star-Chamber cohorts that originated it, and pointed out the ex-Whig leaders by name as traitors to the party they had abandoned, who were traveling, as Junius said of the Duke of Gupton, "through every sign of the political zodiac," animated alone by desire for spoils.   But I was studiously cautious in avoiding any personal reference to opposing counsel, as every lawyer ought to be when conducting a trial.   But Mr. Harris did not observe this courtesy; to turn my batteries, he said without foundation in fact, that "if I am correctly informed, Mr. Hallum belongs to the Know Nothing organization, and ought not to cast stones while in a glass house."   The outrage was too deliberate and flagrant, and I knocked him down instantly, as Judge Joe C. Guild would say "for calarapin" in that way. But be it said, Jesse was a game cock, and all the more to be admired for that, and he rose with his pistol to "back up his calarapin," and we were both in the act of shooting when seized and prevented, and I am profoundly glad, because when he moved for his pistol I was the quicker and would have fired and killed him before he could have fired.   A few cool-headed men prevented a holocaust, an awful tragedy.   If one gun had been fired one hundred would have been fired in that Court house. After order was restored the trial progressed within legitimate limits and White was acquitted.   The Democrats yelled, and old lady White, the mother of the accused, threw her arms around my neck, kissed me and in the rich dialect of Erin, pronounced blessings and benedictions, whilst the beautiful American wife of the defendant held him in her arms, with a countenance radiant with joy.   Poor, chivalrous Harris, he was a noble and brave Confederate soldier, was captured at Island 10, and died in a Northern prison.   Farewell, noble brother, your impulses were strong, your aims high, your life checkered, your repose eternal.

ADDRESS.

On September 2d, 1889, The Southwestern College at Texarkana, Ark., was Dedicated, and the Author Delivered the Following Address to the Board of Trustees, Faculty, and Concourse of Citizens Present.

Hon. T. E. WEBBER, President.

PROFESSORS, ladies, and gentlemen: We have met here in the sacred precincts of this Institution of Learning to perform one of the most pleasant duties which can be assigned a cultured people. I feel doubly grateful for the compliment conferred in the part assigned me. First, to the founders of our Federative System of Government, which looks to the intelligence of the masses as its strongest arm of support ; second, to the Board of Trustees, and this learned corps of Professors and Educators, who have invited me to participate with you all in these ceremonies.

The dedication of a college on American soil carries with it a peculiar significance, which such an event does not embrace in any other division of the globe. Why? Because the web and woof, the heart and the genius of our institutions, appeal for stability directly to the intelligence of the masses. This cannot be said or applied with equal force to any other people or form of Government in the world.

In ours, the masses are the governing classes. This is not so largely the case in any other existing Government. England, with her limited monarchy, is the nearest approach ; she has manifest American tendencies, with a titled hereditary aristocracy ; a nobility who inherit a seat in the House of Lords. But the strongest factor in the governing forces of the monarchy is to-day found in the conservative strength of an elective House of Commons, whose authority and power rests in the will of the people expressed by the ballot.

Republican France of to-day is not to be taken into serious account, or in any way regarded as an exception or qualification to the conclusion indicated. In her spasmodic, and often heroic, struggles between monarchy, empire, and republic, during the last hundred years, she has not determined as to how far the people ought to be educated and trusted, as the major factor in the governing power of the State.

The phenominal attitude which the Swiss Cantons sustain to the Governments of Europe, does not bring Switzerland within the limits of an exception to what we have stated. She owes her freedom more to the isolation and solitude the Alps throw around her, than to the ballot or general intelligence of the masses.

The nearest approach in ancient times to the power the masses exert over our Institutions, is found in the Democracy of Athens. There *vox populi vox dei* found its strongest type, the most vehement expression in the will of the people, at a period when Grecian philosophy, science, art, oratory, diplomacy, literature, and war, in the felicitous language of Lord Brougham "fulminated over Greece," and in that Pagan age dominated the attainments of every contemporary people.

But a successful, pure Democracy, is only attainable in a very limited area of country, where, as in Athens, the people assembled on Mar's Hill, in the Areopagus, and determined all affairs of State.

Our Government is not a Democracy. Brought to such a standard it could not exist. The government of a Democracy, if applied to a vast territory and population like ours, with diversified and conflicting interests, would soon result in chaos and ruin for want of adhesive power.

Our forefathers, in the organic framework of the Government, steered between the evils and extremes of Democracy on one hand, and the odious features of a mouarchy on the other. They amalgamated the better features of both forms of Government. They preserved the inherent power of the people over the Government in the ballot, but neutralized the sudden, spasmodic, and destructive vices of a Democracy, by substituting representative Government.

They eliminated the vices which are inevitable in a hereditary monarchy and aristocracy, and were extremely wise in preserving the strength of a limited monarchy, under the popular form of representative Government; at the base of which they laid the ballot in lieu of that treason to the rights of mankind, which was at one period of the world's history canonized in the heresy which taught "the divine right of kings."

All free Government must necessarily be based on the intelligence of the people. Without the enlightened support of the masses, free Government cannot exist. By free Government I mean that which secures the greatest liberty to the individual, consistent with public welfare, fixed in foundations of law. The farther Government drifts from this mooring, the less its stability will depend on the brain development of the masses, and the less important will be the necessity for education. The manumission of four million of slaves, armed with the sovereignty of the ballot, was the greatest strain our free institutions have ever encountered, save revolution and war. This step of doubtful and more than questionable statesmanship, has greatly enhanced the necessity to strengthen the foundations of the Government in the education of the masses.

In this conviction "The Blair Bill" had its origin. But its provisions clearly point to national guardianship over the whole question of education; and if pushed to its logical sequence would undermine the reserved rights of the States, and ultimately result in centralization. Fearing these results, I am opposed to the bill.

Turning from home for evidence of the impress our example and institutions have exerted abroad, we find they have exercised a powerful influence over the world, and to a great extent have changed its civilization. We see its germinal principles at the masthead of the Mayflower with her Pilgrims freight of human souls, and in the heroic resolve of the Cavalier on the James, and in the organic structure of every Government on the American continent, and we read its fatalism to monarchy. In the recent franchise conferred on a very large body of electors in the British Isles, and the influence these electors exert in shaping the policy of the Government of Great Britain. And the same is true of all her colonies, her vast possessions in India not excepted. There steam, the genius of Fulton, plies its vocation as an inland carrier, and the lightning, caught by Franklin, and harnessed by Morse, performs the office of post-boy for more than 400,000,000 of people in that distant region.

We see it in France, Austria, Italy, the Russian and German empires, and all of their dependencies throughout the world. In fact we see it, and feel and realize it, in every region where the footprints of civilized man are found. We lead the vanguard in this phenominal, this most wonderful of all the ages. Our blood, our people, with Saxon, Norman, and Celtic absorptions, is to-day the dominant race of the world. For all this there is a deepseated cause, underlying great fundamental principles. Their germination is found in the genius of our Institutions, which foster the education of the masses, and opens the door to the most exalted positions. Why do I emphasize these achievements? Because in an Institution like this I feel that we are with the roots, the multiples, the cubes of these mighty results.

Then, Professors, if there is a hallowed vocation on earth, elevating and distinguishing men for the good they

do, and for the influence they exert on earth, it is that of
the teacher. Your work lies at the foundation of society
and Government, and it reaches to the dome. Even the
good Theologian, who sometimes claims an exaltation,
and emancipation from comparison with other callings,
comes to the schoolhouse in the first instance for the good
seed which has germinated so wonderfully in him. There
is nothing good in the development of great brain forces
which does not find in the teacher its best training in
laying deep elementary foundations. The cube of human
attainments always finds its root in antecedent training.
I know no better illustration of this, and a thousand other
things brought to light by patient and laborious investigation all along the whole landscape of the sciences, than
to cite an instance in the ever progressive science of Astronomy. Pythagorus, 500 B. C., taught the revolution
of the planetary system around the sun as a common center. In the second century Ptolemy, an Egyptian Astronomer, discarded the theory of Pythagorus, and taught
that the world is the center of eight crystal, concave
spheres, that the sun is in the third sphere. This theory
obtained for near fifteen centuries. Finally, Copernicus,
a Prussian Priest, and astronomer of great ability,
adopted the Pythagorean theory, and the great Kepler,
and other astronomers, gradually adopted the Copernican
theory. But it remained for the great Galileo, the in-
ventor of the telescope, to prove it. He discovered the
satelites of Jupiter revolving around him. This forever
set the question to rest and established the truth of the
Copernican theory. The cube is often many centuries
from the root of the sciences. So it was long a question
as to whether the sun stands stationary in the heavens or
is sweeping with amazing velocity through the vast void
of space with his retinue of worlds.

But the greatest of all sciences, Mathematics, applied
to astronomical solution, has apparently settled this
question. The sun, with his retinue of worlds, is cleav-

ing the immensity of space at the rate of 400,000 miles
per day, in an orbit around the great star. Alcyone, and
it requires 18,000,000 years to complete the orbital circuit.   The creation of man led up to the splendid achievements of Christianity, through long ages of development.
It is true of an hundred other beauties and glories unfolded in the science of Astronomy, which carries us back
to the Chaldean Shepherds and star-gazers in the remote
past.   And so it may be said of the whole landscape of the
sciences which now encircle the world in a halo of light,
their roots extend back into the laboratories of the brain
over long periods of time.   But because of man's transcendent attainments in this wonderful age, many embrace
the superficial conclusion that the powers of his intellect are yet expanding, with its maximum force not yet
attained.   This is erroneous.   Man's maximum brain
force was attained thousands of years ago.   True, the
range of intellectual vision, and the compass of human
knowledge is greatly enhanced, but this increase of knowledge does not augment the normal standard of brain-
power.

    Oratory, Painting, Poetry, Sculpture, Philosophy, and
Architecture, bear witness that the maximum forces of
the mind in these directions have not advanced in many
centuries.   You teachers toil at the base, you lay the
foundation, but the pupils must build, polish, and finish
the dome.   To the State, you are an indispensable factor,
the greatest necessity.   Strike down and abolish your
high calling, your noble mission, and the pillars of State
will crumble and fall, and our form of Government will
perish from the earth and become a thing of the past.
The attic age of Grecian glory and greatness, lifted that
classic land above all the world.   This was imparted by
her philosophers (which is but another name for teachers.)
They were all teachers, and noble youth drank deep at
the fount of wisdom and inspiration.

    They enjoyed the highest honors and distinction in the

state; they were venerated at home and abroad, and have left an imperishable niche in the Panthean which has survived spires of brass and shafts of marble. They left to the human race an inheritance of learning and wisdom, which has challenged alike the love and admiration of scholars and sages along down the centuries.

This, Professors, friends, teachers, and honored citizens of a great country, is your reward, and will be your reward as long as our children and decendants love the institutions which have made the people who speak the English language the dominant race of the world.

Professors, your reward and praise may not make much noise around you, it may be drowned in the bustle of this busy life, but the influence which you exert for good, will outlive all the coming cycles of time; it will survive the world, and find its reward in the approval of the everlasting God. The cultivated mind is a well of inexhaustible pleasure within itself. The scholar's happiness in contemplating the achievements of the human mind, is infinitely greater and more elevated in all that go to make up the higher types of our race, than all the gold in the world and allurements of power and place can confer.

The student and savant are emancipated from all the sordid and corroding influences which the pursuit of wealth engenders. Such pursuits dwarf the soul and disqualifies it from participation in the pleasures which the scholar finds in all the works of nature, in every field of science. One hour's pleasure which the scholar experiences in his studio, with telescope and spectroscope (that most wonderful of all instruments yet invented by the ingenuity of man), aggregates more unalloyed happiness than that ever felt by all the Goulds, Rothchilds, and Vanderbilts, the world has known.

A ray of light coming from the sun annihilates distance at the enormous and inconceivable velocity of 12,000,000 miles per minute. It is caught in the scholar's room by

the telescope, and handed to the delicate spectroscope, or
solar spectrum, which resolves all the constituent parts
of light into their original elements, and, with absolute
certitude, the little tell tale sunbeam opens its confiding
bosom to the scholar, and names the chemical family composing the vaporous and gaseous elements enveloping
the sun and planets.

The savant, thus equipped in his dark room, sees in
this photographic miniature the composition of the mighty
orb of day, and finds with absolute certitude the existence
of iron, copper, zinc, nickle, cobalt, sodium, hydrogen,
and fourteen constituent elements found in the earth we
live on.   The size, density, and velocity, of the planets
are told with exactness.

Throw the telescope on any luminous body in the
heavens, and the little spectroscope, with the aid of mathematics, will tell the velocity and direction of its flight.
Such are some of the results evolved in the study of the
scholar, the laboratory of the human brain.

I would rather have been Leverrier, with God's patent
of nobility, evidenced by his master genius, when he laboriously and accurately calculated the perturbations
of Uranus, and told where Neptune could be, and was
found, than to have been the wearer of a crown.

In conclusion, we may appropriately allude to the facilities and happy auspices found on "College Hill" for
laying broad and deep the foundations of scholarly and
classic attainment. First, we have an able corps of Professors and experienced teachers, whose names are a
guarantee, an endorsement, of all that is desirable in this
direction.   Second, we have one of the most beautiful
and healthy localities to be found within the limits of the
Southern States.   The air is as pure as the icicles which
hang from the temple of Diana, and the crystal fountains
of water are well-springs of health.

The College building is located on a beautiful eminence
seventy feet higher than the surrounding country,

guarded and shaded by stately, patriarchial pines, which remind us of those attic shades and classic groves, in the midst of which the schools of the Grecian sage and philosopher were located in that renowned, classic land, whose fame will live fresh as the dew drop, as long as the literature of the world is preserved.

Then, noble youth, come hither to these sacred precincts and drink deep at this fount of wisdom and learning. To the mothers and fathers of this sunny land, let me ask: why not build up and foster on a broad and prosperous foundation our home Institution? The many thousands of dollars annually spent in educating our sons and daughters at distant seats of learning could find the most profitable employment in building up our own College. The noble Institution in this hour of its christening, challenges and commands the admiration, the pride and the love of all of us.

May the Infinite, who holds in His hands the growth and destiny of a great people, spread His " healing wings " over the Institution, and make it a powerful factor in the development of the intellectual resources of our sons and daughters to the maximum standard of usefulness.

ADDRESS OF THE AUTHOR TO DRAUGHON'S PRACTICAL BUSINESS COLLEGE, NASHVILLE, TENNESSEE, APRIL 10th, 1895.

MR. PRESIDENT, Ladies and Gentlemen of the College:—Those who know Professor Draughon do not wonder at his phenominal success as a teacher of practical business methods; being eminently practical himself, he makes a success of all he

undertakes.   Such men have in all ages moved and controlled the machinery of the world and always will.

"Keep up with the procession," is the business motto
emblazoned on the Court of Arms of every successful
business man and woman of this generation of toilers.

We live in an age of transcendent and colossal achievement in all the departments of life, which challenges the
physical and brain forces of man, and your presence and
purpose in this Institution admonishes me that you fully
realize the importance of keeping up with advanced business methods and standards of the great business world
of to-day.   The methods followed by the old fogy of yesterday belong to the history and traditions of the past.
They have been swallowed up in the rapid progress of
the business revolutions of to-day in every department of
human action.

It is no exaggeration to say that the business methods
of to-day represent the influx and efflux of a bee-hive, fo-
calizing and radiating the vast energies of art, science,
agriculture, manufacture and commerce in all the business centers of the world.

Success in all the varied pursuits of life, largely depend on thorough knowledge and training for the object
in hand.   The factors which totalize the sum of achievement in all the vocations of men, are as varied and complicated as the multiplied ends to which man directs his
energies.

The arts and sciences, in their application to mechanics have expanded the field of labor and correspondingly
enlarged the necessity for accurate and scientific knowledge in a thousand fields of pursuit, without which
achievement to-day is impossible.   The necessity of this
knowledge in some form reaches every pursuit, from the
delicate ray of light which pencils a photograph in combination with material chemicals, or as co-factor with
scientific mathematics and mechanics weighs the
planetary system and determines the velocity, distance

and specific gravity of each member of the solar system.

The methods of yesterday gave place to the methods of to-day, and the methods of to-day will give place to the march of science and discovery to-morrow. In 1849 the first ocean steamer crossed the Atlantic—that day marked the beginning of a revolution which has changed the face of civilization; overturned all previous business methods. Then a monthly price-current advised of the advance and decline of stocks and commodities. Now price-currents come hourly. Then there was scarcely a Business College on either continent. The knowledge you acquire here of business methods in a few weeks or months was then the product of long and laborious experience, often sandwiched with disaster caused by ignorance. But practical business men of to-day, have overcome the fossil methods of the past.

Science has chained the wildest element of nature to the most delicate machinery, and put it on duty as a post boy around the globe with the price-current of all commercial marts, with daily and hourly delivery. The merchant or broker in any of the business centers of the world can touch the wire in his counting room, and instruct his agents at any business center of the world and energise his financial strength at any given point at a moment's warning. The business man of to-day who fails to keep step with scientific appliances in the commerce of the age, belongs to an era of the fossilized past, and his exchequer is in constant danger of being transferred to the bank account of his alert competitor or a receiver in bankruptcy.

In this connection let me call your attention to a fruitful cause of failure in the average young business man, when he comes from the College or University he is innocent of business methods, but thinks himself possessed of the totals of human wisdom and equipped for the battle of life—that vast attainment is mirrored in his diploma. Such characters point with index-finger to rapid bankruptcy. In other words, when he first leaves his Alma Mater he is a very wise man in his own estimation, but in fact, a business simpleton.

The corner and foundation stones of this Institution are measured by standards best calculated to avoid these errors. Its teachings are best calculated to promote success in all the business relations of practical life. It vitalizes and energises scientific methods looking to success. It stands abreast of the most approved business methods of to-day, and when to-morrow gets here, with advanced improvements, Professor Draughon will be found in line with them.

His utilitarian ideas of system reduced to a business science, methodical and accurate in all departments, keep him abreast of the times. The best evidence of this is found in the great number of banking, commercial, and other houses all over the South, where his students are employed at the highest salaries.

A diploma from this Institution is a passport to business anywhere. In this age of relentless demand on both physical and mental powers—this maelstrom of all the business ages, the Practical Business College is the *sine que non* of all who desire to achieve success. If the attainments which are the ripe fruits of this Institution are not grafted on a business career, sad experience may point to the wrong side of the ledger balance when it is too late to retrieve. The man who ignores the necessity of a business education in the whirling vortex of business life, hugs a false delusion, and he may weep when it is too late at the grave of a fool's ideal.

In this age of steam and electricity, there is nothing of more importance to the countinghouse than thorough knowledge of business demands reduced to the most practical standards. The gradation of attainment from the common school to the College, and from the College to the University, leads the business man to the Practical Business College for final instruction and graduation.

To the ladies of the Institution let me say that marriage is a lottery where many lives are wrecked for time and eternity. This patent fact throughout the centers of civilization, is perhaps nowhere more emphasized than in the United States, and the remedy is largely in your own hands. This phase of the domestic and social problem vindicates your right to seek and apply the remedy, in the noble effort to abolish worthless husbands by becoming independent and self-supporting. The prodigal, dissipated, shiftless spendthrift has no claims on you. They are parasites on the body politic, and have no more right to poison and ruin your high and noble expectations than they have to poison your physical life with corrosive sublimate.

The problems presented for your solution by these domestic cancers, are now being practically solved by many thousands of noble, resolute women who have become competitors with man in a great variety of employments hitherto filled alone by man. Literature, the arts, the sciences, the countingroom, and many other employments have thrown wide open the doors of competition to you with the sterner sex, and your achievements in all of these mark an ominous revolution in the tendencies of society for woman's good. In making this advance over the crystalized prejudices of ages, you have been compelled to fight a great battle, aided at first by only a few great thinkers in the ranks of your fathers and brothers. But now your recruits, grandly won by your superior tact, refinement and grace, numbers untold thousands in every station in life.

It was once feared that your contact with the business world would be at the expense of your superior charms and influence for good, but experience, the last, best, and greatest teacher, after all, has dispelled these idle fears. The elevating influence of your presence is now felt in all the avenues of life. All hail to the day when this onward and advancing civilization will ultimately accord to the

29

gentler sex equal rights in every sphere of life suitable
to your attainments and powers, mental and physical.
Co-education and co-employment of the sexes thus far in
the field of experiment have given satisfactory results,
but much yet remains to be tested before the problem in
all its relations is solved.

To the classes of both sexes in all the departments, let
me here say in conclusion that your Institution here in the
lap of the great South is now supported by the aspiring
youth of both sexes from twenty great States, and that the
usefulness and success of the Institution is now an established fact.   This vast territory is its foster feeding
ground.   The aggregate of its mechanical, mining, agricultural, financial and other resources is vast, but vast
as it is to-day, the boundless possibilities of to-morrow
cannot be estimated.   They reach out and take root in a
brilliant future beyond the conception of Aladdin when
he lit his lamp in Wonderland.   This empire of wealth,
present and prospective, is rapidly rising and advancing
like the fabled Phœnix from the ashes of untold disaster.
The demands of to-day and the ever-increasing demands
of to-morrow require an increased army of business men
and women, and these educated factors and agents must
be supplied by Practical Business Colleges.